Conviction

a sequel to Jane Austen's

Pride & Prejudice

by

Skylar Hamilton Burris

Double Edge Press
TM

Double Edge Press

ISBN 0-9774452-3-2

Conviction: a sequel to Jane Austen's *Pride & Prejudice*
Copyright © 2006 Skylar Hamilton Burris

Cover Artwork: Copyright © Angela Stuckey

This novel is a work of fiction. Names, characters, places, and incidents either are the product of the author's imagination or are used fictitiously. Any resemblance to actual events, locales, organizations, or persons, living or dead, is entirely coincidental and beyond the intent of either the author or publisher.

Acknowledgements

Thank you to my mother, Karen Hamilton, for helping me to polish the text of this 2nd edition even before it reached the desk of my editor. Thank you to the virtual communities the Republic of Pemberley and the Derbyshire Writers Guild, which enabled me to indulge my penchant for writing short, frivolous Jane Austen fanfiction before I tackled the more serious pursuit of novels. And finally, thank you to my loving husband, Steve, who has taught me that happy endings can and do exist.

Introduction

I originally began this sequel to Jane Austen's timeless novel *Pride and Prejudice* as a means of amusing myself. The effort, however, soon grew into a serious project involving numerous revisions as well as a considerable amount of research. In *Conviction*, I have attempted to remain true to the personalities of Austen's classic characters, and I believe I have succeeded. But because I cannot hope to imitate sufficiently Jane Austen's unique and superbly subtle wit, I have authored this tale in my own writing style, while maintaining the sort of formal dialogue one might expect from the time period.

Austen's unique humor is not the only admirable feature of her prose; she also possessed what Sir Walter Scott termed "the exquisite touch," which enabled her to "render ordinary commonplace things and characters interesting, from the truth of the description and the sentiment." Therefore, it is unlikely Miss Austen would have introduced as expansive a political and historical backdrop as I have done. If I make reference to the events and opinions of the times, it is primarily because I feel it enables me to flesh out my new creations.

Jane Austen's novels have long appealed to me, largely because their author insists on realism without at the same time permitting her works to degenerate into pessimism. Although she wrote at the dawn of the romantic age, Miss Austen did not succumb to the popular tendency to deify man. Nor, however, did she make him—as do many modern realists—a slave to his environment, a being utterly incapable of determining his own fate. She gently mocked the society she inhabited, but she also revealed the finer qualities of mankind, always allowing for the possibility of true reform. Her tales were moral without being didactic. If I captured even half her merits in this novel, the time invested in it will have been worthwhile.

Even if you have never before read *Pride and Prejudice*, you can enjoy *Conviction*. This sequel assumes only a basic familiarity with Austen's plotline, which you can obtain by reading a brief summary. Regular consumers of sequels to *Pride and Prejudice* often desire to read more about the unique relationship between Mr. and Mrs. Darcy. And although I have interspersed such scenes throughout my work that should appease this interest, I have not made the couple my novel's primary focus. Rather, I have turned my lens upon Georgiana Darcy along with several original characters. I hope you enjoy the journey.

~ Skylar H. Burris

Conviction

a Sequel to Jane Austen's

Pride & Prejudice

by

Skylar Hamilton Burris

Chapter 1

In spring, a young girl's fancy may well turn to thoughts of love, but Miss Georgiana Darcy's mind was engaged in a more disagreeable task. She was contemplating how to thwart the attentions of her unwelcome suitors. Even now she watched the retreating back of one such gentleman. Mr. Niles Davidson held his head loftily above his towering collar, and his high boots made a proud tripping sound as he departed the drawing room. She could still see the profile of his angular nose, though his blue-gray eyes were now obscured from her sight. The curls of his blonde hair appeared as pretentious in their placement as the owner who sported them.

The young politician had taken an obvious, albeit unrecipro-cated, interest in Georgiana. His regard had at first discomfort-ed and then flattered her, but after a time his company had merely grown tedious. Once the gentleman had safely exited the doors of Pemberley, Georgiana drew closer to her sister-in-law Elizabeth. Miss Darcy loomed a head above her brother's wife. Mr. Darcy had long considered his wife's form to be light and pleasing, but his sister's height made her own figure appear particularly supple in comparison. Georgiana's hair was a less definite shade of brown than Elizabeth's—indeed it was almost blonde—and her eyes were as light as her sister-in-law's were dark. But their unusual bright green hue was now dimmed by discontent.

Mrs. Darcy smiled satirically and issued her verdict: "We must winter in London, where you will, with any luck, encounter more promising possibilities."

"Mr. Davidson is a resident of London," replied Georgiana. Indeed, the parliamentarian had only been vacationing in Derbyshire and would return tomorrow to the city.

"I had forgotten," said Mrs. Darcy. "And although that fact does not bode well for the prospects of London, I still believe that from the wide array of gentlemen you encounter in that quarry, you may perhaps extract a single gem."

Georgiana laughed, but there was a note of uneasiness trapped within the sound. Miss Darcy was aware that she was now expected to be on the lookout for a suitable husband, and her family no doubt assumed she would find a match within the next two years. And yet Georgiana thought herself content to reside at her brother's estate indefinitely; at least, she had no substantial desire to enter the valley of the great unknown.

Every day Miss Darcy dreaded the potential return of Mr. Davidson. He had made it terribly clear to her that he enjoyed visiting Derbyshire often, and he seemed to think the pronouncement brought her pleasure. He was perhaps led to this erroneous conclusion because she had smiled sweetly in response. Yet Miss Darcy nearly always smiled sweetly in response to statements made by gentlemen; it saved her the trouble of having to speak.

Her fears, however, proved unfounded; the young man's political responsibilities must have kept him in London, for month followed month and he did not return. Miss Darcy eventually gave up fearing his appearance, and she focused her energies instead on distracting her other, less diligent suitors. As was expected, she attended both dinner parties and balls, and such a lovely flower must inevitably be plucked from the wall. The dancing did not disturb her; it was the conversation she found difficult to endure. Her brother, Mr. Fitzwilliam Darcy, hoped that with each new event she would grow less timid, but Georgiana's exposure to society had only strengthened her love of solitude.

Spring gave way to summer, and summer faded into autumn. I mention this, dear reader, not in order to insult your intelligence by assuming you do not comprehend the sequence of the seasons, but merely as a convenient means of transition. Autumn brought with it the promise of new life (a symbolic contradiction, admittedly, but unfortunately for the race of authors, humanity often fails to order itself according to literary convention). In this case, the new life was to be that of Jonathan Bennet Bingley, the anticipated child of Elizabeth's sister Jane.

The Darcys journeyed to Hetrfordshire to be present for the birth of their nephew, though the hapless Georgiana was placed in London and left to the supervision of her companion Ms. Annsely, for her brother would not dare deprive her of society. Miss Darcy had hinted that she would not mind, terribly, spending a month or two without the benefit of callers. He in turn had told her that she would not thank him if she were forced to pass her time in the company of his mother-in-law. "It is a price I am reluctantly willing to pay for the privilege of my marriage," he had said. "But you, Georgiana, have no such incentive to endure it."

Thus, Mr. and Mrs. Darcy had traveled alone to Hertfordshire. And so it was that Elizabeth Darcy found herself returning to Netherfield after calling on an old family friend. Such a return journey is of no interest in itself, and it would not even be worth a narrative mention were it not for the fact that she spied a curious sight. As she approached the Bingleys' estate, Mrs. Darcy noticed a stranger walking away from it. He was of above average height and appeared distinguished, though she could not see his face. He walked, however, with a languid gate, and though her own steps on the gravel pathway were by no means quiet, he did not sense her presence. Indeed, she might have deemed him to be wholly oblivious of his surroundings, had he not taken a moment to stoop to the ground, retrieve a stray ball that had been released by a servant's child, and roll it back in the young boy's direction. She watched the elegant stranger's back as he rose from this incongruous crouching position and meandered on to an illustrious carriage, which he entered disinterestedly. Elizabeth had only time to raise her eyebrows before the horses were off.

Mrs. Darcy's first object upon entering the house was to visit with her sister Jane Bingley, who was resting in her room, being in the late stages of an exhausting pregnancy. Elizabeth then rejoined the others in the drawing room. Charles Bingley inquired after his wife with his usual charming eagerness, and Elizabeth assured him that she was well. She then asked about the gentleman she had seen departing Netherfield.

"He is a Mr. Jacob Markwood," said Mr. Bingley, "and he is

considering letting Netherfield from the owner, once we give it up. He is a cousin of my brother-in-law's." Here he nodded to Mr. Hurst, who was sprawled across a nearby sofa, oblivious of the world about him.

"Do you think he was interested?" Elizabeth asked.

"He appeared to be interested, although he really did not speak much. Yet whether or not he lets Netherfield, we intend to move immediately after Mrs. Bingley's confinement. We should very much like to move soon after the child is born." Mr. Bingley was too kind to disclose the reason for his impatience to quit Netherfield, but Elizabeth did not doubt it had something to do with the proximity of Longbourn, and thus of a mother-in-law whose trying attentions would only increase upon the birth of a grandchild.

Upon this mention of the child's birth, Mr. Darcy, who had been absorbed in a book and largely indifferent to the conversation, glanced at his wife. His countenance contained a bittersweet mixture of love, tenderness, and disappointment. She understood that look and returned a half-playful, half-apologetic smile. He in turn shook his head almost imperceptibly, as if to say, "No, no. We have not been married a year; I am not even thinking of a child yet." Yet, if the truth be told, he was.

"Mr. Hurst," said Mr. Bingley to his brother-in-law, loud enough to startle the gentleman from his sleep. "Do you think your cousin will let Netherfield?"

"I really have no idea," replied Mr. Hurst, struggling to raise himself up into a seated position.

"Do you know Mr. Markwood well, Mr. Hurst?" Elizabeth asked.

"Not very. His family and mine are not on social terms. In the past, we did not condescend to entertain them. The Markwoods spent many years in the West Indies, and though they returned to England some years ago, I have not seen my cousin Mr. Markwood until today, and I have met with my uncle Sir Robert but once."

"Not on social terms?" asked Elizabeth, who wondered at Mr. Hurst's airs. Mr. Hurst himself had always seemed rather than behaved the gentleman, and if Mr. Markwood was considering letting Netherfield, if that impressive carriage she had seen were his, and if the dignified appellation of "Sir" before his father's name were any indication of status, then Mr. Markwood could hardly be beneath Mr. Hurst. "Sir Robert, then, is not particularly wealthy?"

"He is now. He gained his fortune in the West Indies, though I have not the slightest idea how he amassed so much wealth in just over a decade. He also managed to procure the honor of a knighthood, but that is hardly an accomplishment in these modern times. As soon as he had that feather to stick in his cap, he was anxious to return to England. He had long desired to secure a seat in the House of Commons."

"But I presume he did not succeed?" interjected Louisa Hurst, the words issuing forth from beneath a condescending chuckle. Mrs. Hurst caught the approving eye of her sister Miss Bingley, who had been uncharacteristically silent during the conversation. Caroline Bingley had, in fact, been too preoccupied with her observations of Mr. Darcy to join much in the dialogue. She still sought his regard, however much he had offended her by his choice of wife. Mr. Darcy, for his part, now favored her only with those minimal attentions that were owed to her as the sister of his close friend.

"No," replied Mr. Hurst. "No, he did not. Some recurring illness he contracted in the West Indies has prevented him from even pursuing the goal. He has transferred all of his hopes and expectations to his eldest son. I imagine Sir Robert plans to see Mr. Markwood elected to the Commons from Hertfordshire when he has completed his studies at Oxford." Mr. Hurst, determined that he had satisfied the inquires of Mrs. Darcy, now chose to resume his former half-supine position upon the couch.

Mrs. Darcy felt a momentary stab of pity for the young Mr. Markwood. The man she had seen depart Netherfield appeared far too absentminded to pursue a calling as a politician. Yet many men before him, motivated either by cowardice or a sense of duty, had successfully followed the paths their fathers had forged for them.

"Mr. Darcy," said Miss Bingley, having at long last given up her efforts to secure his attention through a series of pointed glances. "Has your sister remained at Pemberley during this visit?"

"She is in London with her companion Mrs. Annesley."

"It is not yet the season," she replied.

"No, it is not, but there are enough people in town to occupy her. We will join her at Christmas." Mr. Darcy chose not to expand any further on this response, and Miss Bingley was forced instead to direct her conversation to Elizabeth.

"I understand that you have recently called upon your old neighbour, Lady Lucas?"

"Yes," replied Elizabeth, not unwarily. She could not help but wonder at the direction of Miss Bingley's inquiry.

"I imagine she is quite destitute, now that she has lost her husband."

"She will endure."

"It must have been rather a surprise to the neighborhood that the wife of one of the most prominent landowners in England should call upon a virtually penniless widow."

"Lady Lucas is hardly penniless, Miss Bingley, and I cannot conceive how anyone in the neighborhood should be in the least bit astonished at my visiting the mother of a life-long friend."

Mr. Darcy now looked up from his book and met his wife's eyes with a concerned expression. He did not think that assuming such a raw tone with Miss Bingley would prove conducive to the general welfare. In reply to his warning glance, Elizabeth pursed her lips and spoke challenge with her eyes. She had heard him employ the same tone with Miss Bingley himself, on many past occasions. Mr. Darcy saw her expression and sighed, returning to his book. Very well, he thought. When Miss Bingley's polite wrath was aroused, as it soon must be, his wife could tend to herself.

***

Miss Kitty Bennet attacked her present project with deliberation. She was laboring upon a new hat, and a variety of pins and ribbons were strewn out across the table in the sitting room of Netherfield. The gentlemen had gone out for a little sport, and Mr. Bennet had been particularly glad to be liberated from the confines of Longbourn to join his sons-in-law. Elizabeth watched her younger sister as she wove a piece of ribbon across the brow of the bonnet, and she smiled to herself. Kitty was in many ways still a foolish young girl, but she had been safely removed from the influence of her sister Lydia, and she had begun to pursue her own interests with greater individuality. She was quite the artisan when it came to making all manner of clothing.

"Would you like to return with us to Pemberley?" Elizabeth asked her.

"No, Lizzy," said Kitty. "I stayed with you that first winter, and I was merely in the way."

"You know you are always welcome at Pemberley."

"Yes, by you, Lizzy."

"And by Georgiana and Mr. Darcy."

"I am not so sure of the latter."

Elizabeth was disappointed by her pronouncement, because she thought her husband had made a concerted effort to be pleasant to her sister while she stayed with them at Pemberley. It was true that the girl's perkiness, which was not balanced by a deep wit, tried his patience at times, but he seemed almost to have developed an affection for her, not unlike that which he felt for his own sister.

"Has Mr. Darcy given you any reason to feel unwelcome?"

Kitty frowned. "No," she said. "No, I suppose he has not. And he was very kind to hire the music tutor for me. Still, I felt sometimes as though he would much rather have had you to himself. But it was early in your marriage." Kitty laid down her hat and smiled at her sister. She was certainly not the prettiest of the five Bennet women, but she had grown more beautiful, and the smile set off her twinkling eyes. "Do not worry, Lizzy. I think I will be of more use at Netherfield during Jane's confinement. And then I will help her when she moves—they will leave so soon after the child is born."

"Yes, they are in a considerable hurry to quit the estate. I cannot imagine why."

Kitty was not the cleverest of the Bennet girls, but she was not unwise, and she understood her sister well enough. "I will do what I can to curb mother's attentions during Jane's confinement by drawing them upon myself."

"Your sacrifice," replied Mrs. Darcy, "will be much appreciated, I am sure." Then, to divert the conversation to another, more pleasant avenue, she asked, "How did you enjoy your stay in London with Aunt and Uncle Gardiner?"

"Very much!" replied Kitty. "And despite father's promise to keep me from balls, I was able to attend one through the invitation of a particular friend."

Elizabeth rolled her eyes. Kitty enjoyed the company of military men as much as Lydia, but Mrs. Darcy hoped she behaved more responsibly in their presence. "Were there many officers present?"

"Oh, I don't care about them," she said. "I met a barrister. Well, he was not a barrister then, but he was about to be, as soon as he finished his studies. Mr. Markwood was one of the handsomest men I have ever seen."

"Mr. Markwood?" asked Elizabeth. "He was the gentlemen looking at Netherfield today."

"No, no," replied Kitty. "I hoped it would be him when Mr. Bingley mentioned he would be coming, but that was just his elder brother. It was Mr. Aaron Markwood whom I met."

The conversation proceeded, and Elizabeth soon learned that Mr. Aaron Markwood was not the only gentleman Kitty had thought one of the handsomest she had ever seen. Miss Bennet spoke of dances with several young men, and though Aaron Markwood had been the first in her mind, he was hardly the last.

Chapter 2

The Darcys delighted in the arrival of their nephew, Jonathan Bennet Bingley, before returning to Derbyshire. They set off from Netherfield content in the knowledge that the Bingleys would soon follow and settle in a neighboring county. Although Jacob Markwood had failed to let Netherfield, another occupant had been found. According to Mr. Hurst, Mr. Markwood had relinquished his hopes for the property because he had alienated himself from his father. Sir Robert discovered that his son had abandoned the study of the law and had, in fact, been secretly pursuing theological studies for years. Mr. Hurst reported that Sir Robert had disinherited Mr. Markwood the very day he took orders. The father likewise withdrew all financial provision from the ill-fated gentleman, whom he had previously favored with a regular and generous allowance. Virtually overnight, Jacob Markwood had found himself without a means of support.

Meanwhile, Georgiana Darcy had continued in London. The Darcys, along with their cousin Colonel Fitzwilliam, joined her there for the Christmas holidays. Supported by the arm of the Colonel, Miss Darcy now walked through the streets of London. A light snowfall enlivened the air and lent a contrast of color to the gray and red buildings that lined the streets. She found wandering through the bustling city to be far less traumatic than attending a small dinner party. Though there were scores of people to be found in the byways, conversation was rarely required, and there was a kind of serene anonymity to be gained from dissolving into a large crowd.

Miss Darcy stopped still in the pathway when she noticed an inviting shop. Colonel Fitzwilliam, after ascertaining the reason for her abrupt cessation, escorted her inside. Her goal was to obtain a suitable fabric from which could be fashioned a brilliant new gown. The costume was to be donned at the Pemberley summer ball. The event still rested months in the future, but

Georgiana was already anticipating it with trepidation. It would be among the largest social gatherings she had been compelled to attend, and she was well aware that an inordinate amount of attention would be focused upon her.

Colonel Fitzwilliam had been as patient as a man can be while his cousin attempted to choose an attractive fabric, but he was distracted when he spied an old acquaintance outside the shop window. He temporarily left Miss Darcy to herself as he eased out the doorway to call after Captain Talbot. The gentleman turned. "Colonel Fitzwilliam!" he exclaimed. "It has been years since I last saw you. How are you?"

"Very well. And you?"

"Excellent. In fact, you will have to correct your address. I am a Major now."

"You are not in regimentals," replied Colonel Fitzwilliam.

"I am on leave. London is my home. *Was* my home. I have only an uncle here to call upon now, but it is with him I have spent the holidays."

"You are to be his heir, if I recall correctly."

"Yes."

"And how is your uncle fairing?"

"He is at death's door, as always. Indeed, he is very much as he was four years ago, when I served beneath you. Except this time, I do believe he is knocking a bit more vigorously, and though he has always been a temperamental man, I think I will be grieved to see him go."

"Will you then resign your commission?" Colonel Fitzwilliam asked.

"If there is no war afoot, I believe I will. I do not care for purely ceremonial duties. If I cannot fight in battle, at least I can spend my days fencing."

"And how do you spend your days now, when you are not on leave?"

"Training soldiers," replied Talbot, "trying to turn boys into men so that they might be prepared to meet the French. I rejoin my regiment in a week, and then we leave for France. I would like to have gone abroad earlier, but I am considered too valuable a drill master, and so I have been for many months condemned to that occupation." He nodded toward the window display behind the Colonel, which was adorned with a variety of hats and fabrics. "What brings you to this particular femininely shop?"

Colonel Fitzwilliam suddenly remembered his cousin. "Pardon me one moment," he said and hurried back into the shop. Georgiana was ready to make her purchase, and he assisted her before leading her out onto the street.

"My charge," he said to Major Talbot. "Miss Georgiana Darcy, sister of my cousin Fitzwilliam Darcy. Perhaps you have heard of him."

"I cannot say that I have."

"He is the master of Pemberley."

Major Talbot nodded in understanding. He may not have known of Mr. Darcy, but he was aware of the impressive estate. He now bowed to Georgiana. He must have been accustomed to towering above women of more average height because he brought himself especially low. The effect was somewhat comical, and the gentleman seemed plainly aware of the fact even though he was not in the least embarrassed by it. The open smile that crossed his face on his own behalf revealed a set of uncommonly straight teeth. But it was the half-innocent, half-mischievous twinkle in his sea green eyes that captured Miss Darcy's attention. "Major Arthur Talbot," he said in introduction. "It is a pleasure to meet you." When he had finished speaking, he brushed back a persistent, fallen strand of his rather thick auburn hair.

She curtsied in return. It seemed she would be forced to speak with a stranger after all. So much for the anonymous crowd. Not that she was at all averse to what she saw before her. Major Talbot drew a distinguished figure, and she could not deny that he was attractive. Despite the Major's physical appeal, Georgiana was still alarmed when Colonel Fitzwilliam suggested that they all lunch together.

They found themselves dining in a respectable Inn, and at first the two gentlemen largely divided the conversation between themselves, which came as a relief to Miss Darcy. She learned that Major Talbot would be coming to Derbyshire in the summer to train a group of new recruits who would be marching down from Scotland. "We will be quartered in Lambton for the duration of the training," he said, "about four or five weeks. Then we shall march to Brighton and encamp there. This, of course, is all provided that I am not required to remain in France. I should say permitted to remain, for I prefer the field to the camp."

Georgiana watched Major Talbot as he reminisced with her cousin about their former acquaintance, and she listened to his resonant voice as he spoke about the training of soldiers. "It is very difficult to manage these men when they are so far from battle and so near the comforts of society," he said. "These soldiers need to endure some hardships in order to learn that life is not one long assembly. Most of them have never seen war." Major Talbot appeared to check himself, and he looked hesitantly at Colonel Fitzwilliam, as though he feared he had given offense. Colonel Fitzwilliam, after all, was an earl's younger son, whose commission was largely ceremonial, and who had been actively kept from battle. The Colonel did not look as though he would respond to the remark, and so Major Talbot turned to Georgiana. "Miss Darcy, you have been excessively quiet. I am sorry if we have neglected you."

She protested that she did not feel as if they had, and then she could conceive of no artificial means by which to prolong the conversation. Major Talbot noticed how she hesitated over her words, and he smiled at her shyness. It was the smile that struck Miss Darcy and caused her to temporarily forget herself, long enough, at least, to answer his present address.

"Do you come often to London?" he asked.

"My brother owns a town home here, and he and his wife and I are wintering in London. Most of the year I live with them in Derbyshire."

He motioned to the package she had set on the floor beside her chair. He noted that it contained a selection of fabric. "For a new gown?" he asked.

"Yes," she said and was briefly silent before venturing to continue. "My brother is hosting a large ball in June, at Pemberley."

"I am certain," he said, "that Derbyshire will benefit from such an amusement."

"You ought to come yourself," suggested Colonel Fitzwilliam. "You will be in Lambton then."

"If Mr. Darcy were to issue me an invitation, I would of course be pleased to attend. But I do not expect it, as I am not at all acquainted with the gentleman."

"Well," said Colonel Fitzwilliam, "I will see that he does extend you an invitation."

Miss Darcy was pleased to hear that Major Talbot might attend, but the realization of her own eagerness made her self-conscious, and she soon grew awkward again. Fortunately, the Major made allowance for her shyness, and he sought to put her at ease with his unassuming manner. He asked her direct questions, none of which could be answered with a simple yes or no, but he also understood her responses would be brief. Before she could fall uncomfortably silent for more than a moment, he always followed up with another question. Consequently, she was placed under no pressure to carry the conversation forward and had only to make the effort of replying. Georgiana knew not how he drew her out, but she soon found herself discussing with him her many interests. The meeting, which with any other stranger would have seemed interminable, grew too quickly to a close.

***

Over the next few days, Miss Darcy observed Colonel Fitzwilliam's conversations with her brother, but never once did her cousin mention Major Talbot or suggest that Mr. Darcy extend him an invitation to the summer ball. The subject had simply slipped the Colonel's mind, and he could have no idea what agonies his forgetfulness had caused his pretty young cousin. Georgiana, of course, dared not raise the subject herself.

In a week, Major Talbot had left town, and with him went her hopes. Colonel Fitzwilliam soon followed, as he was unexpectedly called to rejoin his regiment. Not long after, the Darcys were preparing to return to Derbyshire. Normally, they would have remained in London for the season, but estate business had beckoned Mr. Darcy back to Pemberley, and Georgiana had no desire to remain apart from her family in London. She was, in fact, glad to be free of the many new suitors she had unintentionally procured in the city. They were not all as tiring as Mr. Davidson, the young politician who called upon her most often, but during her last two weeks in London, she had found herself reflexively comparing each of her callers to Major Talbot. No man could hope to survive against the romantic standard she had fashioned.

Why, after only an afternoon's meeting, had she drawn such an image in her mind? The Major was certainly dashing, but less so than the handsomest of her suitors; he had seemed informed, but doctors had called upon her in London; he had been kind, but others had been equally well mannered. . . no, it was not his virtues that had captivated her. Major Talbot's good luck lay in the simple fact that he had not carried the weight of their entire conversation.

Georgiana Darcy was not a foolish girl. She was well educated, accomplished, and often thoughtful. But her shyness had long prevented her from acquiring social acumen, and if she remembered her meeting with Major Talbot too fondly, it was because he had succeeded in putting her at ease. Awkward before her suitors in London, Miss Darcy had allowed them to rattle on aimlessly, and such an unguided course could not help but reveal to her their defects, either in style or in substance. At the very least, their monologues must at long last bore her.

Although she thought often of Major Talbot in the weeks to come, Georgiana did not seek to examine the basis of her feelings for him. She never considered that perhaps she had found his company immensely enjoyable primarily because she had herself been a party to their conversation. Miss Darcy had unwittingly made Major Talbot the icon of her heart.

In March, Napoleon Bonaparte abdicated his throne and was exiled to the island of Elba. Georgiana was happy to receive this news for more than patriotic reasons; it also meant Major Talbot would certainly not be required to remain in France. That thought was followed by a second, less encouraging one: now that peace had been achieved, would the Major still come to Derbyshire that summer to train the new recruits?

Whether Major Talbot was thinking of Miss Darcy as often as she thought of him, or with identical fondness, is a subject for speculation. We may assume he thought her beautiful, if for no other reason than that she was, and it is unlikely that he could have been wholly unaware of her sudden admiration for him, which had surfaced at their first and only meeting. It is equally unlikely that such an admiration would fail to make him think very highly of her. But that she was a frequent presence in his thoughts we may doubt, for the blows of time and distance must inevitably make even a very pretty picture fade, especially when one considers that Major Talbot was a man of duty, and a soldier at his heart, with far more pressing things to distract his attentions from romance than a dinner or an easel or a screen.

May came, and with the twilight of spring came the close of life (a more apt metaphor, fortunately, than birth in autumn): the Darcy parish experienced the loss of its vicar through the workings of natural mortality. The Darcy family living, therefore, was in immediate need of a clergyman. The parsonage of Kympton was located just outside the village of Lambton, not far from the grounds of Pemberley. It was the same valuable family living that Mr. Wickham had turned down years before.

The sudden vacancy of a church benefice is an object of profound interest to sundry individuals. There are fathers who seek to establish their listless younger sons in a respectable profession, which, they hope, will curb the extravagance of youth, or at least remove its practice a considerable distance from home. There are impoverished, ambitious curates, who hope to rise above their present levels of indigence by obtaining a more sufficient living. And of course there are vicars, who would be pleased to take on an additional ecclesiastical unit in order to supplement their incomes, though they themselves would not dream of imposing their actual presence on the parish. It therefore came as a surprise to the inhabitants of Derbyshire when Mr. Fitzwilliam Darcy offered the living to a relatively unknown clergyman by the name of Mr. Jacob Markwood.

Jane had recalled the plight of the disinherited clergyman to the attention of her sister Elizabeth, who had suggested to her husband that he ought to consider making Mr. Markwood a free gift of the benefice. Mr. Darcy was aware that other men who were better known in Derbyshire had been recommended for the living, but he had succumbed to his wife's suggestion without much deliberation. If some part of his mind warned him against making a potentially premature choice, he reassured himself that he could at least admire the conviction of a gentleman who would choose the church not because he could rise no higher in society but because he earnestly desired the profession.

"I am glad to hear Mr. Markwood will now have a living," said Jane to her sister. The Bingleys were visiting at Pemberley and not for the first time since their move.

Elizabeth smiled. She was still impressed by Mrs. Bingley's unerring good nature, and she thought no one but Jane could take such an ardent interest in the fate of a man she had met only once. "Mr. Darcy was reluctant at first," said Mrs. Darcy, "to offer him the benefice, knowing so little of his character and reputation, but I related to him the story of his disinheritance, and I tried to imitate your empathy, though I fear I lack your talent for it."

Jane laughed. "Lizzy, I doubt your performance required much to convince him, considering the influence you already wield over your husband."

"Whatever do you mean, my dear Jane? Mr. Darcy is hardly the kind of man to be effortlessly moved."

"No, indeed. It is a Herculean labor, I am sure, to bend his will to anything, which is why I am always amazed to see you accomplish the feat with so little difficulty. Mr. Markwood will be grateful for your abilities, I am sure, though he has no idea to whom he owes his happy fate."

"When will Mr. Markwood settle in the parsonage?" asked Georgiana, joining the conversation for the first time that afternoon. Although the two sisters had almost forgotten her presence, they warmly welcomed her contribution to the conversation. Georgiana had grown comfortable with Mrs. Darcy, whom she regarded almost as her own sister, but she usually became her old, shy self around visitors, even ones as amiable as Jane. "Should we invite him to the ball?"

"Your brother has already extended him the invitation by letter," said Mrs. Darcy. "But he wrote back and politely declined. He will not be arriving until the Thursday before, and he fears he will not have time to settle before the ball. However, he has accepted an invitation to dine with us the following evening."

"Then we shall meet him at Pemberley before we see him at church," said Georgiana. "What is he like, Mrs. Bingley?"

Jane reflected on the question and could only confess that she did not know. She had met him only once, the first time he had toured Netherfield, before she had taken to her bed. She had been shocked to learn from Mr. Hurst that he had been treated so cruelly by his father. She pitied him, but she did not know him. "I feel for him deeply," Jane answered at last. "To be so maligned, and for no other reason than that he wished to serve the Church!"

Georgiana shared Jane's kind temper, though she usually hesitated to express her empathy for others, however keenly she felt it. Yet now her concern was piqued, and she asked, "What has he been doing all this time, since he was ordained and disinherited?"

Jane answered, "I do not know how he has managed to live since then, without his father's support."

The ladies' musings on the new vicar were interrupted by the appearance of Mr. Bingley and Mr. Darcy, who entered the room with the most dissimilar of gates. "I have convinced your brother," Mr. Bingley announced to Georgiana, "that you were justified in commissioning the creation of a new gown for the ball, though he insists that he does not himself understand the necessity since you will hardly be persuaded to frequent the assemblies and since you have not much worn the dresses you already possess."

Mr. Darcy spoke from behind him, "I am sure, Bingley, that she will draw a suitable number of predators, without the assistance of further adornments." If Mr. Darcy encouraged his sister to engage in society, it was not because he sought to marry her off quickly. Georgiana was but eighteen years old, and he had no interest in further encouraging her suitors, who already seemed too numerous and too eager. He only wished that these gatherings, if repeated often enough, would force her to gain a degree of self-assertion, without which she could not hope to survive in the world.

Mr. Bingley moved aside to allow Darcy to take a seat. "Darcy, really, predators? There are many distinguished gentlemen coming to this ball, honorable men, perfectly eligible matches, even for your sister."

Mr. Darcy made a doubtful noise. "Well," he said. "You ought to know. You invited most of them."

"May I remind you, friend, that you gave me permission to invite whosoever I list."

"I assumed you could not know a great many people in this part of the country."

"I do not."

"And yet you have invited a great many."

"Not a great many," said Bingley with a laugh.

"While we were in town today," said Mr. Darcy, glancing at Jane, "your husband issued invitations to seven officers of His Majesty's army, none of whom I know, and five of whom he himself has only met today."

"They seemed perfectly amiable men, Darcy, and really, it is hard on soldiers to be so near the presence of a ball and yet not be invited to attend. Major Talbot said the men are encamped at Lambton only for a month, and then they must march onward once again."

"Major Talbot?" Georgiana asked and hoped that no one noticed her voice hitch.

"Do you know him?" asked Mr. Bingley.

"No," she said hastily. "I mean, I met him once, in Lambton, last winter. Colonel Fitzwilliam introduced us."

"You see, Darcy," said Bingley, turning to his friend, "he is not a complete stranger then."

"So you have invited him?" asked Miss Darcy, trying very hard not to appear eager.

"Yes, I confess I have. And nine or ten others before him. Why, Darcy, you look absolutely stern. I would have thought you would be glad of my services. It saves you the trouble of having to select the attendees yourself, and I know you have no interest in such things."

"My husband," said a smiling Elizabeth Darcy, "has not yet learned to look upon Georgiana's suitors with amusement."

Georgiana witnessed all this with embarrassment. She did not particularly enjoy being an object either of her brother's protection or of Mr. Bingley's encouragement, but she knew both acted out of affection for her, each in his own way. At least Mrs. Darcy's gentle teasing had erased the severe look from her brother's face, and he was now looking at his wife with a silent gleam growing in his eyes.

"Well, now that Darcy has abandoned his attack on my hospitality," said Mr. Bingley, "Let us—"

"It is easy, is it not, to be hospitable with another's home?" asked Mr. Darcy, but he was smiling now.

"Let us," continued Mr. Bingley, simply ignoring the interruption, "engage in a game of whist."

"I would prefer not, Bingley," replied Mr. Darcy, reaching for a book that rested on the stand beside his chair.

"Very well, then I shall assume the responsibility of entertaining the ladies," said Mr. Bingley, directing the three to a table. Mrs. Darcy was not by nature a card player, but she must make up the fourth. Her husband had already succeeded in escaping the entanglement, thus cruelly denying her the opportunity.

Chapter 3

As the music commenced, Mr. Darcy assumed his usual station along the wall. He walked deliberately along its length and eyed his sister's partner as the pair danced.

"Mr. Darcy," said Caroline Bingley as he approached her. She matched her gait with his and trailed beside him. "I see your marriage has not made you any fonder of these diversions."

"My wife is engaged at present," he said, nodding to Elizabeth, who was sitting down at some distance. Mrs. Darcy was involved in an apparently animated conversation with her sister Kitty, who had chosen to sojourn with the Bingleys for the summer.

"But she is not the only lady in the room, Mr. Darcy."

"Is she not?"

Miss Bingley was uncertain how to respond to this question. He had failed to take her hint, and she could not bring herself to press her point. "Dear Georgiana seems to be enjoying herself thoroughly," she said.

"Does she? I cannot determine. She smiles, but her expression seems strained. Do you know of her partner, Mr. Niles Davidson? For I know you are a woman of information."

This Miss Bingley mistook for a compliment, and she gladly related to him what little information she had managed to procure. "Apparently he is a friend of your neighbors and is staying in Derbyshire for part of the summer." This much Darcy knew, and so the statement was of little use to him. Miss Bingley perceived this and offered what she thought would be a unique piece of intelligence: "I understand that Mr. Davidson is a rising star in Parliament."

"So he informed us when he called upon us in London," said Mr. Darcy, disappointing his informant. "He looks rather young to have much influence."

"He is not unconnected."

"You know a great deal about him then, Miss Bingley?"

"Not a great deal," she answered with false humility, "but I am a woman very capable of ascertaining information. I would be pleased to discover anything you like."

"No such effort will be necessary," he replied. He bowed slightly before departing her company, outstripping her pace with his own long gait.

Mr. Darcy observed that, for the next set, Miss Darcy was engaged by a man who donned regimentals. Mr. Bingley answered his inquiry regarding the gentleman by replying, "You know, Darcy, that is the Major we met in Lambton. Major Talbot."

Mr. Darcy murmured something unintelligible in response and then left his friend for the company of his wife. He felt no real interest in Georgiana's current partner. The Major was handsome, to be sure, but he appeared to be at least thirty, which was too old, Mr. Darcy thought, to earn his sister's innocent affections. Major Talbot, he swiftly determined, was not likely to be an object of concern.

Mr. Darcy, perhaps, still overestimated his powers of observation. For had he remained to observe the couple a moment longer, he would have had ample cause for concern. Every time the dance called for physical contact, the Major's touch inspired in Miss Darcy the tints that glow, and though the couple had little opportunity for conversation during the first dance, Georgiana did frequently speak to him with the smiles that win. The second dance of the set afforded the pair a better chance of speaking, and Major Talbot said to his partner, "I do not see your cousin Colonel Fitzwilliam here today."

"He departed for America three weeks after the day we met you in London," she said.

He smiled to hear her calculate the event by using their first meeting as a base date. She obviously recalled their hour together with fondness. His sense of being flattered was eclipsed by a slower realization. "America?" he asked. "Colonel Fitzwilliam has been sent to war?"

Georgiana could hear the surprise in his voice and it made her worry. He must judge her cousin to be an inexperienced soldier—a possibility she herself had suspected—and that fact did not augur well for his chances of survival. When the dance allowed her a chance to speak again she said, "Yes. Do you think he will be in much danger?"

"A man of his profession must occasionally find himself in the course of danger," he replied. At the moment, he was insensitive to her concern for her cousin's safety because he was brooding over the injustice of what he perceived to be Colonel Fitzwilliam's good luck. "I would love to be able to do my duty by my country and actually serve where I am needed, on the battlefield, instead of squandering my time here."

This declaration produced an instant frown upon Miss Darcy's face and thrust her back into her familiar silence. By that expression, Major Talbot could not remain unmoved. He quite literally bit his tongue, a sort of involuntary self-castigation for his thoughtlessness. "I apologize, Miss Darcy, I certainly did not mean to imply—" The movement of the dance prevented him from continuing, but when he was near enough to her again he said, "I only meant that I am training boys in Lambton, dedicating myself to mere exercise when I could be of greater use on the field. But I am most certainly not sacrificing my time here tonight; I cannot imagine a more pleasant use for it, than to have the honor of sharing the floor with you." This soothed Miss Darcy's discontent partially, but it was not until they danced a second set together later that evening that he was able to fully restore himself into her good graces. His expressions of concern for her cousin's safety and his repentant attentiveness to her at that time dispelled the lingering effects of his earlier *faux pas*.

Kitty Bennet also had the opportunity of dancing with Major Talbot at the ball. And though she could not deny his appeal, she had observed Georgiana's apparent interest in the gentleman and had consequently decided to focus her energies elsewhere. Kitty, though no less romantic than her sister Lydia Wickham, was less foolish; she might be young and unschooled, but when it came to the subject of courtship, she could mentally calculate all manners of probability, quickly and without recourse to paper.

Kitty knew her own dowry to be virtually nonexistent, her fortune to have been entailed away, her accomplishments to be mediocre, and her beauty to be beyond the norm yet nothing in comparison to Georgiana's. She had a delightful liveliness and a certain willingness to assimilate to the opinions of others, the latter of which, in particular, was considered an attractive trait by many men. She was determined to enjoy her time by dancing with as many gentlemen as possible and to pass her youth in the pursuit of amusement. Unless she thought it predictably productive, she would not focus her powers on any one man. But she had every intention of securing a husband before her looks began to fade. She would throw herself, she thought, at the mercy of the first willing man who was able to support her, and because he may or may not be worth spending a lifetime beside, she would not abandon her diverse merrymaking until the specter of that frightful, old-maid began to breathe hot upon her neck.

***

The parade of gentlemen who had sought to dance with Georgiana Darcy all averred they had been drawn by news of her singular beauty and diverse accomplishments, but her elder brother suspected that the promise of an expansive fortune had not been a deterrent. "I should have been at peace had she never been allowed out," he said, somewhat edgily, as he fell into his favorite chair by the fireplace. The ball had concluded and the house was now solemnly quiet, save for the crackling of the single fire, which had been lit to provide a reading light. Elizabeth Darcy let her eyes depart momentarily from the pages of her book to honor him with an amused glance, but she was soon reading again by firelight.

"And what do you mean by that look?" he asked, feeling himself settling back at ease after a tiresome night, which had required him to converse amiably with a great many strangers. He had performed admirably, but he was nonetheless glad to return to his own small family circle. Now that Georgiana and the family's various houseguests had retired for the night, Mr. Darcy could finally be alone with his wife.

"Why I mean nothing at all by it, Fitzwilliam," Elizabeth said, archly returning her eyes to his face.

"Hmmm," he murmured, clearly unconvinced. "You think me, perhaps, too cautious an elder brother?"

"I did not say so, my dear. Yet I think it may not be necessary to interrogate every gentleman who happens to dance with Miss Darcy."

"Interrogate!" he exclaimed in mock protest, knowing full well her statement had been light-heartedly hyperbolic. "I was merely attempting to ascertain their characters."

"And how did you get on?"

"About as well as you when you first met me, I imagine."

"You thought them all despicable?"

"No. I only mean that I had not the necessary information to draw an informed opinion."

"Unfortunately, that consideration did not stop me when I first drew a fixed opinion of you. Had I been less hasty in solidifying my prejudices, perhaps, our courtship would not have been so—tumultuous."

He winced. "It is equally true that had I been less arrogant and more of a gentleman—"

Elizabeth stopped him with a slight raise of the hand. "It is enough. We have been married for well over a year now, and I think we can put our humble beginnings behind us."

He nodded. They sat silently for a moment as he watched her face. At times, he still stared at her in that same odd manner; it was a look she had once mistaken for offense, but which she now knew meant he was either struggling to arrive at some conclusion or striving to control some emotion. In this case, she suspected the former and asked quietly, "What are you thinking?"

"I am hoping that my sister will be able to make as fulfilling a match as I have done. But I fear. . . I fear it will be difficult to tell if she is sought for herself or for her thirty thousand pounds. Appearances, as we have both learned, can be deceiving; men know well how to don masks in society. Of course, it has never been a particular talent of mine."

"No, it has not. And although I once took umbrage at the fact, I have since learned to respect you for it. But do you not trust your sister's feelings to be a reliable guide in this matter?"

He raised his eyebrows. It was not a well-thought question. Georgiana had almost eloped with the disreputable Mr. Wickham, who was now married to Elizabeth's sister Lydia. Indeed, even Elizabeth had been temporarily persuaded by his seemingly fine character, and she did not have quite the innocence of Georgiana.

"Then at least, love," she continued, "do not worry yourself about any of them until your sister should take a particular preference to one. Then perhaps you could inquire after him in a. . . subtle fashion."

"Invite him over in company for dinner; observe his character."

"Yes, exactly. And you will, no doubt, be sure he sees you have just finished cleaning your guns when he arrives."

He smiled. "You always know how to lighten my spirit, Elizabeth."

"It is certainly an arduous task," she sighed, "but I assume the burden as my domestic duty, and I will continue to persevere."

She had intended to tease him further, but he had already crossed the room and was now sitting beside her, his arm extended across the back of the couch, his eyes dancing with hers.

"Take pity on me, my darling wife, and do not tease me tonight. Social exertion before strangers is for me an exhausting exercise, and having engaged in such efforts all evening, I fear I do not now have the energy to spar with you."

"Why should you feel drained, Fitzwilliam? You are not shy like your sister."

"No. But I am easily bored. And I don't much enjoy speaking casually on such an enormous host of trivial topics."

"Ah, yes. I had forgotten. You are above such discourse."

"You rebuke me. Perhaps not undeservingly."

"No, dear, I will assign credit where it is due. You were all charm tonight, the single exception being the thirty minutes you spent in the corner watching your sister and Mr. Davidson dance."

"Did you not think he was a bit too familiar with her?"

"Yes, and so did Miss Darcy. I assure you she is not interested."

"And in whom would you say she did take an interest?"

"I am never one to disclose easily my opinions."

Mr. Darcy laughed. "Yes, indeed. You are quite guarded in your judgments, Lizzy. You have always been the epitome of restraint."

"And now it is you who rebukes me. Is it really true, then, that you have no energy remaining for the night?"

"Oh, I have energy enough," he hastened to clarify, "just not for a prolonged battle of wits."

"Then for what, Mr. Darcy?"

He looked as though he would begin to answer her, but instead he hesitated, attempted to speak, and again fell silent. She marveled that he could ever seem unsure of his reception, especially given the passion that—when it had first surfaced in response to his own—had surprised and almost frightened her by its intensity, but which she had since so often and so freely shown to him.

Mr. Darcy leaned closer. "Do you not think," he said, taking her hand in his, "as it is growing late, perhaps we should. . . that is, Elizabeth, do you wish—"

Her lips silenced his, and he responded to the kiss with fervor. He felt her draw very near to him, and when the faintest whisper of pleasure reached his ears, he knew he had his answer.

Chapter 4

The following evening brought a partial stranger to Pemberley. He was known well by name, and his advent in Derbyshire had engendered much speculation, but no member of the party could claim the slightest intimacy with him. Mr. Jacob Markwood's addition, as Miss Caroline Bingley helpfully pointed out, would make for an even number. The party already included Mr. and Mrs. Hurst, Jane and Charles Bingley, Elizabeth and Fitzwilliam Darcy, and the three single maidens, Georgiana, Kitty, and Caroline. The Gardiners, who had also been staying as guests of the Darcys, had journeyed on that morning to Lambton, where they would take a short vacation before returning to London. Elizabeth regretted that her aunt and uncle would not be joining their party, but she understood they had other people and places to visit in Mrs. Gardiner's home town.

As the company awaited its expected guest in the drawing room, Georgiana took a place next to her brother on one of the couches. Before Elizabeth could be seated on the other side of him, Caroline Bingley had assumed the spot. Elizabeth was more amused than disturbed by Miss Bingley's usurpation, and she amiably departed her husband's company to sit instead with her sister Jane, where she proceeded to admire her nephew Jonathan.

"He is crawling quite profusely now," Jane told her, scooping the active boy from the floor and placing him in his aunt's welcoming arms. "Kitty has immensely enjoyed playing with him, and she has been quite an attentive aunt."

"You have been a very positive influence on her, Jane," Elizabeth replied, glancing at her younger sister, who sat engaged in conversation with her brother-in-law Mr. Bingley.

"I am sure, Lizzy, the work was all yours, when she last sojourned at Pemberley."

Mr. Darcy smiled across the room at Elizabeth as she held the baby in her arms, and he was struck by a sudden twinge of jealousy. They had still not been so fortunate as to conceive a child, and he had begun to fear the happy day might never come. While he watched his wife and nephew, Mr. Darcy gradually began to realize that Caroline Bingley was attempting to engage him in conversation. Instead of encouraging those efforts, however, Mr. Darcy turned his attention to Mr. Hurst, saying, "Your cousin Mr. Markwood, I understand, has been residing in Oxfordshire?"

It was early in the evening, and as Mr. Hurst was not yet either comatose or inebriated, he managed to carry on a coherent exchange. "Yes," he said. "Ever since his disinheritance, he has worked as a curate there."

"It seems cruel of Mr. Markwood's father to cut off his son so entirely," said Georgiana, quietly braving the waters of conversation.

Mr. Hurst replied, "Mr. Markwood did expressly disobey his father's wishes. I believe Sir Robert hoped that if my cousin were forced to endure the life of a poor curate, he would relent his new ambition and return to Oxford to study the law."

"Not all curates are poor," suggested Kitty, who was eager to join in a new conversation now that Mr. Bingley had wandered off to amuse his son. "The curate in this parish, Mr. Bailee, is actually quite comfortable, and he even lets a small cottage of his own in Kympton."

Indeed, Peter Bailee had been allotted a healthy income by the former vicar. This would seem to speak well of the vicar's generosity, but it may have been something other than liberty that motivated him to open wide his hand. Peter Bailee, like many a curate, had conducted the real work of the parish, and finding his income insufficient, he had begun to intimate that he might seek another profession altogether. The vicar, unsure that he could obtain as dependable a replacement, was determined to keep him. Not only was Mr. Bailee's income above the norm for a curate, but, as a single man, he had been able to live quite cheaply. All this Kitty knew because the curate often managed to corner her after church, feeling, perhaps, that she was neither too common nor too genteel for his conversation.

"Perhaps," replied Mr. Hurst, "but it is not so with most curates, who we all know to be the poor relations of the church. Mr. Markwood's income in Oxfordshire was certainly very meager, and the fact that such a state of poverty did not drive him to reconcile with his father I can only attribute to sheer stubbornness. I have heard that after Mr. Markwood's ordination, he and his father exchanged harsh words, and I can certainly believe it. I knew Jacob Markwood as a child, although the family was absent from England for many years, and I have not much known him since. But in his childhood he was certainly headstrong."

"But surely," suggested Georgiana, "he would not have ignored his father's wishes had he not felt a real calling?"

"Who can guess his true reason for entering the Church?" replied Mr. Hurst. "Sir Robert, at least, believes his son took an express joy in rebelling against him. Jacob Markwood utterly flouted his father's wishes, despite the expense Sir Robert had incurred to educate him. The father, therefore, now pins all his hopes—and his fortune—on his younger son Aaron Markwood."

Mr. Darcy had never considered that Mr. Markwood had perhaps chosen the church not as an act of conviction, but as an act of rebellion. The thought now concerned him. He did not know the man, and yet he had acted on mere suggestion when offering him the living at Kympton. Mr. Darcy was not an obviously religious man—at least, he seemed to be no more religious than convention would naturally dictate—but his conscience pained him when he thought that he might possibly have chosen a more worthy clergyman. Mr. Markwood's fate at the hands of his father had garnered Jane's easy sympathies, and she had conveyed them to Elizabeth, who should have known her sister well enough to know how quickly she thought the best of everyone. To please his wife and sister-in-law by offering Mr. Markwood the living had been quick and easy.

Mr. Darcy had acted more frivolously than was his nature, and he began to fear he might regret it. He had also begun to wonder why so many people seemed to know of Mr. Markwood's misfortunes. It is true that word spreads quickly in a society that relies on gossip for its foremost entertainment, but Mr. Darcy had also known men—one, indeed, whom he must now call brother-in-law—who had boasted proudly of their imaginary calamities. In hope of learning something more reassuring, he asked, "And what was Mr. Markwood's reception when he assisted in Oxfordshire?"

"Oh," said Mr. Hurst, "I have not heard too much of it. There were some, I know, who thought his pastoral attentions were too indiscriminately bestowed, in that he failed to make the appropriate distinctions of class which we all know to be essential. Apparently, he spent a great deal of time in the homes of certain poor families—not, I do not mean, performing his right duty by them—but actually fraternizing with them. Then, in turn, he behaved quite indifferently toward the better elements of society. I hope he shall exhibit himself better here, Mr. Darcy, as you have insisted on giving him the living despite my better advice."

"I was unaware you had offered any advice on the matter."

"I said something to Mrs. Bingley, you know."

"So, then, Mr. Markwood was not well liked?" Mr. Darcy asked.

"He certainly gave some important persons in society occasion to murmur," replied Mr. Hurst. "But I have heard that he was once permitted by the vicar to preach a sermon, and it was apparently well received because it was brief, and although it contained some words that inspired offense, it at least provided no inducement to sleep."

Georgiana smiled at the remark, but then she thought she should not make light of the divine office of preaching, and she forced herself to frown in order to avoid laughing. Meanwhile, the anticipated guest had arrived and was being escorted to the drawing room, where he met his host with a bow. After some brief conversation, and after all the introductions had been made, the company began to move toward the dining room. This time, Mrs. Darcy claimed her rightful place beside her husband.

As they were seated, Georgiana remarked to Mrs. Darcy, "You failed to mention how handsome Mr. Markwood would be." This statement was evidence of an abiding trust in her sister-in-law. It was but a spontaneous overflow of unfiltered thought; it was no serious reflection, and Georgiana had no fear it would be regarded as one.

Nevertheless, even Elizabeth's light hearted teasing caused Miss Darcy to blush. When Mrs. Darcy noted that Georgiana had recently begun to pay more careful attention to single gentlemen, she replied in a fluster, "Yes, Lizzy, but I only comment to you." She glanced toward her brother as she spoke these words, caution in her voice.

Making sure not to be overheard, Elizabeth said, "Be assured, dear sister, that all your confidences are safe with me. I am not in the habit of discussing with your brother your observations on the appearances of various men, nor did I mention to him that you wished Major Talbot could have danced three sets with you last night instead of just two."

Georgiana's blush deepened and she quickly took her seat. Major Arthur Talbot had indeed been an object of her admiration, and why not? He had first earned her attention that afternoon in Lambton, and even now the vision of his gentle smile lingered in her mind's eye. Georgiana's pleading look, when she finally raised her eyes to her sister-in-law, told Elizabeth that the conversation on the subject of Major Talbot must come to an end.

The new vicar was called upon to say grace, but if the guests were expecting his words to provide insight into his character, they were disappointed. His prayer was brief and his text was borrowed. The meal began.

"So, Mr. Markwood," Mr. Hurst called from several seats away as he plunged full-force into his meal, "You do not have a wife."

The clergyman looked up from his plate as if confused. He glanced in the general direction of his cousin. "Pardon?" he asked.

Mr. Hurst, realizing he had not been heard the first time, now repeated loudly, "You do not have a wife."

Kitty was glad to see that the vicar had been addressed as she hoped that his conversation might eventually lead to the subject of his brother Aaron. Kitty had gradually forgotten the gentleman after their dance in London, but the appearance of his brother at Pemberley had drawn the young man once again to her attention. She now determined that Aaron Markwood was indeed someone whom her mind would be content to dwell upon. Unfortunately for her, the conversation never meandered onto such a happy subject.

"No, cousin," replied the vicar to Mr. Hurst. "I do not have a wife at present. But I am not yet eight and twenty, and so I am sure the situation is not quite as desperate as your tone implies."

Mr. Darcy did not much care for Mr. Hurst's outburst either, but the subject did raise his interest. "And yet," he said to Mr. Markwood, who sat directly across from him, "the position of a clergyman is somewhat unique in regard to marriage in that a congregation wishes its shepherd to be settled. A parson has the kind of position that might require him to visit—that is to say, the propriety of certain situations would require him to be wed."

"I understand you, sir," replied Mr. Markwood. "Marriage is likewise important, I think, in order to give a man some concept of the great mystery that is represented by Christ and His Bride, the Church. I do envy those who happily inhabit the blessed state. Yet God has not chosen to so grace me at present, and I have learned to be patient with Him."

Mr. Darcy was so concerned with reading the vicar's character that he did not think to be polite, and he defaulted instead to bald directness. "That is all very well," he said, "so long as patience with God is not used as an excuse for passing up a satisfactory opportunity in pursuit of unrealistic expectations."

"I am, sir, already known to have passed up a satisfactory opportunity—at least with regard to profession—for my concept of God's will." When next he spoke, Mr. Markwood sounded vaguely defensive. "But never, I think, would I mistakenly do so in the case of marriage. Of course, I suppose we may possibly disagree with regard to our definition of the word 'satisfactory.' Our standards, on that point, may not be the same." Mr. Markwood looked at Mrs. Darcy, who was in excellent beauty that evening, and who had just then been watching her husband with a mixture of tenderness and amusement. "Yet," he said, continuing to observe Mrs. Darcy, "upon consideration, I do not think that our definitions could much differ."

Darcy caught the hint, but he was unsure how Mr. Markwood intended it. This ambivalence prevented him from taking offense. Instead of responding, he changed the subject. "And how do you like the parsonage, Mr. Markwood?"

"Very well, sir. It is humble, yet somehow elegant. It has been designed, I think, by a true workman. If I were forced to complain of anything, it could only be the lack of a suitable library to house my books."

"You have a large collection, then? I understood you were currently without fortune of any kind."

"Without an allowance, and without the hope of inheritance. But not without fortune. While we were yet on good terms, my father was generous. Whenever I saw a volume I wanted, he saw that I had it, even before we were wealthy. He obtained for me in two decades more than many families acquire in two generations."

"And when you ceased to be on good terms, he did not keep them for his own library?"

"His interests are confined to law, politics, and philosophy. Mine, on the other hand, tend toward poetry and theology. My collection was the one thing he let me take from home. I had acquired a great many books before. . ." He looked down, abruptly mastering some emotion, but whether it was anger or regret Mr. Darcy could not tell. When he had conquered himself, Mr. Markwood resumed, ". . . before I displeased my father." After a moment of uncomfortable silence, he continued, "But I suppose it is quite wrong to say I am without hope of inheritance. For I hope for a very great inheritance indeed."

"Oh?" inquired Caroline Bingley as she leaned forward to look down the length of the table to where the vicar sat. She had not taken much interest in the clergyman until the word 'inheritance' had forced her to become suddenly engaged. "From what source?"

"From the Dayspring, madam, from God Himself. I have an inheritance awaiting me one day. We all do, I hope."

Miss Bingley's interest was considerably diminished by this

response, but she nonetheless nodded with seeming politeness. Mr. Markwood continued, "It should go without saying that there are greater treasures in this life than those we store up upon earth."

"It should go without saying," announced Mr. Hurst, who was now well into his cups. "And yet you say it. You clergymen are always forcing the conversation onto spiritual paths, are you not? You cannot rest for a moment, it seems, without introducing a lecture." He motioned for the servant to refill his glass. "Now that's a treasure," he said, taking a sip before falling into his more familiar state of silent lethargy.

Mr. Darcy eyed his friend's brother-in-law with distaste. Mr. Hurst was a tolerated visitor to Pemberley but fortunately not a frequent one. While Mr. Hurst absorbed himself with his plate, Mr. Darcy directed his conversation once again to the vicar. "We have offered your archdeacon our hospitality when he comes tomorrow with the bishop for your induction. He will stay with us for the duration of his visitation."

"Are you acquainted with him?" asked Mr. Markwood.

"No. He has been with your bishop only three years, and I have not had the opportunity to meet him during any of his former inspections. But I assume you are acquainted with him?"

"A little."

"What sort of man is he?"

Mr. Markwood blinked and was silent for a moment. Gradually, he seemed to realize he had been asked a direct question. "The Venerable Dr. Ramsey?"

"Yes," replied Mr. Darcy, striving to mask his irritation. Although he had learned to regard pride as a weakness and had for some time endeavored to approach others without prejudice, he was still accustomed to having men pay close attention to his words. "That is the name of your archdeacon."

"Yes, it is," agreed Mr. Markwood, but he did not address the question.

"And what sort of man is he?" Mr. Darcy asked again. "Is he sensible?"

"He is capable of reason."

"Is he pious?"

"He is fond of quoting the Bible."

"Articulate?"

"His pronunciation is accurate."

Elizabeth observed Mr. Markwood as he continued to answer the queries of her husband. How strange, she thought, that she had not noticed he was handsome until Georgiana had drawn the fact to her attention. Since Elizabeth had fallen in love with her husband, she had rarely bothered to observe the appearance of other men. It had long been agreed by all that Mr. Darcy was among the handsomest gentlemen in society, and love had given to Elizabeth an even more admiring vision.

Yet now that she thought of it, Georgiana was right. Mr. Markwood was singularly handsome. The light hue of his uncommon eyes contrasted sharply, but not unattractively, with his raven hair. At times those eyes looked brown, at others green, and in a certain light, almost gray. His face too was remarkable, sculpted like the work of some Italian artist who had sought to imitate a bold Greek hero. He held himself with poise, and yet he seemed somehow distant. Although he conversed actively and politely enough when directly addressed, he initiated conversation with no one. When he was not a party to the discussions, he looked somewhat absently about the table. At times, Elizabeth thought she observed in his deep eyes a kind of sadness. She did not think it could be the loss of a mere monetary fortune that had produced such feeling. But what weight burdened the disconsolate clergyman, Elizabeth Darcy could not guess.

Chapter 5

After enjoying their port, the gentlemen moved to the drawing room to rejoin the ladies. There Mrs. Louisa Hurst entertained the company with her playing on the pianoforte. Her husband had already procured for himself an entire loveseat, and he was soon partaking of a deep sleep, which rendered him inconsequential to the rest of the party.

Mr. Markwood watched Mrs. Hurst play with some disinterest; he gazed in her general direction, but his thoughts were clearly elsewhere. When she had completed her playing, he continued his reverie while the others politely clapped. The sound seemed to draw him forth, and looking mildly embarrassed, he joined in with the applause at the precise moment when it had ceased.

Elizabeth wondered if Mr. Markwood's behavior could be attributed to shyness, but she did not think so. For one, he had chosen willingly to be a clergyman, an uncomfortable calling for a timid man. What was more, he had no difficulty expressing himself when he did respond, although he usually hesitated before speaking as if he had not been listening and was just then catching the echo of words.

"Mr. Markwood," said Charles Bingley, with easy charm, "I have not much heard your conversation this evening. I see you had a lively interchange with my friend, Mr. Darcy, but from my position at the table I was not privileged to enjoy it. How do you like Derbyshire?"

The pause that succeeded these words was more than brief but not quite so long as to be uncomfortable. "From what I have seen so far," said Mr. Markwood, "I like it considerably, although I have just now settled. I am grateful for a benefactor," he nodded toward Mr. Darcy, "and for the opportunity to serve in this parish."

Jane Bingley was pleased with the turn of the conversation, for she always liked to hear positive words. "And what," she asked Mr. Markwood, "have you liked about Derbyshire so far?"

"The grandeur of the land has much inspired me. And residing so close to Pemberley—long known to be one of the most beautifully maintained estates in the country—is a kind of day-to-day honor. I have enjoyed the city, but the scenery here is more conducive to the kind of reflection that befits a man who is striving to know his Creator."

Caroline Bingley believed she had been too long omitted from the conversation, and in an attempt to vault herself back into its midst, she issued forth at once a criticism and a quip. "I cannot imagine, Mr. Markwood, what you mean by saying that you are striving to know your Creator. After all, you are to be the new vicar in this parish; you don't mean to imply you do not already know your business?"

Mr. Markwood responded, "I know my business, madam. But I do not think I shall ever fully know my God. Though I try to comprehend His feeling, though I delight in His slightest encouragement, and though I desire nothing more than that He should condescend to grace me with His presence, I am never fully sure of myself. I am forever longing for some. . . for some gentle touch from God."

"Why, you speak like a lover!" snorted Miss Bingley. "This is hardly appropriate language for religion."

Although Mr. Markwood's response had lowered him in Miss Bingley's esteem, it had raised him in Mr. Darcy's. The possibility that Mr. Markwood's choice of profession had been an act of rebellion now seemed far less likely to him. Nevertheless, Mr. Darcy still wished to learn more of the clergyman's character since he had not made a proper effort to discern it previously. He asked, "You possess no bitterness, then, even though you have lost your fortune for your profession?"

"For my profession, sir?"

"Yes. No regret?"

Mr. Markwood appeared confused. "I do not comprehend you."

"I believe my question was straightforward. Do you regret that your choice of profession has caused you to fall out of favor with your father and to lose thereby any hope of earthly inheritance?"

"I think. . ." Mr. Markwood hesitated and then resumed, "I think, sir, that you have been misinformed with regard to my current situation. While it is true that my father and I have suffered an estrangement, its cause was not my choice of profession. I understand that the employment of the church is not often the ambition of a gentleman, and it is certainly not expected of the elder son of a wealthy knight. Nevertheless, after less than a year at Oxford, I elected to pursue studies in theology rather than law. My choice disappointed my father, but it did not alienate him. Rather, he supported me. Sir Robert paid my way through Trinity College. He planned one day to secure for me a respectable living, but after our alienation from one another, I was forced to rely on my own resources. Were it not for your generosity, sir, I should still be a humble curate, without a living, and without glebe lands. Thanks to your kindness, I need no longer dread either poverty or obscurity."

"But," said Jane suddenly, quite surprised by these revelations, "I had thought. . . I mean, your cousin, surely, told me your ordination was the reason you had lost your fortune."

"My cousin, Mrs. Bingley," he said, glancing at the slumbering Mr. Hurst, "has no better sources of information on the subject than do you. He has never been particularly close to my family, and his assertions are evidence of nothing more than Rumor, who is a shifty Lady, and not long to be trusted. I have heard many interesting tales regarding the source of my misfortune; I did not know this was the particular one with which my cousin had presented you. I am sorry for the misunderstanding."

"If your father already knew you were to be a clergyman," wondered Jane aloud, "why was he planning to let Netherfield for you?"

"It was not intended for me, madam. Sir Robert was looking for an estate for my brother, Mr. Aaron Markwood." The reader may safely conclude that—in spite of anything she may have been thinking, or saying, or doing at this point—Kitty Bennet's concentration was instantly redirected toward the speaker. "As my brother had just entered his profession in London," continued the vicar, "he was too busy to tour Netherfield himself. He has a home in the city, but he wished also to have one in the country. He decided against the estate and has since settled on another in the shire of Buckingham where my father also resides."

Miss Bennet was not alone in directing her attention to the present exchange; Caroline Bingley was likewise engrossed by Jane's conversation with Mr. Markwood, but for a different reason: she sensed in it the presence of the delicious fruit of gossip. She could hardly wait to learn the secret of his misfortune so that she might later delight in sharing it with her friends. "What then," she asked Mr. Markwood, "was the source of the estrangement between you and your father?"

Mr. Markwood did not answer. Instead, for the first time that evening, he turned his conversation toward an individual who was not directly addressing him. "Miss Darcy," he said, bowing toward the young Georgiana, "I have heard from Major Talbot that you have a great love of music. I should very much like to hear you play."

"Major Talbot?" she asked, surprised by the mention of his name. "How do you know him?"

"We met at Oxford some years ago. He is three years my senior, and he completed his legal studies at about the same time I abandoned mine. Everyone thought he would be a successful barrister, but he has a peculiar streak of patriotism, which finally overcame the world's expectations. He purchased a commission, and oddly, it proved a profitable choice; he is a stronger fighter on the battlefield than he ever would have been in the courtroom."

"So you are in contact with him still?" asked Georgiana.

"I chanced to see him in Lambton this morning, though I had not seen him for years. He is quartered there, you know. I mentioned my living at Kympton, and he, almost immediately, mentioned you."

Georgiana reddened. Her change in color did not escape the notice of Mr. Markwood, nor indeed of Mr. Darcy, who regretted that he had not had the opportunity of conversing with the Major. He had been so busy questioning the other younger gentlemen who attended the ball that he had not thought much of Major Talbot, who must be eleven years his sister's elder. And now it seemed he had let the most pertinent one escape.

Mr. Markwood, sensitive to the embarrassment his words had caused Georgiana, hastened to add, "That is, when I mentioned I would be dining here tonight, he told me what he knew of the family, and the conversation naturally. . . that is, we were speaking of the whole family, and he happened to mention that you had a particular love of music, which seemed to lend a real spirit to your playing."

Georgiana had indeed played a song at dinner before the dancing had begun, but she was unaware that, in so doing, she had impressed Major Talbot. Had she been less humble, she might have considered this fact a small victory. Instead, the idea merely flattered her.

"In short," concluded Mr. Markwood, "I should like to hear you play, if you would grace us."

Georgiana agreed, eager to escape from any further mention of Major Talbot and from her elder brother's concerned gaze. She quickly made her way to the pianoforte and began to play. Mr. Markwood watched her, equally grateful to have eluded Miss Bingley's inquiry. But his relief soon gave way to real pleasure when he realized that Major Talbot had not just been speaking as a prejudiced admirer; Miss Darcy truly did play with spirit. This time, when the song ended, his applause was prompt. But his reprieve did not last long.

"Mr. Markwood," exclaimed Miss Bingley when Georgiana had reclaimed her seat. "We have been distracted from our conversation. You did not answer my question! What was the source of the estrangement between you and your father?"

Mr. Markwood supposed it would be too much to ignore her a second time, and so, taking a deep breath, he braced himself for his own reply.

"It was not because I refused his choice of profession," said the new vicar. "It was because I refused his choice of wife."

No other person in the company, except perhaps her own sister Louisa Hurst, shared Miss Bingley's lust for the sensational; but there was now no one who was not at least curious.

"Whatever do you mean?" asked Miss Bingley.

"There was a longstanding engagement," he answered, "or rather, I should say there was an understanding between my father and the parents of a certain Miss Grant. She and I had long been intended for one another. Her family resided in Oxfordshire, and I was encouraged to court her while studying at Trinity. My father had taken great pains to encourage me to love her; and for a time, I suppose, there was something in my demeanor which may have led him to believe that I did. He assured his friend that the match would be final as soon as I secured a respectable living. But I failed to fulfill the engagement. This deeply offended her father, and my own thereby lost a crucial political ally. My father's illness has prevented him from active involvement in politics; he has labored quietly behind the scenes. My father had hoped that Mr. Grant would enact the political vision he himself could not bring to fruition. But my decision destroyed that possibility. Sir Robert has not forgiven me."

"This is astonishing!" exclaimed Miss Bingley. "What possible reason could you have for refusing her? It is not as if you ran off and married some other young lady presumably for love, as some young men are apt to do these days." Mr. Darcy shot her a perturbed glare; he was not indifferent to the true direction of her barb. She smiled at him as if in excuse and returned her attention to Mr. Markwood. "What was there in her character to offend you?"

"Nothing at all, madam."

"You do not expect to pass scrutiny with such a cursory response as that, do you, Mr. Markwood? Was she unattractive?"

"She was—is—beautiful."

"Dull?"

"Her mind is quick."

"Poor?"

"She is of the same position as my family: greatly wealthy, albeit only lately so."

"What then? I must know!"

"It was simply that she did not love me."

"What do you mean?"

"I mean what I say. She did not love me."

"She, then, was the one to refuse you? But why then did you speak of failing to marry her?"

"She did not refuse me. She would have married me to please her father without so much as telling him it pained her. She would have settled for me."

"And little doubt," persisted Miss Bingley, "you feared she might every day remind you she had settled."

"It is not that. She would have respected me. But she would not have loved me. She made that clear enough, though not with any malicious intent. She wanted only to be honest, wanted only that my expectations should not be disappointed. I could have had her hand, but because I knew I could never hope to have her heart, to her own great relief, I declined her. My father lost much political ground because of my refusal, and he never deigned to ask me the reason for it. Perhaps my decision was unwise. But it was made and it cannot be unmade. And I hope that, in time, my father will understand that the past cannot be revived by his anger, and then we will reconcile."

"Then you may be wealthy again?" asked Miss Bingley, whose interest in Mr. Markwood was steadily growing.

"I may. But I am content with my present state, except for the loss of the good regard of a father whom I still love. Yet this is enough. I have answered all your inquiries, and I have spoken of matters that are too personal for polite society."

These words affected Miss Bingley, and she became suddenly aware that she had descended into country manners. How had she allowed that to happen? She could be malicious, but she always remained within the bounds of society's rules. She spread rumor only when the subject was not present, and she made her snide comments only among friends. She selected juicy appetizers from among the gentry's gossip and passed them gleefully about society's table. But to have been so frank a questioner while a guest in someone else's house, and while among new company—it was unlike her.

She excused herself, however, on the basis that Mr. Markwood had been too secretive and with the confidence that she had done Mr. Darcy a favor by exposing the vicar's past. After all, it was clear that Mr. Darcy had been concerned about Mr. Markwood's character. Had she not helped him to know it? That the master of Pemberley did not seem grateful for the information, but rather mortified by her conduct, was a misfortune that disturbed her. She had always hoped Mr. Darcy would choose her for a wife, and ever since he had settled, instead, for a woman below his sphere, Miss Bingley had held for him a strange mixture of admiration and contempt. It had compelled her sometimes to forget societal norms and to offer both unsolicited praises and all-too-public stings.

Charles Bingley, who had been discomforted by the rash line of questioning pursued by his sister, quickly seized the opportunity to redirect the conversation. With great enthusiasm, he began to speak of hunting: "Mr. Darcy and I simply cannot wait until autumn for the organized drive. We are determined to pick off a few pheasant of our own next weekend before I return home. Of course, it will be very difficult with such a small party, and so long before the season, but we're just out for the fun of it. We'll be stalking our prey in the field of one of Darcy's farmers, a tenant. Darcy has an excellent Springer spaniel that will help us flush out the birds. Pheasant are fabulous hiders, you know. Would you like to join us for the hunt, Mr. Markwood?"

"I should be glad to, and I am honored that you would condescend to invite me."

Bingley laughed, "Condescend? Why no, not at all. We should be delighted with your company I am sure, shouldn't we Darcy?"

"We will be pleased to have you join us, Mr. Markwood. I can lend you your choice of arms, should you have need."

"I have a shotgun, sir, I believe will suffice."

"Well enough."

"But I do thank you for the offer."

"No need."

The two men had difficulty continuing the conversation as both had been equally brief and direct in their replies. So Bingley asked, "Will Mr. Gardiner be joining us, Darcy?"

"I have invited him, but he has business to attend."

At this, Caroline Bingley raised her eyebrows, anticipating the sweet savor of criticism. Mr. Gardiner was a mere attorney, and he must forgo the gentlemanly pleasures of hunting in exchange for labor. Miss Bingley had once enjoyed abusing Elizabeth's relations with Mr. Darcy, and she hoped they might now share that common pleasure again. But to her disappointment, nothing further came from the gentleman's lips. Instead, Caroline heard her brother say, "That is a shame. I rather enjoy his company."

"As do I," replied Darcy, and here he glanced at Elizabeth. It was not merely that he enjoyed the company of his wife's uncle; he also felt indebted to the gentleman since the Gardiners had been the means of bringing Elizabeth back into his life after all hope of winning her seemed lost. Mrs. Darcy returned her husband's smile. "Will you," he asked her, "grace us with a song? You have not played this evening."

"Only because we have had more worthy performers to prevent me."

"Well, Mrs. Darcy, if you are fishing for flattery, you will not catch it with self-deprecation. I insist that you assume your place on the bench."

"Very well, sir." She curtsied before sitting before the pianoforte. "I am not known to thwart your commands."

Miss Bingley was taken aback by Elizabeth's ironic tone, and she glanced at Mr. Darcy, expecting to see him offended. Instead, he only smiled satirically and replied, "No, Mrs. Darcy, I am quite sure you would not dare."

Caroline Bingley did not deem this exchange to be at all in keeping with Mr. Darcy's dignified character. Her sister Louisa shot her an expressive glance, but both women refrained from commenting as no one else appeared affronted. Kitty, the Bingleys, and especially Georgiana had grown accustomed to such scenes, and Mr. Markwood seemed wholly unaware that anything was amiss.

Elizabeth began to play. Mr. Darcy, as always, listened to her with admiration, for though she was not the most proficient player, few things gave him greater pleasure than to hear the vibrant music her graceful fingers managed to extract from those simple ivory keys. As the evening wore on, Mr. Markwood resumed his pattern of speaking only when spoken to, and his answers grew increasingly short, his expression ever more distant. At length, he politely took his leave and expressed his wish of seeing them all in church the following morning.

Chapter 6

A chorus of voices rose as the loitering parishioners awaited the arrival of the clergy. The gossip had that morning inexorably turned to the new vicar. Why had he received the Darcy family living? How had the Darcys first become acquainted with him? Who knew anything of his character? There were rumors that he had been deprived of his fortune because he chose the church. Others said it was his penchant for gambling while at Oxford that had persuaded his father to cut him off, and that he had sought orders only in order to secure a means of economic survival. One of the parishioners claimed to have heard that the loss of Mr. Markwood's fortune related somehow to a shadowy liaison he had conducted with a distinguished lady who was far beyond his social grasp. Miss Bingley, however, denied the rumor, and proudly indicated that she—and perhaps she alone—knew the true story.

Immediately, and much to her delight, Caroline Bingley found herself to be the center of attention. She began to divulge her news; but something checked her. Was it a scruple? Miss Bingley was aware that she had long been in want of a husband. Mr. Markwood's father was wealthy and recently distinguished, and there was hope that the vicar might reconcile with him, thereby regaining both place and fortune. True, he was a minister now, and that would never do, but once he had his fortune again, she could begin to lead him on to higher paths. And the fact that he was handsome, well, that would just serve to draw more attention to her. . . No, she would not indulge in sensational stories with these petty women. She would not make Mr. Markwood appear in an uncertain light. He was a gentleman's son; he must be known to be a gentleman himself.

Not all of the parishioners desired to know the details of their new shepherd's history. Some actually wondered what kind of preacher he would make. The former occupant of the position, if he had been dull, had at least been honorable. He had known his Scripture well, and he had always said the proper thing at the proper time. His doctrines had been correct. But would Mr. Markwood's be? These parishioners were more spiritually minded. They came to church with the sole intention of listening—and listening carefully—to every word of the sermon. If Mr. Markwood proved flawed on some point, they would be more than delighted to correct him.

And so began the first Sunday of the first week that Mr. Markwood would serve in Derbyshire. The congregation milled about, and the buzz of conversation was finally silenced by the dramatic approach of the bishop. Intermittent exclamations of "my lord" could be heard as the bishop led Mr. Markwood up to the church door and ceremoniously placed the clergyman's hands upon it. The bishop's presence in the parish was a rare one, for he appeared only when a new clergyman was to be inducted, and he always departed as swiftly as he came.

When at last Mr. Markwood rose to recite the thirty-nine articles, there was a sudden murmur of feminine voices. Now that the ladies of the congregation had a good view of their new vicar, they felt that they were not likely to disapprove, and they began to show their reverence. Once the induction ceremony was complete, the real service could begin. Prayer books were rustled, yawns were suppressed, voices were unevenly lifted, and at length, Mr. Markwood ascended the pulpit to deliver his sermon.

Georgiana Darcy watched nervously. She wished Mr. Markwood a good reception and knew that society could be critical, and yet, it was not for him that she was nervous. Major Talbot was standing immediately beside her. The Major, having ventured in somewhat late to church, had seized the first available opening in the crowd, and in so doing, he had brushed unintentionally against her arm. "My apologies, Miss Darcy," he whispered, and then, "Why are you not in one of the reserved pews?" Her family was wealthy and would certainly have owned their own pew. He was therefore surprised that all of the Darcys appeared to be standing. Miss Darcy pointed toward the pew where Mrs. Bingley held her young son. Next to her sat two elderly, feeble ladies. It seemed the Darcys had surrendered their seats. Major Talbot smiled at the generosity, and whispered, "A new entry in your book of virtues."

Georgiana did not have time to feel flattered by the remark, because she could feel the gaze of her elder brother, who was eyeing Major Talbot with some consideration. He had not intended to be obvious, and he did not know how peculiar his attention appeared; his concern was reflexive. Elizabeth placed a hand on her husband's, and when the pressure caused him to break his steady gaze from the Major in order to turn to her, she whispered, "Subtlety, dear."

Mr. Darcy sighed and returned his attention to the service. He was able to concentrate, despite the near presence of his sister's suitor, because he genuinely wished to observe Mr. Markwood's presentation. He still faulted himself for having gifted the living so hastily; he had not considered what a crucial role a clergyman must play in maintaining the balance of society. Mr. Darcy desired to know that, by promoting Mr. Markwood, he had not failed in his own duty to the community.

Jacob Markwood looked silently about the congregation. Elizabeth began to anticipate his words with some interest. Church attendance, for her, had become an unwelcome obligation these past several months. It had required all of her self-discipline to concentrate on the former clergyman's sermons. Because she had heard Mr. Markwood speak so feelingly of God the evening before, she now hoped he might have the ability to inspire her sincere attention. But when he first began to preach, she was at once astonished and disappointed. He breathed hellfire and damnation.

It was not that Mrs. Darcy was among those who considered it impolite for a clergyman to mention sin. It was just that he was so vehement, so merciless, in his condemnation. He described the state of mankind in the most desperate and graphic terms. Men were vile; they were but worms, incapable of pure understanding; they were proud, backbiting, gossiping creatures who wounded each other more with weapons of speech than with weapons of war. Mr. Markwood's manner was articulate; his voice was powerful; and his words were not unpoetic. But his tone was bitter and unrelenting. After an escalating barrage of critical accusations, during which he described man as an invalid choking on his own vomit, Mr. Markwood fell suddenly and unexpectedly silent.

The congregation shifted. Was he done? Was that his message? How long until the benediction, when they would be freed to flee from this miserable, uncomfortable moment? They could only hope the preacher had reached the end of his sermon. But Mr. Markwood was not finished.

The vicar spoke again, only softly this time, almost inaudibly. "And yet," he said, stopping a moment to inhale a heavy breath. "And yet, while we were yet sinners, while we yet inhabited the wretched state that I have just described, our Lord did die for us." He continued, his voice no longer so low, but still gentle, still full of quiet awe. "While Judas's kiss still lingered on His lips, filled with the rancid taste of man's hypocrisy, our Lord did die for us." He turned now to the left, and looked with almost dampened eyes at that part of the congregation. "While Peter's denials still echoed in His ears, amplified by the pathetic cries of man's cowardice, our Lord did die for us." He turned to his right. "While the spit of His mockers still pooled in the scars they had torn on His back, bent by the burden of man's measureless sin, our Lord did die for us."

Mr. Markwood looked down. He seemed to be wrestling for composure. "Our God," he said, pronouncing his words slowly and clearly, "Our God feels for us an inexplicable love."

The clergyman raised his eyes again to the congregation, speaking now with less emphasis but with no less feeling. "We read today in our gospel lesson how 'Moses lifted up the serpent in the wilderness,' and we read that 'even so must the Son of man be lifted up: that whosoever believeth in him should not perish, but have eternal life.' Our Lord has given us life through His death. He has been lifted up on the cross, that we might likewise rise up from the ashes of our old selves. Because, in this sacrificial way, He has first loved us, we are able to learn to love Him. It is this gratitude that fuels us as we soar with injured wings to greater heights. It is this sacrifice that compels us to shake off the weight of our own indifference. It is this condescension that moves us to put off the outer clothing of all our selfish pretensions, and to stand, naked in spirit, before our God. It is His love that inspires us to love one another. And it is with His grace that we can begin to reflect His image once again, as we did in the Garden of Eden, in the age of our innocence, in the midst of the presence of God."

Mr. Markwood looked toward one of the church's stained glass windows; he seemed as though he would try to look through it. In time, he returned his attention to the congregation. "Brothers and sisters," he concluded, "let us love one another. For there will be help in this world, and there will be joy on this earth, if we but draw from the fountain of grace, and pass the cup of charity from one man to another."

***

As the congregation exited the church, it was considerably less gregarious than when it had entered. There was conversation, and pleasantries were exchanged. But there was no more discussion of Mr. Markwood. No more speculation about his lost fortune. And no one said a word about the sermon.

Kitty Bennet had not been long in the sunlight when the curate approached her under pretense of discussing the weather. Mr. Bailee had noticed her over a year ago, the first time she sojourned with the Darcys. As long as they spoke, she found his easy jollity amusing, but once she was out of his presence, she rarely thought of him at all. She assumed he spoke frequently with her because she was vaguely pretty and only slightly ashamed to condescend, but she never would have credited him with any serious designs. He was, after all, just a curate, dependent on the charity of the parish.

Consequently, Kitty could not help but think that Peter Bailee was beneath her. True, he had enough income to support himself, while she on the other hand was wholly without fortune; but she was connected by marriage to the illustrious Mr. Darcy, and Mr. Bailee—well, Mr. Bailee was the offspring of an honest, respectable, but obscure man. Had he been handsome, his position in society may not have borne so much weight with Kitty, for she had flirted with many a lowly officer. But Peter

Bailee was an unremarkable man. He was of average height, and if only he had been an inch or two taller, his figure might have been attractive. As was, Miss Bennet thought him slightly pudgy. His hair was a dull brown, though well trimmed, and his eyes would have been excessively plain were it not for the small, constant twinkle that brightened their otherwise dreary shade.

As Mr. Markwood approached his curate, Kitty parted quickly from the scene. The vicar said something to Mr. Bailee just as she left, and it made the curate laugh. That sound was perhaps Mr. Bailee's only truly distinguished feature. The laugh was surprisingly masculine, considering that it emerged from such a mild-looking man. It was also evidence of an uncomplicated nature, of a willingness to be pleased.

What Mr. Markwood might have said to elicit such an extraordinary sound, I will leave to the reader's imagination; I will only venture to hint that it had something to do with the archdeacon Dr. Ramsey, who had accompanied the bishop to church that morning and who would remain in Derbyshire to inspect the parish.

Mr. Markwood had only just met his curate the day before, but already he felt at ease with the merry man. In response to some words from Mr. Bailee, the vicar said, "I appreciate that you will execute that duty for me. I must dine with the Darcys this afternoon."

"Must?" said the curate, somewhat enviously. Though he was generally well liked, Mr. Bailee was not the sort of man to be invited to dine with the wealthy. Normally, he accepted this fact as an irreproachable condition of the society he inhabited, and he was not given to coveting the company of the upper classes. But now, Miss Kitty Bennet was once again a resident of Pemberley, and Mr. Bailee was not opposed to her company. What was more, he knew that his chances of enjoying it were quickly diminishing as she would soon return with the Bingleys to their estate.

"Dr. Ramsey will also be dining with the Darcys," said Mr. Markwood, "as he has been invited to reside with them during the course of his visitation."

This declaration effectively beat down the hoary head of jealousy, which had begun to raise its olive brow, and the curate gave his new vicar an almost sympathetic glance.

Dear reader, if you are wondering why both these gentleman should seek to avoid the archdeacon's company, you will know anon, as we are about to open the curtain wide upon this luncheon scene. But I must first pause to remark that a third person, other than Mr. Markwood and Dr. Ramsey, had also been invited that afternoon to Pemberley. Major Arthur Talbot now sat across the table from Georgiana, who occasionally rallied enough courage to shoot him a furtive glance. He seemed amused by her shyness and flattered by her apparent, but not excessive, admiration.

Had there been time enough for Miss Darcy's infatuation to evolve into something deeper, something more like love? Only she herself could know that, and I daresay it was a question she had failed to ask. It was better to enjoy the present moment, better to ask for nothing either more or less than her current giddiness. That she still enjoyed Major Talbot's company was plain enough. He possessed, after all, that special way of putting her at ease, a lucky talent that made him the continued recipient of both her smiles and—rarer still—her words.

And that vital question—had Major Talbot asked it of himself? Dear reader, I fear he had not, merely because he never thought to debate the finer points of such distinctions. He was serious about his profession, serious about words like 'honor' and 'duty', and serious, too, about keeping his promises—but beyond this, there was little he could regard with solemnity. To him, infatuation passed well enough for love, and so he was a man in love.

Mr. Darcy observed the pair's exchanges with subtle caution until he was distracted by the archdeacon's words. "Mr. Markwood," Dr. Ramsey was saying, "you preached today as though you were an Evangelical."

Mr. Markwood tilted his head ever so slightly; this physical reply was ambiguous to all who beheld it, and no one could guess whether he were affirming or contradicting the accusation. Dr. Ramsey, however, who was content to rely on his own assumptions without support from Mr. Markwood, warned, "The Anglican way, Mr. Markwood, is not the way of fervency. The English Church has always provided a via media." Here the archdeacon looked toward Georgiana, and, assuming that such a young, pretty girl could not possibly be familiar with common Latin, explained, "the middle way." She smiled warmly and nodded just as if he had not been patronizing, but she turned her attention away as quickly as possible and caught Major Talbot's eye. The two conducted their own silent conversation while the archdeacon continued, "Do you not think, Mr. Markwood, that it is dangerous for a man to be fervent?"

"Well," replied the vicar, "I imagine that depends on the subject of his fervency."

"Excess is never a virtue!" exclaimed the archdeacon. "Do you imply that it is?"

"I was not speaking of excess. I concede that excess, by its very definition, is never a virtue. If it were, it would not be called excess."

"Then we understand each other?"

Mr. Markwood glanced at Major Talbot, who offered his friend unspoken sympathy. The Major then said aloud, "I am quite sure he understands you, venerable archdeacon."

"Well," said Dr. Ramsey, not catching the true intent of Talbot's words, "you may think he understands my meaning, but I must be more plain. Tell me, Mr. Markwood, is our bishop aware of your predilection? For it is good to ask, as do some in the Bible, 'By what authority doest thou these things, and who gave thee this authority?'"

Mr. Markwood replied hesitantly, "The Pharisees asked that of Christ, I believe."

"It may be so," said the archdeacon hastily, "but Jesus Himself says, 'For I am a man under authority'."

"I believe it is the centurion who says those words."

"The point, Mr. Markwood, is that we are called by our Lord and Savior to be submissive to the hierarchy. Every man has his station in life. A great landowner like Mr. Darcy"—here he smiled at his host, attempting to ingratiate himself with a man

whose wealth he hoped might prove beneficial to the Church—
"inhabits a different sphere in society than a mere solicitor in
London. Likewise, as a vicar, Mr. Markwood, you ought to regard the opinions of your superiors. Even more so, for you are
called to submission not by societal, but by divine law."

Mr. Darcy now more fully understood Mr. Markwood's earlier
answers to his inquiries regarding the archdeacon, and for the
moment he regretted that hospitality must be among the Christian virtues. Dr. Ramsey would reside with them for another
few weeks, and the Darcys had not been prepared for the sort
of company they had procured.

"Has the bishop any objection to my 'predilection'?" asked
the vicar. "He said nothing to me after the sermon."

"The bishop," said Dr. Ramsey, "is a man of few words. As he
prefers contemplation to articulation, I always endeavor to
serve as his mouthpiece. I am at once his servant and his emis-
sary, and he relies on my judgment so thoroughly that he
sends me about the countryside to inspect the parishes of his
diocese more often, I daresay, than any other archdeacon in all
of England. Not only this, but he believes my ability to be so
keen that he desires me to stay for long periods of time among
the parishes of his dioceses. So implicitly does his lordship
value my opinion that he is always entrusting me with some
task or another, so that I am scarcely a day in his presence."

"That is confidence indeed, venerable archdeacon," said Mr.
Markwood, hopeful that Dr. Ramsey had distracted himself from
his preoccupation with the vicar's 'predilection'. "The bishop
must value you immensely to use you with so little reservation
and with such frequency."

"Indeed I believe he does, Mr. Markwood. In fact, just last
month, his lordship—"

For the next several minutes, the entire dinner party was
treated to the archdeacon's prolific description of the many
duties that the bishop had, in his great confidence, assigned
him. The list might have been expanded had not Elizabeth's
uncle outstripped his own sphere in society by interrupting Dr.
Ramsey's monologue in mid-sentence. "Mr. Markwood," he said
in a cheerful voice. "I, for one, was pleasantly surprised by the

conclusion of your sermon, and I found it inspired much reflection. When you began, I had been expecting something quite different. . . but the negativity of the first portion of your sermon ultimately served to accentuate the beautiful hope of the last. Mrs. Gardiner and I were both very quiet on the walk back to Pemberley. We thought it. . . very moving."

Mr. Markwood nodded with an appearance of earnest gratitude and said, "Thank you, sir, I am glad you found it so."

"Yes," said the archdeacon, "I understand why some in the merchant class might very well find something in an evangelical lesson to suit their tastes—"

"I likewise found the sermon affecting," said Mr. Darcy, a-bruptly and decidedly. "Major Talbot," he continued, redirecting the conversation onto a path he hoped would bring the entire party relief, "how long will your regiment be stationed in Lambton?"

"For but a few more weeks," he replied. "We march to Brighton in the near future, where we will join with another regiment for further training." He saw Georgiana's disappointment and opened his mouth to offer some comfort, but his words were swallowed by the archdeacon, who managed to find an immediate portal back into the conversation.

"But now that Napoleon is exiled on Elba," said Dr. Ramsey, "why train with such fervor? Why not allow the men more time to mingle in society, which is always a much needed civilizing influence on soldiers?"

"I was not aware that soldiers were so desperately in need of civilizing, venerable archdeacon," replied the Major.

"I did not mean the officers, sir. I hope I do not offend."

"No, indeed." Major Talbot glanced at Mr. Markwood, who returned him a suppressed smile.

"I believe you are an evangelical," announced Dr. Ramsey suddenly, turning from the Major and resuming the very subject Mr. Markwood hoped he had escaped.

"The idea should not much strain your credulity now, venerable archdeacon, as you have but recently assured me of the fact yourself."

Fortunately for Mr. Markwood, Dr. Ramsey was entirely impervious to sarcasm. Had he discerned the subtle insubordination that lay behind Mr. Markwood's words, the archdeacon might have reacted in defense of his privileged position. Instead, he said, "I mean I should have known you were because the bishop mentioned to me yesterday that he knew you to be a generous contributor to the London Evangelical Mission Society."

Mr. Markwood opened his mouth slightly as if to speak, but no words were forthcoming. He closed his lips and then opened them again just long enough to murmur, "Yes, I am."

Before the archdeacon could pursue the topic any farther, Elizabeth Darcy came to the vicar's rescue by suggesting to the ladies that it was time to retreat into the drawing room. How Mr. Markwood faired from thenceforth, we can only speculate, but when the six gentlemen at long last emerged from the dining room, their opinions were seared upon their faces. Mr. Darcy's countenance was marked by contempt, Mr. Gardiner's by weariness, Major Talbot's by boredom, Mr. Bingley's by discomfort, and Mr. Markwood's by embarrassment. The last face alone glowed with happiness, and it belonged to the venerable archdeacon, who was still speaking.

Chapter 7

The Wednesday following Mr. Markwood's unusual sermon, the Darcy family butler swung wide Pemberley's substantial front door in order to answer the impatient pounding of Mr. Niles Davidson. "I have come," the politician said, "to call upon Miss Darcy."

The butler replied, "She is not expecting visitors, Mr. Davidson. The family and guests have gone to town for the day. Only Miss Darcy is currently at home; she was feeling a bit tired and remained behind."

"What a wonderful coincidence," Mr. Davidson said, already stepping up into the hallway, which caused the butler to stumble back.

"As I mentioned, sir," cautioned the butler guardedly, "the rest of the family is away from home. Perhaps you would care to call when others are also present?"

He snarled an emphatic "no." Niles Davidson would never have taken such a tone with a superior, but he was sore displeased by this defiance from a servant. "I care to call now. Tell Miss Darcy I have arrived. I am sure she will be happy to receive me."

"Very well, sir." The butler nodded and retreated farther into the estate.

Mr. Davidson stood looking around the impressive foyer, attempting to determine what sort of London home he could secure with 30,000 pounds. Eventually, he spied a mirror and walked toward it. Niles Davidson was an exceedingly good-looking man, but he knew it, and that awareness tended to diminish his appeal. He straightened his cravat as he gazed admiringly at his own reflection. The mirror's frame was gilded with an intricate and creative carving, which did not fail to impress the visitor. But then, Mr. Davidson had never encountered a looking-glass he did not like.

"Miss Darcy will see you in the drawing room, sir," announced the returning butler, leading the gentleman down the hallway. When he had deposited Mr. Davidson in the presence of his mistress, the butler warily departed.

"Mr. Davidson," said Georgiana. "I am afraid you find me alone this afternoon. Mr. and Mrs. Darcy, along with our guests, have gone to Lambton for the day."

"It seems my good luck is holding strong, Miss Darcy," he said, and sat down in the most prominent armchair in the room. Georgiana likewise took a seat, clasping her hands together nervously in her lap. "And how are you, Mr. Davidson?"

"Exceptionally well, Miss Darcy. As you know, I have already obtained a seat in the House of Commons, and I hope one day soon to be among the most prominent of parliamentarians."

"How pleasant for you."

"And for you, Miss Darcy."

The statement flustered her. Unsure how best to respond, she said simply, "I do not understand you."

"I meant, Miss Darcy, that it will not require any condescension, on your part, to be seen with me, as I have succeeded so thoroughly, and will continue to succeed."

"I would not be embarrassed, Mr. Davidson, to be seen with any man of good character and education." Georgiana had never possessed any societal airs, though her shyness had been mistaken, at times, for aloofness.

"You should be more discerning, Miss Darcy. But a sweet young lady such as yourself—such openness becomes you. Not quite so well as that dress you are wearing, and I admire the way you have chosen to arrest your hair, just so. . . .."

While Miss Darcy attempted to derail Mr. Davidson from his present course of adulation, the butler opened the front door to a second caller. Major Arthur Talbot stood on the doorstep, his posture emanating an odd mixture of dignity and ease. "Is the family at home?" he inquired.

"As I have already told the other gentleman," replied the butler, somewhat curtly, "they are in town, and only Miss Darcy remains behind."

"I am sorry," said the Major, preparing to leave, "I certainly would not wish to invade her privacy." But as he began to walk down the great stairs that led to the courtyard, he turned. "The other gentleman?"

"A Mr. Davidson, sir."

"Davidson?"

"Yes, sir."

"On second thought," the Major climbed the stairs again, "Would you show me in to Miss Darcy?"

"Certainly, sir."

Mr. Davidson rose and greeted Major Talbot with a bow when he came into the drawing room, but the young politician was obviously displeased by the intrusion. He was likewise unsatisfied by Miss Darcy's reaction to the Major's entrance, for she greeted him with a great deal more warmth than he deserved.

Georgiana was not just pleased to see Major Talbot, she was relieved. Mr. Davidson would not presume to court her so recklessly in his presence.

"Your family, Miss Darcy, is in Lambton this afternoon?"

"Yes, Major," responded Georgiana. "The Bingleys are still with us, as are Miss Bennet, the Gardiners, and the archdeacon, and they have all gone together to town."

"You did not accompany them? I hope you are not unwell."

"Only a little tired."

He looked at her with concern. She seemed something more than tired, but it was not sickness that had marred her brow. Perhaps it was her company. He felt like he should leave her to herself, but he could not abide the idea of leaving her alone with Mr. Davidson. So he pretended that the moment was not awkward, and he began to speak: "I would like to keep your guests clear in my mind. The introductions that were made at dinner Sunday, I must confess, have not remained with me." He could not resist glancing at Mr. Davidson. He wished to watch the politician's reaction as he learned that Major Talbot had been an actual dinner guest of the Darcys. The Major was not disappointed. Mr. Davidson's irritation was apparent. Having received this trifling satisfaction, the Major returned his eyes to Georgiana and asked, "Mr. Bingley is your brother-in-law?"

"No, he is an old friend of my brother's." Miss Darcy thought for a moment and then continued, "Oh, but yes, he is a kind of brother-in-law now, as he is married to Mrs. Darcy's sister."

"And Miss Bingley, of course, is his sister."

"Yes."

"Miss Bennet is Mrs. Darcy's sister. And The Gardiners?" asked the Major.

"They are Mrs. Darcy's aunt and uncle. They live in London, but they are staying with us for part of the summer."

"Major Talbot," said Mr. Davidson before his rival could continue his conversation with Georgiana, "you are not staying long in Lambton, are you?"

"No sir, I leave before July, at the end of the month."

"Excellent. All of this socializing does not exactly become a soldier, does it? After all, even though Napoleon has abdicated and is safely exiled on Elba, the armies of England must always be on alert, do you not think? And there is also the matter of that disturbance with the former colonies, which has yet to be resolved."

"Our forces are prepared for anything, Mr. Davidson. And I am not exactly on leave, sir. My regiment is only encamped in Lambton. We are actively training, even now."

"Then why are you here, Major Talbot?"

"My day, sir, begins before sunrise. My present duties have been fulfilled, and I happen to have the rest of the afternoon at liberty."

"Strange that you should employ that liberty to travel over five miles from Lambton to visit the Darcys, who barely even know you."

"You, Mr. Davidson, have employed your liberty likewise."

"I have but come from next door. In so far as I am staying with their neighbour, I think I have a more reasonable claim to visit."

Before Major Talbot had a chance to address this taunt, Georgiana asked, "Have you heard any news of my cousin Colonel Fitzwilliam?"

"I am sure you would have heard from him before I," said the Major, turning his gaze away from the politician and back to the lady. In the process, the heat which had begun to rise to his cheeks lost its intensity, and his voice became cordial once again. "We are not on intimate terms, I fear. I served under him years ago; we are acquaintances, but not friends."

"I mean—I only mean, have you heard anything of his regiment through military channels? I only ask because we have not received a letter from him."

"I would not be concerned, Miss Darcy. It may only take a short time for letters to travel from America in peace time, but when a war is raging, there are so many opportunities for epistles to go amiss, and soldiers often do not have either the time or the resources to write."

Georgiana was eased somewhat by his assurance. "Do you think he will have to go into battle?"

He did not lie to her. "It is likely. I know your cousin has a ceremonial commission. . . but, ceremonial or not, he is under the General's command, and he has been called to war." He then offered her the following reassurance, and though it eased her heart, it could not uphold her countenance: "Your cousin, I think will prove a brave soldier."

She responded gloomily, "I still do not understand America's quarrel with us."

"They are upset about the blockades, and they claim we are illegally impressing their citizens." She had not wanted an explanation; she had only wanted his sympathy, and he realized that a moment too late.

"But we were not, were we?" she asked. He intended this time to ignore the question she asked and to offer instead the comfort she needed, but he was prevented.

"We," interrupted Mr. Davidson, "have impressed only our own former citizens, one-time British subjects who, for all we know, have defected from the British navy. Because some of them have become naturalized American citizens, Brother Jonathan insists on claiming them for himself."

Major Talbot looked at Mr. Davidson with some distaste for the gentleman's style of expression, but he did not contradict him.

"But really, Major Talbot," Davidson continued, "surely you are well bred enough to know that politics is one of the topics to be avoided in polite society. You should not encourage Miss Darcy to worry herself with these complex deliberations."

Again, Major Talbot made no reply. Instead, Miss Darcy actually interposed herself to guide the conversation forward. "And will you," she asked the Major, "likewise leave the country when you depart from Lambton?"

"It is a possibility," he replied. "Our current orders do not specify what the future may hold. We are to pull up stakes at the end of the month and march toward Brighton, but where we go from there, I cannot say with any certainty at present. I should like to do my duty by my country in America, rather than remain aimlessly at Brighton. But whether I am permitted to do so is a decision that rests in the hands of my betters."

"After dinner last Sunday," she said, gathering her courage to ask the question that most weighed upon her heart, "you mentioned that as soon as ever you are able to settle, you would like to return to Derbyshire. Is that still your wish?"

"Yes, Miss Darcy. I have seen much of the country since joining His Majesty's army, and I do think Derbyshire one of the most beautiful counties in the land."

"As a young child, I grew up here," said Georgiana. "Although I am not as well traveled as you, I do think it one of the finest areas I have seen."

"You would not ever care to settle far from Pemberley," surmised the Major.

"No. I do not think I could bare it."

"And yet," Mr. Davidson rejoined the dialogue, "would not a woman of your character and accomplishment eventually grow bored in Derbyshire?" Her attachment to the country was stronger than he had guessed, and Mr. Davidson had every intention of carrying her away from the area. He would not settle outside the city. "London has far more to offer you. It is the seat of parliament, the cradle of law and culture."

"True," she replied hesitantly, "Derbyshire does not have as much to offer in the way of culture." After a pause, she asserted herself a little farther, "But if I am surrounded by my friends and family, they will satisfy my need for intellectual stimulation. I have access to an immense library, so I am never in want of literature. And I enjoy art myself, and I paint from time to time. The unsoiled scenes of nature here, I think, afford a better subject than, for instance, would the filthy Thames."

"But London is alive, Miss Darcy!" exclaimed Niles Davidson. "It is teeming with activity. What better subject could you desire?"

"I am sorry to disagree with you, Mr. Davidson. I have lived in London, and it has its advantages. But I would not desire to settle there. I do not even like to visit for more than two months at a time."

"You do not know what you are about. If you thought for a moment, you would see how much more you would grow to love the city—"

"You paint often, Miss Darcy?" interrupted Major Talbot.

"As often as I can. Lately, I have grown to love it more than music."

"I would be gratified to see your work, sometime, if you would allow me."

Mr. Davidson agreed. "Indeed, Miss Darcy, I would be even more appreciative of your artistry. I am sure you paint with a profound passion."

"Not passion, really," replied Georgiana. "But I do enjoy my work. It brings me pleasure."

Soon, Georgiana was showing her two suitors a series of paintings. Major Talbot was complimentary, but his accolades were brief. Mr. Davidson, on the other hand, soliloquized at great length on the subject of her talent, showering her with copious praise. The visit wore on, both men reluctant to leave the other alone in the young lady's company.

"Do you not need to return to your regiment, Major Talbot?" asked Mr. Davidson.

Major Talbot rejoined, "And do not you, Mr. Davidson, need to prepare for your return journey to London? Surely you do not intend a lengthy vacation in Derbyshire, since you apparently think it pales in comparison to your own city."

And so the exchange might have continued, had not Georgiana courageously intervened. "Gentlemen," she said. "I have some household business I fear I must attend to before the evening arrives. I am sorry that you will both have to take your leave of me."

Major Talbot responded graciously, afraid he had already overstayed his welcome. Mr. Davidson was more loath to depart, but by the time Major Talbot had reached the lane, Georgiana had succeeded in timidly prodding the ambitious politician out onto the steps of Pemberley. He left reluctantly but with confidence. Major Talbot would be gone from Derbyshire in a month's time. The Darcys would, Mr. Davidson hoped, winter again in London, where he could see Miss Darcy frequently. Then he would visit Derbyshire again in the spring. . . yes, all in all, he would have ample opportunity to win her for his wife. And with such a prize in London, his career would know no bounds.

***

While Mr. Davidson was speculating on his glorious future, Major Talbot was waving to the vicar from a distance. He called out a greeting to his old school friend, and when the two were within ten feet of each other, Talbot asked, "What are you doing in these parts?"

"I was coming to call upon the Darcys," replied Mr. Markwood, stopping in the lane. Finding the spot was shady, he removed his hat and began to tinker with its rim.

"I was just there," said Talbot. "They are away from home. Only Miss Darcy stayed behind. But I do not think she would like another visitor today."

"You have wearied her already?" the vicar asked with a half-smile, turning away from Pemberley and following the Major back down the lane.

"I think it more likely that Mr. Davidson was the one to weary her."

"Mr. Davidson?" Markwood asked, returning his hat to his head and adjusting it over his puzzled brow.

"He is not a native of your parish, so do not fear that you do not know the name. But even if he were, how could you know everyone in but a few days?"

"I have visited as many of my parishioners as possible this week. I am determined to know them all."

"You take your profession very seriously."

"It is not precisely a profession," said Mr. Markwood.

"Your calling, then."

"Was Miss Darcy unwell that she stayed behind?" the vicar asked.

"Only tired. But I fancy she revived when I arrived."

Mr. Markwood shook his head with amusement. "So you admire her."

"Who could not? She is a vision."

"Visions fade, Talbot," he replied with a laugh. "I hope she is not a vision."

"You must know what I mean. You used to be a romantic."

"Yes," replied the vicar in good humor, "but I have striven to temper my idealism with regular readings from the Calvinists."

"Well, you certainly worked that darkness into your sermon last Sunday."

"Only to make a greater point of the light. Or were you too distracted by other sights to listen to my conclusion?"

Major Talbot flashed a smile that seemed to cry, *You cannot embarrass me; I admit I am besotted.* But he said, "The sermon really did begin dismally, Markwood."

"So did mankind. I saw things on some of the plantations in the West Indies, Talbot. . ." he shook his head and clenched his teeth, growing suddenly serious.

"Yet your idealism endures. You have a sense of man's great potential, and you believe in the power of love, do you not?"

"Yes. But with regard to Miss Darcy, let me advise you, my friend, to proceed with caution."

"What do you mean?" the Major shot him a mixed look. He thought his friend might possibly be impugning Miss Darcy's reputation.

"I mean her brother is exceedingly wealthy, as I am sure you can observe, and you are not."

"I am by no means poor. I have recently been left an inheritance by my Uncle. Unfortunately, his estate is tied up by some legal complications, and it may be a year before I can disperse it and settle in Derbyshire. Once that is done, however, I will be able to settle quite comfortably. And having my wealth bestowed upon me rather than earned will make it all the more respectable."

"Ah, yes. Then you will no longer be tainted with the vice of labor, as was my father, and as I must now be."

"If you chose, you need not labor at all. You could assign all of your work to your curate."

"As do many vicars. I abhor the practice. Mr. Bailee is a diligent man, but I could not trust him with everything."

"Being acquainted with your personality, Markwood, I would venture to guess that you will entrust him with nothing. You will insist on performing all of your duties yourself."

"Stubborn, is it not?"

"Excessively. And yet, despite your vice, despite your unrespectable inclination for labor, you seem to be growing in Miss Bingley's regard."

"Regard? Is that what you call it?" asked Mr. Markwood.

"She observed you rather carefully during dinner on Sunday. She spoke to you as often as she could. That is to say," he laughed, "when the archdeacon was not speaking to you. And she is aware of the extent of Sir Robert's wealth."

"She is likewise aware that my father has disinherited me."

"And why was that, by the by?"

The recollection of this estrangement must have dampened Mr. Markwood's spirits because Major Talbot could see that his question had pained the vicar. Like most men, the Major was not one to force intimacy from his friend, and so he sought to distract him. "What do you think of her?" he asked.

"Miss Bingley?" he asked, in a baffled tone, as though the answer should be obvious.

"No," replied Major Talbot. "What do you think of Miss Darcy?"

"She seems a sweet girl."

"And is that all the judgment you will render?"

"That is all the judgment I can render. I have been in her company but two times, which is two full times fewer than have you."

"I sense that you mock me, Markwood. Many men, you know, have admired women upon far lesser acquaintance."

"Many men have done many things." Mr. Markwood kicked a small rock from the pathway, and after a moment added, "So why do you admire her, Talbot? I mean other than for her beauty, which a man cannot help but admire."

"For her virtue."

Mr. Markwood smiled. "How can you know it?"

"Does she not seem virtuous to you?"

"All women *seem* virtuous to me."

"Do you question her honor?"

"Not at all. I question your ability to know it at the present moment."

"I admire her for her spirit," insisted Major Talbot. "I first heard her play after dinner at the ball, and I told you—well, you have heard her."

"Yes. I will concede the point. She has spirit, and her playing also provides evidence of self-discipline."

"You admit it then, Markwood. I do have cause to admire her!"

"You have my permission to do so."

Major Talbot laughed at this and would have told his friend that he did not require his permission, but they had reached a fork in the road, and Mr. Markwood took his leave to call upon another member of his congregation. "I will see you at lunch tomorrow, I suppose," he said before parting.

"Yes," replied Talbot. "I managed to garner an invitation to join your little hunting party. Granted, it is not Mr. Bingley and Mr. Darcy I desire to see, but it will be pleasant to put a firearm to use again."

Of course, he was already using firearms daily, drilling the soldiers quartered at Lambton. But he hardly deemed that to be a useful application. These recruits were like children who es-teemed their weapons no more than toys and tired of them just as easily. They did not seem to understand that war was not a game to be played for an hour and then be put aside without regret. He would break that indifferent attitude, he knew, but it was taking more time than he had imagined, and were it not for Lambton's proximity to Georgiana Darcy, he would have wished for an instant transfer to the field.

"Well, you shall see her at lunch," concluded Mr. Markwood, as he waived a casual goodbye. Major Talbot took the other road, and the two friends, so unalike in personality, so alike in virtue, drifted to their separate destinations.

Chapter 8

Elizabeth Darcy sat at her private writing desk and drafted a letter to Charlotte Collins. Over two years ago, when the former Miss Lucas had, in true mercenary fashion, accepted the marriage proposal of the Bennet's self-important cousin William Collins, Elizabeth had concluded that no real confidence could ever again subsist between them. But after her own marriage, Mrs. Darcy had come to accept her sister Jane's gentle observation that not everyone can share the same disposition. As Elizabeth's judgment against Charlotte was removed, so too was the impasse to their friendship. The two had renewed all of their former intimacy, although distance now required them to communicate primarily through epistles. Elizabeth penned the date upon her page, *Saturday, June 11, 1814*, before beginning her missive:

> *Dearest Charlotte,*
>
> *Mr. Jacob Markwood, the new vicar, and Major Arthur Talbot are to come for lunch today, after which the men will enjoy a hunting party. It is early in the year for birding, but my husband is determined to enjoy his time with Mr. Bingley, who must depart tomorrow. The archdeacon Dr. Ramsey remains with us, but fortunately he is often absent from Pemberley as his inspection of the parish keeps him occupied.*
>
> *Mr. Darcy begins to be more confident that he has made an appropriate choice for the living. As for Major Talbot. . . Georgiana appears to have taken a real liking to him, and the fact worries her poor brother comically. He commented to me that the Major seemed a bit old for her. "Indeed," he said, "I believe the gentleman is my senior." When I reminded him that he had found fault with some of her other suitors for being too immature, he relented somewhat, but*

I half think he has invited the Major today merely to observe him.

At least my husband may reassure himself that Miss Darcy's most forward suitor—the politician Mr. Davidson, who has been in Derbyshire on holiday—has thankfully returned to London. He will not be missed. Major Talbot, on the other hand, will be leaving Lambton with his regiment at the end of the month, and Georgiana does not look forward to the parting.

Although he is originally from London, Major Talbot has had no permanent residence since first receiving his commission. When he is able to establish a firm home, he said, he should very much like to settle in Derbyshire. My dear Mr. Darcy took this as a hint and told me he doubts the Major will have much luck when he does finally return, considering the immense pageant of suitors that must meanwhile pass through the halls of Pemberley. I cannot help but agree; if Major Talbot desires Georgiana's hand, he must secure the promise of it within the next few weeks. I doubt it shall be free when he returns.

I am sorry to end this letter so abruptly, but the housekeeper has just informed me that my guests have arrived. I eagerly await your reply. You are the most sensible friend I have ever had the fortune to possess, and I value your correspondence most dearly.

Sincerely,
Elizabeth Darcy

Mrs. Darcy sealed her letter and rose to greet her guests, but she felt suddenly faint. Returning to her chair, she gripped its sides. It was just a headache, she thought, and would pass.

A few minutes later Mr. Darcy looked in on her. "I sent the servant to tell you the guests had arrived. Did she not come to you?"

"She did," said Elizabeth, "I—"

"My darling, you look pale."

"I do not feel well, Fitzwilliam."

He was at her side immediately. "Should I summon the physician?"

"No, no dear. It is just a little headache. I need only to lie down for a while and it will pass. Please make my excuse to the guests. I should be well by evening."

While Mr. Darcy was leading Elizabeth to her bed, Georgiana, not knowing what had become of her brother and sister-in-law, was forced to play the hostess. "You have met Mr. and Mrs. Bingley and Miss Bingley already," she said as she led her guests to the sitting room. Mr. Markwood and Major Talbot bowed their greetings to the rest of the party before being seated. "How convenient," continued Miss Darcy, "that you should both arrive at the same time."

"It was no coincidence," said Major Talbot, "but sheer premeditation. I stopped at the parsonage on my way in order to collect Mr. Markwood."

Mr. Markwood nodded in agreement, but he seemed content to let the Major carry the conversation.

"We," continued Talbot, "have just been recalling our days at Oxford. My studies there overlapped his by only a year, but we were fast friends even in that short time."

Miss Darcy asked a few generic questions about those school days, and Major Talbot gladly answered them. He inquired after Miss Kitty Bennet, also, and was told she was now staying with her Aunt Gardiner. Mr. Markwood heard this news and pitied his smitten curate. He had perceived quite clearly—in that single Sunday conversation—Mr. Bailee's affection for the girl, and he had seen that she did not return it. But he suspected Miss Bennet's absence from Derbyshire would not be permanent, and perhaps Mr. Bailee would have some future chance of seeing his attentions returned. Mr. Markwood never considered that the girl might think herself to be above his curate. Nor did he know how many other gentleman paraded in her head, and he would certainly not have guessed his own brother was among them.

Soon, Mr. Darcy approached his guests, and the men immediately stood to exchange bows. "I am afraid," said their host, "that my wife will not be joining us for lunch. She has had a sudden headache."

Georgiana expressed her concern. "It is not serious, I hope?"

"She was not warm to the touch," responded Mr. Darcy, "and she assures me the pain is minimal. She is probably only in need of some rest."

"She did rather exert herself last week in order to help me prepare for the ball."

"I am sure that had nothing to do with it, Georgiana," said Mr. Darcy, who knew how easily his sister could make herself feel guilty for the smallest of things. Wishing to distract her from her unhappy thoughts, he promptly ushered his guests into the dining room.

"And how do you like Derbyshire, Major Talbot?" asked Jane during the course of the meal.

"It has," said Major Talbot, glancing at Georgiana, "much to recommend it."

"Such as?" inquired Mr. Darcy, perhaps a little too sharply.

"Such as the beautiful grounds of Pemberley, for one," said Major Talbot, immediately taking his eyes from Georgiana to address her more formidable brother. He had heard much of Mr. Darcy, though the reports could never be easily reconciled. Either he was an arrogant and disagreeable man, or he was the most liberal of landlords and the wittiest of gentlemen.

When Mr. Darcy replied this time, he was careful to temper his instinctive wariness. He suspected he was being too protective, and he feared that, as a consequence, he was failing to be polite. Therefore, he now made a sincere attempt at affability when he said, "You shall soon have the chance of seeing those grounds at a closer vantage point."

"We should ride out to within a mile of the field," said Mr. Bingley, "and then dismount and walk the rest of the way so that Mr. Markwood and Major Talbot may have more time to take in the scenery."

"I agree," replied Mr. Darcy. "It is a beautiful day to view some of the land."

"I for one," interjected Caroline Bingley, "am immensely looking forward to enjoying the pheasant you will no doubt bring home this evening, Mr. Darcy. For I am certain you are the best shot in all of Derbyshire."

Mr. Darcy did not acknowledge the compliment. He had never directly encouraged her adulation, but perhaps it had once flattered his ego. Now that he was married, however, he wished her to understand that he considered it inappropriate.

After an uncomfortable silence, Georgiana ventured an address. "Major Talbot," she asked, "do you have any idea, yet, when you might return to settle in Derbyshire?"

"Not, I am afraid, for at least one year." Georgiana appeared keenly disappointed by the reply. "And yet, Miss Darcy," he said, "if I may have your permission to write, I will be glad to keep you informed of my activities in Brighton, or wherever it is that my regiment is put to use."

She replied eagerly, a new brightness forming in her eyes, "I should very much like to hear about your adventures."

Their conversation was interrupted by the sound of Mr. Darcy's chair scraping across the hardwood floor as he stood. "Major Talbot," he said, with strained calmness, "you are reputed to be an excellent marksman. You must have an interest in firearms. I have two Holland and Hollands, and a Purdey, among others. Would you come with me to view my collection?"

Major Talbot was so pleased to have elicited the delight of Georgiana that he did not immediately discern the reason for Mr. Darcy's abrupt reaction. He was uncertain why the invitation seemed extended to him alone. But in a matter of seconds, he realized that his offer to correspond with a young lady to whom he was neither related nor engaged had been improper. He had instinctively sought to assuage Miss Darcy's unhappiness by any means necessary, and he had consequently failed to think before speaking.

Major Talbot rose reluctantly from the table. He was not afraid of Mr. Darcy. Georgiana's brother was his junior by a few months, and the gentleman had never been seasoned by the kind of trials a soldier must endure. No, the Major was not afraid of him, but he was afraid of offending him. He was disturbed by the possibility that Mr. Darcy might now forbid him to see his sister.

Major Talbot, in all his travels, had met and—it must be confessed—sometimes fancied beautiful women, as well as wealthy ones, but he had never known a lady to be both without at the same time being entirely preoccupied with herself. Georgiana had never sought to draw attention to her person; she had never solicited the praise of men. Her shyness had attracted the Major when it might have repelled another man.

As the men departed, Georgiana shot her brother a warning glance. It was perhaps the first time she had ever dared show him the slightest sign of reproof. He returned to her a stern gaze, but it was not precisely steady. His care for her softened what he had intended to be a reprimand. But his harshness, mixed though it was with tenderness, had its affect. Once they were gone, Georgiana looked down at her plate and swallowed as she struggled to suppress the tears that threatened to well in her eyes.

Mr. Markwood's powers of observation were selective. He could become deeply involved in the conversation about him, but there were times, also, when he seemed lost to the room, when he was caught up in the festivities of his own mind. There was one thing, however, that he never failed to notice: another person's pain. And when he saw it, his compassion was so instinctive that he could see nothing else.

Mr. and Mrs. Bingley saw it too. But Charles, good natured as he was, could settle on no right course of action. And Jane, though she felt compelled to comfort Georgiana, was beaten to the task by the vicar.

Mr. Markwood rose from his seat and occupied the one the Major had vacated. He whispered to Georgiana, "Do not worry; your brother, I gather, is a fair man. Major Talbot was mistaken to say what he did, but I am certain he had no blameworthy intent. Your brother will see that."

Georgiana was greatly relived by Mr. Markwood's words. When he saw that she was more or less at peace, he retreated to his own chair once again. Caroline Bingley, who had been made exceedingly uncomfortable by the entire situation, attempted frivolous conversation. Georgiana replied distractedly; she had been comforted, but she was naturally still preoccupied. Jane tried to carry the weight of the conversation for her. At length, Caroline grew tired of the ladies' dialogue and turned her courtesy instead to Mr. Markwood.

"Mr. Darcy made some admiring comments about your sermon the other day," she told the vicar. "You seem to have earned his respect. And as he is among the most distinguished of gentlemen, and the nephew of the great Lady Catherine de Bourgh, his compliments must reflect well upon you."

"I. . . thank you," replied Mr. Markwood, unsure whether he were receiving a compliment or an insult. Miss Bingley had already paid him some strange attentions after church the previous Sunday, and he did not know what to make of her behavior. Major Talbot had called it regard, but the vicar would have chosen a different word. It was clear enough that she had nothing but contempt for his current station in life, and yet at the same time, she seemed to desire to ingratiate herself with him. What was more, she seized upon every opportunity to express her concern about his misfortune, and to inquire about the potential of reconciliation with his father.

Indeed, she was in the middle of just such a comment when his wandering mind began to return to the present. ". . . your father. . . to reconcile. . . learns. . . Mr. Darcy's esteem," he heard, the words progressively rising to clarity in his conscious, ". . . not long. . . a clergyman. . . hold it against you. . . Especially when he considers that, having been thrown into the company of very good society, you will have the opportunity of gaining an even better wife with far superior connections."

The table was silent. Miss Bingley was anticipating his response. Had she gone too far again? Been too personal? Her words, she thought, had been an encouragement.

"Mr. Bingley," said the vicar hurriedly, simply ignoring her, "I should very much like to see Mr. Darcy's stables. Do you think he would mind if I walked out there now and met you gentlemen later when you are ready to depart?"

"I do not think he would mind in the least," said Mr. Bingley.

Mr. Markwood excused himself from the table, noticing as he departed the apologetic smiles of Jane and Georgiana, two women who understood Miss Bingley's intentions better than did he.

Chapter 9

"I don't see him," came Mr. Darcy's voice.

"Maybe he already rode past the stream," replied Mr. Bingley.

"He would have told us if he was planning to go on," insisted Mr. Darcy. "He said he would meet us at the stables."

"Perhaps he's inside," suggested Mr. Talbot.

"I doubt that." Mr. Bingley chuckled as he spoke. "It sounds like a couple of servants are having an extremely hearty laugh in there."

"I hope Thomas has not neglected his duties and has prepared our horses." Mr. Darcy passed through the stable doors and was surprised to find his servant in animated and familiar conversation with Mr. Markwood. Upon seeing his master, the groomsman fell solemnly silent, but Mr. Markwood's expression did not alter.

"He is inside," called Mr. Darcy to the Major and Mr. Bingley as he walked toward his groomsman. "Have you saddled all the horses, Thomas?"

"Yes, sir."

"Very well then. Lead them out."

Thomas looked at Mr. Markwood and raised his eyes, gesturing his head toward Mr. Darcy. Mr. Markwood nodded to him, and Thomas began leading the horses out of the stable.

"I wondered, Mr. Darcy," said Mr. Markwood, rising from the bale of hay where he had been leaning, "if you would be willing to let Thomas have some time Monday. With your permission, he has consented to help me build some pews in the church."

"Pews?"

"Yes, sir."

"Why are you building them yourself? Has not the family who purchased them paid for the work?"

"No, sir. These are to be free pews that anyone may use. I have taken the lumber from the trees on my own glebe lands, and I have engaged several men to volunteer their labor, Thomas among them, if you will."

"I will give him his liberty for the day, if you can use him."

"Thank you."

"What is the cause of the delay?" Charles Bingley asked, poking his head through the stable door and peering curiously around its frame. When he spied Mr. Darcy, he said, "Major Talbot has already mounted, and his horse is chomping at the bit. I am eager to move on myself. What do you say, gentlemen?"

"I say let us proceed," replied Darcy, following Mr. Bingley from the stable.

Once the party had ridden out from Pemberley, the men dismounted their horses and determined to walk the remainder of the way to the field that would serve as their hunting ground. Lingering back together at some distance, the Major and Mr. Markwood fell easily into conversation, the eclipse of several years having interfered but little with the warmth of their friendship. Mr. Darcy's dogs seemed to have taken a liking to the Major, and though their master called back to summon them, they remained at Talbot's heels. At last Mr. Darcy gave up, but not without a little resentment. He began a discussion with Mr. Bingley, leaving Major Talbot—and his dogs—well behind.

Mr. Markwood said to his friend, "It has been good to see you again, Talbot, these past several days."

"And you as well, Markwood. It has been too long."

"The army is a demanding mistress, is she not?"

"So, I imagine, is the Church."

"Yes. Sometimes more than you can imagine," said the vicar. "But at least it allows a man to stay settled in one place. To start a family."

The Major glanced at him. "Was that a hint?"

"Well, apparently you are considering the possibility, if you are offering to correspond with a woman you have courted—if you can justly call it courting—for what, two weeks now?"

"Do not rebuke me, Markwood. I rebuke myself."

"I know you meant no impropriety," said the vicar in softened tones. "You are a well intentioned man, but you can be rash."

"Some have called my rashness courage."

"One seed has produced two branches." The vicar smiled. "Your lunchtime *faux pas*, however, does not seem to have permanently injured you. How was your conversation with Mr. Darcy?"

Major Talbot looked toward the man. "I explained my intentions to him as best I could. I think I was convincing; at least, he granted me permission to write the family as a unit. But he nonetheless proceeded to show me his extensive and most impressive gun collection. He asked me if I was in the habit of offering to write all of the young ladies, or just his sister; and he mentioned something about how duels were gradually going out of fashion, but he indicated that if someone dear to him were ever hurt, he might invigorate the waning trend."

Mr. Markwood laughed heartily. It caused Mr. Darcy and Mr. Bingley to look back, but they soon resumed their own conversation. When it was clear that the other gentlemen would not be observing their exchange, Mr. Markwood sputtered, "You're not serious, Talbot."

"It is conceivable that I have resorted to hyperbole," he replied. "Mr. Darcy's words were far more subtle. But that, I gather, was his meaning."

Mr. Markwood shook his head. "He must have had some trouble with that girl before."

"What is your implication?" asked the Major, drawing himself up straight and rigid.

"I certainly meant no mark on her character, my friend." The vicar hastily explained himself in an effort to soothe the offense he had inadvertently inspired, while simultaneously struggling not to laugh at the indignant concern of the would-be lover. "She seems the very fountain of innocence. But there are men in the world who will seek to abuse such simplicity. No doubt Mr. Darcy is only trying to protect his sister from them."

"And am I to be considered such a one as this?"

"You are a noble man, my dear Major. But have patience. Mr. Darcy does not know you. And men are not always as they seem."

By now they had nearly caught up with Mr. Darcy and Mr. Bingley. As anything they said might be overheard, conversation on the topic of Georgiana Darcy inevitably ceased. Instead, Major Talbot switched to another subject. "On that topic," he said to the vicar, "remember the fellow you scuffled with back in Oxford? That Cambridge man?"

"You mean the right honorable Mr. Wickham?" Mr. Markwood laughed.

Mr. Darcy came to an instant standstill. The Major nearly bumped into him. Mr. Darcy began walking again, this time beside them. When Mr. Bingley discovered that he stood out alone, he too fell back into formation. As neither gentleman spoke immediately to them, Major Talbot and Mr. Markwood continued their dialogue.

"The very one. And would you guess? He has found his way into *my* regiment."

"So he, too, must have renounced his legal ambitions. I wonder how long he's been a soldier."

"I would imagine for some time. He was banished to the regulars before he found his way to me. The only reason I thought of him now," said Major Talbot, "is that he claims to have a special relationship with you, Mr. Darcy—I am speaking of this fellow we met once back at Oxford. No doubt it is another one of his illusions of grandeur."

"No doubt," said Mr. Markwood. "He pretended to be a gentleman when we first met him. Remember what he said— 'vacationing at Oxford to enjoy the culture it afforded'. He probably just needed a new place to carouse. Cambridge, no doubt, had grown hackneyed to a Casanova such as he."

"He was in general a rake," Major Talbot said to Mr. Markwood, "but what was your particular inspiration for confronting him? I only heard about the encounter as I was leaving Oxford. I regret that I had not the pleasure of witnessing it."

"He had aimed his pretensions at Miss Grant, you know."

"Surely she was not taken in by him?"

"Not for more than a moment. But when she made it clear that she perfectly fathomed the variety of man he was, he began to abuse her subtly behind her back. I squelched those rumors, fortunately, before they could grow."

"What became of Miss Grant, Markwood? I would have thought for sure you had married her by now."

"It was not to be," he said in dismissal.

"I am sorry to hear that," Major Talbot told him privately, in lowered tones. "You began to court her, I know, merely as a duty to you father, but I thought you might eventually fancy her. Beautiful, intelligent, graceful—I'm rather surprised you didn't."

"Yes, well, but enough of that," replied the vicar, and then, in a louder voice that could be heard by the entire party, "What is the claim that Mr. Wickham makes on Mr. Darcy?"

Major Talbot looked at Mr. Darcy, who appeared quite stern. Perhaps the joke would lighten his mood. "He claims, Mr. Darcy, that you are his brother-in-law. The presumption! And from such a man! It is truly laughable."

"Mr. Wickham," said Mr. Darcy, "is indeed my brother-in-law."

The Major's jaw dropped. The vicar's heart sank. Major Talbot was sure he had just lost any hope of Georgiana Darcy, and Mr. Markwood feared he had offended his only benefactor beyond repair. Mr. Darcy observed their discomfort, and he would have hastened to erase it if some small part of him had not taken a momentary delight in torturing the poor Major. But soon he reproached himself for his own pettiness, and said, "Mr. Wickham is wed to my wife's sister, Miss Lydia Bennet. He is indeed my brother-in-law. But I never sought the connection. Mr. Wickham is not now, nor will he ever be, welcome in my home."

The faces of both friends were washed with relief. His expression half-surprised and half-amused, Mr. Bingley observed the conversation without comment.

"Major Talbot," Mr. Darcy asked, "do you know how or why Mr. Wickham was transferred to your regiment?"

"I do not know who orchestrated the change. I know he had incurred a great many debts in Newcastle. He was ordered to quit them and accept a transfer. My regiment—though fortunately not my own company—received the happy honor of having him added to our number."

"I have heard nothing of this," responded Mr. Darcy. "Who quit his debts?" He knew his wife had practiced sufficient economy to send her sister small gifts here and there, but she cold not have supplied enough to satisfy his creditors entirely. "Bingley?"

Charles Bingley looked abashed. "For the sake of Mrs. Bingley, Darcy, you understand. . .."

"We have discussed this, Bingley. You know he will never learn financial responsibility if you continue to relieve him in this manner. You must be more resolute, Bingley, for his own good, if not for yours."

"I am aware, Darcy, I am aware. But Mrs. Wickham stayed with us in the spring, remember, while Mr. Wickham was away. And he could not afford to provide properly for her comforts with all of those debts. We could not leave Mrs. Wickham at such a disadvantage, you understand?"

"You and your wife are both too good natured for your own well-being. Fortunately, you can afford such generosity. I am not so confident that Mr. Wickham can afford to receive it. Let us restrict our future aid, Bingley, to advancing his career only. Then he may have the dignity of supporting his wife himself."

"You are quite right, Darcy, quite right. Next time, I shall tell Mrs. Bingley that we absolutely cannot assist the Wickhams. Next time, I shall put my foot down."

"Is that so?" asked Mr. Darcy. Even he knew how hard it was to resist the persuasion of a beautiful wife, and Mr. Bingley did not have half his resolve. Yet his friend had sounded determined. At any rate, Darcy would not press the matter further. He must allow Charles Bingley to be his own man. Mr. Darcy had once before improperly applied his influence on his friend's easy character, and the intrusion had nearly resulted in a serious loss of happiness for both.

"Mr. Markwood," said Mr. Darcy, finally allowing poor Bingley to escape his scrutiny, "how did you both escape unscathed? Did no one have the upper hand?"

"Excuse me, sir?"

"When you dueled with my endearing brother-in-law. Who prevailed?"

"It was nothing so honorable as a duel, sir. It was more of a brawl. The confrontation was hardly befitting a gentleman, and it would have been unpardonable had I then been a clergyman. I should have behaved more appropriately, had my anger not got the better of me. But I am a man who is not easily offended, and so I have had little practice disciplining such emotions. Fortunately, there were few witnesses to the impropriety, and my main object—that of silencing Mr. Wickham's rumors before they could be heard by anyone of consequence—was achieved."

Mr. Darcy made no response to this explanation. Let the clergyman think he disapproved if he must. Mr. Darcy certainly would not admit to condoning such crude behavior, however much he may have secretly envied Mr. Markwood his moment of physical triumph.

When the hunting party had made conquest of a few of its prey, the gentlemen returned to the stables. To the astonishment of all, Mr. Markwood had proved to be the most accurate man in the group, and his bag was laden with several pheasant. He was looking happily forward to a hearty meal as the men dismounted.

"Look Bingley," said Mr. Darcy, as he handed the reins of his horse to his groomsmen Thomas. "Here comes your wife toward us now."

"She looks terribly upset," said Mr. Bingley, clearly concerned. He walked quickly toward her. After they had lowered their heads in conversation, he ran back to Mr. Darcy. "Mrs. Bingley was about to send for us when we arrived. She believes you should summon the physician as soon as possible. Mrs. Darcy appears to have taken a turn for the worse."

"My horse," cried Darcy violently, turning toward Thomas, who was just then returning the steed to its stable.

"Send one of the servants, Darcy," said Mr. Bingley. "You are too alarmed to go yourself."

"A servant will not be quick enough."

"Then let me ride for you," interceded Major Talbot. "I am a skilled horseman, and I give you my full assurance that I will be as swift as humanly possible. You should stay with your wife."

Mr. Darcy relented and handed the reigns to Major Talbot, who rapidly mounted the steed. With a spurring kick to its side, he was instantly gone.

***

Mr. Darcy paced back and forth in the hall outside the bedroom. He was tracing his own footsteps with his eyes, and he just avoided tripping over the emerging physician. "Her fever has broken," the physician told him. "And it is all I can do tonight. I believe she will be well in time, but the fever may return. If it does, summon me again."

Mr. Darcy's reply was merely mechanic. "Thank you, Mr. Henry," he said.

"You should go into her now. She is awake for the time being, but she will need her rest later. Be sure that she gets it."

"Certainly."

"And Mr. Darcy," said the physician as he began to leave, "do not worry yourself too much about the child. It is still my hope that the sickness will not injure the pregnancy."

"What?" asked Darcy, the disbelief more apparent in his eyes than in his voice.

"You did not know?"

Mr. Darcy moved, still in a daze, to the bedroom, and he shut the door behind him. He sat by Elizabeth's bedside and took her hand in his. "The physician said—"

"That I am getting better. The fever is broken, but it may return. And I know, I am to rest for at least a week."

"No. I mean he also said—he said that you were expecting."

"I did not want to tell you until I was sure. I dared not raise your hopes prematurely; we have been wishing for some time."

"Then it is true? You are—you are carrying my child?"

Elizabeth smiled. "Yes."

He kneeled before her and placed his hand reverently upon her. "When—how long?"

"Almost two months."

He laid his head softly upon her stomach, and shut his eyes.

Suddenly he sat up. "You must be hungry. You have not eaten all day," he said with alarm. "Let me summon the servant at once."

She smiled feebly. It was all the amusement she could muster. She adored him, she thought, this man who felt so deeply, yet controlled his emotions so tightly until they could not be contained and overflowed. "I have no appetite, but I will make myself eat for the sake of the baby."

Mr. Darcy rang for the servant and then returned to her side.

"My sister will stay, then, until I am well?" she asked.

"Yes, of course she will. Bingley, unfortunately, must still return to his estate. But your sister will stay, and in addition, I have already sent for your father. I. . . I was not sure how serious your sickness was going to be."

"I am glad that you did send for him, my love, even if I am not exactly at death's door."

"He will come on horseback, and I expect he will arrive within the next few days. Is there anyone else you should particularly like to have with you while you recover?"

"My aunt and uncle."

"Major Talbot has already brought them back from Lambton with your younger sister. They had not yet left for London. Would you like to see them now? They have not yet retired for the evening. Indeed, no one has." He took her hand in his own and kissed it tenderly. "We were all worried about you."

"Yes, please do send them in."

As he walked toward the door, he turned back. "Do you mind, Lizzy, if I share with Georgiana the good news about the child?" It was, he feared, too soon to reveal the fact to others as the risk was not yet passed. But he knew his sister had longed to be an aunt for as many months as he had desired to be a father.

"Do tell her. And send my sisters to me also, that they may know from me."

Jane, Kitty, and the Gardiners entered Elizabeth's bedchamber just moments after Mr. Darcy had departed. Elizabeth's sisters and aunt sat in chairs by her bedside, while Mr. Gardiner stood smiling down at his niece. "You gave us quite a scare," he said. "When we arrived, we learned you were getting better, but when Major Talbot originally came for us, the situation seemed quite desperate."

"It was kind of the Major to ride for you. He also went for the physician, I understand."

Mrs. Gardiner looked pleased. "Well, he is a fine gentleman. He was very gracious to us, and obviously very concerned for your well being—no doubt because it must have an effect on your sister-in-law."

Before Elizabeth could respond to the hint, Miss Darcy herself entered the room, all aglow and obviously eager to talk. Mr. Gardiner, perceiving that the ladies had affairs to discuss among themselves, excused himself on the pretense of consulting with Mr. Darcy. After he had taken his leave of them, Elizabeth shared with her aunt and sister the good news that already shone in Georgiana's happy countenance.

All four ladies were immensely pleased that they would soon be aunts, particularly Miss Darcy, who alone would experience the privilege for the very first time. Jane and Kitty had already assumed the honor at the birth of Lydia Wickham's daughter, but they were far more delighted by the prospect of a little Darcy.

Chapter 10

Mr. Markwood wandered hazily into his drawing room. His mind had been drifting again, and he must compose it before meeting his guest. When his manservant had announced the presence of the archdeacon, the vicar had received the news with little pleasure. Dr. Ramsey had been in Derbyshire for his visitation for almost two weeks, but until now, he had not come to call at the parsonage.

It was not that Mr. Markwood feared the archdeacon would issue a bad report to the bishop. The bishop had been taciturn when they had met, but Mr. Markwood did not perceive any dislike on his part, and he inferred that His Lordship was not as fond of his archdeacon as Dr. Ramsey wished to believe. It was only that the vicar must now endure the archdeacon's conversation without the moral support of other gentlemen. It is a universal truth that misery loves company, and that a torture, by virtue of being shared, is rendered less acute.

The vicar greeted Dr. Ramsey and asked him to take a chair. As they were seated, the archdeacon suddenly started, looking with alarm about the room. "Mr. Markwood, do you keep your library in your drawing room? That is most unusual indeed."

The vicar glanced at the books that were stacked haphazardly in piles against the parsonage walls. "I keep my library in my library. But it seems it was there insufficiently contained, and it has since crawled out into my drawing room."

"I believe," said the archdeacon, "that reading is not the most productive use of a clergyman's time."

"I do not sacrifice my clerical duties for reading, venerable archdeacon. My parishioners are my first priority. But I am a bachelor, sir, and I have more than sufficient time to read in the evenings."

"Yes, Mr. Markwood. . ., but so many books! Christ warns, 'of the making of books there is no end, and much study is a weariness of the flesh.'"

"Solomon, rather."

"Pardon me?"

"I was just saying that it is Solomon who discovers that knowledge is a weariness, but only if one seeks after it with the false expectation that it will fill the void only God can occupy. Nevertheless, the same writer also says, 'say unto Wisdom, thou art my sister; and call understanding thy kinswoman.'"

"Yes, of course, Mr. Markwood. I have no objection to theological study. I have several volumes of commentary myself, as well as many collections of sermons. Yet you have a large number of books piled here; I did not think so many religious texts had been written."

"I will grant you that not all of my books are religious. There are a great many volumes of poetry among them, as well as novels."

"Novels!" exclaimed Dr. Ramsey.

Had Mr. Markwood been more circumspect, he probably would not have allowed the word to slip so recklessly from his tongue. Now that it had fallen and the archdeacon had seized upon it, however, Mr. Markwood had no recourse but to change the subject. "How was Mrs. Darcy when you left her?"

"She was, I am afraid to say, very ill." Dr. Ramsey's voice took on a sudden dramatic tone as though he were delivering a rehearsed sermon. "The fever that we all believed had been vanquished returned yesterday evening, and the tragedy was intensified by an unfortunate miscarriage. The family now fears the sickness may threaten her own life as well. I would consult with her at this moment, to be assured of her spiritual state, if only Mr. Darcy would permit me. But he jealously guards her bedside. Though his vigilance has left him drained, he will not yield. He has not slept a minute since the fever returned. He clings too much, I think, to the things of this world, and he does not comprehend the importance of allowing me to minister spiritually to his wife as she nears that valley of the shadow of death, through which we all must one day journey, where there will be wailing and gnashing of teeth, and where every tear shall be wiped away from their eyes."

Mr. Markwood had not heard enough to notice that the

archdeacon was mixing his metaphors. Dr. Ramsey's last sentence was lost to him, because he was severely distressed by the others. The vicar shifted uncomfortably in his chair. "This comes as a shock," he said, and his countenance confirmed that it did. "When I last called at Pemberley, Mr. Darcy told me he thought his wife was well on the way to recovery. I did not even know she was with child. You say she has lost the baby?"

"Yes, and it is my opinion that—"

"I have mistakenly believed these last two days that she was getting better. Had I known otherwise I would have. . . I know not what I would have done. No one truly knows how to help in times such as these. But I wish I had known sooner."

"I believe," said Dr. Ramsey, "that a clergyman can and should be of help in times such as these, and I take some small pleasure in the belief that I myself have, in that capacity, brought a measure of comfort to the inhabitants of Pemberley. I have shared with them all of the pertinent scriptures, and I have urged the family to petition God in prayer. I have not, since Mrs. Darcy's fever returned, had the opportunity of sharing these ministrations with Mr. Darcy himself, but I do fully intend to extend this comfort to him when I return from your parsonage today."

"I will return with you," said the vicar, rising from his chair and already heading to the door.

"Oh, no," said the archdeacon, following after him. "Do not trouble yourself, Mr. Markwood. You have been clergyman in this parish for but a short time, and I myself have resided as a guest of the Darcys for as many days as you have had this living—"

"As they are my parishioners, it is my duty, nay, my desire—"

"They have," said Dr. Ramsey firmly, "one clergyman in the house already, and I really do not think it appropriate for you to call at this moment."

Mr. Markwood despaired of convincing the archdeacon, and he was unwilling to defy openly his superior. He was no man's sycophant, but nor was he an intentional insurgent. So he offered up a compromise. "Perhaps tomorrow morning, venerable

archdeacon, I may grant you a reprieve in your pastoral duties."

"I do not think that will be necessary–"

"I will call upon them tomorrow morning." Mr. Markwood had
not meant to allow those words to escape his lips as a decree,
but his tone had hardened before he could control it. Seeing the
anger flash into the archdeacon's eyes, the vicar hastened,
"Venerable archdeacon, your services to the bishop are far too
valuable to be disseminated in such a way. I am a lesser minister. Let me take upon myself tomorrow morning this mundane
task of sitting with the Darcys, that you may be free to pursue
the greater projects that have been ordained for you."

Contrived though his words were, they worked. Dr. Ramsey
consented to the compromise and seemed satisfied that the
vicar had recalled his place. But a greater humbling was in order. Dr. Ramsey insisted that Mr. Markwood return to the drawing room, where he proceeded to examine him on all matters of
Christian orthodoxy.

***

Though the archdeacon returned to Pemberley in the afternoon, he did not venture to approach Mr. Darcy until later that
night. The door to the bedroom where Mrs. Darcy lay had been
left open, and the archdeacon received this fact as an invitation
to address her constant husband.

"Mr. Darcy," he said, entering the room with a pronounced
air of seriousness. "It is at this time, I think, one should be
mindful of the scriptures, which say that God is faithful, who
will not suffer you to be tempted above what ye are able; but
with the temptation will also make a way to escape, that you
may be able to bear it. You are tempted at this time perhaps to
lose faith in Him, who for His own reasons has permitted the
loss of your unborn child, and who for a time has allowed your
wife to endure this sickness—or perhaps not for a time, for we
know not whether it is God's will she should ever recover—and
who can search God's ways? They are inscrutable and past finding out, and yet, I believe, it is clearly His will at a time such as

this that I should extend comfort to you. . .."

The archdeacon's words gradually faded into silence, and he became speechless in the face of Mr. Darcy's bitter gaze. But he could not remain so for long. "Do you wish, sir, that I should pray with you at this time? For it is written that the prayer of a righteous man can availeth much; and, as I am not a mere clergyman but also an archdeacon, I feel that it is not presumptuous of me to believe that there might exist within my own prayers a certain power—"

"I wish you to leave me alone," interrupted Mr. Darcy, his tone measured and hard.

"Very well," said Dr. Ramsey, surprised by the cold response, but unwilling to force himself any longer on a wealthy patron of the Church. "Do call upon me if you feel I may be of any service." He bowed once as he walked backwards through the door and into the hall, where he bumped into Mr. Markwood. Mr. Darcy had not closed the door, but he had turned his back to it and was staring out the window. The vicar looked past Dr. Ramsey to where the suffering husband stood.

"Mr. Markwood," said Dr. Ramsey, "I had not expected you until tomorrow morning. That, I believe, was our agreement." The vicar did not reply and so the archdeacon continued, "I have just been ministering to Mr. Darcy."

"Miss Darcy informed me that you were in the process of," he cleared his throat, "ministering to Mr. Darcy. I asked her if I might see him myself, and she thought I should."

"If you will," said Dr. Ramsey, "though I do not think it is likely you can be of any further service to him. He stubbornly refuses to be comforted."

"He has just lost his child, venerable archdeacon. He may lose his wife."

"And it is at just such a time of loss that my ministrations would have been most beneficial to him, had he not hardened his heart. I have nothing more to accomplish here. Consequently, I will depart tomorrow morning to give my report to the bishop."

Mr. Markwood bowed to the archdeacon, who retreated angrily down the hallway. The vicar approached the open doorway, where he stood with his hand resting on the door's frame and with one foot in the hall, as though to imply that he did not desire to force himself upon the mourning man. "Mr. Darcy," he said tenderly, "I just today learned of this sad news, and I have come to offer your family my service, however you may require it."

Mr. Darcy turned from the window, looked down at his sleeping wife, and remained silent. Mr. Markwood neither moved nor spoke.

How long would the clergyman stand there, Mr. Darcy wondered, before allowing him to be alone with his grief? "Well, Mr. Markwood," he said, an acid tone creeping deep into his voice, "have you no scriptures to quote me? No pretty words of comfort? Can you not extend to me the great consolation that the death of my child and the suffering of my wife are well within the will of God, and therefore to be considered with equanimity?"

"No, sir."

This was not the response Mr. Darcy was expecting. He hadn't known what the vicar would say, and he hadn't cared; he had just desired to provoke a target for his anger. But this unlikely answer distracted him from the mounting rage. "No?" he asked.

"No, sir. I have not the talent of Dr. Ramsey, who, I am sure, had he been privileged to live in the days of the patriarchs, would have had the ability to comfort even Job."

Mr. Darcy was surprised by the sound of his own laughter. For a moment, he was not even sure it was he who had laughed. But there it was, a sweet second of reprieve, as unexpected as the sickness that had overtaken his wife. Almost as suddenly as it had come, his levity vanished, and the great weight of sorrow that had hung upon him these past two nights returned with all its brutal force.

"I have," continued Mr. Markwood, taking a hesitant step forward, "only my empathy to offer you. You need speak but one word, and I will instantly leave this room."

Mr. Darcy began to tremble, almost imperceptibly. The tears that had been welling in his eyes now burst forth, and he wept without a sound. Mr. Markwood immediately closed the door and walked toward him. "Do you wish, sir," he asked, "that I should pray with you?"

It was the same question Dr. Ramsey had asked. And yet it was not the same. Darcy stumbled backward one step, falling to his knees. He buried his head face down on the bed and grasped at the sheets that covered his dying wife. His *dying* wife. It was the first time he had allowed himself to think the word. His cries now became audible, and with a great sob he looked up at Mr. Markwood from where he had fallen. He tried to speak, but he could not make his voice heard. The clergy-man kneeled beside him, leaning closer as Darcy desperately whispered, "I. . . I cannot, Mr. Markwood. I cannot pray."

"I believe you are praying already."

Mr. Darcy's expression was one of utter confusion.

"In our most fervent and most honest prayers," explained Mr. Markwood, "The Holy Spirit intercedes for us with groanings that cannot be uttered."

Mr. Darcy had heard that phrase. He did not doubt that he had read it once. But he had never begun to comprehend it until now. A tremor ripped through his body as though he were racked by some great sickness. His sobs caught silently in his throat, almost choking him. And then, without any warning, something wholly unfamiliar swept over his spirit, and in an instant, the pain was gone.

"What is this?" he asked Mr. Markwood. "What is this feeling?"

"It is peace."

"How long will it last?"

"Long enough."

As Mr. Markwood slipped out the door, Mr. Darcy climbed into the bed beside his wife, kissed her brow, and curled up like a child beside her. In seconds, he was asleep.

Chapter 11

The fever subsided later that night, although Mr. Darcy did not know it. He was awakened by the gentle pressure of his wife's hand upon his face as she stroked him.

"I am the one who is sick," she said, "and yet I feel as if I need to be caring for you." He gathered her into his arms, held her close, and felt a deep sense of gratitude overwhelm him.

The physician, after seeing Mrs. Darcy, assured the family that the worst was most certainly over. Elizabeth's father, who had arrived just as the sickness had turned desperate, now exclaimed, "Thank God!" Kitty felt more pleasure than she knew how to express; the Gardiners issued a joint sigh of relief; Jane smiled sweetly, and Georgiana—dear, quiet Georgiana—let out a sudden shout of joy.

After Elizabeth had taken several days to recover, Charles Bingley returned to Pemberley to reclaim his wife, and the ubiquitous Caroline Bingley followed in his wake. But Mrs. Darcy was not willing to part with her sister's company yet. She persuaded all of their guests to stay another day and proposed a dinner party for the following evening.

"Are you sure your spirits will tolerate such a gathering?" Mr. Darcy asked her.

"If yours will," she replied.

He understood her answer. She had been deeply saddened by the loss of their child. It had seemed to both that as soon as hope had breached the emptiness of longing, it had been crushed and ground into despair. But for Elizabeth, keeping friends and family at hand would bring relief. Entertaining guests would divert her attention from unhappy thoughts. For Mr. Darcy, however, society would not prove a consolation, and it might even increase his burden. He could endure that, though, so long as it brought comfort to her. He said, "I can bear it," and even suggested that they invite Major Talbot, who was soon to leave Lambton with his regiment.

During Mrs. Darcy's sickness and recovery, the Major had called almost daily to ask after her health. He had also sought to console and encourage Georgiana during each of these visits. Mr. Darcy observed their courtship without comment. The near loss of his wife had softened his reserve, and he had reconciled himself to the fact that his little sister must one day leave Pemberley to be mistress of her own home.

He thought his sister's admiration for the Major—and his for her—had perhaps developed upon too short an acquaintance and that it had taken too shallow a root, but he had discerned no permanent fault in the Major. Georgiana would have to wait for Talbot if she desired him; he had said it would be at least a year before he could return and settle down. Yet Mr. Darcy believed that his sister, once she had made her choice, would have the conviction to carry it out.

***

Major Talbot's attentions to Georgiana during the dinner party were apparent but not immoderate. Mr. Darcy watched his sister and saw her regret; she was too keenly aware that the Major would be leaving when the month came to a close. Therefore, when dinner drew to an end and the ladies went their separate way to the drawing room, Mr. Darcy compassionately determined not to keep the gentlemen long at their port.

"Darling," said Mr. Gardiner to his wife as the gentlemen emerged from the dining room, "let us take a look at the gardens before it grows too dark." Mrs. Gardiner took his arm and the couple excused themselves from the party, thanking the Darcys for a satisfying dinner and promising to rejoin the group later that evening. They asked Kitty to join them and she consented but only because Miss Darcy had already staked her claim to the most appealing gentleman in the room. Not that Jacob Markwood was physically unattractive—far from it! He was, she thought, nearly as handsome as his brother. But Kitty could not seem to take an interest in him. His conversation was too distracted, and she always feared that his profession would eventually lead him to moralize. Past experience with her cousin Mr. Collins had taught her to avoid clergymen. The vicar might have proved useful to her had he been inclined to discuss his brother Aaron, but he almost never mentioned the young man, and Kitty could not determine how to inquire after him without appearing suspicious. So she resolved instead to join her aunt and uncle.

After the Gardiners and Miss Bennet had taken their leave, Mr. Markwood spoke to Mrs. Bingley. "I have never had the opportunity of hearing you sing, but at dinner tonight Miss Darcy remarked that you were very talented."

"Miss Darcy flatters me," replied Jane nervously. "I do not have her skill. I am not at all proficient."

"Oh, but your voice is quite beautiful," encouraged Georgiana. "If Lizzy will play, will you sing?"

"I am willing to accompany," said Elizabeth. "Jane?"

Jane smiled her consent and the two sisters proceeded to entertain the company. Mrs. Bingley stood apprehensively next to the pianoforte while Elizabeth began to play. She had never sung before an audience such as this. Mr. Markwood took an armchair near the candelabrum and listened with general pleasure, if not with absolute attention, to the performance. Major Talbot eased gracefully next to Georgiana, who now sat sandwiched between her suitor and her brother. The other couch was claimed by Mr. Bennet and his most agreeable son-in-law.

Soon after Jane had commenced her song, Miss Bingley approached Mr. Markwood and claimed an empty chair next to his. After a time, she attempted to engage him in a hushed conversation. "Mr. Markwood, I understand that you wrote to your father recently?"

"I write to my father regularly, Miss Bingley."

"And has he replied? What did he say?"

"He has not yet honored me with a reply." Mr. Markwood answered his inquisitor, but he did not look at her. Instead, he watched Mrs. Bingley sing, amazed that such a powerful voice could emerge from such a delicate frame. It reminded him of another voice, which he had heard during his Oxford days, and which he was, perhaps, still struggling to forget.

"But you still hope for the restoration of your fortune, do you not?"

"I still hope for reconciliation."

Miss Bingley smiled with optimism. "Then you do expect that one day soon you will be a wealthy man once again. When do you think it will happen?"

As Jane concluded her song, Mr. Markwood clapped heartily. "Mrs. Bingley sings beautifully," he said, now turning to look at Miss Bingley for the first time in the course of the conversation. "Do you not think so?"

"Yes, she has a considerable talent. It is especially amazing when one considers that her background might not have afforded her the finest education." She then whispered, "Mr. Gardiner is a merchant, and lives in Cheapside."

"Yes, I know. Did I not hear from your brother that your own father made his fortune in trade?"

Miss Bingley, who had leaned forward to disclose the shameful secret of the Bennet's connections, now drew back and stiffened. "I only meant—"

"Yes?"

"Mr. Markwood," interrupted Mr. Darcy, relieving Caroline Bingley of the necessity of explaining herself. "You have never seen my library."

"No sir, though I hear it is exceedingly comprehensive."

"I will show it to you now, if you like," he said, rising from the couch. He then turned to his father-in-law. "Mr. Bennet, I have some new volumes that will interest you."

"You are forever acquiring objects of interest to me," he replied, smiling at Elizabeth as he stood to follow his son-in-law.

Mr. Darcy did not need to extend his invitation to Miss Bingley, who, having judiciously forgiven Mr. Markwood for his insinuation, was immediately at his side. As he left with his guests, Mr. Darcy shot an expressive glance at Charles Bingley, who nodded almost imperceptibly.

When that portion of the party had departed for the library, Mr. Bingley approached his wife. "My dear," he said, "You are looking a bit flushed. Would you like to walk with me to the gardens, where we might breathe some fresh air and join your aunt and uncle?"

Before rising to take her husband's arm, Jane leaned over and whispered to her sister, "It appears Mr. Darcy is attempting to clear the room. I presume he trusts you to follow his lead."

Elizabeth doubted that the master of Pemberley would intentionally seek to leave any suitor alone with his sister, and yet she could not think of an alternative explanation for the convenient succession of events.

Major Talbot was somewhat nervous to find himself the only man in the room, certain that he would be expected to guide the conversation. At least his attentions to Georgiana would not now seem disproportionate. Nevertheless, he thought he had better address Mrs. Darcy first. "You look in excellent health, Mrs. Darcy."

"Yes, thank you Major," she replied, taking up some needlework she had put aside earlier that afternoon. "And I feel it too. With the good care of friends and family, I have made more or less a full recovery. Thank you, Major, for riding to summon the physician that night."

"There is no need to thank me, madam. I only wish I could have been of more service."

Mrs. Darcy let out a slight cry as she pricked herself with the needle. "Oh dear," she exclaimed. "Please do excuse me while I attend to this."

And then there were none.

***

While Miss Bingley began to inform Mr. Markwood in vague but feignedly-learned terms of the contents of the various books that inhabited Mr. Darcy's library, the vicar slouched down into an enormous armchair. He soon found himself enamored with an old volume of poetry. Miss Bingley abandoned her efforts to garner his attention and turned her energies instead to Mr. Darcy, who was slightly less dismissive.

As Mr. Markwood read, he let one arm rest on the table beside the chair, and in so doing, he had pinned down the day's newspaper, which was of particular interest to Mr. Bennet.

"*Ahem*," the gentleman cleared his throat. "You have no interest in today's papers, have you Mr. Markwood?"

The vicar was unaware that he was blocking access to any literature. He looked up, believing that Mr. Bennet was attempting to solicit his conversation. Mr. Markwood was not at that instant inclined to chat, but he endeavored to be polite. "Well," he answered, "as the American President Thomas Jefferson once said, 'The man who reads nothing at all is better educated than the man who reads only newspapers.'"

"I meant," said Mr. Bennet, "may I have those," and he motioned to the pages.

"Of course," said Mr. Markwood, suddenly sitting up straight in the chair. "By all means."

Mr. Bennet half-bowed but did not reply. He was as eager to read as was the vicar, so there was no need to prolong the conversation.

"Your collection is superbly organized, Mr. Darcy," Miss Bingley was saying. "I don't know of any estate in Derbyshire with such a well-arranged library."

"That would be owing more to the expertise of my servants than to any act of mine. I merely make my wishes known, and they do all the work."

"Yes, Mr. Darcy, but without the educated mind to engineer great thoughts, what would be the use of any man's labor?"

Mr. Darcy was spared the necessity of answering by the appearance of his wife. Elizabeth eased quietly into the library, almost as if she were hiding, shutting the door behind her.

"Lizzy," said her father, "I knew you could not avoid such a cerebral party for long."

She crossed to her father and placed an arm affectionately around his and then smiled across the room at her husband. She was searching his expression to determine whether or not he had really planned for the courting couple to be alone together. His face gave her no clue, but as he later appeared reluctant to let his guests depart too soon from the library, she suspected Jane had been right after all.

Whether by design, or whether by chance, the would-be-lovers found themselves alone together, but the discovery had been met only with silence. Georgiana did not understand why Major Talbot would not speak. He had been lively enough with her on his past few visits, but now it seemed she would be forced to initiate the conversation.

"We regret that you will be leaving so soon," she said. "My family will miss you."

"Your family?"

"Yes. I think Mr. and Mrs. Darcy have both enjoyed your company these past few weeks."

"And you, Miss Darcy?"

"Oh! I have too, of course." It had not occurred to her that she might have excluded herself when she said 'my family'. She thought her regard was well-understood.

"You are a sweet and patient lady, Miss Darcy."

The compliment flattered her, though it was unexpected.

"Do you know the extent of your patience?" he asked.

"I do not understand."

"If you wanted a thing, how long do you think you could wait for it?"

"It would depend, of course, on what I was waiting for."

Major Talbot rose from his chair and walked to the fireplace. He ran one hand nervously across the mantle. He turned around again and walked toward her, sat beside her, and took her hand. He looked at her with some measure of hope in his eyes, but there was no certainty. "And if you were waiting for me, Miss Darcy?"

Georgiana was distressed. She could not think of a proper way to respond. She understood what he was asking her, but he was not asking directly. If she answered the question behind his question, then she would be accepting before he had officially proposed. And what if her interpretation had been flawed? But the look of disappointment her hesitation had inspired in the Major's countenance erased all her caution. "If I were waiting for you, Major Talbot, I could be as patient as a turtle."

He laughed. He might have been overjoyed at her encouragement; he might have gazed upon her with lavish gratitude; he might have told her how, with her gentle sweetness, she had endeared herself to him from the very first moment they had met. Instead, he nearly fell off his chair.

"A turtle, Miss Darcy?" he asked, still guffawing, "a turtle?"

"Turtles are patient!" she insisted, clearly upset by the sudden change in his disposition.

The Major took two deep breaths, half-regaining himself. He was no longer laughing, but his smile still stretched from ear to ear. "Yes. Yes they are, my sweet, innocent Georgiana. Turtles are the most patient of creatures."

Chapter 12

So Major Talbot had, in his own way, proposed to Georgiana, and she, in her own way, had accepted him. Given this succession of events, one might reasonably assume that Miss Darcy had concluded she was legitimately in love with the Major, rather than simply enamored. But just because an assumption is reasonable does not mean that it is true. Georgiana Darcy had, in fact, never felt compelled to reflect upon the nature of her attraction. Major Talbot desired her. His company pleased her; she liked him, and she liked none better. What then was to prevent her from thinking him the best possible choice of husband?

Major Talbot made his case to Mr. Darcy, and Georgiana's brother consented to the match but not without at first scrutinizing the suitor. "I assume you will not remain a soldier once you are wed," he said from behind his massive desk.

Major Talbot sat nervously across from him, his back to the closed door of the study. "No, sir. I will resign my commission in a year and retire."

"Why not resign it now? Why make my sister wait so long?"

"A year is not an excessively long engagement," the Major suggested tentatively before rising straighter in his chair. He was angry with himself for allowing this man to intimidate him, even for a moment. He had stared down far greater threats on the battlefield, and without so much as blinking.

"It is a long time when you consider the distance," suggested Mr. Darcy. "You will be in Brighton; she will be here, at Pemberley."

"Miss Darcy said the three of you will vacation at the shore this spring when I have leave."

"That is eight months away."

"There is another matter. Legal complications prevent me from accessing my fortune at this time. I cannot afford to settle presently, but in a year I will be able to do so very comfortably."

"You could settle on my sister's fortune now," said Mr. Darcy, trying to gauge how much the Major valued that particular asset.

"I wish to settle on my own. I am sure you understand that, sir."

This answer seemed to please Mr. Darcy, although other questions followed, and it was with no small amount of relief that Major Talbot exited Pemberley an hour later. He walked with Mr. Markwood down the lane toward Kympton while leading his horse beside him.

To Talbot's surprise, the vicar also asked him why he wished to wait a year to wed. When he had explained himself, Mr. Markwood responded, "Nevertheless, a year is no short time."

The Major laughed. "Why are you in such a rage to see me married, Markwood?"

"Because then it would be certain. Then it would be settled. You have seen the number of suitors who have journeyed up this lane to Pemberley in the last month alone."

"They will desist when they know Miss Darcy is engaged."

"Some will."

What had been amusement was slowly turning to annoyance. "Her brother, I am sure, will see that they *all* do."

"There must still be balls, Talbot, and parties, and dances. She will not retreat from society for an entire year. I do not mean that any man would dare to court her openly, while she is engaged, but they may use subtlety—"

"Markwood, you do not doubt her conviction, do you? You do not doubt her ability to keep a promise?"

"I know her less than you do, Talbot. If you believe she is steady, then I trust your judgment. I have seen nothing but sense and kindness in her actions and in her words—her very *few* words. I only mean to say that the wait will not be easy for her. You are placing her in a difficult position. I do not suggest she will not prove firm, I only suggest that the struggle would be unnecessary if you would simply retire and settle immediately."

"We are at war with America and with France. Even if I could afford to settle, it would not be honorable of me to desert my profession now."

Mr. Markwood thought this motive, which he doubted Major Talbot had disclosed to Mr. Darcy, was the truer inspiration for his decision to wait. "Not France, my friend. Napoleon is no longer a threat."

Talbot's horse neighed and the Major reached out to soothe the animal. "It is his name," he said, by way of explaining the steed's response.

"An odd name to give an English horse."

"I respect Napoleon. One must be sure not to underestimate the enemy. And you may believe he is no longer a threat if it pleases you to do so."

"If we are not at peace in a year, will you still return to Derbyshire and wed Miss Darcy?"

Major Talbot did not answer.

"You will have your fortune then," continued the vicar. "You will be able to settle."

"I suppose, if we were still at war, I could wed her when I am on leave and then return to my regiment until the war ended. I do not think it right to give up my commission until we are at peace."

"Then you risk leaving her a widow."

"What would you have me do? I am a soldier."

"Yes, you are. But you have led the Darcys to believe—perhaps you have even led yourself to believe—that you desire to be a gentleman. You are smitten with this girl, Talbot. She is sweet and beautiful and she admires you, and so how can you not admire her in return? You are thirty, and perhaps you think it is high time you should be wed. But still you have not renounced your highest priority."

"What, can only men of no profession mate?" Talbot was perturbed.

"Of course not, but some professions are more conducive to marriage. You may believe you wish to settle down and live a gentleman's life—"

"I do, Markwood," said Major Talbot through clenched teeth. "When we are at peace." He glared at the vicar before continuing, "I do not recall, clergyman, asking for your advice."

Mr. Markwood was shamed by his friend's anger. He let his eyes fall to the ground. He had never been inclined to judge his parishioners or to dispense unsolicited advice. He had been a subtle but effective guide, a humble helping hand, a dreamy laborer, or a silent listener, but never a Dr. Ramsey. He was less circumspect with Talbot, however, because the Major was a friend. But friendship need not always call for frankness. "I am sorry," he murmured.

Major Talbot was fully disarmed by Mr. Markwood's penitent tone. "I am engaged," the soldier said softly. "It is too late to imply I should not be. And my engagement cannot be what troubles you, my friend. Tell me, what weighs you down?"

Mr. Markwood did not respond, and Major Talbot, of course, did not force his confidence. Indeed, the Major was prepared to embark upon another subject altogether when Mr. Markwood asked, "You know what my father wanted me to be?"

"Yes."

"I wonder sometimes if I chose a lesser calling."

"You doubt whether you were called to the Church?"

"No. I doubt whether it matters that I was. I doubt whether the good I can do here, in my natural calling, is as great as the good I could have done in the profession that was chosen for me."

"It was chosen for you by man, not by God. That is what *you* told me, anyway, when we were students, when you first decided to abandon the law. Mr. Darcy is a reserved man."

Mr. Markwood started. Major Talbot's dialogue was disjointed, his final sentence highly incongruous. "What has that to do with anything?"

"I understand he was in agony when his wife was seriously ill," answered Major Talbot. "Miss Darcy told me she had never seen his face wrought with so great a pain, and yet he would not speak to her, certainly not to the archdeacon—he would not even pray to God. But somehow, you went into that room, and. . . Miss Darcy says he did not pace the floor that night. He actually slept, and in the morning, his wife was well. She thinks you worked a kind of miracle."

"Me? Of healing? I made no such pretension."

"Not of healing Mrs. Darcy, but of healing her husband."

"Oh."

"You do not really believe your calling is futile. When you chose to leave the law, did you lose Miss Grant? Is that the real reason for your regret?"

"No, I did not lose her because of this calling. The break came long after I had abandoned the law, and it was my choice. I knew she loved another." The vicar winced and studied the earth. Always the wheel turned round. He would forget her after a tireless struggle, and then she would be recalled to him again. "That, Talbot, is why I advise against a long engagement. Miss Grant was *not* a dishonorable woman. She did not seek to betray me, and she even would have married me as she had promised, had I not released her from that obligation. It is an awful thing, my friend, to lose the woman you love; but it is still more awful to marry one who does not love you in return."

"You did the right thing, then, to break with her. And you have my sympathy for your own suffering. But my situation, Markwood, is quite different. My relationship with Miss Darcy was not orchestrated by our fathers. Both of us have entered this engagement without encouragement from outside sources. It is not as though you had Miss Grant's heart and then lost it during the course of your long courtship. You simply never had it."

Mr. Markwood shut fast his eyes, brought his hand to his brow, and rubbed it as though a sudden pain had risen there.

The Major regretted the words, which were spoken in his own defense. "I do not say this to be cruel."

"I know you do not. You never say anything to be cruel. But intentions are not everything, Talbot. Words and actions matter too." The subject was dropped; the rest of the way to the parsonage was traveled in silence.

When they bade each other farewell, however, their parting was warm. Mr. Markwood knew he would not see Major Talbot for some time. The Major would spend his last moments in Derbyshire with Georgiana, but the vicar would not see him until he resigned his commission. Their friendship must now endure yet another hiatus.

"Pray for me," asked Talbot. He was not himself religious, but nor was he merely resorting to convention. He knew what the request would mean to Mr. Markwood. The vicar nodded, clasped the Major's shoulder in a gesture of farewell, and retreated into the parsonage.

Talbot rode on to Lambton, slept fitfully, and rose early. He trained his men by day, beneath a sweltering sun, and took pleasure in the rough sounds of clashing, shouting, marching. His evenings he passed quietly at Pemberley beneath the soothing showers of his beloved's smiles, delighting in the sounds of her sighing, her whispering, her laughing. So passed the last few days of June. On that final morning, he found himself not at the front of his soldiers, but by the side of Georgiana, strolling slowly down a pathway, which wound its way across the scenic park.

"I am glad we could have this moment alone," said Georgiana. "I will not have the opportunity of seeing you for some time."

"You will be in Brighton in the spring. I will have leave then, and I can see you daily for a week."

"Yes," she said quietly, and it was apparent she was not reassured.

Major Talbot avoided the thorny issue of his impending absence. Affably, he said "So, now that Mr. Bingley, Mr. Gardiner, and Dr. Ramsey are all gone, poor Mr. Darcy will once again be relegated to a house full of women."

"There are worse fates, Major Talbot."

He smiled down at her as they rounded a corner, "My dear Miss Darcy, I cannot imagine a happier fate than being confined to *any* habitation with you."

She lowered her head shyly and refused to meet his eyes. Though seemingly glib, his praises were never insincere. Intellectually, he may not have meant precisely what he spoke, but at the moment he felt it, and what he felt he said. He did not press her for a response. Instead, they walked silently through the park, simply enjoying one another's presence.

When they returned to a small side door where Miss Darcy

normally entered Pemberley, she asked him if he was to come in for tea.

"I wish I could. I truly do. But I will have to gallop as is to return to my regiment in time." Georgiana appeared disheartened. "I am sorry," he apologized. "I will write to you at least once a week, as long as it is in my power to do so. You have my word. "

"Every day would be better." Her smile pled with him.

"I do not make grand promises, dearest. Only those I am certain I shall never break. I will not swear, but I will try."

"I do not mean to be unreasonable. I am merely sad to see you go. You would not like if I were not, would you?"

"No, I suppose I would not. And yet I hate to see you saddened. I hate to be the cause."

She smiled at him with that wide-eyed innocence he adored, and he felt a pride swell into his heart. He swallowed. "I am thirty," he said, "and yet sometimes you make me feel like a bashful schoolboy."

Georgiana laughed. "How did you manage to stay unwed so long?"

"For many years, I was at war."

"My brother once told Mrs. Darcy he thought you were too old for me," said Georgiana. "But I think he likes you better now. He knows you are mature enough to care for me, and yet you have a youthful spirit."

"And what about you, Miss Darcy. What do you know?"

"I know that you admire me—and for myself."

"For what else could I admire you?" he asked, taking her hand.

"For my fortune. For my family's reputation."

"Two very attractive things, neither of which repelled me. But nor could either have secured my affection and my fidelity, as you have done."

She was obviously pleased by his words, but she did not know how to respond. He let go of her hand and instead placed his own gently on her cheek. "Georgiana," he said, and as always, the tender, familiar use of her first name caused a blush to grace her cheeks. "Georgiana, nothing could make me forget you, and yet I'd like to have something to remember, to look back on . . . might we. . .?"

"Yes," she whispered, and he almost did not hear her.

"I may kiss you farewell?"

This time, she only nodded. He leaned forward and brushed her lips with his, very gently, like the faintest sigh. She was almost disappointed when, unexpectedly, he returned his lips more firmly to her mouth. She clung to him, wishing to live on in the moment, but knowing in her rational mind that time would not stand still and that the present scene would prove all too fleeting.

Chapter 13

The summer passed without event. The Darcys heard once from their cousin Colonel Fitzwilliam, who was encamped somewhere along the eastern coast of the United States and who had not yet seen battle. He expected, however, to enter the field in the near future. Georgiana wrote to Major Talbot to share the news, and although part of the Major secretly envied Colonel Fitzwilliam his position, he expressed only concern for Georgiana. Major Talbot wrote nothing of his own desire to be put to use in the service of his country. He had hinted at this fervor before, and always it had disturbed her because she feared he would be killed or injured. So for the sake of her tranquility, he sought to keep these feelings to himself. His letters consisted mainly of passing comments about the weather and the amusements to be found in Brighton, mixed with praises of her beauty, and crowned with inquiries about her well-being.

Miss Darcy wrote to the Major, at first, daily. But by September, her writing had fallen off to match his, and she produced a letter only twice a week. She still eagerly devoured each of his epistles when they arrived, but she did not mope about the house listlessly awaiting the post. She concluded, at length, that one could perhaps remain engaged without at the same time proving wholly useless, and she continued to pursue her music, drawing, and reading with all of her pre-engagement vigor.

Mr. Markwood became a regular caller at Pemberley and could have boasted of the number of times he was invited to dine there, if he had been inclined to boast of such things. Instead, he declined as many invitations as he accepted because he felt it important to call upon his other, less illustrious parishioners as well. When the vicar did come to Pemberley, however, Mr. Darcy was fully at ease with him as though Mr. Markwood belonged in the estate. That night of spiritual wrestling had eroded the social barrier that normally puts a distance between men.

Even Georgiana was relaxed in the vicar's presence. Miss Darcy had at first exerted herself to converse with him because he was a valuable source of information on a topic of considerable interest to her: Major Arthur Talbot. He knew the Major better than did any member of her family, and he always seemed willing to discuss him with her. The comfort that his candor on this subject had established soon expanded to other areas of conversation, and Miss Darcy found, in time, that she spoke to Mr. Markwood on a host of topics, only one of which was Arthur Talbot.

The Bingleys and the Gardiners, along with Kitty Bennet, joined the Darcys for the autumn drive, which came early that year. Mr. Markwood once again succeeded in procuring the largest number of birds. The company now relaxed in one of the sitting rooms while the pheasant were delivered to the kitchen for dinner. Mr. Markwood helped the servants to carry some of the prey to the cook. It was a most unusual condescension, and although Mr. Darcy wondered whether Mr. Markwood should engage in it, he made no verbal judgment. A clergyman, he supposed, even an educated one, must behave more openly than other gentlemen.

After handing over the pheasant, the vicar took a seat at the kitchen table where the servants usually dined. He began toying absently with a knife, twirling it around the single point where he had thrust its tip into the wood.

"I don't think," said the cook, "that Mr. Darcy will take kindly to your scarring his kitchen table in that manner."

"When does he ever come in here, Betsy?"

The cook smiled broadly, the wide grin further enlivening her plump but appealing face. "Well now, you have a point there Mr. Markwood."

"On the other hand, if *you* do not take kindly to my deface-ment of *your* kitchen table, I will desist."

"Thank you, sir. I'd appreciate it."

Mr. Markwood put down the knife and motioned to the pheasant. "What are you going to do with those?" he asked.

"Why I imagine I'm going to cook them."

"Yes, of course. I meant, how?"

"That's for me to decide." The cook brushed a stand of auburn hair from her face and asked, "Why aren't you up in the sitting room with everyone else? They're going to start wondering why it's taking you so long to deliver a few pheasant to the kitchen."

"Why now, Betsy, don't you enjoy my company?"

"All of us enjoy your company, Mr. Markwood," she replied, and with a half-smile she continued, "I would like to have seen Mr. Darcy's expression when you said you wanted to come take these birds down to the kitchen!"

"Mr. Darcy's reaction was unremarkable."

"You don't think it took him aback?"

"Probably. But as he has not droned me out of Pemberley, and as he still seems to expect me to dine with the family this evening, I will assume he is willing to tolerate my actions." Mr. Markwood's hands had been free far too long. He looked around the table for some object. He picked up a pair of kitchen shears and began to open and close their blades.

"Mr. Darcy is a generous master," said the cook. "Always has been. He's even seen to the education of some of us servants. But he certainly doesn't fraternize with us, Mr. Markwood. And I'm not sure if he approves of you doing so either."

"Well if I offend him, I am sure he will tell me, and if he does not, then that is his concern, not mine." As indifferent as Mr. Markwood appeared, he did, in fact, care about Mr. Darcy's opinion. It pained him to think he might offend the man he had respected as a patron and had begun to regard as a friend, but he could not shun the powerless in deference to the great. He had learned that he could not relate to his lower-class parishioners, could not genuinely serve them in their times of need, if he approached them merely as servants. He attempted to refrain from affronting the sensibilities of society, as far as that was possible, and he kept his interactions with the classes separate. But he was also aware that his pastoral style somewhat violated societal convention, and he knew that he might be censured for it. Although he was willing to suffer that consequence should it come, he certainly did not invite it.

"For a parson, you don't much care what people think of you."

"I do care when what they think is relevant."

The cook let out a great laugh. It made Mr. Markwood smile just to hear her. "You are more jolly than my curate," he said.

"Your curate? I don't know him."

"Peter Bailee. He has been in this parish much longer than have I. You *might* know him, Betsy, if you came to church more often. Your husband does."

"You don't need one more woman swooning at your altar, vicar."

"What do you mean?"

"You know what I mean. The ladies half come to church just to look at you. And then when you are friendly with them—"

"I do not flirt, Betsy," he said, feeling a compelling need to defend himself, for he was not wholly unaware of the wide spread admiration he had inspired in the feminine portion of his congregation. He did not seek to foster it, but nor did he know how to discourage it politely.

"No, sir. I did not say you did. I said you were friendly. And you are. Most women don't need any more encouragement than that."

"Then that puts a man in a very unfair position," he lamented. "Either I must be rude to the ladies, or I must falsely and inappropriately encourage them."

"If you had been ugly, Mr. Markwood, you could have been as friendly as you liked."

"Well, that is some consolation."

"*Hmph*," she said, and grabbed the shears from his hands. "I'll be needing those later."

She turned back to her work and asked, "What's he like?"

"Who?"

"Your curate."

"Mr. Bailee is a ruddy fellow. He is not in the least bit pretentious. And he is a dutiful curate, despite the fact that he is clearly there for his belly and not for his soul." Mr. Markwood could not help but like Mr. Bailee, even if it peeved him to see a man enter the church without a calling. But not everyone was fortunate enough to have a father who would labor rigorously to ensure the education of his children; some men had to support themselves by whatever means they could find. And Peter Bailee had obtained a decent income, far better than what Mr. Markwood had once earned as a curate.

While he was reflecting on these thoughts, the cook had become preoccupied with her own chores. Discovering moments later that he was still there, she commanded, "You go on now, Mr. Markwood. I have cooking to do, and I can't be entertaining you."

"Yes ma'am," he said and rose to leave, but he remained a-while longer to observe and comment upon her cooking, until she threatened to drive him off with a less than ominous spoon.

***

When Mr. Markwood entered the sitting room, Mr. and Mrs. Bingley were engaged in amorous whispering in a corner by one window, while Mr. Darcy was writing a letter from his desk under a second. Kitty was engaged in some needlework, Elizabeth and Georgiana were both reading, and Miss Bingley was pretending to. The Gardiners, who never ceased to be amazed by the beautiful grounds of Pemberley, were once again taking a stroll before dinner.

Mr. Markwood sat next to Miss Darcy. "You smell like pheasant," she said with a slight smile. That morning before the hunt, he had mercilessly teased her about Major Talbot, and she now felt obligated to return the favor.

"Perhaps," he said, glancing at Elizabeth, who sat nearby, "Mrs. Darcy can direct me to a place where I might refresh myself, so that I do not offend the entire room."

"Certainly," said Elizabeth, who rose to summon a footman to assist the vicar.

When Mr. Markwood returned, he interrupted Georgiana's reading for a second time. "Am I now acceptable to you?" he asked with a grin.

"You are much improved," she replied, and then looked up as

Miss Bingley approached them.

Caroline strode toward the vicar with a stately gate and placed a hand upon the arm of his chair. With the familiarity of a confidant she said, "I have heard, Mr. Markwood, that your father has recently made a number of transactions that have increased his already substantial fortune."

By now, Mr. Markwood was wholly aware of Caroline Bingley's intentions. She considered him a potential husband, but one who would be of no use to her until his fortune was restored. He knew this, but he still did not know how to distance her. He had tried subtlety, and it had failed. He now resigned himself to the uncomfortable fact that he must be less polite in the future. "I am not in correspondence with my father," he replied, "so I can neither confirm nor deny your information. He has always had an instinct for the investment of money, so if your report should prove true, I would not be shocked."

"Are you not attempting to reconcile with Sir Robert?" asked Caroline.

"Presently, I am attempting to read this volume." He pointed to the book he had secured before he had taken his seat. Miss Bingley gave him a forced smile and continued her walk around the room.

When she was gone, Mr. Markwood put his book down and eyed the volume Georgiana held. He read the title with disbelief: "Blake's *Marriage of Heaven and Hell*?" Miss Darcy was an innocent sort of girl; it was not the kind of book he expected her to read. "Your brother lets you read these unorthodox writings?"

Hearing this, Mr. Darcy glanced up. He had no idea what his sister might be reading.

"I took it from his library," she said tentatively, not wishing to alarm her brother. Mr. Darcy had never censored her reading. Surely, she thought, he would not keep upon his shelves books he thought improper, and if he did, he could not blame her for reading them.

When Mr. Darcy looked at Mr. Markwood, he saw that the vicar was not genuinely affronted by his sister's choice of reading. The vicar seemed surprised but also slightly amused. Mr.

Darcy therefore returned to his letter. When she saw him relax, Georgiana issued a sigh of relief. "What do you make of the book, Mr. Markwood?" she asked.

"It is intriguing, but blasphemous."

He may have been half-joking, but his pronouncement troubled Georgiana. She had not really been reading a blasphemous book, had she? Would not her brother disapprove? And would not Mr. Markwood judge her for it? "But when Mr. Blake writes the proverbs of hell," she asked nervously, "do you not believe he is being ironic?"

Mr. Markwood blinked. She was more perceptive than he would have imagined. "Yes, I think he is. I mean, I thought he was, when I first read it. And then I was not so certain, when I read it a second time. The whole strain of the work is at odds not just with Christian orthodoxy, but with Christ's own teachings."

"Are those two things not the same?"

"Not always."

"Which," she said, "I suppose is precisely Mr. Blake's point."

"Yes," he said, his voice tinted with amazement, "you are quite right. You have encapsulated the theme precisely. Yet I think Blake takes that point, which has a seed of truth, and runs wild with it. His conclusions are untenable."

"And yet you must have read Blake, if you are familiar with this work." In speaking thus, she was partly continuing an interesting conversation and partly defending herself for having been caught with the questionable book.

"Like John Donne, he has glimpses of some great mystical vision. But unlike Donne, he does not, I do not think, interpret it aright."

"Dr. Donne, then, is a favorite of yours? He has rather fallen out of fashion."

"Not a favorite, Miss Darcy. He is the most passionate poet of God I have ever had the privilege to read."

"Not *just* of God, Mr. Markwood."

It took awhile for her implication to dawn upon him. Miss Darcy was clearly an accomplished woman, but she possessed such a semblance of innocence that he never would have anticipated the suggestive wit that had just now fallen from her lips.

"No," he said. "Dr. Donne also has somewhat to say on the subject of *human* passion. And I am not averse to those poems either."

"Questionable reading for a clergyman," she said. She tried to make it sound like an accusation, but the smile that curled around her lips belied her.

"A clergyman wrote them." He turned in his chair to face her more completely, and asked with amusement, "You would not like it half as much, Miss Darcy, would you, if I were a model vicar? For then you could not entertain yourself by mocking me."

This time, there was only sincerity in her voice. "Oh," she replied, "but you are a model vicar, Mr. Markwood."

She had spoken artlessly. She had no idea how those words would gratify and relieve him. He had been fearing that the inhabitants of Pemberley might one day frown upon his method of ministry. This reply gave him hope that they would not. It was not the words that affected him, but rather the manner in which they were voiced. The same declaration coming from Miss Bingley would have meant nothing.

He let the conversation end there, and he returned to his own book. He seemed to read, but his mind was not upon the text. He was wondering about Miss Darcy's character. He had formerly considered her naïve. Yet their recent conversations, particularly this latest one, had convinced him that she possessed a rare intellect that was the product of an independent mind and not the offshoot of a rehearsed education. Had Major Talbot perceived all this in but a month?

Mr. Markwood supposed it was possible. Talbot had, after all, drawn her out of her shell long before she had been comfortable with the vicar. Yet he suspected that his friend had not known this depth in her. Major Talbot, he believed, had seen her surface virtues, and those alone had been enough to satisfy him. He had beheld a single shiny coin, and had dug it from the earth, little knowing he had struck a treasure chest beneath. The Major had been fortunate, because he was a man willing to take risks. Mr. Markwood, on the other hand, was cautious with his opinion and guarded with his heart.

Chapter 14

Autumn had arrived on cold and muddy wings, and with the drifting leaves came a new family to Derbyshire. Sir Andrew Atwood and his wife procured a country estate, though they were expected to spend most of their time in London. To fight the bleak weather they announced a ball and invited every respectable member of the neighborhood.

Georgiana wrote to promise her fiancée that she would not dance more than a single set with any one partner. She would strive, also, to avoid taking to the floor with any man who was 'to handsome'. She concluded her missive: *Yet I do not make grand promises, dearest, only those I know I shall never break. I will not promise, but I will try.*

Major Talbot was amused by her vow, but he also understood her timid rebuke. She was, of course, quoting what he had said when they parted. It was not as though he was being intentionally neglectful with regard to his writing, and he *had* more than kept his minimal promise to send a letter weekly. Nevertheless, he was often mired in the concerns of his profession. Even when his time was free, he could usually think of little new to write. He did not feel he should share with her the details of his drilling, which he was sure could only bore her. And he had already exhausted all the news of Brighton.

Her most recent letter, however, he answered immediately, reproving himself for having been less diligent in the past. He wrote that he wished he could join her for the ball and told her to dance with as many young men as she liked, provided she told each one that she was engaged. He confessed to her, also, that he was beginning to feel aimless in Brighton. Though he worked earnestly at his duties, he now feared that the training he was bestowing upon his men would prove futile. *We do nothing,* he wrote, *but eat, sleep, and train to confront an enemy we will not be sent to fight. We are ready, but ready for what? They leave us here to stagnate upon the English shore.*

Miss Darcy did not comprehend his zeal to put that training into use. If it were not necessary for him to enter the battle-field, why should he seem to desire it? She was grateful he had avoided the snare her cousin Colonel Fitzwilliam had been un-able to escape.

***

Sir Andrew's estate of Hartethorn had been carefully prepar-ed for the ball, and when its doors were thrown open, it shined in all its glory. Seeking amusement wherever they could find it, the guests circulated from the dance hall through the various open rooms of the house. Mr. Markwood remained somewhat closer to the side of the Darcys as he had never grown fully ac-customed to formal gatherings, which he had attended only sporadically in his eight adult years in England and not at all while he lived in the West Indies.

As Mr. and Mrs. Darcy stood speaking to the vicar, Miss Caroline Bingley spotted them and eagerly joined their circle. "You will be most surprised, Mr. Markwood," she said, "to learn the maiden name of Sir Andrew's wife. You will know it when you see her."

Mr. Markwood looked across the room in the direction of La-dy Sarah Atwood. She stood arrayed in an exquisite gown that managed to remain unpretentious despite its ornate, lace ac-cents. The light red fabric of her dress accented the dark blue hue of her eyes, which in turn made a vivid contrast with her fair skin. Mr. Markwood was not, in fact, surprised by what he saw, but such a strong emotion crossed his face that Miss Bing-ley considered it astonishment.

"Miss Grant, I believe," continued Miss Bingley, "was to be your intended. I am happy to inform you that she is now wed and has assumed the name of Lady Sarah Atwood." He was to understand that one avenue of marriage—at least—was no longer open to him. "Sir Andrew," she continued, "is a baronet, and a man of substantial fortune. The fact that Miss Grant has made such a beneficial match, I think, should give her father some ease. Your own father, I do not think, can long remain estranged from you."

"No, indeed, madam. We reconciled some weeks ago." Ever since his disinheritance, Mr. Markwood had written his father regularly to seek a reconciliation, and Sir Robert must seem a cold man indeed to have failed to respond for so long a time. Yet it must be confessed that in all of his missives to his father, the words 'I apologize' never fell once from Mr. Markwood's pen. A penitent man may be quickly forgiven, but Sir Robert had at last granted his son's request for reconciliation even though the vicar himself would admit to no wrongdoing.

"Oh?" said Miss Bingley with delight. "Then your fortune has been restored?"

Mr. Markwood nodded.

"What course shall you then pursue?"

"Course, madam?"

"Will you be returning to your father's estate in Buckingham-shire, or will you be taking a house of your own in town?"

"I shall do neither, madam. I am to remain at the parsonage where my duties require me."

"But you are not now to remain an active clergyman?" Miss Bingley's voice rose with disbelief. "At the *very* least, you will allow your curate to perform your duties. You are only required to preach one sermon on Sunday. And with your fortune restored, you may retire to lead a gentleman's life or press on to the episcopate."

"Nothing has changed for me."

"Why everything has changed, Mr. Markwood. Your father has reinstated your inheritance. He will support you generously now, and—just think—when he is gone, you will be wealthy indeed!"

"I am sorry to disappoint you, Miss Bingley," he said with acerbic emphasis, clasping his hands tightly behind his back, "but I do not anticipate my father's death with such cheer. As for the money he affords me in the meantime, I will spend it as *I* see fit."

"Well," sniffed Miss Bingley, as she indignantly fluttered a-way, "I never."

"That was an interesting performance," commented Mr. Darcy, who was becoming increasingly baffled by Miss Bingley's character. He had never profoundly respected her, but he had always considered her more than suited to society. This past year, however, the unwed woman had developed a sort of desperation that had loosed her hidden nature to the public eye. "And now she is accosting the Atwoods."

"One seems to have escaped," remarked Elizabeth, who lingered at the elbow of her husband.

Lady Sarah approached them from across the room. She walked gracefully, drawing attention by virtue of her beauty and not by any planned effort of her own. She smiled as she arrived before them. "Mr. Markwood, it has been some time."

"Yes it has, Miss Grant—Lady Sarah." The two names followed one another in rapid succession as the vicar quickly regained his composure. "Mr. and Mrs. Darcy," he said, "allow me to introduce you to Lady Sarah Atwood. I formerly knew her in Oxfordshire as Miss Grant."

The Darcys greeted her pleasantly.

"I understand, Lady Sarah," continued Mr. Markwood, "that I am to congratulate you on your recent marriage."

Lady Sarah's happiness shone without speech. As Mr. Markwood smiled back at her, Elizabeth could well understand why his father might once have perceived something in his demeanor to suggest love.

"I have indeed recently wed, Mr. Markwood."

"And you are happy?"

"Immeasurably so. A fact I owe, in large part, to a generous friend."

"I have always desired little more than your happiness."

Sir Andrew now joined them. The man was not so unusually handsome as the vicar—he was a good six years older, and a premature grayness had begun to creep about the temples of his russet hair—but there was a confidence in his air and a nobleness to his demeanor that made him undeniably attractive. "My dear," he said to his wife, "the ballroom is in need of dancers, and I have somehow found myself engaged to a certain Miss Bingley. You will not be without a partner, I hope?"

Lady Sarah glanced wordlessly at Mr. Markwood.

"I would be pleased," the vicar replied to her unspoken suggestion, "if your husband would consent to allow me to dance with you."

For a baronet to encourage his lady to dance with a country vicar might seem an enormous act of condescension. But Sir Andrew knew Mr. Markwood's father was titled, and he was aware that the vicar anticipated a mighty future fortune. None of this was so important, however, as the simple fact that he owed the man his very wife. "I have heard a great deal about you," said Sir Andrew, "and I feel safe investing my wife into your hands."

Mr. Markwood bowed and took Lady Sarah's hand. The Darcys followed them to the floor, although it had required some skill on Elizabeth's part to persuade her husband to join the merriment. This was the first time anyone had seen Mr. Markwood dance. He had been present at such amusements before, but never had he solicited the hand of a woman. Mrs. Darcy had once ventured to ask him why, and he had replied, "Dancing is not a particular talent of mine. Consequently, I always think it better to reserve for the ladies more suitable partners." Yet, thought Elizabeth, he had clearly underrepresented his abilities. For he danced with a certain easy grace, and if his steps were not always perfectly accurate, the fact was owing more to a lack of concentration than to a lack of natural talent.

When the dance was concluded, the couples parted, and conversation was sought in the various corners of the hall. As Mr. Darcy left Elizabeth to sit with Georgiana, the gentleman sought out a corner he had determined, upon his entrance, to be a likely observation point. But he found Mr. Markwood already inhabiting the spot.

"Mr. Markwood," he said, "it seems you have usurped my designated hideaway."

"Most unintentionally, sir," he replied. "It merely seemed like a good retreat, and one likes to rest from society, from time to time."

Mr. Darcy agreed. The men stood silently together for some time, watching the ball. Mr. Markwood's intense eyes followed

Lady Sarah as she danced with her husband. Mr. Darcy sensed in him the same sadness Elizabeth had once witnessed. "Some time ago," he said, "you helped me to obtain peace in a time of great agony. Do you not now take possession of that same peace for yourself?"

"I know what you are asking me, Mr. Darcy," the vicar replied. "May I speak directly?"

"Certainly."

"It is true that I once loved Miss Grant. And it is true that seeing her here tonight has somewhat aggravated those feelings that I thought I had fully suppressed. There was a time when I had only to say the word, and she would have been mine. She loved Sir Andrew even then. Although their match seemed highly unlikely, she held out a hope, and I could not extinguish it by taking her hand. She has since made the conquest, and I think her husband will prove a devoted one. I am happy in her happiness. It is a kind of peace."

Mr. Darcy nodded. "In time, no doubt, you will love again."

"It is not impossible. My only prayer is that—if I do—that love will be requited. But God has always provided for me in every way. I have faith that He will either fulfill my desire for domestic bliss or else take the desire wholly from me."

"Although I admire your faith, Mr. Markwood, it is commonly said that God helps those who help themselves. There are a number of young ladies who are, at present, without partners for the next dance."

"You are correct in that, sir. I shall now then take my leave of you."

The men bowed to one another, and Mr. Markwood had every intention of seeking out a single lady. But he found himself pausing, instead, by the chairs where Mrs. Darcy sat with Kitty and Georgiana. He had no intention of asking any of them to dance. Kitty was the only available woman among them, and he dared not make himself the envy of his curate. He did, however, begin to exchange pleasantries with them.

As Mr. Darcy passed by, he leaned toward Mr. Markwood and said quietly, "That is not what I intended, Mr. Markwood. You see, *Mrs.* Darcy is spoken for." The vicar returned his wry smile. Mr. Darcy took his wife's hand and led her to the floor.

"I am sorry your brother could not join us," said Kitty. "He has yet to visit you here."

"He finds his profession very consuming," answered Mr. Markwood, pleased to be distracted by conversation. "But he will come in time. You shall all have a chance of meeting him."

"I have met him already," replied Kitty. And this time, she did not have to recall the long ago dance in London. For the past several months, she had stayed with the Gardiners, and she had seen Aaron Markwood in the streets of London. He had even remembered her and had greeted her warmly although their conversation had not been long. Kitty's aunt and uncle, unfortunately, tended to move in a social circle quite different from that of the young Mr. Markwood, and that one chance meeting had been their last. She could only hope he would find his way to Derbyshire at a convenient time—when she, too, happened to reside at Pemberley.

"You have?" Mr. Markwood asked, not expecting such an answer. She explained their acquaintance, but she did so casually. The vicar perceived no sign of infatuation in her words. He would have discussed his brother further, had Kitty not been claimed by an anonymous young man who wished to dance a set with her.

"Do you not dance, Mr. Markwood?" Georgiana asked, when Miss Bennet had departed. "I have not seen you do so the entire evening."

"I danced with Lady Sarah."

"Ah, I did not see. Mr. Davidson, I am afraid, captured my attention." The politician had made his way from London under the pretense of visiting a friend; his true intention, however, had been to attend the Hartethorn Ball and to woo Miss Darcy. Georgiana had made it clear to Mr. Davidson, in the course of their conversation, that she was engaged, and yet the fact did not seem to affect his attentions any. He had made an offhanded remark about 'long engagements' and had said that 'war may alter matters'. Then he had continued to flatter her. Georgiana now dispelled his frustrating image from her mind and said to Mr. Markwood, "I thought that perhaps, as an evangelical, you disapproved of dancing altogether."

"No," said Mr. Markwood. "I could hardly do so with much success, when the Bible itself depicts the diversion."

"But in the Bible," said Georgiana, "dancing is a religious ceremony, performed only for the glory of the Lord. And it only occurs in the Old Testament, under which we are no longer bound." Georgiana was not seeking to fuel the position against dancing. Indeed, she enjoyed the amusement and regarded it as a retreat from the more pressing demands of society. But she was curious to see how Mr. Markwood would respond to these traditional arguments, which she had gleaned primarily from books. Based on the accumulated evidence provided by his sermons, his contributions, and his treatment of the lower classes, most of the parish had come to assume that the vicar was an evangelical. Yet there were times, Georgiana thought, when he did not act like one, and he himself had never used the word.

"Ah but," responded Mr. Markwood. "in the New Testament, when the prodigal son returns, there is dancing. And I think it safe to assume there was dancing at the wedding in Canaan. It is not any scruple that restrains me—" His voice dwindled into silence as he observed Miss Darcy's growing apprehension. "Does something trouble you?" he asked.

Georgiana did not know if she should tell the vicar the reason for her agitation. Normally, she would not have answered such a question, but she was nearly as much at ease with him as with her family. "Mr. Davidson is approaching," she said. "I fear he will ask me for another dance, and I do not think it would be proper to accept. We have already danced a set."

"He knows you are engaged to Major Talbot?"

"Yes."

"Then he is not likely to ask. One set is certainly harmless enough, but under the circumstances he would not pay you the inappropriate attention of requesting a second."

"Oh, but he will. He was on the verge of doing so earlier when we were interrupted, and I only narrowly escaped."

"Then tell him you are not inclined to dance."

"But if I do, then I must sit down for the entire evening. I could not say so and then dance again, and yet I would like to dance again." She was growing increasingly nervous. Niles Davidson had been temporarily detained, but he was now just a few strides away.

"Then tell him," said Mr. Markwood hastily, "that you are engaged to me for the next set. I will not be an impressive partner, but I will endeavor to concentrate, and I promise not to embarrass you."

Georgiana smiled. She suspected he was being overmodest, and she seized upon the suggestion. To dance with Mr. Markwood would be a pleasant escape. She could enjoy the freedom of movement and the sounds of the music without having to endure the burden of socializing. She could talk to him without discomfort. Better yet, she could be silent in his presence without unease. He was only Mr. Markwood, after all.

***

Georgiana, having secured another partner the moment she was released from her enjoyable dance with Mr. Markwood, managed to avoid Niles Davidson for two sets. But upon the advent of the next set, the politician confronted her, and she was forced to say she intended to rest for the remainder of the evening. She therefore took a chair by the wall and watched the vicar as he attempted to heed Mr. Darcy's advice.

Mr. Markwood danced with two very pretty young ladies as well as with one rather plain one, but he could not manage to manufacture an interest in even one of them. Each was pleasant enough, in her own way, but none exhibited any intellectual depth. There was only so much, he thought, that he could say about the weather or the place settings or the ballroom decorations. All three women had been thrilled that such a handsome man had approached them, but when he had failed to engage in routine flirtation and had actually attempted to learn something of their characters, their interests partially waned.

He gave up his quest after the third dance and planted himself alongside the wall, next to Georgiana. "I saw Mr. Davidson speaking with you," he said. "I am sorry you could only escape by taking up permanent residence in this chair."

She laughed. "At least I have enjoyed four sets this evening. One in particular."

"Ah, well, I have eclipsed you then, for I have danced five." He crossed his arms across his chest and leaned back into his chair. He looked strangely casual, there among the many rigid gentlemen, but Georgiana had grown accustomed to his conduct. He was watching Lady Sarah again, but there was now less intensity in his gaze. He felt relaxed. Talking to Miss Darcy was easy, comfortable. He did not have to worry about how he appeared. He did not have to concern himself with games of courtship since she was already engaged, and they could be no more than friends. Granted, he was no longer seeking to "help himself," as Mr. Darcy had suggested, but at least he was now *enjoying* himself, which was far better than what he had been doing before.

"But surely you are not finished dancing for the evening," she said. "Or are you also avoiding someone?"

"No one in particular," he replied.

She suppressed a smile. "Mr. Markwood," she admonished, "look at all the handsome young ladies in this ballroom. Do you not realize that you are squandering your time by sitting here with me?"

"Did your brother instruct you to say that?"

"My brother?"

"He, too, has been encouraging me to seize the day."

"Then why don't you seize it?"

"The day has turned out to be less appealing than I imagined."

She shook her head. How could he possibly think it was more interesting to sit here with her than to dance with some beautiful, eager woman? She did not understand his preference, but she happily accepted it, and she no longer pressured him to leave. Georgiana hated that she could not dance again, and she feared roaming the ballroom might subject her to some vapid conversation with a relative stranger. She was safe here in this corner, sitting with the vicar, and speaking of whatever crossed her mind.

Chapter 15

Major Talbot returned to his quarters after another weary day and threw himself into a chair. He began to sort through the small stack of mail he had received that day. He opened first his latest letter from Georgiana, which he read with a smile. He perused next a slightly longer epistle from his friend Markwood. The vicar wittily related to him his heroic attempt to rescue Miss Darcy from the attentions of Niles Davidson, and the Major laughed at virtually every line of the letter. He was glad the vicar had been at the ball and glad now that he himself had not, for he could not have faced Davidson with grace. He would have found it difficult to restrain himself. He was also pleased to see that his friend now admitted what he would not confess in their earlier conversation—that Major Talbot did indeed have cause to admire Miss Darcy.

As he reached the bottom of this letter, however, his grin faded. The vicar mildly upbraided the Major for not writing Georgiana more often. "I know how taxing your profession is," he wrote, "but Miss Darcy has hinted, on more than one occasion, that she would prefer more than two letters a week." That was it. One sentence, but the reprimand was strong enough to strike him.

He went straightaway to his writing desk and began to draft a letter to his fiancé. He wrote out *Dearest Georgiana,* thought for a moment, and then mustered a praise or two. These compliments were sincere, but, he feared, they were beginning to sound hackneyed. He wrote that the winter weather was bleak and inquired after the health of her family. He asked how her music skills were progressing and said he missed her playing. Then he found himself a little perplexed.

Perhaps he could tell her about his day. These boys they had sent him were as a green as the English countryside in springtime, and they were requiring a great deal of effort to discipline. But today, he felt he had at long last shattered their apathy and had taught them to respect both their weapons and their profession. He trained them longer, on average, than any of the other companies were required to drill, and they resented the fact slightly, but they did not complain. They respected their Major because he was a true gentlemen but also a true soldier. He was less crass than the common men who had overseen them in the past but also less soft and arrogant than the ceremonial officers they had suffered beneath. His men desired to please him, but they were inexperienced and sometimes lazy. He felt, finally, that he was making short strides of progress.

He did not express all this to Georgiana, however. He told her only that matters were improving and that he was enjoying his labor. He did not know how to explain to her how much he loved his work. Major Talbot had never thought of referring to soldiering as Mr. Markwood referred to his own profession—as a calling. That, he imagined, was too strong and pure a word for what was, in the end, a violent employment. If he had thought about it, however, he would not have been able to conceive of a better word for what he felt.

But why write about that to Georgiana? It mattered little how he regarded his career. He was going to abandon it as soon as he married her. He had promised her as much, had promised her brother, had promised himself. He couldn't very well make a devoted husband traveling about the world with his regiment; and he couldn't very well make a useful soldier passing his time in a country estate. He had to choose one or the other, and he had chosen. He would sell his commission as soon as he secured his Uncle's fortune. He had been constrained to accept that fate the moment Georgiana accepted him.

In proposing to her, he had operated by instinct. He had seen a worthy and inviting woman and had clutched her to himself before she could be lost. He now conscientiously struggled not to doubt whether that instinct had been just.

***

Mr. Markwood peered out his window before he answered the

door. It was an odd hour. The Pharisee Nicodemus, he remembered, had in Christ's time come by night so that he would not be seen of men. But standing before his door this evening, under shadow of twilight, was no secret Christian. It was the bishop.

He opened the door hesitantly, and the bishop hurriedly pushed his way in. "A word, Mr. Markwood," he said as he strode into the drawing room. Mr. Markwood followed him and quickly ordered his manservant to light the candles. He had known the archdeacon would deliver a bad report, but Dr. Ramsey's visitation had been nearly five months ago. Mr. Markwood had concluded, by now, that the bishop did not care.

Both men sat down. The elder visitor had a stately posture, but he drummed his fingers peculiarly on the arm of the chair. Then, suddenly, he began to speak. He said more than Mr. Markwood had ever heard him say. His words came rapidly. He seemed in a rush to dispense with an uncomfortable situation. "The venerable archdeacon had a few choice words to say about your behavior in this parish. He said you publicly defied his authority, fraternized with questionable members of society, drank to excess, frequented houses of ill repute, and contradicted the doctrines of the Church."

Mr. Markwood was astounded. He had expected a negative report from the archdeacon, and he thought he might suffer some mild repercussions, but he had not suspected that blatant falsehoods would be delivered to the bishop; he had not, for a moment, actually feared for his position.

"What have you to say in response to these accusations, Mr. Markwood?"

"Only," he murmured distraughtly, "only that they are not true."

"Two weeks ago, Mr. Markwood, I would have been inclined to believe you. There is a pettiness to my archdeacon that could hardly escape my notice. When he first brought me his report, I assumed you had somehow managed to irritate him. I therefore concluded that his accusations were at best an exaggeration, at worst a sheer fabrication. I decided to ignore them."

The bishop seemed to be waiting for some kind of response, but Mr. Markwood could think of nothing to say. He was still staggering. His mind was racing with fears for his future, fears for the present.

"What piqued my concern," the bishop continued, "was a conversation I had last week with a certain gentleman who will remain nameless. I was dining at his house, and he mentioned having been in Lambton last August. He mentioned also having seen you just outside a brothel. He was quite indignant about the whole affair although he had forgotten it, apparently, until I dined with him. These gentlemen so often are indignant, you know, when they remember to be and when the object is another man's sin. But as he is a wealthy patron of the Church, I of course would not dream of inquiring what he himself happened to be doing there. You, however, are a clergyman, and one under my direction. So I *must* inquire what you were doing there."

Mr. Markwood was about to deny the accusation entirely when a thought occurred to him. Perhaps he *had* been seen outside such a place last summer; indeed, perhaps on more than one occasion. "I. . ." he stammered, feeling trapped and hopeless. "I. . . I perhaps twice, maybe even as many as three times, spoke to two women in that area."

"For what purpose?"

"I wished them to know that they did not have to live like that."

The bishop shook his head and rolled his eyes. "Mr. Markwood," he said in exacerbation, "you insufferable, idealistic parson. What is the name of the imaginary world you wake up in every morning?"

"Pardon me, sir?"

"I have seen enough clergymen in my day to know the real from the counterfeit. You're the real thing, you poor fool."

"Then you take my word?"

"Yes, I do. I see the kind of vicar you are. But give it time. You'll end up disillusioned, and then you'll learn to play the game." He looked Mr. Markwood up and down as if sizing up an opponent. "Yet who knows," said the bishop, "perhaps you have the conviction to press on. What was the result of these two or three conversations?"

"One of the women renounced that life and became instead a servant. The other. . . the other fell very ill and died."

"And for that outcome, you were willing to risk the potential murder of your reputation?"

"I had not thought. . . I certainly did not try to make myself seen. We were some distance from the house. I aimed to be discreet. You see, the way it happened was that one of them—"

"It does not concern me how it happened, Mr. Markwood. I know precisely how it happened. Your compassion mastered your sense."

The bishop rose and began to walk to the door. Mr. Markwood quickly followed him. He was still nervous. Was that the end of the interview? Where was the judgment?

"Mr. Markwood," said the bishop at last, "if you cannot learn to ignore your compassionate impulses like so many other clergymen pragmatically do, then at least be a little more cautious about how you follow them. Do your good deeds in secret, as the Bible says. In utter secret. So that absolutely *no one* sees you. Am I understood?"

"Yes, my lord."

"Very well, then. We will assume I was never here. And that anonymous gentlemen who saw you will be persuaded to remain silent on the matter or risk exposure himself. That hint, however, will cost the Church a pretty penny."

"I regret that, my Lord."

"No," said the bishop. "You do not regret it. You consider it insignificant. And that is why you will forever prove a thorn in my side."

"My Lord—"

The bishop raised his hand and waived him into silence. "Do not trouble yourself, Mr. Markwood," he said. "You have nothing to fear from me." He opened the door and left as hastily as he had come.

Mr. Markwood stood shakily by the door and issued a strained sigh. He had become a clergyman because he could not imagine being anything else. He had been prepared for struggles, had been prepared, even, to witness and occasionally suffer injustice; but he had not been fully equipped to endure the everyday meanness of men, who were so quick to think the worst of one another. He had not been ready, either, for the politics that wove a tangled web behind the scenes.

Georgiana Darcy had once called him a model vicar. What would she call him in another ten years? He wished, desperately, to live up to that accolade. But he now knew how vigilant he must be to avoid inciting judgment.

The vicar glanced out the window and saw the bishop's carriage jerk to a start. His Lordship was returning to the seat of power, under mask of night, to hush up what never should have been considered a crime. *There*, thought Mr. Markwood, *goes the husk of a man who was once as I am now.*

He vowed never to follow that example. He would be more cautious, yes, but he would not abandon his ideals. He must not allow his life to end in shadows.

Chapter 16

It was the habit of the Darcys to pass the winter in London. The weather, however, had hindered a long distance journey, and Georgiana was glad of it. She could not abide the thought of being so near to Niles Davidson. Mr. Darcy, for his part, also had few regrets. Now that he was married, he was not as enamored of the city as he had been in seasons past. He still believed the country to be unvarying, but as he could be secluded there with his wife, he found it required little effort to forgo London society. And now that he had discovered a clever mind in Mr. Markwood, he received intellectual stimulation from yet another source. Indeed, their budding friendship ensured Mr. Markwood's routine presence at Pemberley, and this, Miss Darcy soon discovered, was posing an unexpected problem. Her mind had become inexplicably preoccupied with the vicar.

As Miss Darcy sat looking out one of the great windows in her brother's estate, she made a New Year's resolution. She would not, she determined, permit her mind to stray. She would not allow her thoughts to dwell on Mr. Markwood. If she were forced to speak to him, she decided, she would speak of Major Talbot. Indeed, she would think of Major Talbot. In fact, she would reread his letters this very moment and remind herself of his many virtues.

So when Mr. Markwood came to call upon them at Pemberley the following week, Georgiana avoided meeting his eyes as much as possible. Mr. and Mrs. Darcy, anxious to see the snow-fall that had gently blanketed the grounds of Pemberley, had gone for a walk earlier that afternoon. Mr. Markwood sat with her in the drawing room and listened for the second time as she said, "My brother and sister should be returning any moment." He wondered at her uneasiness. He knew her to be shy, but he believed time had tempered that trait, and for months she had not been awkward in his presence. What had changed?

"I saw your easel as I came in. Have you been painting this

winter scene?" he asked.

"When Major Talbot studied at Oxford," she replied, "did he excel?"

He was startled by the change in subject but answered, "Indeed he did, Miss Darcy. You have won for yourself a very clever man."

Georgiana blushed. "I think it was most honorable of him," she suggested, "to give up a comfortable and respectable profession in the law so that he might serve our country, and at great risk to himself. Do you not think so, Mr. Markwood?"

"The Major is a man of conviction. Even though he had already completed his legal studies, he thought nothing of that lost cost, and did instead what he believed to be right. Indeed, it was his example I followed. I abandoned my law studies at the same time he completed his. When he purchased his commission, I took up theology."

Georgiana's good intentions were frustrated. Mr. Markwood had somehow managed to redirect her mind onto *him* at the very same moment he was complimenting her fiancé. It was hardly just; she had been so careful. She tried once again to focus her thoughts. "Napoleon is safely on Elba," she said, "and now that the Treaty of Ghent has been signed, the Major will certainly not be sent to America."

"Will your cousin Colonel Fitzwilliam be returning soon?"

Her former loquaciousness was quieted. She said softly, "We have not heard from him recently. But we hope to every day now."

It was obvious she was concerned about this lack of communication from her cousin, and the vicar attempted to offer her some comfort. He concluded, however, that his style must have been inadequate, for she abruptly changed the subject: "I hope to see my fiancé at the end of March. We would have gone this winter—I suggested it—but the weather has been too harsh to travel such a distance, and Major Talbot says he will not have leave until the spring."

Mr. Markwood nodded; he was not under the impression that she was seeking a verbal response.

"I am so pleased, Mr. Markwood," continued Georgiana,

"that you will be officiating at our wedding. Major Talbot has said he will be glad to have you assume that role because, when it is you who admonishes him to enter reverently into the state of matrimony, he cannot help but take your words seriously."

"And yet," said the vicar, "I suppose I should not speak so assuredly of a state with which I have so little experience."

When this remark was met only with silence, Mr. Markwood spoke again. He departed from the subject of Major Talbot with caution as though testing the waters. "Did your brother tell you I intend to build a school?"

"Yes," she murmured. Mr. Darcy had remarked that Mr. Markwood would continue to live off his income and that he would use his newly regained allowance to support a small country school. Mr. Darcy himself was donating a parcel of land for the site, and the Bingleys were contributing to the project. Georgiana had thought the idea admirable and had been especially impressed to learn that Mr. Markwood intended to educate the poor, both boys and girls.

"I am going to attempt to pare down my library," he said. "I have not space enough to contain all of my books. I would like to donate some to the school so that, when it opens, it will have a small library of its own. You are young still and not quite as far from your childhood as am I. Perhaps you can advise me as to which volumes would be best for the school. Mr. Darcy has agreed to help me select them tomorrow afternoon. Would you assist us?"

"I am sure the school would be fortunate to receive whatever books you are willing to part with."

"I am not wholly willing to part with any of them. And yet I think the school will have more immediate need of my boyhood volumes than I. I would genuinely appreciate your advice."

"You are far more learned than I, Mr. Markwood; surely you do not need my help on that score."

He did not know the motive behind her reluctance, and he thought her hesitation stemmed only from humility. "You will resist," he said. "Very well. Then I shall keep back the Mary and Charles Lamb."

"Not the *Tales from Shakespeare*!" she exclaimed, suddenly forgetting her resolution to remain uninvolved. "If you would donate anything, you must donate that. It is specifically written for children, and will, I believe, serve wonders to inspire their love for the literature of our nation's greatest playwright."

Mr. Markwood smiled. "Miss Darcy, it appears you have taken the bait."

Georgiana was disarmed by his maneuver, and she no longer sought to remain aloof from the dialogue. "But that work is not above seven years old," she told him. "It cannot have been one of your boyhood volumes."

"No, it cannot have been. Yet I will confess to occasionally purchasing books based upon the presently tenuous supposition that I will one day have an heir." From that point forward the conversation involved literature, and it was much enlivened by the return of Mr. and Mrs. Darcy, who had a great many opinions to offer on the subject.

***

Georgiana decided that it would be too dramatic to avoid Mr. Markwood's company. He was a friend of her brother's, and any active effort to shun his presence might draw suspicion upon her motives. She was ashamed of herself for thinking of him so often and with such high regard. Her actions were pure, her commitment was firm, but her thoughts would not be brought under control. She regularly attempted to focus her meditations upon Major Talbot, and although she possessed as tender as ever a feeling for him, she had begun—far too late—to wonder whether that emotion were really the equivalent of love.

How, one may wonder, could such a sensible woman have failed to ask herself that question before? Georgiana was not foolish; she was only inexperienced. What she had felt for Major Talbot was the strongest affection she had ever possessed for any man; she could not help but regard it as love. But when the Major departed for Brighton, she suddenly found herself with more than adequate time for introspection. While he had been present, she had not much observed the world around her; she had observed only him. He was handsome, kind, attentive. . . she hardly had time to think about anything else. But in his absence, she had begun to notice again her brother's marriage, and to assess the depth of the love that couple shared. She saw anew the way they looked at one another; she witnessed their battles of wits and their exchange of thoughts.

That union had long been her model. But now, when she compared it to her relationship with Major Talbot, she wondered whether such a high standard had simply been unrealistic. Major Talbot had looked at her with affection—indeed, with attraction—but he had not looked at her the way her brother looked at her sister-in-law. His admiration, she began to think, was of a different kind. Major Talbot had praised her for her sweetness, her beauty, her innocence, and for her excellence in those fields society deemed 'accomplishments'. Yet he knew little of her mind and soul. She had told him the names of her favorite painters, her favorite authors, and her favorite musicians. But she had not shared with him even a thimble-full of the thousands of thoughts that swarmed within her mind, ever changing and evolving with each new book she read. And he, for his part, had not revealed to her his trials as a soldier, or exposed in detail his opinions about the things nearest to his heart—patriotism, duty, service, self-sacrifice, and the protection of his brothers in arms.

But was she expecting too much? She was very fond of Major Talbot, and a marriage built on fondness and mutual respect had a significant chance of happiness. It was true that she had once been almost as fond of George Wickham, but that was a different matter. She had been far less mature then and not very talented at interpreting character. Her discernment had since improved, and—if nothing else—she knew her present affection was superior because its object was superior.

Perhaps, she reflected, their courtship had been too hasty. The specter of distance had frightened her into seizing the bird at hand. Nevertheless, her promise had been given; their engagement was now public knowledge, and they *did* at least care for one another. Georgiana must content herself with the hope that once they were married, they would have a meeting of minds. Then she would learn to love him more profoundly.

In the interim, more time in the vicar's presence ought to reveal his defects and thus make her fidelity as steadfast in thought as it was in deed. Besides, it was not as if she were in love with Mr. Markwood. She was, she assured herself, only distracted by him.

Therefore, she consented to accompany her brother to the parsonage the following afternoon. Her brother's presence, she expected, would serve as a form of protection, but managing to absent himself in a corner of the parsonage where he became engrossed in a book, Mr. Darcy left all the work of selection to the vicar and his sister.

Eventually, Georgiana relaxed just enough to enjoy Mr. Markwood's company. "William Blake?" she asked, taking a volume from the vicar's shelf. She recalled their earlier exchange regarding the poet and asked with a hint of playful accusation, "Is he not a bit unorthodox for a clergyman's library?"

"Perhaps. And yet, who else could conceive of that brilliant metaphor: 'And the hapless Soldier's sigh / Runs in blood down Palace walls'?'" He took the volume from her hands and turned it over lovingly. "My friend the Major," he continued, "may not appreciate Blake's anti-imperialism, but even he would have to admit that it is a stunningly powerful image of the selfish manipulation our forces sometimes suffer."

"You are an aficionado of morbid poetry, Mr. Markwood?"

"I am afraid I am, Miss Darcy. Does it lower your opinion of me?"

"Not at all. And yet, I certainly would not call the carriage that takes a woman from the church on her wedding day the 'marriage hearse,' as does Mr. Blake."

"Nor I, nor I, when all is right, which it so rarely is."

"You are a pessimist?"

"Not as such," he replied. "For I do believe, despite all I have seen of man's inhumanity to man, that with God's help it is possible for a man to work a change in society itself, though he may begin with but a single heart."

He climbed the ladder that was poised against his bookcase

to return Mr. Blake's volume to a different shelf, which was now half emptied. When he descended, he landed very close to Georgiana, and she felt a sudden need to escape his nearness.

"To where has my brother wandered?" she asked, taking a step backward and looking down the hallway.

"I believe he is in the other room reading." The vicar extended his arm to Miss Darcy. "Should we join him and persuade him to advise us on these volumes?"

Georgiana eyed his arm cautiously, but eventually she took it. There could be no danger, she reasoned, in a simple touch.

Chapter 17

In the late hours of a moonless night, Mr. Markwood was a-wakened by a loud pounding on his parsonage door. It was not unusual for the clergyman to be summoned from bed in the middle of the night. Because his concern for his flock was sincere, his parishioners—whatever their station in life—felt no discomfort sending for him at any hour of need. He dressed quickly now, grabbing the clothes he had laid by his bed that night, as he did every night, for times such as these. Still buttoning his shirt, he arrived at the door and opened it.

Mr. Darcy's man Thomas stood before him with a lantern in his hand and an urgent expression on his face. "Mr. Markwood, sir, there has been a break-in at Pemberley."

"Dear God! Is the family safe?"

"They are. Miss Darcy woke when she heard the silver crashing to the floor. She went to investigate, and the thief ran past her. He threw her to the wall."

"Is she injured?"

"A scrape. A bruise or two. Nothing serious. She's badly shaken. Mr. Darcy sends for your assistance. He and the other servants are hunting the thief."

"I will come instantly," replied Mr. Markwood, grabbing his boots and vest, dressing as he walked out the door. He jumped back when his stocking foot hit the muddy snow on his doorstep. He had not been expecting it; it was already March. Mr. Markwood quickly pulled on his boots and hurried out. It was then he saw that Thomas also held the reins to two horses.

"Mr. Darcy did not wish you to lose time saddling your own," explained the servant. The vicar leapt atop one of the horses, and soon the two men were galloping up the lane toward Pemberley.

Mr. Darcy met Mr. Markwood as he dismounted, tossed the vicar a rifle, and pointed east. "You head that way with Thomas and some of my other men; I'll take the west with John and

Mark here. We have heard crashing in the woods from both directions, and he could be running in either." Mr. Markwood nodded and began the hunt.

The moon had just begun to appear for the first time that night as an obscuring cloud moved slowly from the path of the rock's reflecting light. By its gentle glow, Mr. Darcy followed an almost imperceptible sign, but as he moved further into the woods, the tracks became clearer, and he was instantly aware that they were not human. He was about to taste the bitter gall of disappointment when a cry form the east raised his hopes. The thief must have been apprehended.

Mr. Darcy ran with his two servants to join the other party, only to find Mr. Markwood on the floor of the woods, propped up by Thomas and groaning in agony. In the faint gleam of the lanterns' flames, Mr. Darcy could see the fabric that lay flayed around the clergyman's left leg and the dark blood that had begun to ooze through its tattered remains. Mr. Markwood had stopped moaning, but he was now gasping heavily, his breath forming dense clouds in the frigid air. To the vicar's side, Darcy saw the ferocious glint of metal.

"Thomas," he said as he stared at the contraption that the servants had pried from Mr. Markwood's now mangled leg, "help me get Mr. Markwood up to the house. John, you ride for the surgeon. Mark, fetch the constable and tell him a thief is on the loose in these woods."

***

Elizabeth cried out in shock when the bloodied man was carried into the parlor and laid on the couch. Retrieving towels and water, the servants immediately went into action while Georgiana looked on in silent disbelief. She felt a sickening sense of fear growing in the pit of her stomach.

Mr. Darcy took out his pocket knife and cut away the fabric from the bloody man's wounds. He pulled back the material as gently as possible and then began to reach for the towels. "No, Darcy," insisted Georgiana, "you are weary from the chase. Let a servant clean his wounds."

"Very well," Darcy agreed, stepping back from the couch. As a house servant took over the care of Mr. Markwood, Darcy led his wife to a secluded corner for a private conference.

"This is my doing," he said, and clenched his teeth together in anger at himself.

"What do you mean? What has happened to him?"

"He was caught in one of the man-traps the game keeper laid out for the poachers."

"You can't blame yourself for that, Fitzwilliam. You couldn't have known your men would have cause for running about the woods at night—"

"I should have recalled they were there. Mr. Markwood generously came to my aid, and I did not so much as remember to warn him of the danger—" Before he could continue, Mr. Markwood uttered a painfilled cry. The Darcys hastened back to him.

"Do not attempt to move, Mr. Markwood," the servant was saying, "wait until the surgeon arrives."

The vicar fell back on the couch. He closed his eyes and was silent.

"Mr. Markwood," said the servant, apprehensively, "Mr. Markwood, can you hear me? Are you conscious?"

After a seemingly interminable delay, he whispered, "Yes."

"Where is Georgiana?" asked Mr. Darcy.

"She went to the door, to wait for the surgeon," replied the servant.

Apparently Miss Darcy had anticipated the surgeon, for although the others had heard no knock, Georgiana now led him into the parlour. As Mr. Witherspoon approached the patient, he said, "Why don't you ladies leave the room?   We will keep you informed of his condition."

Reluctantly, Elizabeth and Georgiana took their leave of him.

***

The excess of blood had made the wounds appear deeper than they really were. The vicar's leg was indeed mangled, but the trap had not maimed him as badly as had been feared. Once the gashes were washed and treated, the situation appeared far less drastic. The patient was carried into one of the guest bedrooms, where he was told by the surgeon he should rest and recover for a number of days. Soon, he could begin walking with the assistance of a cane, and eventually, he would regain full use of his leg. Georgiana was relieved to hear of his quick improvement as indeed was Elizabeth. The two sat by the fire and discussed the riotous events of the night while Mr. Darcy talked to Mr. Markwood in his room.

"You will not be returning to the parsonage, Mr. Markwood, for some days," the gentleman said. "You will remain here at Pemberley where we can see that you receive the proper care."

"Mr. Darcy, I cannot long impose—"

"It is no imposition. You know by now the reason for your injury, and you know I am accountable for it. I shall never allow another such trap to be laid out upon my estate, poachers notwithstanding."

"Accountable, sir? You are much too severe upon yourself. You are placed in a difficult position by our game laws." A rehearsed speech began to trip from his tongue, one he had heard from the mouth of his brother Aaron many times. Aaron shared with their father a solid political ambition, and he was something of a firebrand in the privacy of his own home, among his family and sympathetic friends. How vocal he was in other company, however, his brother did not know. But Jacob had heard Aaron speak passionately about his desire to see the game laws softened, and those sentiments now fell from the vicar's own lips, though in a much more tempered form:

"These laws are presumably enacted for your benefit to support your place in society as a property owner. Yet it is the very strictness of these protections that have lent impetus to the poachers by making their illegal trade viable. Man-traps have been made necessary, and yet they are as likely to injure the innocent as the guilty. If. . ." Mr. Markwood allowed his words to trail off into silence. Mr. Darcy's expression had altered to one of stern concentration, and the vicar could not know whether he was offended by this political opinion or whether it was merely a new, and not wholly infuriating, idea to him.

Whatever he thought, Mr. Darcy did not share it with the vicar. All he said was, "We will delay our trip to Brighton until we are sure you are recovered."

"Do not do so on my account. Miss Darcy, I am sure, must be eager to see her fiancé."

"It will only be a matter of days, and we will arrive before his leave is in effect. Then we will spend the entire spring there. I think it will not be long before they are wed. Major Talbot should be able to secure his inheritance soon. Frankly, I do not understand why he has not secured it already, and I wonder if he is as eager to wed as Miss Darcy thinks he is."

"You do not think, Mr. Darcy—you do not suspect Major Talbot's willingness to honor his commitment to your sister?"

"I do not know the man as well as I would like."

"I believe you do not know him at all," said Mr. Markwood, offended by the insult to his friend's character. Admittedly, he had himself considered Major Talbot's engagement to be a hasty act, inspired more by flights of fancy than by any profound attachment. However, he did not doubt the man's essential integrity; having committed himself, Major Talbot would prove firm. "I thought you approved of him."

"I do," replied Mr. Darcy. "He seems honorable. But one never knows the extent of a man's character until it is tried."

"I can assure you of Major Talbot's conviction. Or do you doubt me as well?"

"I do not doubt you, Markwood. I consider you a true friend. You must know that by now."

Mr. Markwood's resistance softened. He was gratified to be assured of Mr. Darcy's friendship, and the fact that the reserved gentleman had now ceased to preface his surname with 'Mr.' did not escape his notice. "Then believe me when I tell you that my friend will prove a loyal husband to your sister."

There was a creak in the hallway. Mr. Markwood strained to see through the open door. "Miss Darcy, is that you? I hear you lurking about."

Georgiana peeked in hesitantly. "I just came to see if I could have a servant get you anything. Do you need something to drink?"

"No, Miss Darcy. I think we could all use some rest."

"Then you are well for the night?"

"Quite. But if you must be of service, in the morning, you might have some books brought to me. I am ordered not to move from this bed, and I must be entertained."

"Are there any in particular you would like to read?"

"I trust your judgment."

"Very well then," she said, and curtsied before retreating.

"She has been very concerned for you," said Mr. Darcy. "She is grateful, I think, that you have been willing to entertain her with tales of her fiancé."

"For awhile, that was nearly all she desired to discuss."

Mr. Darcy caught a hint of something unsteady in the vicar's voice and wondered why the fact should seem to concern him. "What do you mean? She speaks of many things."

Mr. Markwood merely mumbled "yes, yes." Having convinced Mr. Darcy of the steadiness of Major Talbot's commitment, he did not wish to raise questions about Miss Darcy's. However, he himself had begun to question the old adage 'absence makes the heart grow fonder', and he now wondered if another was not more accurate: 'out of sight, out of mind'. He believed that Georgiana was persistently reminding herself of the Major because her feelings, which perhaps lacked a solid base, were beginning to fade.

Talbot did not write her often enough; his letters (Georgiana had recently admitted to the vicar) had fallen to once a week. Mr. Markwood felt it was vital that the Darcys travel to Brighton as soon as possible. If the Major could stand beside her in all his handsome glory, the vicar thought, and shower her with the gentle attentions that once had won her, all would be restored.

And it was fitting, Mr. Markwood believed, that all should be restored. He respected his friend, and though he thought the Major's feelings for Miss Darcy to be somewhat superficial, he believed they would intensify in time when he knew her value better. He believed Major Talbot was worthy of her affections, as worthy, at least, as any man could hope to be. For Mr. Markwood had come to realize there was a greater depth to Miss Darcy's character than he had at first acknowledged. Her virtue did not stem merely from innocence, but from a secret inner strength; every day he was learning that she was not as naïve as he had once imagined.

The vicar scrutinized the darkness into which Georgiana had retreated and thought that beneath her pleasing veneer of simplicity, a complex spirit rested.

Chapter 18

Later that night there was a quiet knock on Mr. Markwood's chamber door. "Enter," he announced, assuming it was the servant come to dress his wounds with clean bandages. The door drifted open slowly, creaking timidly. He saw the light of a single lantern, and behind its glow was a striking feminine figure. His eyes adjusted slowly until he could just make out the familiar features. "Miss Darcy," he said with alarm, sitting up in his bed and pulling the covers tighter about himself. "This is not–"

"I know, sir," she said. "I know it is not appropriate for me to be here by myself at this hour. But I must speak to you alone. I must have your advice as a minister. I did not know how else to see you privately."

He was uncomfortable with the situation and feared, in particular, that the servant might come at any moment, see her in his bedchamber, and draw his own conclusions. She was clearly distressed, and he desired to give her whatever reassurance she required. The bishop's visit, however, had taught him to place a greater weight upon appearances. He thought he must send her away, and he intended to, but he found himself saying, instead, "Remain in the doorway, and speak to me from there. If someone should approach–"

"I understand," she replied.

"What concerns you?"

"I recognized the thief, and I don't know what to do."

He processed this revelation as she waited nervously. "Identify him," he said simply. "You did not tell your brother? Was he a servant?"

"No, sir," she said, with dread in her voice. "He was not a servant. I did not reveal his identity to my brother because . . . " She seemed unable to continue.

"Miss Darcy," he said gently, "justice must be done. He threw you to the wall. He is a violent man. He may hurt–"

"No," she averred. "He did not intend to harm me. He only

meant to escape."

"Miss Darcy, you must tell me your relationship to this man. I cannot advise you otherwise."

She was quiet for a long time. She looked down the hallway and blinked to prevent the advent of tears. "He is the husband of Mrs. Darcy's youngest sister."

"Mr. Wickham?"

She turned immediately back to face him, "You know him?"

"I met him once, yes. But he. . . he is in Brighton, with Major Talbot's regiment."

"No. I received a letter from Major Talbot some days ago, in which he cautioned me that Mr. Wickham had been given leave in order to return and satisfy his creditors. It seems he ran up some more debts while he was stationed at Lambton. Major Talbot wrote me and told me to ask my brother to relieve him."

"And did you tell your brother?"

"No," she cried; it was a sob of guilt. "No. I. . . I was still angry with Mr. Wickham for a past wrong he tried to do me. I thought. . . I thought it was time someone put him in his place." Then, more quietly she said, "I was vengeful. I did not know he would try to steal from us. I did not know his debts were so severe. I thought his creditors would only scare him and that it might change him for the better."

She should have told her brother, but it was senseless to tell her what she should have done. She knew her error, and she felt it keenly. He longed to comfort her, but he could offer only this consolation: "Miss Darcy, even if you had told Mr. Darcy, I doubt very much that he would have relieved Mr. Wickham."

"I would have told," she said, "had I known the whole truth. Mr. Wickham, when he saw that it was me he had pushed aside, stopped suddenly. He tried to explain himself. He told me that his were not normal business creditors. They were threatening to harm his wife and daughter. He was desperate. He is not a good man, Mr. Markwood, but he is not evil. I do not think he would have done it if he were not desperate."

This, thought Mr. Markwood, explained why Major Talbot had advised her to persuade her brother to quit Wickham's debts. After what Mr. Darcy had said during that hunting party so many months ago, the Major would never have suggested such a course if there had not been a compelling reason to do so. It was likely, therefore, that Wickham had told the truth about his motivation.

But why had the Major not communicated the entire story to his fiancé? Talbot, the vicar concluded, had affectionately sought to protect her; he still regarded her as his sweet, innocent Georgiana, who required shielding from life's sordid realities. The Major had probably assumed she would simply heed his advice. He must not have known about this past wrong, which had influenced her to act differently.

And what, the vicar now wondered, had Mr. Wickham done to her? A variety of possibilities entered his mind, and each enraged him. Her brother, no doubt, had dealt with it, whatever *it* had been. But the scars had not been permanently healed. That much was clear.

Georgiana did not take his pensive silence as a condemnation, but it disturbed her nonetheless. Frantically, she said, "Mr. Markwood, please advise me. If Mr. Wickham should be court martialed, he may be put to death or at the least imprisoned. And then Mrs. Wickham would suffer so much shame and depravation! She does not deserve such humiliation simply because she made a foolish choice in a husband. Women can be foolish when they are young. They should not have to suffer for it all their lives." She was thinking of her own narrow escape from a union with the very same man.

"You should be telling this to your brother, not to me."

"I am afraid he will be angry with me for not telling him before."

"He will not be angry."

Georgiana did not speak. The lamp light quivered in her hand.

"He will not be angry. Tell him. Let him guide you. This will affect him too, as much as you. Mr. Wickham is his wife's brother-in-law. He ought to have a say in this."

She knew the course he suggested was right, had known it, perhaps, before she had sought his advice. But she had needed the impetus before she could summon the courage. She thank-

ed him for listening, apologized for her impropriety, and retreated from the room.

***

Early the following morning, Mr. Darcy entered Mr. Markwood's chamber. He had come, he said, to seek advice. He related to Mr. Markwood the entire story of Wickham's robbery as
though he expected the vicar to know no part of it. It was wise,
Mr. Markwood thought, that Miss Darcy had not shared with her
brother the fact of her late night visit.

Mr. Darcy sat easily in the chair by Mr. Markwood's bedside.
There was no formality in his manner. It was clear to the vicar
that he was now considered a friend rather than a mere social
inferior.

"My inclination," said Mr. Darcy, "is to seek justice. Mr. Wickham has led an unscrupulous life. He has—I did not tell you,
but he once attempted to elope with my sister, for the sake of
her fortune. I prevented it, thank God, but. . . Georgi was so
innocent then."

Mr. Markwood would never have asked for this truth, but he
was glad to finally know it. He had suspected as much but had
feared even worse, and relief now cooled his heated temper.

"On the other hand," continued the gentleman, "this would
ruin Mrs. Wickham, and thereby wound my wife. I did not think
he had this in him. I knew him to be a spendthrift, a womaniz-
er, and a liar. . . but I did not think him to be a thief."

"I do not think he is a thief at heart, Darcy." Mr. Markwood
now followed the gentleman's lead in assuming a friendly familiarity. When Mr. Darcy accepted the informal address without comment, the vicar continued, "It is likely he petitioned Mr.
Bingley for the money first. Your friend was so resolved not to
err again, he no doubt refused him. Mr. Wickham must have
thought, then, that he could stand no chance with you. If Major
Talbot advised your sister to solicit you for the money, then the
case must have been serious indeed. I do believe, as much I
despise Mr. Wickham, that he acted from desperation and for
love of his family. Perhaps you should just remain silent for the

sake of his wife and yours." Then, allowing a light sigh to escape his lips, he concluded, "And for the sake of your sister, who little doubt already blames herself."

This, Mr. Darcy thought, was well reasoned. Yet he feared that he had once before done a wrong by keeping Wickham's character hidden from the world. That silence had enabled the scoundrel to elope with Lydia Bennet. How could he fail to speak now? "But shouldn't he be punished?" Mr. Darcy asked. "Shouldn't his character be exposed to society? If justice is not brought to bear upon him, will he not grow worse?"

"I do not think so," answered Mr. Markwood. "Georgiana saw him, spoke to him. He knows that by now you must know. If you do not pursue justice, he will take it as mercy. Having sunk to this level, and having been forced to bear the shame of your forgiveness, he may be motivated not to incur debts again. It may work the same change in him that punishment would work, without the injury to his family—or to yours."

"Is it wrong, however, not to tell the constable?"

"Had he robbed another man, I would answer yes. I would tell you that you had no right to keep this secret. But the crime that was done was done only to you and to your sister. You therefore possess the authority to forgive him. You may do so, if you choose, without remorse. Your sister, I gather, is inclined to forgive." He said, 'I gather'. He dared not say, 'I know', although of course he did.

"She is." Mr. Darcy sat in quiet contemplation, and then concluded, "Thank you, Markwood, for your advice." He did not say whether he would heed it.

***

After leaving Mr. Markwood's chamber, Mr. Darcy immediately sought out his wife. They had a lengthy conversation regarding Mr. Wickham and came to a conclusion together.

"I believe," said Elizabeth, "that Mr. Markwood's advice was sound."

"You would not. . . you would not think ill of me for keeping silent? I did your family an injury once, by not revealing Wickham's character. I—"

He was silenced as she placed a finger on his lips. She had been sitting beside him on the couch in their most comfortable sitting room: the one that only family used. "I made the same decision then, too, love."

He kissed the finger that suppressed his speech. She had not been expecting the physical response, and to her surprise that simple gesture produced in her a small shiver. He smiled to see her reaction and took her hand from his lips, kissed its palm, and laced her fingers together with his own. Elizabeth let her free hand stroke his cheek and then lose itself within the thick curls of his hair. "Do not judge yourself so harshly, my dear. You are too conscientious."

As he drew closer to her, she could see the appreciation in his eyes. She had been hard upon him once, long ago, but he knew by now that he was the only one to regret his past transgressions. From her, he could expect only admiration and support. "Be glad of that conscientiousness, Lizzy. It keeps me from growing too proud."

She might have replied, but he had pressed his lips to hers, and the thoughts she had been forming seemed to scatter. She enjoyed his lingering kiss and responded to it willingly. When they parted, however, she prevented him from claiming a second. "You had better write Mr. Wickham now," she urged, "or I suspect the letter will not be ready in time for the post."

"Why?" he asked with a thinly concealed grin. "What might prevent me from completing it in time?"

He leaned toward her and she playfully pushed him away, saying, "Later, my love. . .."

He feigned defeat and forced his growing smile into a mock frown. "Very well," he sighed, rising from the couch and making his way to his writing desk. He turned back once, however, to give her a fiery look, as though to tempt her with what she had brushed aside. It almost worked, but in the end he found himself taking hold of several sheets of paper and sitting at the desk.

As he began to draft the letter, his anger soon distracted him from thoughts of his deferred pleasure. He resented that he could exact nothing from Mr. Wickham, but he knew this decision was best for both families. He let his rage roam about the letter's pages, although he concluded by saying that, for the sake of the innocent, the crime would go unreported. Then, just before signing his name, he warned the prodigal that if he ever erred again no mercy would remain.

Chapter 19

Mr. Darcy's next course of business, upon completion of the letter, was to locate his sister and tell her his decision. He would have preferred to preoccupy himself with other interests, but he felt Georgiana should know immediately. Though she was often too shy to express openly her heartfelt wishes for others, he knew she harbored a quiet compassion for the people about her, even for those whom, like Lydia Wickham, she had never met. It would have pained Miss Darcy to see the wife suffer for the sins of her husband. Her brother's verdict therefore unburdened her, and Georgiana could not help but think she was indebted to Mr. Markwood for that relief.

She wished to thank the vicar, and so she insisted on bringing him the previously promised books herself. Of course, she could not enter his chamber alone. Her brother accompanied her. But she spoke her gratitude by silent expression. The vicar saw her eyes and understood. He only wished that he could assure her, in words, that she owed him nothing. Instead, he merely asked, "What did you select?"

"Burns, Shakespeare, and Defoe," Miss Darcy answered.

"The first two I admire, but Defoe I cannot endure."

"Not even *Moll Flanders*?"

"Ah, no. You've hit upon the one exception. I feared you had brought me *A Journal of the Plague Year* or some such monstrosity."

Mr. Darcy laughed. "Defoe's *Journal* is a fine book for a bedridden man," he said.

"Yes. Very encouraging. There is nothing like a tale of black death when you are laid up for the week." The vicar turned to Georgiana. "If you could choose only three, Miss Darcy, what Shakespeare titles would you recommend I read this week?"

"*Much Ado About Nothing*," she replied.

"His finest comedy," he replied.

"*King Lear*," she continued.

"His finest tragedy."

"And *Richard the Second*," she concluded.

"Hmm. Not one I would have thought to place in the top three. And yet, that king is among his finest characters."

"You think Richard the Second is one of the bard's finest characters?" asked Mr. Darcy, leaning forward a little in his chair, poised for an engaging argument.

"He's magnificent," replied the vicar with feeling. "The way Shakespeare portrays his overthrow—the sensitivity of his speech—it never ceases to amaze me. Why, who is your favorite invention?"

"Hamlet, without contest. He has the best lines."

"The best lines, yes. But do you not think he is a rather insipid figure himself?"

"There is something to your criticism," conceded Mr. Darcy. "And yet, I could re-read his speeches daily and never tire of them."

"And what about you, Miss Darcy?" Mr. Markwood asked. "Who is your favorite?"

"I have always been fascinated by Cordelia."

"Now there's an intriguing personality," mused the vicar. "Cordelia's?"

"Yours, Miss Darcy. Why do you choose Cordelia?"

Georgiana answered, "It interests me that she insists on the utmost honesty, even with her own father, when it would be both easier and more rewarding simply to be polite."

"You admire frankness?" he asked. "Society does not."

"I did not intend to say frankness. Or perhaps I did. No, I believe I only meant sincerity. Speaking directly prevents misunderstanding, which is always good." The instant her opinion was spoken, she began to revise it. "Or perhaps not," she continued. "Directness can injure those who are not accustomed to candor."

She blushed because she had only been able to articulate her thoughts in stages, and she assumed she must appear to him as a foolish child. Yet the vicar was fascinated by her thought process, and he delighted in witnessing the unpredictable, introspective workings of her mind.

"True," ruminated Mr. Markwood, "one may be too direct. And yet Christ did instruct us to say yes when we mean yes and no when we mean no."

Georgiana was relieved that he addressed her points as though they had been serious reflections and not senseless out-pourings of the mind. When she spoke again, therefore, it was with less self-consciousness. "He also instructed us through his apostle Paul to do nothing that would offend our brother." She had leapt from one verse to another; she had been thinking that perhaps one ought to avoid directness in order to avoid of-fense, but she was now unsure whether her use of the biblical allusion, which she had quoted without preface, would be com-prehensible.

Mr. Markwood responded as if it were. "I understand what you mean to imply, Miss Darcy. But the instruction is to avoid doing that which causes your brother to offend his own consci-ence, not that which causes him to *be* offended. Some people are quick to take offense, and the fact cannot be helped. Christ, I am sure, did not meet His brutal fate because He went about seeking to ingratiate Himself."

"No, indeed," she agreed. "He is the Great Offense. But. . ." Nervous though she was, Georgiana was unwilling to concede the argument. "But we are not God. *We* cannot presume to speak with such authority, with such little concern for conse-quence. Our judgments may not always be informed. Our vision may be obscured by some invisible beam."

She awaited Mr. Markwood's response, but he appeared only befuddled. She thought she must have sounded ridiculous. She could not know her words had startled him because her depth still startled him. It beat against the current of his former judg-ment; it failed to fit the first image he had drawn of her, an im-age he was redrawing almost hourly. In the course of his artistry, he must sometimes pause for breath, for, in taking her portrait, he was forever erasing lines only moments after making them.

Mr. Darcy took this as an awkward silence and wished to put the company at ease. Lightheartedly he said, "I just realized who you two remind me of at the present moment." Both turned to him with expectation. "My sister-in-law Mary Bennet."

Georgiana smiled. "My brother censures us, Mr. Markwood. We must change the topic of conversation. Mr. Darcy means to imply that our tone is somewhat too moralistic for such a fine Wednesday morning."

"The analogy is perhaps unjust," Mr. Darcy admitted. "For yours is hardly a textbook discussion. Nevertheless. . .."

"Nevertheless," the vicar smiled obligingly as he spoke, "I will be happy to entertain less weighty subjects. And by way of changing the topic—have you heard from your cousin, Colonel Fitzwilliam?"

That, as it turned out, was not a lighter subject. "We have not," Mr. Darcy replied, looking at Georgiana with caution. Mr. Markwood followed his glance and saw that Miss Darcy was visibly upset.

"America is a long way away," the vicar remarked. "And I have heard that a battle was fought as late as January. But now that the United States has ratified the treaty, I am sure you will hear from your cousin soon. Perhaps he has already set sail to return to England."

"That is our hope," said Mr. Darcy, looking at Georgiana with encouragement. The girl's face did not brighten, and her brother thought it altogether better not to dwell on the subject. "What were the West Indies like, Mr. Markwood?" he asked. "You never speak of them."

"They were much like England, I imagine, except that social conventions were ever so slightly relaxed. And there was the difference of scenery. And the heat. And the slaves."

Georgiana was disappointed by what she perceived to be his casual mention of slaves. Some recent reading had led her to consider the question of slavery, and she had begun to doubt whether its existence ought to be tolerated by any civilized society. If Mr. Markwood were indeed an evangelical—as some in Derbyshire hoped, and others feared, he was—then he would almost certainly oppose the institution. She had hoped he did. But now she was suddenly reminded where the vicar's father had made his fortune.

She tried not to fault Mr. Markwood for this apathy. A man,

she supposed, believes more or less what he is raised to believe. She asked, "Your father had many slaves, then?"

He surprised her by looking shocked. "No, indeed," he said quickly. "He is an abolitionist."

Miss Darcy's perplexed silence worried him. He knew not where the Darcys stood on the slavery issue. Such a topic had never arisen, and there was no reason to believe they would share his family's feelings on the matter. Mr. Darcy was of the landed gentry, and he might be perfectly satisfied with the status quo.

"But I understood," said Mr. Darcy, "that your father made his fortune in the West Indies."

"In a sense, he did. But not from the plantations. Not on the backs of slaves." Mr. Markwood winced. The last sentence had been a condemnation, and what if they did not agree with his position? The vicar believed that the surest way to change individual minds was to take a gradual approach and never to let the person know you were sanding down those jagged edges. His father, however, had said that the law could accomplish in one sweeping arc what the vicar hoped to achieve mind by mind. And that law, averred Sir Robert, could only be worked on in the open, with fervor, like a man driving a violent chisel into a block of stone. Had he not experienced repeated illnesses, Sir Robert would have made his way to Parliament. He had wished to see his eldest son there. But Jacob Markwood had convinced him that he himself was called to walk a quieter path.

Yet was he walking it? Had he feared offending Mr. Darcy because it might impair his ability to make an abolitionist of him, or had he feared it because he sought the praise, not of God, but of man? How strangely fragile is the human will! Mr. Markwood believed he would die rather than renounce Christ, but there were times when he hesitated to pronounce His truth for fear of social embarrassment.

The vicar rebuked himself and shook off that concern. "My father," he continued, "moved us to the West Indies after my mother died. We went to live with his half brother on his plantation. What my father saw there horrified him. It was not that my uncle was cruel; it was that he was indifferent. He would in-spect the slaves like chattel on Saturday evening, and then go to church Sunday morning. He would hear the reading—about how, in Christ, there is neither Greek nor Jew, neither male nor female, neither slave nor free—and he would nod in agreement. He would think he was living Christianity. How easily we all convince ourselves that we are living it! My father left the plan-tation, became the steward of a small but profitable farm that did not use slave labor, and at the same time worked as a soli-citor as he had in England."

"Then how did your father become so wealthy?" asked Geor-giana. It was, perhaps, too direct a question. But she did not ask it with either the morbid curiosity or the social grasping of a Miss Bingley. She asked because she desired to understand the vicar better.

"My father, as I said, had two professions, and he worked at both intensely. We lived very frugally, and he invested his ex-cess earnings in England. When the master of the farm my fa-ther managed died, he died childless. My brother and I had been like children to him, and so he left half his fortune to our father for our education and our support. Meanwhile, my fa-ther's investments were paying off remarkably well, and he needed only return home to claim his newfound wealth."

Mr. Markwood had just confessed that he was the son of a steward and a solicitor, and he knew that the fact might place him in an unfavorable light. Since his return to England, Sir Robert had regarded himself as a gentleman, and he had typic-ally been treated as one. Men with significant wealth are rarely slighted, even if they are not deeply respected. But Mr. Mark-wood could never quite predict the idiosyncrasies of society, and he never knew whom his background might offend.

The vicar had not sought the acknowledgment of any elite, but nor could he bear the open censure of society without pain even when he knew that condemnation to be unfounded. He looked hesitantly toward Mr. Darcy, but he saw no disdain in the gentleman's expression. Mr. Markwood glanced next at Georgiana and was surprised to see that she looked rather more pleased than she had a moment before.

Mr. Darcy asked, "Is that why Sir Robert wanted to be a parliamentarian? To campaign for abolition?"

"Yes," the vicar answered. "And when his illness would not permit him to persevere in that quest, he passed the mantle to me. I disappointed him, and he forgave me. Then I alienated Miss Grant's father, a powerful man who might have become a close friend to the cause because his daughter was inclined to favor it. And for that, it took my father somewhat longer to forgive me."

Mr. Markwood recalled the former Miss Grant, whose hand he had refused. He was pleased to discover that he could now think of her almost without pain. He considered himself a healed man, but he sensed also that those scars had not dissolved utterly and that they might be made to smart again if proper pressure were applied. He wondered if his heart would ever be quite whole. He was certain it must be, if only he could give it to another. But in the absence of that possibility, he hoped that time would eventually bury the few lingering effects of unrequited love.

"A clergyman can do as much good for abolition, if not more, than a politician," Mr. Darcy suggested.

The comment surprised and relieved Mr. Markwood. It could only mean that the gentleman was not offended by the cause. And if he were not offended, perhaps his family could prove actual active friends of the movement. That hope the vicar deferred, however. The Darcys, he thought, were moral but complacent members of society. They were guided by duty, not by religious or political zeal. He might persuade them, eventually, to contribute to the cause, but he could not expect too much of them too soon. What was more, he himself had chosen a different passion, and he no longer considered it his place to recruit fellow abolitionists.

Mr. Markwood answered his friend's remark by stating that he had no intention of using his pulpit as a pounding board for the anti-slavery movement. "Although I share my father's views on slavery," he said, "I have felt called to answer the less dramatic needs of my parish. And if in so doing I can affect men's hearts for the cause of abolition, so be it. But it is not, nor will it be, my driving focus. God uses different men for different purposes. My younger brother, however, will pursue my father's vision, and although Sir Robert has not yet perceived it, I think he will find that Aaron Markwood is far more suited to the vocation."

The conversation soon shifted to other topics, and Georgiana was more than a little relieved when the bell rang for lunch. Miss Darcy was no longer grappling with mere thoughts. She was now struggling to conquer her very heart. Unfortunately, too much time in Mr. Markwood's company was causing her to lose ground in the battle.

Though she continued to fight valiantly against her wayward emotions, there was no reinforcement to be found. That day, the post brought some unwelcome news from the camp at Brighton:

Dearest Georgiana,

When I take up this pen, I falter. I know this letter will be a source of great disappointment to you, and it pains me to have to write it. I had looked forward to seeing you in Brighton this spring, but our meeting is not to be. Napoleon has escaped from Elba. I am at this moment about to cross the Channel with my regiment, and I cannot tell you when I will return. I am sure you understand that I cannot renounce my commission now when the nation that has nurtured me has fallen under so great a shadow.

I will write to you as often as I can, but please do not fear if my letters should seem infrequent. The distance will be considerable, and the circumstances may not permit me to write as often as I should like. I do not intend to be lost in battle; I will not succumb to death but will struggle to return, even as I remain,

Faithfully yours,
Arthur Talbot

Faithfully yours. The words leapt forth from the page like an accusation. Guilt was a severe drill master, which could and must be obeyed; but though it could discipline the will, it could not train the heart.

Chapter 20

For the second time after a calamitous event, life at Pemberley once again returned to normal. Georgiana worried about Major Talbot's safety and meditated on him with real affection, but she also worried about her failure to turn that affection into a love that would admit the thought of no other man. Fortunately, however, Mr. Markwood did not remain long beneath her brother's roof. His wound healed well, which allowed him to return quickly to the parsonage and to resume all his duties with full vitality.

And so it was that one fine Lenten Sunday morning, while Major Talbot marched beneath a foreign sky and while Napoleon prepared to ascend a second time to the throne, that, mounting his pulpit, Mr. Markwood opened—to the shock of certain members of his congregation—not the Bible, but a book of contemporary poetry. "And said I that my limbs were old," he recited, "And said I that my blood was cold, and that my kindly fire was fled, and my poor withered heart was dead, and that I might not sing of love? How could I to the dearest theme, that ever warmed a minstrel's ream, so foul, so false a recreant prove! How could I name love's very name, nor wake my heart to notes of flame!"

Murmurs rippled through the congregation. What did he think he was doing, reading Sir Walter Scott in the house of God?

"In peace," he continued, "Love tunes the shepherd's reed; in war—" Mr. Markwood glanced toward Georgiana Darcy "—he mounts the warrior's steed." The vicar had only wanted to call her attention to the verse, but his sight was staid upon her longer than he had intended; he did not know quite what had arrested him. This distraction he soon shook off and resumed the recitation more forcefully. "In war, he mounts the warrior's steed; in halls, in gray attire is seen; in hamlets, dances on the green, Love rules the court, the camp, the grove, and men below, and saints above; for love is heaven, and heaven is love."

He shut the book, put it aside, and took up the Bible. "In the New Testament," he announced to the congregation, "the gospel writers use four precise words that we translate as, simply, 'love'."

He placed the Bible back on his podium before continuing. "The first, 'agape', is the kind of perfect, divine love that God feels for us. It is the unfathomable, inscrutable, overwhelming, sacrificial passion I described to you the very first time I preached a sermon within these walls. It is a love we are called to aspire to obtain, for as our epistle reading this morning said, 'Let this mind be in you, which was also in Christ Jesus: Who, being in the form of God, thought it not robbery to be equal with God: But made himself of no reputation, and took upon him the form of a servant, and was made in the likeness of men: And being found in fashion as a man, he humbled himself, and became obedient unto death, even the death of the cross.' And, as it is elsewhere written, 'Greater love hath no man than this, that he lay down his life for his friends'."

"The second kind of love," continued the vicar, "is 'philos', or brotherly love. It is a sincere love, but it is devoid of romantic passion. It is characterized most fully by a sense of mutual respect. We might call this kind of love friendship.

"The third love is 'storge', an instinctual love, like the affection a mother feels for her child, a brother for his sister. And finally," he said, "the last, but I do not believe the least, of the loves is 'eros', or romantic passion. It is the unique kind of love, one hopes, that a man feels for his wife, and a wife likewise for her husband."

The vicar noticed Mr. Darcy glance at his wife as these words were spoken and saw the way she returned his attention. For the first time, Mr. Markwood envied his benefactor. All the glory of Pemberley had not excited his jealousy, but that one look, which seemed at the moment to encapsulate the pure union of two complementary souls, caused him to turn away in resentment. It was strange that it should have affected him so; he had been witness to their marriage for some time now, and he had felt only happiness for his friend. It was not that he was now suddenly more aware of the love that couple possessed; it was rather that he had begun, of late, to feel more acutely what he lacked.

The congregation was looking at him expectantly. How long had he stood there in silence? He swallowed. He could feel the nervous sweat begin to break across his brow. The poetry reading had been shock enough for them, he was sure; it was worse that he had fallen speechless. He grasped the side of the podium and steadied himself. He must complete his sermon. He was preaching to himself as much as to the congregation; for these words, he believed, had been laid upon his heart by God although he himself was unsure why.

"And what of these four types of love?" he asked, and the congregation looked relieved to see him continue. "Can we step easily from one to another, as if climbing or descending rungs on a ladder? If we feel eros, can we subdue it into philos? If we feel philos, can we, with romantic sentiments, goad that affection into eros? Can we learn to love, and to love appropriately, and if so, how?

"Christ, as I have preached to you before, taught us to love Him because He first loved us. It was a hard lesson, a bitter lesson, but He taught us the only way He could, through His death. We have read in the Gospel today how they that passed by reviled Him, wagging their heads, how the chief priest likewise mocked Him, how He felt as if God Himself had turned His back upon Him, and how He cried out in His desperation and loneliness, '*Eli, Eli, lama sabachthani?*' that is to say, 'My God, my God, why hast thou forsaken me?' He taught us to love Him by loving us. What splendid passion! What exquisite torture!

"But we, at times, are slow to learn. And if God must suffer such condemnation simply in order to teach us, how can we hope to instruct one another in the depths and heights and varieties of love?"

Jacob Markwood continued to preach, although he ultimately failed to answer his own question. He let his query linger there, uncertain, while he exhorted his parishioners to love one another.

Christian love was Mr. Markwood's favorite subject, and he had now returned to it after that strange diversion into the realms of eros, philos, and Sir Walter Scott. Thus far no one had admitted to growing weary of the theme. Some, indeed, embraced it, for it had made church-going a more pleasant experience. The sermons were no longer a springboard for theological arguments and bitter disputes. Passing through the congregation after services was now less like walking through a paddling line. In times past, it had seemed that certain parishioners could always succeed in mustering at least one disparaging word about another. (Mrs. Darcy's dress, perhaps, had been a bit too revealing one Sunday. Mrs. Smith, really, had not seemed to grieve suitably for the loss of her husband. Mr. Taggart never appeared reverent enough, and Major Talbot, during his brief attendance there, had been embarrassingly inattentive.)

It was not that Jacob Markwood did not have his critics or that his parishioners had suddenly embraced one another unconditionally; it was rather that the vicar had succeeded in silencing certain elements of his flock. These individuals brooded resentfully from their seats in their special, reserved pews. They might make a snide comment to him from time to time, but never in public, never before other congregants. It had become difficult, they regretted, to render proper judgments on the sermons, and it had become almost impossible to divulge to the light of day the imperceptible faults of other parishioners. With the vicar preaching virtually every Sunday on the topic of love and Christian unity, one might risk appearing petty.

So when the service concluded and the crowd dispersed, these congregants did not linger long. They delivered to Mr. Markwood a warning look as they passed through the receiving line, or they drew him aside and reproved him in hushed tones, and then they returned, still dissatisfied, to their private dwellings.

***

Georgiana was grateful that Mr. Markwood chose to dine with other parishioners that afternoon. She saw her brother approach him after the service and knew he was extending an invitation. But when Mr. Darcy returned to Pemberley alone, her mind was as relieved as her heart was disappointed. Today, at least, she could eat her lunch in relative peace.

She showed her plate no mercy, however, and toyed with her food like a child. Her brother watched her with cautiously raised eyebrows and was about to tell her to behave in a more lady-like manner when Elizabeth gripped his leg beneath the table. Surprised by the sudden and intimate touch, he turned to look at her and saw her shake her head almost imperceptibly. It was a warning. He remained silent, and when Georgiana asked to be excused from the table, he let her leave without comment.

When Miss Darcy had shut the door of the dining hall behind her, Mr. Darcy turned anxiously to his wife. "What do you know?"

"Only that something is disturbing her," she replied. "I do not know what. But it did not look as though what you were about to say would have been any consolation."

"I did not think her distraction so dramatic. She has had difficulty, at times, because of her shyness. She has not always performed according to social mores. That was all I was trying to correct."

"You are too hard upon her, my dear. She is very cultured."

"Yes, yes, but it has all come with painstaking practice and not by nature."

"Fitzwilliam!"

"I mean no insult, Lizzy. She is an intelligent, caring woman, a sister I am honored to claim as my own. But her shyness has been an obstacle to her. It is not easy to combat one's own nature; I know that well myself. I had hoped she had conquered that shyness. Indeed, I thought she had months ago, but today it seemed to return. I believe she is still suffering from the effects of this morning's social exertion. You saw how difficult she found it to speak to Mr. Markwood; you saw how she avoided his company." The fact had disturbed Mr. Darcy, who thought his sister to be wholly at ease with his friend, who thought her, indeed, to have vanquished her social terror. He did not understand why the shyness had suddenly returned. "And our neighbor tried to speak with her also, and she could not even manufacture an interest."

Elizabeth smiled. "It would take a factory full of laborers to manufacture an interest in that man."

Her husband laughed. "True enough, my dear." Mr. Darlson was a rather dim-witted gentleman. Despite his proximity to Pemberley, he was rarely invited to dine there. His company was something less than desirable, and he seemed to sport the most inadequate taste in friends. Niles Davidson, for instance, was known to sojourn at his estate. "Then you think something else is disturbing her, Lizzy?"

"She looked positively dejected, my love."

The earnestness with which Elizabeth spoke these words caused Mr. Darcy to lose color. He felt, first, a stab of guilt for not seeing that something more than shyness pained his sister, and then he felt an urgent need to see her comforted. "I wish you would talk to her," he said. "I cannot. She trusts me, as a protector, but she is not open with me." He regretted, sometimes, the distance he had placed between them, but it had been necessitated by their circumstances. She was more than ten years his junior, and she had become his responsibility at an early age. He had made himself a father to her more than a brother. He felt that loss now, but he knew also that nothing could be done to redraw those ties. He was grateful she had found a sister in Elizabeth. Indeed, he had long ago considered his sister's approval of his wife to be a prerequisite to his marriage, and he had been instantly gratified to see Georgiana open up to Lizzy.

Elizabeth, who had reproached him for his near thoughtlessness at lunch, now reached out to touch him again, but this time it was a caress of love. She was moved by the tenderness he seemed to feel for his sister and by his desire to see her at peace. He pressed his forehead against her own as she caressed his cheek. They sat there quietly, leaning against one another, until by instinct she intensified her touch. She had meant only to console him, not to excite him, and she was therefore surprised when his lips captured hers in a heated kiss.

She must be more careful, she thought. He was so reserved in public that she often forgot how easily he was aroused in private. And she forgot, too, how quickly she could find herself responding to his passion. She pulled away, but he mistook her resistance for an invitation. He thought she was only freeing her neck for his ministrations, and soon he was trailing kisses all the way down to her collar bone. As tantalizing as his lips were upon her skin, she at length made him desist, though only after he had managed to elicit a tiny moan from her closed lips. He moved aside, sat back in his chair, and looked at her with confusion. "Do I displease you, my love?"

"Georgiana, dearest. We were speaking of Georgiana."

"Of course," he said, dropping his head in self-rebuke. "I entirely forgot myself. It was not intentional selfishness, Lizzy. . . I. . . You have no idea how you affect me."

"Oh," she said, with the ghost of a smile, "I think I have some idea."

"You will go to her now?" he asked. "You will discover what ails her?"

"I will try."

"Thank you." He leaned forward to kiss her in gratitude, but she placed a finger upon his lips to prevent him.

"I do not think," she said, "that it will stop there. Not in your present agitated state."

"You are wise," he replied, and kept his distance as she rose to leave the dining room. "For there is something in your manner that has a means of. . . agitating me."

***

Elizabeth found Georgiana secluded in her favorite spot, a great windowsill in the hallway where she could sit and read by brilliant sunlight. As Lizzy approached, Miss Darcy drew herself up and swiveled about so that her legs were now hanging over the sill and part of the area was freed. Elizabeth accepted the invitation and sat beside her.

"What were you reading?" she asked.

'What were you *not* reading?' may have been the more appropriate question, for Georgiana had been staring at the page with a vacant gaze.

"*Songs of Experience*," she answered softly. "Blake."

"I did not know your brother owned that volume."

"Mr. Markwood lent it to him."

They sat silently for some time. Georgiana did not seem inclined to talk to Mrs. Darcy, but nor did she attempt to push her away. At length, Elizabeth chose directness. "If you wish to speak of what upsets you, I am here to listen."

Georgiana did not wish to speak of it. She was ashamed of it. She said instead that she was worried about Major Talbot's safety, and worried, also, about her cousin, from whom they still had not heard. And it was true that part of her heaviness had resulted from such concerns.

Elizabeth offered her what consolation she could, but she perceived that it was of little effect. She was about to leave the girl to herself when Miss Darcy ventured, "Lizzy?"

"Yes?"

"How did you know my brother was the right man for you?"

Neither Mr. nor Mrs. Darcy had ever revealed to her the entire story of their courtship: that initial proposal, the rejection, and the reformation. She knew her husband was ashamed of his former manner and certainly would not wish to share his errors with his younger sister. Mrs. Darcy kept his confidence, but she struggled to determine how to answer Georgiana without referring to the change she had witnessed. "I knew," she said at last, "because I watched him behave with honor for my sake." She was referring to his rescue of her sister Lydia, when he had forced Wickham to marry the compromised woman. But she thought also of the reformation of character that had been inspired by her reproof.

"Many men behave with honor, Lizzy. Do you love them all?"

"Of course not."

"Only my brother."

"Yes."

"Why?"

"Our dispositions complement each other perfectly, it seems. I love him. I cannot precisely say why."

"Yet you know it."

"Yes."

"I do not know it with regard to Major Talbot. I do not know it as you know it."

So this was the crux of her present misery. Not just fear for the Major's safety but fear for the shallowness of her own emotions. Elizabeth had not been expecting it. She could not think how to respond. Instead of rolling out the carpet of advice, she asked, "Did Mr. Markwood's sermon inspire these doubts?"

Georgian's distraction had not become obvious until that morning, and the vicar had, after all, preached about the varieties of love. He had asked, if she recalled correctly, whether it was possible to urge friendship into romantic love. Perhaps his preaching had raised that very question in Georgiana's mind. The vicar had offered no answer; Miss Darcy, it seemed, feared the answer was no. And that, Lizzy thought, may have been why Georgiana avoided the vicar after church. She did not wish to be reminded of his message.

Georgiana answered, "He did seem, almost, to be preaching to me. Yet the origin of my doubt is older than that."

"Distance, perhaps, has made you question your feelings," suggested Elizabeth tentatively. "When Major Talbot is near you again, matters will appear differently." Mrs. Darcy tried to believe her own assurance. She had not seen a deep love spring up between them, but she had witnessed mutual affection and attraction. Most marriages in society were contracted upon far weaker grounds; she had been glad for Georgiana that the girl could secure at least that much happiness.

"Perhaps," Miss Darcy replied, sounding unconvinced.

"But you do respect him, do you not?"

"Yes, of course. And I feel warmly toward him. And he is an attractive man."

"Do not feel guilty, dear Georgi, if you are not always in the throes of passion when you think of him. It cannot always be like that. A woman would be consumed if it were."

Georgiana knew this. She was not a romantic in the sense that she expected love to always be like a raging fire. She knew the quieter flame was the truer flame. But even a quiet flame must sometimes suddenly spark, and glow into a flash of fire, before being soothed back again. She feared a marriage that did not mix tenderness and friendship with moments of intensity and longing. Talbot had made her cheeks glow and had caused her heart to flutter; but she now saw that was giddiness, not passion. The few times Mr. Markwood had touched her, however, to dance or to lead her by his arm, she had felt almost a jolt, which she could only imagine to be the dormant seeds of her own desire.

Yet it was not the lack of passionate feeling that concerned her most. She could be happy with a man, she thought, even if he never stirred her body, so long as he stirred her soul. She could be content if only they could share a deeper union, what Shakespeare had deftly termed "the marriage of true minds." Talbot had put her at ease; he had enabled her to speak without fear for the first time. He had drawn her out of her cloistered realm, but he had not drawn out her very spirit; he had not encouraged her to share her deepest reflections, her sincerest opinions, her innermost self. Mr. Markwood had done all this, without open flattery, without courtship, without a desire to gain anything in return except the pleasure of sharing thoughts with a woman he respected. She *did* love Talbot. But she felt certain it was not the type of love, as Mr. Markwood had preached, that "one hopes a man feels for his wife and a wife likewise for her husband."

Elizabeth reached out to touch her gently, concerned by her silence. "Georgiana?" she asked.

Miss Darcy drew herself from her reflections and answered the gentle inquiry. "I know it cannot always be like that, Lizzy. But what if I never. . . *never* feel like that?"

Elizabeth did not know what to say to this. She could not imagine a marriage—for herself at least—that had no root deeper than affection. But she knew many who lacked the kind of complete accord she enjoyed who were yet content in their marriages. It was possible. The ideal could not be realized in every union, and not every disposition required it. Jane had tried to teach her that when her friend Charlotte had wed Mr. Collins. Then her sister had tried to warn Elizabeth not to condemn others because their standards were somewhat more flexible than her own.

What could she say to Georgiana? The girl had promised herself. She could not, with honor, reject that promise now. And as far as Mrs. Darcy knew, there was no greater prospect, no more likely candidate to inspire her love. "You care for Major Talbot?"

"Very much."

"It will suffice. In time, perhaps, you will grow to love one another more deeply."

That was precisely what Georgiana had been telling herself. She had even believed it, at first. But by now she had admitted to herself that the emotion she suffered for Mr. Markwood was *not* a mere distraction. She knew she did not love Major Talbot as a wife should because she now knew what real love was. She had for some time known that her love for the Major was not intense, but until today, she had not fully confessed to herself how deep was the love she felt for the vicar.

Yet she had committed herself to another. And even if she had been free, what then? She had received no indication that Mr. Markwood loved her in return. He respected her, perhaps even esteemed her. He seemed, also, to enjoy her company, but if he loved her, he offered her no perceptible hint.

If Miss Darcy had told Elizabeth of her love for Jacob Markwood, she may have received different advice. But Georgiana could not bring herself to reveal those secret feelings even to someone she trusted as thoroughly as Lizzy. It had been hard enough to reveal them to herself.

It brought her relief, at least, to share her doubts about Major Talbot. And it brought her comfort to hear Elizabeth assure her that it was not an inevitable tragedy to marry without that special kind of love, that happiness might still be possible. She thanked Mrs. Darcy for her kindness, begged her not to disclose a word of her doubt to her brother, and received Elizabeth's promise of confidence.

Mrs. Darcy told her husband only that his sister was worried about the safety of her fiancé and her cousin. That seemed to him adequate grounds for her disconsolate state. It was enough, also, to cause him to pay Georgiana deeper kindness and to show her greater patience. For days thereafter, he walked about her as if treading on eggshells, but by the end of the week, she seemed to be at peace again. He assumed it must be because they had at last received the good news that Colonel Fitzwilliam was safe. And that happy information had brought her relief. But the greater measure of her peace stemmed from the fact that Mr. Markwood was too preoccupied with his newly resumed duties to call upon them. It is far easier to suppress emotions when the object that inspires them remains at a comfortable distance.

Chapter 21

Mr. Markwood was standing outside of Pemberley and laughing heartily with the gardener when Mr. Niles Davidson approached. "If you are finished socializing," he said to the vicar, "then will you please show me to your young mistress?"

Mr. Markwood looked at him in disbelief. "My mistress?"

"You heard me, man!" exclaimed Mr. Davidson. "I would be shown in to your mistress."

The gardener looked curiously from Mr. Davidson to Mr. Markwood.

"I do not have a mistress," responded Mr. Markwood. "I am a bachelor."

Mr. Davidson appeared deeply affronted. "I do not take kindly to mockery from servants. I doubt Mr. Darcy tolerates this kind of speech from you."

The gardener let out a yelp and gripped his sides as though the humor would hurt him.

"I am not a servant, sir," explained Mr. Markwood, more amused than offended. "I am the vicar of this parish and a friend of the Darcys."

Niles Davidson was nearly shocked silent, but he always managed to summon speech. This time, however, his words erupted in a stammer. "I—but—I thought. . . thought. . . you were a ser—ser—"

"No, not a servant," said Mr. Markwood.

The gardener shook his head and waved a gesture of farewell.

By the time the gardener had departed, Mr. Davidson had composed himself. "I apologize for the misunderstanding," he said, "But surely you understand—given your behavior when I approached—why I might have made the mistake. You are not in a clergyman's dress."

"No, but nor am I in a servant's livery, sir. And you see my collar." He pulled his outer jacket forward to reveal the mark. "I was about to go call on the Darcys myself, if you would like to join me."

"Certainly."

The two men began to walk together toward the house, and the disparity in their gaits would have been amusing to observe. Jacob Markwood was the slightly taller or the two, but he took shorter steps, walking with greater leisure, still aided by the use of a cane. Niles Davidson strode pompously forward, his footfalls fraught with purpose. Mr. Davidson had to stop to allow the vicar to catch up before asking, "Is Miss Georgiana Darcy at home today, do you know?"

"I have no idea. I have not called in over a week. I was quite busy with my parish duties. You see," he said, motioning to his leg with his cane, "I had been confined."

Mr. Davidson merely nodded and did not bother to inquire about the injury. He was no longer embarrassed by his earlier faux pas. In fact, he had begun to feel a bit put out. *This clergyman, this impudent vicar,* he thought, *behaves like a yeomen and then has the audacity to grin when I mistake him for one.* Mr. Markwood's manners reminded him of an old Cambridge acquaintance, a self-confident gentleman who shared with the vicar an identical surname. "Are you any relation to Mr. Aaron Markwood? A cousin perhaps?"

Mr. Markwood answered, "He is my brother."

"Is he indeed?" asked Mr. Davidson, as though the relationship explained some mystery he had been contemplating. "How very interesting. I thought he was a second son."

"He is. I am the elder, though there is barely twelve months between us."

"Why would you, the eldest son of Sir Robert, become a clergyman?"

"I was called."

Niles Davidson half-smirked at this response, though he hid the expression and asked only, "How is your father?"

"Very well, thank you."

"So what does a knighthood go for these days, Mr. Markwood?"

Jacob Markwood abruptly stopped walking. The two were

now at the foot of those majestic stairs that led up to the main door of Pemberley. Mr. Davidson continued to speak in the face of the clergyman's cold silence. "I was simply wondering. I would like to be called Sir Niles myself someday."

Mr. Markwood responded with calculation. "If you mean to imply, sir, that my father somehow purchased his honor, you are very much mistaken. He would never stoop to such an action. He would not consider it good politics."

"But he is not a politician, is he? He never made it to Parliament. And how, pray tell, did a middle-class solicitor, who ran away to the West Indies in order to scrape together a questionable fortune, manage to earn His Majesty's recognition?"

"I feel no need to defend my family to you, sir," replied Mr. Markwood before quickly ascending the steps and knocking aggressively on the door. Mr. Davidson followed and stood beside him. The politician looked far too satisfied.

When the housekeeper Mrs. Reynolds answered the door, she greeted the vicar enthusiastically. She acknowledged Mr. Davidson.

When Mrs. Reynolds had left them to alert the family of their presence, Niles Davidson asked, "Doesn't Mr. Darcy have a butler? He is certainly wealthy enough."

Mr. Markwood replied, "Mr. Darcy's butler has recently married and sought employment in another estate where his wife works. Mr. Darcy has yet to find a suitable replacement. So the position is still open, sir, if you have an interest." He regretted the insult once he had spoken it. He was still angry with the gentleman for his earlier remarks, and he had not yet mastered that resentment. He did not wish to return Mr. Davidson's impropriety with a dose of his own, but he could not prevent himself.

Mr. Davidson had just begun to issue his incensed reply when he was interrupted by none other than Mr. Darcy himself. "Markwood," said the master of the house. "Mrs. Reynolds just told me you were here. I am pleased to see you. Will you—" here he noticed Mr. Davidson— "And your name sir?"

"Mr. Niles Davidson, Mr. Darcy. We met at the summer ball

in Pemberley and again at Hartethorn in autumn."

"Oh, yes. You danced with my sister, I recall."

"Yes, sir."

"And you have come to call. . .."

"I am in Derbyshire for a short time, and I thought to call to inquire after Miss Darcy's health and happiness. And yours and your wife's, of course."

The afterthought irritated Mr. Darcy. He knew well enough what Niles Davidson was about; he had witnessed the politician's inappropriate attentions. "Of course," he echoed almost sarcastically as he turned to walk away. Mr. Markwood followed him agreeably, while Mr. Davidson stood motionless, appearing exceedingly perplexed by this indifferent reception.

"Well, come along, Mr. Davidson," said Mr. Markwood as he motioned back to him. "If you wish to inquire after Miss Darcy's health and happiness, I think you will find both in good order."

When they entered the drawing room, Mr. Markwood was surprised to see his brother among the company. "Aaron!" he exclaimed. "Why are you at Pemberley?"

Aaron Markwood rose from his seat and crossed the room to embrace his older brother. Drawing back he said, "I got your letter. I'm sorry I couldn't get away sooner. When you were not at the parsonage, a neighbor told me you might be here. It seems I have preceded you."

"Yes. But you didn't need to come all this way, Aaron. I am perfectly well."

"So it would appear. It was a minor wound?"

"I was not out of commission for long. Father wrote to tell me that you are already an outer barrister. You are not missing any important briefs, I hope?"

"No. Nothing that can't wait."

"Aaron Markwood, a barrister. Will wonders never cease?"

"I hope not, because I expect to have a seat in the Commons within the next few years."

Mr. Markwood was about to reply when he realized that he had not yet greeted anyone else. "I apologize," he said, moving further into the room and bowing to the ladies. "I was rude. It is only that I have not seen my brother in some time."

"That is perfectly understandable, Mr. Markwood," said Elizabeth.

Mr. Davidson audibly cleared his throat. He had faded into the background, and he did not care to remain there.

"Mr. Davidson," said Mr. Darcy. "You have met my wife and sister. Apparently you encountered Mr. Jacob Markwood outside. And this is Mr. Aaron Markwood."

Niles Davidson looked at the other guest, and his eyes narrowed. "We have met," he said, declining to bow. He walked indifferently past the young Markwood and, without waiting to be asked, took a chair across from Georgiana. "Miss Darcy, it is a pleasure to see you once again."

She acknowledged him with only two words: "Mr. Davidson."

Meanwhile, Mr. Markwood had drawn his younger brother aside into the doorway. "What inspired that exchange?" he asked-ed.

"Niles Davidson is the one I debated at Cambridge, the one who vowed to see that I never sit in the House of Commons."

"Does he have any real influence?"

"He thinks he does. Whether or not his judgment on that point is sound, I do not know."

"I suspect not. Why does he oppose you? Because of your stance on abolition?"

"No. He considers that position a mere child's fantasy. But he sees election reform as a legitimate threat, and I support fully extending the franchise to the middle-class."

"Which, I assume, would not help his future any."

"His is a pocket borough. He has apparently ingratiated himself with some large landowner, and his position was bought. He may seem ill-mannered here today, but he can be a genuine sycophant when the occasion requires it. His obsequiousness has carried him but so far, and he fears the technique will not prove as successful with the average man."

Both Markwoods glanced over at Mr. Davidson, who was still attempting to goad Miss Darcy into conversation.

"His flattery," said Aaron, "does not seem to be furthering his reputation with Miss Darcy. Nor would I imagine it could. She is too far above him in every particular."

Mr. Markwood saw how his brother looked at Miss Darcy as he pronounced this assessment of her character. "Aaron, I hate to disappoint you, but Miss Darcy is engaged."

Aaron frowned. "But she is so young."

"No younger than many brides and more mature than most. Major Talbot has secured her hand."

"Your friend from Oxford?"

"Yes."

"And is he worthy of her?"

Jacob glanced at Georgiana and let his eyes rest upon her for a moment before answering. "I imagine he is as worthy as any man can be. She happened to choose him."

"He's much older, isn't he?"

"Only three years older than I," the vicar answered.

"When are they to be married?"

"When he returns from war. Whenever that may be."

The younger Mr. Markwood sighed. "Then I had best not throw my hat into the ring."

"No, Aaron, it would be neither wise nor proper."

"Yet Mr. Davidson does not stand down."

"I would not advise modeling your behavior on his," Jacob Markwood chided.

"I would not dream of it. However, I am determined to spare that lady from the torture of his conversation."

His elder brother took him by the shoulder as if he would restrain the young barrister.

"I am only going to provide a service, Jacob," he said, removing his brother's hand. "I am not going to trifle with her." Having issued Mr. Markwood this assurance, Aaron walked toward Georgiana. "Miss Darcy," he said, as soon as Mr. Davidson had taken a breath, "My brother tells me you are an excellent painter."

Georgiana looked hesitantly from one brother to the other. She wondered when Jacob Markwood had communicated this information. Had he drawn his brother aside for that purpose? Aaron, in fact, had only deduced her interest from the paintings he saw adorning the hallway he had entered that afternoon.

"I would be glad to show you my collection," she said, eager for any excuse to escape Mr. Davidson's conversation. The two began to leave together, and Mr. Davidson rose to join them. Mr. Darcy prevented him.

"Sit down, Mr. Davidson," he said, "and tell me about London. We've missed the season this year."

Still watching the retreating couple, Mr. Davidson returned reluctantly to his chair. Jacob Markwood sat not far from him and glanced at him with irritation. The look was only brief, however. The vicar was soon directing his attention toward Mr. Darcy, to whom he said, "Have you received news from Colonel Fitzwilliam?" Mr. Markwood was glad he had the opportunity to ask the question in Miss Darcy's absence, in case the answer was negative. He had pained her before by inquiring after her cousin, and he did not wish to see that injury repeated.

"We have," said Mr. Darcy. "And he is well. A little better than well, perhaps." He then related to Mr. Markwood the contents of Colonel Fitzwilliam's letter, which had reached their grateful hands just days before. The Colonel had managed to procure for himself a wealthy and beautiful American wife. Indeed, he wrote as though the Darcys should know this fact, asked why they had not replied, and speculated that they might be wroth with him for having wed and remained with the enemy. It seemed this letter was not his first on the subject, but what had happened to that initial missive on its journey across the seas, no one knew. "I sent him our congratulations," continued Mr. Darcy, "and expressed all our best wishes for his happiness. Just to be safe, however, I think I shall send two additional copies of the letter, each on a different day."

Mr. Markwood smiled. "I am relieved to learn of your cousin's safety. Miss Darcy, I assume, must now possess a measure of peace. I have heard from my friend the Major, as I am sure has she. He, too, appears to be safe. But as he enters the battlefield, she will likely hear from him less often."

"Soldiering is quite the dangerous occupation," interrupted Niles Davidson, who was now aware that Mr. Darcy had not detained him in order to discuss London. It was clear the gentlemen wanted to keep him apart from his sister. That could only be, thought Niles Davidson, because she was engaged. He ought to remind Mr. Darcy, therefore, that her fiancé could be lost in war. "Miss Darcy may be in need of future consolation." The politician's implication did not escape Mr. Darcy. "Let us hope not," he said. "But should she be, she has friends enough, here at home, to provide it."

There was a bitter edge in his voice, which Mr. Davidson found insulting. He forced himself, however, to remain calm. The politician, for all his self-importance, was beginning to perceive that he was not particularly welcome. Thus, after a short but painful time of exchanging polite dialogue laced with insincerity, the frustrated suitor took his leave.

When Aaron and Georgiana returned, the young barrister appeared innocuously self-satisfied. His brother Jacob looked at him with an expression that seemed the hybrid offspring of a suppressed laugh and a calculated rebuke. Georgiana knew nothing of this brotherly communication. She noted, only, that her inconvenient suitor was absent, and this observation she made with considerable relief. "Has Mr. Davidson truly departed?" she asked.

"He has," replied Elizabeth, "and I rather doubt we will be seeing him again."

"How regrettable," pined Georgiana, with a mock sigh.

Jacob Markwood smiled at her uncharacteristic sarcasm, and then he caught her eye. She let her vision linger on the vicar, she thought, a bit too long; he had only meant to share a joke, and in a moment he had turned.

Chapter 22

The steps of the two Markwood brothers fell lightly on the earthen trail as they walked back toward the parsonage. The day's shadows were beginning to disappear, though the trees looming beside the trail still provided patches of darkness along the way. Society would likely have deemed the younger Mr. Markwood the more handsome of the two, for his features were subdued, symmetrical, and pleasing whereas his brother's, although attractive, were arguably stark and, some might think, unsettling. Aaron's hair was several shades lighter than Jacob's, so that it was difficult to distinguish whether it was brown or black. His warm but dark eyes were a solid shade of brown, unbroken by anything like the multicolored flecks that permeated his brother's.

The young barrister was the first to break the silence. "I am sorry I can only stay two days. I have to meet with Thomas Buxton next week."

Jacob recognized the name. Sir Robert had mentioned in his last letter that he believed Mr. Buxton, a friend to the abolitionist cause, would be the next Member of Parliament from Weymouth. "Are you going to assist him with the next campaign?"

"Yes," answered Aaron. "He, in turn, may later help my career. I have a great deal of respect for the man. Unlike Mr. Wilberforce, he is not satisfied with merely ending the slave trade."

William Wilberforce, a parliamentarian from Hull, had used his influence in the House of Commons to push through a bill abolishing the slave trade, but he did not approve of emancipation. The news of the bill's passage had greeted Sir Robert upon his return to England. It had sailed through the Commons by 114 to 15 votes, though in the House of Lords the margin had been narrower. Sir Robert actually wept to learn that the slave trade had been brought to an end. But his joy was short-lived.

When he read Mr. Wilberforce's pamphlet, in which the MP argued that it would be wrong to emancipate the slaves, Sir Robert flew into a rage. He read aloud to his sons Wilberforce's words: "To grant freedom to them immediately would be to insure not only their masters' ruin, but their own."

Sir Robert had thrown the pamphlet to the floor. He had stormed across the drawing room of his new estate to where Jacob stood gazing out the window, mesmerized by the great extent of the land his father now possessed, and by the house itself, which was nothing like his boyhood home. He turned at the sound of his father's footsteps. As usual, he had not been listening to Sir Robert; his mind was elsewhere. His father proceeded to tell his son that when Jacob was a parliamentarian—when, not if—he must push for emancipation.

Jacob's brother had readily agreed. "Complete emancipation," Aaron had said, "is the only way to alleviate the unutterable suffering of those men. This £100-per-slave fine is well intentioned. It may curb the trade. But it will not crush it. There are slavers who will simply press on with their twisted industry, and should they happen upon a British ship, they will merely throw their human cargo overboard to avoid paying the fines." Jacob watched his brother speak almost nervously; he had never grown accustomed to Aaron's sudden changes of disposition. Aaron was by nature light-hearted, but there were times when he would grow fiercely intense, especially when the cause was mentioned. And when he spoke on that subject, his voice was magnificent, commanding the attention of every ear near enough to catch its cadence. Sir Robert's friends and allies had observed this; many had begun to whisper that Aaron Markwood might be the last great hope for the cause. Sir Robert alone seemed unaware. He still expected Jacob to fill that role.

"Yes, yes!" Sir Robert had exclaimed, looking at his younger son only long enough to agree and then returning his concentration to the elder. "You must take the cause to its inevitable extreme, Jacob. You must not compromise."

As the two brothers now walked farther and farther from Pemberley, Jacob's drifting mind leapt forward in time to the day he had told Sir Robert he would cease to pursue the law.

His father had been disappointed at first, but when Jacob explained that he felt a calling, Sir Robert grew cheerful again. "Then God will use you for the cause through the Church, Jacob. Of course! I had not thought of it. . ." Sir Robert quickly revised his expectations for his son. Jacob would not be a member of parliament; instead, he would one day be something far more powerful—the Dean of St. Paul's.

It was therefore with great carefulness and some trepidation that Jacob had been forced to explain that God may or may not plan to use him in that way, that he himself did not seek to wade into the mire of earthly politics, and that he would follow his Lord wherever He might lead even if that path were not the road of agitation, but some other more common byway. His father accepted this calling and did not actively pressure his son to pursue the cause. He even supported Jacob's theological studies and planned to secure a living for him. Nonetheless, Sir Robert still entertained a silent hope that Jacob might change his mind. And with a beautiful, persuasive wife such as Sarah Grant at his side, Sir Robert had not doubted that the alteration would be forthcoming. His son's break with Miss Grant had meant, to him, more than the loss of her father as an ally. It had meant the destruction of his one last hope for the future of his son.

Jacob Markwood now reached up and snapped a twig from the branches of a nearby tree. He began to twirl it around the fingers of one had. Aaron eyed the mobile piece of wood and wondered why his brother could not perceive how annoying his habitual actions were. Finally drawing his eyes away from his brother's fidgeting fingers, Aaron said, "I heard that you read poetry in church last week."

"M'hmm," Jacob murmured.

"What was the response?"

"A few parishioners drew me aside to question privately my salvation. But I'm still vicar, aren't I?"

"I don't know, are you?" asked Aaron with a smile.

"Yes."

"Have you really amended matters with Sir Robert?"

"He can be a fickle man, but yes."

"Fickle! Father? What did you expect, Jacob? You refused to tell him why you broke off the engagement."

"I did tell him."

"Yes, in a letter," replied Aaron, "but not in person and not until two months after he had disinherited you."

"I told him at the time I had my reasons," said Jacob, "and he should have trusted me. I did not think an explanation should be required."

"In other words, you were stubborn."

When Jacob replied, he did not sound repentant but only discouraged. "I did not at that time see fit to divulge Miss Grant's emotions to him. I considered it a private matter, and I thought I had already earned his faith in me."

"He needed an explanation, Jacob. And what is more, he deserved one."

Here Mr. Markwood's expression altered. It was tainted with annoyance because it is hard for an older brother to accept instruction from a younger, but it was also mixed with uncertainty and something like shame.

"After mother died," Aaron continued, "he could easily have deposited us with some strange relative, but instead he committed to raising us himself. He ensured that we had the best tutors in the West Indies, regardless of the price. He worked himself to the point of sickness, Jacob, so that his sons would not have to, so that we would have the luxury of pursuing the cause without concern for our income. And when you first turned your back on that mission, he accepted your decision because you made an effort to delineate your reasons to him before taking any action. Had you done the same with regard to Miss Grant, there would have been no riff. He deserved an explanation."

"He eventually got one, Aaron, and for months after that he *still* refused to respond to my pleas for reconciliation."

"He was waiting for you to admit that you were wrong: not wrong to break it off, but wrong because you did not instantly tell him why. He regretted his rage, I think, the moment he learned your reasons. He approved of your action when he knew its root. That sort of nobility was just what he would have wanted of his son."

"Then he should have forgiven me at that moment instead of months later."

"You could have said that you were wrong, too, Jacob. You could have said it even if you did not believe it. That was all you had to do!"

"Well, we are reconciled now."

Aaron shook his head in frustration. The barrister liked to argue. It seemed he was constantly striving to get the better of his brother as though he could only earn approval by conquest. But this, he knew, was Jacob's dismissal sentence. His brother was saying he did not wish to continue the argument. Aaron sighed. He would surrender. The battle was never any fun, anyway, once Jacob had stepped abruptly off the field. "Then I really am back to being a younger son after all," he pined. "Sans inheritance."

"Alas, poor Aaron, however will you endure?"

"Belittle me if you will, my dear brother. We cannot all be inured to the finer things in life."

"I am not. I imagine we just have different ideas about what constitutes the finer things."

"Don't get sanctimonious with me, Jacob. I am the one who will be fighting the good fight; I'm the one who will be taking up the banner for the cause. You could not be inconvenienced." He snatched the twig from his brother's hand and threw it aside. "Religion is free, Jacob, now that you have a living. But politics has its price."

"You mistook me, Aaron," Mr. Markwood replied, looking disconcertedly at his fallen twig and shoving his restless hands into his pockets. "My statement was not intended as a criticism. I know your quest cannot be easy. But neither is the life of an active vicar. Whatever you may believe, I did not run into the arms of the Church in order to retreat from the cares of the cause."

"Then why did you? Why be bred up for politics and then suddenly switch horses in midstream? You never mentioned theology a day in your life, Jacob. And the next thing I know, you're at Trinity College, pursuing a masters in divinity."

"I fell in love."

"And because Miss Grant did not love you in return, you threw away your future? Did you really think, Jacob, that if you left Oxfordshire for some village parish—that if you left the cause—you could forget her? And now here she is, Lady Sarah Atwood of Derbyshire, and you are forced to see her gorgeous face at balls and parties and dinners. Was it worth it? Why didn't you marry her when you had the chance?" His brother was silent, and so Aaron persisted, "It wasn't enough for you just to have her. You had to make her love you."

"I meant, Aaron, that I fell in love with God."

"Meaningless. The slogan of divines."

"Not to me, it isn't."

Aaron stopped walking and looked at his brother's determined profile. "You're serious aren't you?"

"Yes."

"I never would have guessed—"

"I was a student of divinity, Aaron, long before I freed Miss Grant of our engagement. You know that! I didn't choose this profession to be rid of her memory; I chose it while I still thought of her as mine."

"I thought you knew all along she wasn't going to return your love. I presumed you were merely biding your time to ensure that father continued to pay your way through Trinity before you ended the engagement. I thought you had long intended to walk away from both her and the cause and that the Church was your predestined escape hatch."

"No. I believed I could be both a clergyman and her husband. I did not know she did not love me until it was too late. I waited a long time before I surrendered her my heart, Aaron— and yet not long enough." The vicar was riled now; he was angry that his own brother had so wildly misconstrued his intentions. "This is your assessment of my calling? An *escape*?"

"I mistook your motives. I see that now. My conclusion was unkind. You told father why you abandoned the law, but you never told *me*. You're something of an enigma to me, Jacob, you always have been."

The vicar's voice softened. "I wish, sometimes, that we knew one another better."

"So do I. You, for instance, think me a libertine, and the judgment is not accurate."

"I never said any such thing."

"Jacob, the second we stepped out of Pemberley tonight you made it immediately clear to me that I was not to work my arts upon Miss Georgiana Darcy."

"I saw the way you looked at her." Mr. Markwood adjusted his hat so he would not have to look at his younger brother. "You cannot deny it."

"I have no desire to deny it. I find her attractive. Do you mean to tell me *you* don't?"

Aaron could not see how this question worked upon the vicar's countenance. Had he been able to view his brother's face, he might have seen hesitation mingled with unconscious regret. But he heard nothing unusual in the vicar's voice when he answered, "Aaron, there is no avoiding the fact of her beauty, or indeed of her other more substantial attractions, but she is—"

"I am well aware she has pledged her troth elsewhere, and whilst I was admiring her paintings, she made it quite apparent to me that she has no intention whatsoever of violating that promise."

"Tell me now, little brother, why did she feel the need to make that fact plain?"

"I cannot imagine."

"Can't you?"

"Jacob, I do not have, nor have I ever had, any intention of infringing upon another man's territory."

"That's a crass way of putting it," replied the vicar.

"Too unromantic for you, Jacob? You have always been a dreamer of dreams."

"And do you fancy yourself to be a passionless fountain of reason? You are as much an idealist as I, or you could never invest so much energy into the unrealistic cause of abolition."

"Now, Reverend Markwood, surely you know that whether or not a thing is likely has nothing to do with whether or not it is right."

Jacob Markwood smiled ever so slightly. "Well said."

Aaron looked back some distance to the pond they had walked past, and he watched as the rays of the setting sun rippled across the water's surface. "Do you think Mr. Darcy would let me swim in there? Spring has come. The weather has turned unexpectedly warm."

"Maybe," answered Jacob. "But it would be rather forward of you to ask him as you have met him just today. Sometimes I think you have even less social acumen than I."

"We both of us had a strange upbringing and, for many years, no mother to teach us man-made mores."

"Quite true. For example, I have learned that, although some people think it very peculiar for a vicar to attend a farmer's party, they have absolutely no objection to his presence at a ball."

"And I have learned," returned Aaron, "that the dean of Cambridge does not take kindly to a knight's son playing the piano in a local tavern."

"Ah, the things we cannot learn from books alone."

The two men walked on for a time in silence, both staring at the path ahead of them and smiling. At that moment, they looked liked brothers indeed.

Jacob put an arm around his sibling and leaned in, laughing. "Would you guess, Mr. Davidson mistook me for a servant."

Aaron let out a manly roar. "I would love to have seen the look on his face when you told him who you were."

"It was rather entertaining."

"The Darcys obviously did not care for him either. But they were very welcoming to me although they had no reason to be."

Jacob expressed his good opinion of the family, but he focused his accolades on the master and mistress of the house.

"And Miss Darcy?" asked Aaron.

"What of her?" returned his brother.

"I hoped you could answer that. She was content enough to leave with me to escape Mr. Davidson, but then I could hardly extract eight words from her. Would you describe her as somewhat muted?"

"Georgiana Darcy, you would be surprised to learn, is extremely articulate when persuaded to speak, but it takes rather a lot of effort to unhinge her mouth."

"You are well acquainted, then?"

"We have spent a lot of time together since Major Talbot departed. She likes to hear tales of her fiancé."

"And you like to deliver them?"

"I like. . ." Jacob had always despised those moments when he discovered he had not been listening and that he must answer he knew not what. That single second of recognition brought a sinking sensation to his stomach. And though this time his mind had been firmly present, and he had heard well his brother's words, he still did not understand what had just been asked or how to answer. Aaron squinted his eyes in reaction to his brother's bewilderment, as though that would help him to perceive the vicar better. The question had seemed to the young barrister a very simple one; he had not injected it with innuendo, and he had not foreseen his brother's shaky pause.

"Ah, see, there it is," said Jacob, with a tone of excitement too great to be congruous with the moment, "my humble parsonage!" They had rounded a hill, and their new position permitted a view of the house.

"Not so humble. Rather impressive, actually," replied Aaron. He let the awkward moment pass, uncertain why it should ever have surfaced at all.

The two brothers entered the home and lit the fireplace. Aaron threw himself down in a chair and let his legs fall listlessly before him. "Why are all the pretty ones taken?" he groaned.

Jacob sat down opposite him. "Still thinking of Miss Darcy?"

"No, actually, I was thinking of Miss Grant. Excuse me, Lady Sarah. Do you talk to her often?"

"No, not often. We exchange casual conversation when we meet. Beyond that, I no longer have the faintest idea what is in her mind."

"Do you regret it ever, Jacob?"

"Regret what?"

"You know."

"Not here," he said, tapping a finger against his forehead.

"But here," his brother responded, reaching over and touching Jacob Markwood's chest, where frail human flesh covered the one muscle that, once strained, caused the greatest agony of all.

Chapter 23

Social mores notwithstanding, Aaron Markwood did ask Mr. Darcy if he could swim in his pond. The master of Pemberley thought the request a little unusual, but he consented readily enough.

Early in the morning, the young Markwood swam laps through the deepest length of the water while his brother stood guard to ensure no ladies wandered across the gentleman in such an informal state. Kitty Bennet, who was even now in a carriage bound from the Bingleys' estate to the Darcys', would have been bitter indeed to know she was missing this scene.

Aaron emerged from the pond and fully clothed himself. The two brothers lay back upon the bank and looked up at the shifting clouds. The younger said, "I intend to swim from Sestos to Abydsos, just like Byron."

"Oh, and when do you propose to do that?"

"In late summer when I can get a break from my case load."

"How do you like being a barrister?"

"It's not the purpose of my life. But it's a useful tool in the cause; it's a sturdy stepping stone."

Jacob didn't want to talk about the cause. He sensed his brother was still angry with him for choosing to expend his life on a more subtle mission. "When did Byron become an idol of yours?" he asked.

"Isn't he every man's idol?"

"At least every libertine's."

Aaron only grunted in return. Jacob turned and grinned; he hoped to show his brother that he had meant the words in jest. The vicar continued, "I thought you imagined yourself to be unsentimental."

"Byron is a realist, whatever the populace may think of him. He writes satires, after all." Aaron strained his head to the side as though trying to decipher something in the sky above. "Remember when we were boys," he asked, "and we used to look for pictures in the clouds?"

"Yes. I still do, sometimes. Or maybe I'm looking for a sign."

"Do you ever see one?"

"No," said the elder Markwood. "But I keep looking."

"So you fell in love with God, did you?"

"Yes."

"What exactly does that mean, Jacob?"

"It means I serve His creation in the most mundane ways imaginable. It means I sit with poor old widow Smith as she complains about her corns. It means I spend half the day weeding widow Warren's garden because she refuses to admit it is unsalvageable. It means I endure the repetitive play of orphan children, who never tire of their games and who always accompany their activities with incessant shrieking."

Aaron propped himself up on one arm and looked down doubtfully at his brother. "Sounds magnificent."

"But I love it, Aaron, every minute. I belong here, in Derbyshire, in a country parish."

Aaron shook his head and fell back on the ground where he lay languidly until the sound of footsteps stirred him. The young Markwood leapt up and began to brush the grass from off his trousers. "Quick man," he instructed Jacob, "someone's coming. Look dignified."

"Who?" asked Jacob, rising with less urgency and likewise striking the blades from his clothes. Aaron was straightening his cuffs, but when he saw the figure was merely a footman, he ceased.

"Hello, James," said the vicar.

"Good day, Mr. Markwood," replied the servant, who was carrying a small table, which he erected under the shade of a tall oak tree. "If you are properly disposed, sirs, the ladies would like to join you for tea. I am instructed to bring them you're answer. Servants will follow with refreshments and chairs."

"Well, I for one am disposed to have some tea," said Aaron.

"No," said the footman, "I meant if you were properly disposed, what with the swimming—"

"He knew what you meant," interrupted Jacob. "Tell the ladies we would be honored if they would join us."

As the footman walked away, Aaron mused, "I wonder who 'the ladies' are? I certainly hope my beloved is among them."

Jacob viewed him guardedly. Aaron only smiled; he apparently enjoyed provoking his brother. The two eyed the horizon, from whence appeared two feminine figures. Gradually, it became clear that one was Elizabeth Darcy, the other Georgiana.

"This is shaping up to be an enjoyable day, is it not?" asked Aaron, winking at his brother. He then ran off to meet the women and returned with them. After the servants set up the tea and chairs, the Markwood men waited for the ladies to be seated before joining them at the table.

Aaron smiled at Georgiana. "It was very considerate of you, Miss Darcy, to think of us."

"Oh no," she insisted, "it was Mrs. Darcy's idea. She realized you had both been out in the sun for some time, and she thought you could benefit from some nourishment."

Jacob watched his brother guardedly. Aaron could sense his gaze, but he never broke his own from Miss Darcy. Jacob sought to stir him up, and so he asked Georgiana, "How is Major Talbot?"

"He seems well. My fiancé is now overseas, Mr. Markwood," she said, addressing the younger brother, "and so his letters are taking longer to arrive."

"But I'm sure he writes you every day," suggested Aaron, "for how could he resist?"

Georgiana colored, and Mrs. Darcy looked displeased. Elizabeth did not care for Aaron's attentions to her sister-in-law, but she was willing to tolerate the young man. After all, he was the vicar's brother, and she did not believe he had any malicious design. He appeared to be only amusing himself with no expectation of harm. Indeed, he seemed surprised that his words had upset Miss Darcy, and he looked remorseful. He did not know her embarrassment was not so much the result of his flattery as the offspring of her own doubts about her relationship with the Major. To ease the discomfort of both, Elizabeth addressed the vicar. "Mr. Markwood, I have finished the George Herbert volume you leant me."

"And what do you think of his verse?" he asked.

"I found it very moving. Very sincere."

"He was a painstaking divine, to be sure."

"He is a gentle poet," she reflected, "unlike so many of to-day's popular lyrists. Lord Byron, for instance."

"Poetry and politics," announced Aaron Markwood, resuming his usual lively temper, "are the two subjects Lord Byron has suggested should never fall from the lips of women."

"And we all know how well Lord Byron knows women," replied Elizabeth.

Aaron half-bowed his head. "Touché, Mrs. Darcy."

"Hasn't he recently settled?" asked Georgiana.

"He married a certain Miss Milbanke," answered Aaron, "but I don't think that can end happily."

The small party continued to discuss both poetry and politics, despite Lord Byron's injunction to the contrary. When the servants returned to collect the dishes, the men took their leave of the ladies. Aaron Markwood glanced back at Georgiana as they struck out for the parsonage, and he smiled at her. She returned the favor, and he thought he saw in her smile more than a passing flirtation. It frightened him. He had not sincerely intended to excite her interest; he thought she must know he was only sporting. But there she stood, looking after him, with the warmest expression on her face. He assumed it could only be directed at him. After all, no one stood beside him, except Jacob, who had done little more than wave a hesitant farewell.

* * *

As the Markwood men were leaving Pemberley, Mr. Darcy approached them. "Did my pond prove a sufficient swimming hole, Mr. Markwood?" he asked the vicar's brother.

"Yes, sir," replied Aaron. "I thank you for its use."

"I understand you are leaving tomorrow afternoon."

"Yes. I would like to have visited longer with my brother, but I have. . . I have some pressing business." Aaron was vague in his response, for although he believed in abolition wholeheartedly, he was still loath to disclose his activities to relative strangers. Jacob was surprised by his brother's reluctance, especially considering that Aaron had rebuked him for his own lack of active commitment to the cause.

"Well, if you gentleman have the time and the inclination," said Mr. Darcy, "I am on my way to Darrington House. My friend, John Scott, is an aficionado of fencing, and he has somehow managed to turn his great hall into a sort of informal salle. Are you interested in sparring?"

Aaron Markwood appeared more than eager. His brother Jacob, however, was rather more reluctant.

"You are coming as well, Markwood?" Mr. Darcy asked. "Your leg has not healed enough to spar. But you could keep us company. Mr. Scott will be glad to have you. Although, he *is* a nonconformist." This elicited no reaction from the vicar, and so Darcy asked, as a slight glimmer stole into the corner of his eye, "Unwilling to stand beneath his roof?"

Mr. Markwood smiled. "Of course not."

"Then let me have Thomas bring round my horse and your brother's." Darcy had been housing Aaron Markwood's steed in his own stable. "You may borrow one of mine, Markwood, rather than returning to fetch your own."

Mr. Scott was pleased to have more than one competitor grace the hall of his estate. First, he set up a match between Aaron and Mr. Darcy. Privately, Mr. Scott advised his friend to spar lightly with Mr. Markwood. "He is a young barrister, whose father has only recently risen in society. It is unlikely he has spent much time at the diversion. And you are one of the best fencers in Derbyshire. Spare him his dignity."

"I fully intend to," replied Mr. Darcy, and he gripped his rapier in his weaker hand in order to give the barrister the advantage. But when Aaron Markwood almost immediately scored a hit, Darcy quickly shifted back to his dominant hand. He then moved forward with confidence, and still the barrister scored again.

"Very well," said Mr. Scott, as Darcy drew back to begin the next round. "You can start trying now."

"I am," replied the gentleman, before re-entering the fray with angry passion, this time scoring.

"Aaron," cried the vicar from where he stood leaning against the wall. "Stop toying with him."

The younger Markwood nodded at his brother.

Mr. Darcy looked at the barrister with disbelief. He hated to think his recent success was due only to a lack of effort on his opponent's part. "You had better fight me sincerely," he said.

"I will."

The two men met once again, each pushing the limits of his own skill. In time, Aaron emerged the victor, though the triumph had required far more energy than he was accustomed to expending.

"Where did you learn?" Mr. Darcy asked, knowing that the Markwoods' family had become wealthy only in the last eight years. He doubted the barrister could have learned such prowess in so short a time.

"My father taught us both from a very young age."

"But where did he learn?"

"From his father."

"And where did he learn?"

"From his—"

"Forget my question. Is your brother as skilled as you?"

Aaron smiled. "Rather more I'm afraid. I would love to see you spar him if he did not still possess that unfortunate limp."

"I will give you time to rest before the next match."

Aaron smiled indulgently. "I hardly need to, sir."

This self-confident expression irked Mr. Darcy. "If you think so," he returned, now determined to put the upstart in his place.

Darcy was pleased to score the first hit, and he was glad to see the arrogant smile fade from Aaron Markwood's face. But with the smile went the young man's frivolity, and he was soon responding to the bout with all of his vigor. Mr. Darcy failed to score even once more. He was frustrated by this second defeat, but he conceded it generously enough, and he complimented the younger Markwood on his form. Nevertheless, Mr. Darcy was not eager to fight another bout.

Mr. Scott and Aaron Markwood fought the next match, and the barrister actually lost, no doubt wearied from his former battles. Mr. Darcy was well rested when he engaged his friend, and so he beat Scott rather easily, which he regarded as a kind of victory by syllogism. After this match, Mr. Darcy suggested it was time to return to Pemberley.

"Leaving so soon, Darcy?" asked Scott. "You and I have had a chance to spar but once."

"I regret that, Scott. But if these gentlemen wish, they may remain behind. I am sure Aaron Markwood will keep you well preoccupied. I, however, must return in order to receive a guest. My sister-in-law is coming to stay at Pemberley for a time."

"Mrs. Bingley?" asked the vicar.

"No. Another of my sister-in-laws. You met her. Miss Kitty Bennet."

Mr. Markwood nodded. "Yes, of course," he said, remembering his curate's infatuation with a smile. The poor fellow; it would be a taunt to have her back in Derbyshire. He could only see the girl for a few moments after church. Mr. Bailee would have to work very hard in that short time if he wished to earn her affections.

Mr. Markwood considered the girl a decent enough match for the man. She had been rather vivacious and not particularly deep, but he thought her natural excess of spirit had been tempered by the instruction of her elder siblings. Consequently, Miss Bennet behaved respectably while at the same time appearing capricious. As for her apparent intellectual shallowness, Mr. Markwood saw signs in her conversations that it, too, was being altered by the care of her sisters. With a year or two of additional tutoring, the vicar suspected, Miss Kitty Bennet would emerge a very attractive woman, no longer just in form, but also in personality.

"Miss Kitty Bennet?" asked Aaron, and Jacob heard something in his brother's voice that aroused his caution.

"Yes," replied Mr. Darcy. "Are you acquainted with her?"

"I met her at a ball some time ago in London. And I saw her again in the city, just this summer. But I understand she lives in Yorkshire."

"Sometimes, yes, with her sister Mrs. Bingley, and at other times, here at Pemberley with us. She also visits her aunt and uncle in London, which is why you saw her there."

"So she is arriving at Pemberley tonight?" asked the barrister.

"She is," replied Mr. Darcy.

"And how long will she be staying?"

"For approximately a month. She will spend some of the summer with her aunt and uncle."

"And how is her health?"

"Very well."

"And she is still studying music?"

"We have hired a tutor for her." Mr. Darcy half-smiled. "Well, Mr. Markwood, if you did not have pressing business drawing you away from us, I would invite you to dinner tomorrow night, and you might address your questions directly to the lady in question. As is, I do not have time to serve as an intermediary, and I must depart." He bowed to the Markwoods and his host Mr. Scott before heading to the door.

"Mr. Darcy," called Aaron after him. "I was earlier discussing with my brother the possibility of staying on just one extra night."

"Were you?" asked Jacob.

Aaron, in a seemingly friendly gesture, placed a hand on his bother's arm, but his grip was anything but friendly.

"Yes, brother," he said. "You recall. I. . . my business can wait one day. I did not have a set day of meeting but only an appointed week."

"Well then," said Mr. Darcy, "the offer still stands. Will you both be joining us for dinner tomorrow night?"

"We would be honored," replied Aaron.

Mr. Darcy, however, awaited the vicar's response. He sensed that Jacob Markwood was less than pleased by the idea. "Markwood?" he asked.

The vicar nodded. "We will attend."

"Scott?" asked Darcy, thereby extending the invitation to his friend.

"No, Darcy, sorry, not tomorrow. Lady Mary is coming to dinner. The old mother-in-law, you know."

After Mr. Darcy had left, Jacob sought the first available moment to have a word alone with his brother, but the opportunity did not arise until after Aaron had sparred Mr. Scott. When their host departed to solicit a servant for refreshments, Jacob Markwood asked, with a tone of mild accusation, "Miss Kitty Bennet?" and awaited his brother's response.

Aaron ignored him for the moment and lazily cut the air with his rapier.

"Aaron?"

"Yes, Jacob?"

"What of Miss Kitty Bennet?"

"What of her? I met her at a ball and took a fancy to her. And what is that to you?"

"Well, it is only that I think my curate fancies her too."

"Your curate, Jacob? Your curate?"

"Yes, my curate."

"She's the sister-in-law of Mr. Darcy, Jacob. She isn't going to be enamored with anybody's curate. Not even *yours*."

"You cannot know that."

"What are you, the village match maker? Has this fellow contracted for your services?" Aaron laughed heartily. "All's fair, dear brother, in love and war."

"I wouldn't mind if I thought you might be serious. It is just that you seem to take a fancy to a great many women."

"A great many women are worthy of fancy. You know, Jacob, we were raised by the same father. We were instilled with the same values. You can trust me. 'Who have my sighs harmed?'"

"Aaron, you know it is important that a man avoid even—"

"—the appearance of evil. Yes, I know. So I show a little interest here and there. Where is the evil in that?"

"You see no evil in breaking the hearts of young, vulnerable women?"

"Name the owner of a single heart I have broken, brother."

The vicar prepared to rattle off the names of women he could recall his brother flirting with, but he checked himself before the first fell from his lips. None of those women, he realized, had ever anticipated a proposal from Aaron Markwood; all had enjoyed themselves, and all had parted amiably. What was more, they had ended up happily wed to other men, most of whom had been recommended to them by Aaron himself. "Nevertheless," he said at last, "you cannot know they will not love you sincerely. You gamble with their hearts."

Jacob had always possessed an excessive concern for his younger brother, ever since Aaron had, at ten years old, criticized a slave master's son, which resulted in a severe beating. Aaron had returned home a bloody mess. That was when their father had begun to teach them fencing. He had been forced to sell off their mother's jewelry to obtain sufficient equipment for his sons.

Sir Robert's own father had never possessed any fortune to speak of, but he had once worked as a steward for a fencing instructor, and he had been treated to private lessons. He had passed that knowledge onto his son, who served as a stern taskmaster to his own two boys. Sir Robert had been reluctant to depart with the treasures that had belonged to his late wife, but he was even more reluctant to allow his sons to grow soft, especially considering that he had every intention of giving them an unpopular mission and then thrusting them into an unwelcoming world.

"Well," grunted Aaron, who was growing weary of his brother's lectures, "if I were to take my instruction from you, then I would believe a man should delay as long as possible in showing his interest. But what if you lose her heart to another in the meantime, Jacob? What then?" It was a cruel stab and he knew it. He had spoken in the heat of argument, and when he saw written upon his brother's face the injury his words had inflicted, he repented of them. He thought the vicar was pained because he still loved Miss Grant. In fact, Jacob's former feeling had finally faded. He was only wounded because he longed to love and to be loved, and because he feared he may never again have the opportunity. Aaron hastened, "Jacob, I did not mean—"

"I understand your allusion perfectly. It is wisest, you suggest, that a man express interest even before he is sure of his own feelings; that way he risks only the woman's heart and not his own."

"You think me more selfish than I am. Had any one of those women sincerely loved me, had any sincerely anticipated a proposal, I would have given her one."

"You would have married a woman even if you did not love her?"

"Jacob, I could make myself love anyone."

"A man cannot make himself love—not in *that* way."

"Is love a feeling or an action?"

"Both," answered Mr. Markwood.

"And can a man control his actions?"

"Of course, but—"

"Aha!" exclaimed Aaron, satisfied with his victory.

The vicar was weary of this argument, and so he altered the path of their conversation, joking, "I thought you considered Miss Darcy to be your Juliet."

"No, brother, she was only my Rosaline."

"Except you met Miss Kitty Bennet first. But I will forgive you the sequential inaccuracy and let the analogy stand, for one's Juliet should not be engaged."

"No indeed. So I have your blessing to pursue Miss Bennet?"

"As usual, I do not believe you are sincerely interested. You never are. What is more, you only met her twice."

"I have never been in the presence of one woman long enough to become sincerely interested. But Miss Bennet's vivacity struck me. I had put her out of my mind because I never expected to see her again. But now that I have the chance, I would like to learn what she has to offer."

Their conversation was cut short by the return of Mr. Scott, who invited them to take a break from their exercise to enjoy some tea and sandwiches. Aaron followed him happily, daydreaming of his almost-forgotten Juliet.

***

When Mr. Darcy returned that evening to Pemberley, his wife said, "I hope you did not put the young Mr. Markwood to shame."

"Oh, fear not," replied her husband. "I did no such thing." Then he crossed the room to give his sister-in-law a brotherly greeting. He now regarded her with affection although she had once been little more than an embarrassment to him. "Kitty," he asked, "how did you leave the Bingleys?"

"In very good health. I am sure they are glad to be rid of me, though. They need some time alone together. Their house is always occupied by some guest or another."

"Well, we are glad to have you," said Mr. Darcy. "We'll be having some guests for dinner tomorrow evening: the vicar and his brother, Aaron Markwood. Do you know him?" Given the young Markwood's obvious interest in Miss Bennet, Mr. Darcy was curious to see Kitty's reaction when he mentioned the name. The girl, however, seemed unmoved. He said the name again, deliberately, "Aaron Markwood."

"I am certain she heard you the first time, darling," Elizabeth said with laughter, amused by her husband's peculiar behavior and expression. "If we are having dinner guests tomorrow, I had best go speak to the cook." Mrs. Darcy departed their company.

"Thank you, Mr. Darcy," said Kitty, "for sending for Mr. Jameson to tutor me while I am at Pemberley. I begin my lessons tomorrow."

"It is our pleasure. You have not met Mr. Aaron Markwood?"

Kitty seemed to consider for a moment. Of course she remembered Aaron Markwood, but she wouldn't give Mr. Darcy the satisfaction of appearing interested. "You know, I think I may have," she said. "At the ball in London. Yes, yes I did. We even danced once."

"What sort of impression did he make?"

Kitty laughed dismissively. "Mr. Darcy, how *unlike* you, to ask after a girl's interests. Really. I suppose he was pleasant enough. But it is hard to keep track of all the many young men these days. I hardly know who is who anymore."

This reaction, thought Mr. Darcy, did not bode well for the moonstruck Aaron Markwood. But once the gentleman had arrived for dinner the following day, Kitty appeared less disinterested. He heard her whisper to Georgiana, "He is much more handsome than his brother, do you not agree?"

Mr. Darcy did not, however, hear Georgiana's reply. "I will only concede," she said, "that he is more *conventionally* handsome."

Throughout the meal, Kitty directed most of her conversation to the young barrister. Later, in the drawing room, he managed to find a chair next to hers, and the pair seemed temporarily to forget that they were not the only people in the room. To draw her away from what might appear like an excess of attention, Mr. Darcy suggested Kitty play the pianoforte, but this only gave Aaron Markwood an excuse to watch her more intently. As she played, he gazed at her with barely concealed admiration.

That evening brought Aaron more than the pleasures of flirting with a pretty young girl. It also granted him a measure of relief; for although Georgiana Darcy had, in his mind, been easily eclipsed by the more available Miss Bennet, he did take a moment to glance at her, and he was glad to learn his attentions to another had excited no jealousy on her part. Apparently he had mistaken her earlier fond gaze, and he chided himself—with more amusement than severity—for his own vanity. He was willing to believe that a flaw existed in his perception, but he was not able to consider the possibility that the look had been real and yet cast at another. It never occurred to him that Miss Darcy might be in love with his brother.

Aaron lost himself in the moment, there at Pemberley, in the presence of Miss Bennet. There was nothing in her looks or manner or character that was inherently more attractive than that of other women he had known, but he had somehow taken a deeper fancy than usual, and he could not have explained why he enjoyed her glances and her company anymore than he could have explained why he preferred Byron to Herbert, or ale to port.

Until now, Aaron had always danced very happily and very clearly outside the limits of anything resembling sincerity. Tonight, however, there were occasional moments when he forgot to ensure that his flirtations appeared only in jest. The young man, it must be confessed, had often regarded romance as something of a hobby. He was skilled at the diversion, but he had no intention of making a profession of it. He knew his limits, and his emotions were always subject to his will.

That is not to say he had no thought of ever marrying. He

assumed, as a matter of course, that he would one day obtain a wife, and he rather liked the idea of having a channel, other than abolition, for his passions. He approved of marriage and accepted it as a gentleman's inevitable fate, but he could not precisely envision it. He simply did not see himself as a permanent domesticate, tied to any one place. He was not like his brother, who had always hoped to complement his professional calling with his domestic joys, who felt most at home when settled quietly, who had thought of marriage as a little mirror for divine love, and who had longed for it just as urgently.

As Mr. Darcy observed Aaron Markwood, he began to be glad the barrister must leave the following morning. Part of him had hoped for a match; he had never before believed that Kitty could rise so high in society. But the barrister's attentions were too pronounced, and they had been inspired too easily. Mr. Darcy did not trust him. He did, however, trust the man's brother, and when he looked to the vicar with concern in his eyes, Jacob half shrugged and returned him an expression that seemed to say, "Do not trouble yourself. He is innocuous."

Nevertheless, thought Mr. Darcy, it was well that the young Markwood would depart on the morrow. Juggling the suitors to his own sister had been wearisome enough; he did not wish to be put on guard once again.

***

Before Aaron Markwood set out from Derbyshire the following morning, he called on the Darcys to thank them for their hospitality. He managed to ascertain when and for how long Miss Bennet would next be in London with her aunt and uncle. She informed him that she would arrive in late May, but she regretted she would be staying only through the end of July.

"What a time you picked!" exclaimed Aaron. "The summer is the worst season to visit London."

"I know," agreed Kitty, "but my uncle cannot often get away from his profession to come to the country. And I do love to see them."

"And I would love to see you," said Aaron, "when you come

to town." He received her answering smile and departed with a bow.

While he journeyed to meet the politician Mr. Buxton, Aaron Markwood wondered what Miss Kitty Bennet would think of his cause. He had not mentioned it to her despite the fact that it was the central purpose of his life.

He asked himself what game he was playing with this girl. He could not go on like this, living one life here and another there, letting some people know him as a fiery abolitionist, others as a harmless rake. He had to have the courage of his convictions. He must learn to talk about his beliefs even when among those who might disagree with him, as he had done in his childhood, before discovering that the truth often has unpleasant consequences.

Chapter 24

One tranquil evening at Pemberley, weeks after Aaron Markwood had departed Derbyshire, the three Darcys relaxed in an informal sitting room. They were joined by Kitty Bennet and Jacob Markwood. Georgiana half closed the book she was reading and looked across at the vicar. It was awhile before he noticed her attention and returned it. Though she still loved him, Georgiana was no longer uncomfortable in his presence. She had resigned herself to the thought that he could never be more than a friend, and she was now determined to make as much of that friendship as possible. She felt a need to learn his thoughts on a matter that had been plaguing her. "Mr. Markwood," she said, "you oppose slavery."

"Yes," he replied, ready for an engaging discussion. He found it very easy to talk to Miss Darcy. . . and yet, not easy. He was comfortable sharing his ideas with her; he felt free to speak his opinions without fear of judgment. But she also challenged him. She was not like most women he had known, who would agree with a man simply to satisfy his ego. And she was always refining her own thoughts, incorporating new information, and honing her opinions. She made him think more quickly, more deeply than he had ever been compelled to think before, and when he was with her, he hesitated to take anything for granted.

"And you are a Christian," she stated. "My question is—how then do you reconcile your abolitionist beliefs with the fact that the Bible permits slavery?"

She did not disagree with his position, he knew. She simply never arrived at a belief without first considering every objection to it. He admired that about her, but he wished his brother were here to answer. Aaron knew every argument in favor of slavery and every convincing response. Yet Aaron could not be his mouthpiece now.

"I. . ." He gathered his words before continuing. He was very aware that Mr. and Mrs. Darcy were now listening to him as well. Politics was not his calling in life, but a door had clearly been opened, if only for a moment, and it would be unjust of him to refuse to walk through it. This was what he had wanted—not to be a politician, or an attorney, or an orator—but to live out quietly his priestly calling and to use his subtle influence whenever opportunity arose. Unprepared though he felt, somehow the words came. "Are you speaking of the law?"

"Yes."

"The law regulates slavery in the same way it regulates lust or greed. That is not the same thing as endorsing it."

"So what are you saying? That slavery, if regulated, is permissible? Do you believe it is ever permissible?"

"No," he said, feeling a little helpless. He knew what he believed, and he knew he had the support of his religion, but he could not seem to voice those thoughts. After considerable mental struggle, he replied, "Let me give you an example. The law permitted a man to give his wife a bill of divorce. Does that mean God is pleased with divorce, that He endorses it?"

She shook her head.

"No," he continued. "It does not mean that at all. Moses gave men that law because of the hardness of their hearts. Men *will* abandon their wives. Better, at least, that those innocent women should be afforded some protection—which a written bill of divorce would provide."

She waited for him to continue. She was not inclined to question him further until he had sorted his thoughts and laid them completely before her.

"Slavery is something like that," he said. "Man—every culture, every creed, every race—has kept slaves for centuries upon centuries. The law regulated how a man could treat those slaves: what punishment he must bear if he abused them, when they should be freed. Yet that does not mean God does not hate bondage or that a Christian should endorse it."

"But does not Paul himself endorse it, when he tells slaves to obey their masters?"

He paused for a moment before answering. He was only gathering his thoughts. He was not afraid to argue with her; he did not fear offending her. He knew now that she was not so fragile as her initial shyness had implied. She had a strong mind and a spirit that was willing to brave challenge. At length he answered, "He tells all men to obey authority. He told Christians to obey their rulers, and at a time when the emperor was dipping them in oil and setting them aflame as human torches to light his garden. To tell a man to obey his master is not to tell him his master is right. But a man draws less rage upon himself when he refrains from defiance."

"Then why not refrain now? Why support abolition now?"

"To everything there is a season. I believe the time is now ripe for abolition. Now that the institution has deteriorated into a more heinous crime than ever, men have become more open to the possibility that a society can persevere without slavery."

"More heinous than ever?" she asked.

"Oh indeed," he replied. "Worse because it is unregulated, because it is crueler, because it is now based solely on race, because it is a permanent state. Modern slavery is a sickness that eats away at the heart of man, and it must be opposed. Men may take these verses at random and find some petty support for their faltering consciences, but the whole tenor of the Bible cries out against the modern institution. If the Bible truly supported slavery, how could it be then that slavery's most ardent opponents, both here and in America, are so often to be found among the ranks of the evangelical Christians?"

"That is true," she conceded. "Yet there are men enough who keep slaves who are Christians. *Most* slave owners are Christians."

"*Most* Englishmen are Christians, at least in name, as are most Americans. You might as well say most slave owners have two legs."

"The fact remains, Mr. Markwood, that people professing to be Christians own slaves and quote the Bible to support the institution."

"Christians who own slaves do not own slaves *because* they are Christians, Miss Darcy, they own them in spite of the fact. If it were truly the Bible persuading them to own slaves, then they would keep its law with regard to slaves, which they clearly do not. The law forbids dividing families. The law requires slaves to be freed in the year of Jubilee. The law insists that runaway slaves from other countries are not to be returned their owners, but given asylum. The law requires a man to free his slave if he knocks out his tooth. Do you see modern slave owners obeying these laws?"

"No."

"Christian slave owners do not turn to the Bible to seek out guidance for the kind of life they *ought* to live; rather, they turn to it looking for support for the life they have *already* determined to live. Monetary gain, or pride, or some other force—not Christianity—inspires them to place men in bondage. They feel in the innermost depths of their hearts that what they do violates every commandment of God, and *that* is why they turn to the Bible for excuse. But Christians who are abolitionists, Miss Darcy, are not abolitionists despite their religion, they are abolitionists *because* of it. The knowledge that in Christ there is neither slave nor free, the belief that man is created in the image of his Maker, the understanding that the second greatest command is to love your neighbor, the awareness of the cardinal rule—that we are bid to do unto others as we would have them do unto us—*these* are the things that compel the Christian abolitionist! Do you not see the difference, Miss Darcy? Do you not see the difference between the man who manipulates his religion to serve his own will, and the man who is driven by his religion to serve God's?"

He grew suddenly quiet. He had allowed his emotions to carry his thoughts so that he spoke rapidly and with a tremble in his voice. He was not so zealous as his brother might have been, but he had shown feeling enough. Every eye was now focused upon him, even that of Kitty Bennett. He wondered what she thought of his mild outburst. If she were really as uncomfortable as she looked, then she would, he believed, have a difficult time dealing with Aaron Markwood. For Aaron could be far more passionate on the subject, and Jacob felt sure that his brother was called for the public arena, however much he may have hesitated to reveal his aspirations while at Pemberley.

The tension was alleviated when Georgiana replied softly, "Yes, Mr. Markwood, I do see. I do."

He almost said, 'Thank you', before he realized it would be a ridiculous thing to say. He had certainly never before thought to thank a person for agreeing with his opinion. Either his beliefs were right or they were not; he could not be swayed by the consensus of others. And yet he did feel a sense of gratitude for her gentle reassurance. A sense of gratitude and. . . something else he could not quite define. That indecipherable something else caused him to mutter, "Yes, well, very well, then," and to pick up his book and bury himself in its pages.

The scene about him faded back to normality. Kitty resumed her needlework; Georgiana picked up her volume; Mr. and Mrs. Darcy talked quietly about subjects of interest to one another. The vicar read or pretended to. He was no longer a visitor who needed to be entertained; rather, he had become an accepted part of the family structure. No one observed him when he rose, half an hour later, and wandered silently into the halls of Pemberley.

***

Mr. Markwood now felt very much at ease in the estate though it had once intimidated him. He had never lived long in a mansion himself. Their home in the West Indies had been modest, and not long after the Markwoods returned to England, Jacob had left his father's estate for Oxford.

More than a few minutes passed before his absence was noted, and then only by Georgiana. Nonchalantly excusing herself from the company, she put down her book and rose. Miss Darcy was curious to discover where the clergyman had absconded, and although her reason told her not to seek him out, her feet, this time, obeyed her heart.

Guided by the sound of a piano, she found him at last in the music room. She had not realized he could play, but she knew it could not be a servant who was using the Darcys' instrument. She stepped inconspicuously into the doorway and observed him as he began to sing the words to a song she had never heard:

Be thou my vision, O Lord of my heart.
There is none else, my ruler thou art.
Be thou my study by day and by night
Be thou the goal of my sleeping sight.

Thou my conviction, and thou my one Word,
Be ever with me, and I with thee Lord.
Thou art my father, and I am thy son
Dwell thou with me, and we shall be one.

Mr. Markwood had led hymns at church, but his singing had always been obscured by that of the congregation. Georgiana had no idea his voice harbored such resonant depths. It was not a clean voice, nor a particularly attractive one, but it was accurate, powerful, and fervent. The vicar continued:

Be thou my war-shield, and be thou my sword;
Be thou my honor, and make me thy ward.
Be thou my shelter, and be thou my hold;
And wrap me with angels into your fold.

Breath to my body, and life to my soul,
Be thou my kingdom; Christ make me whole.
Thou, thou alone art the chief of my heart
There is none else, my captain thou art.

Before Georgiana was aware of the fact, she had already walked well into the room, and she now stood mesmerized by the unusual hymn. Were Mr. Markwood not himself absorbed, he would have noticed her. Instead, he sung on:

'Til in thy hands I come to my rest,
Be thou my treasure, beloved bequest.
Be thou my noble and awesome estate
Riches I need not, menpleasers I hate.

Be thou the constant guard of all life
Whether at peace or whether at strife.

Our corrupt longings shrivel and die
Under the gaze of Heaven's strong eye.

King of all Heaven, victory once won,
Grant me this joy: the gift of your Son.
Heart of my own heart, whatever befall
Be thou my vision, oh Ruler of All.

When he stopped playing, she asked with pronounced wonder, "What was that?"

He jumped. "Miss Darcy!" he exclaimed, apparently embarrassed. "I had not known you were there."

"I. . . I just happened in and heard you singing. What was the hymn? I don't believe I have ever heard it before."

"You would not have heard it," he responded. "It is an Old Irish incantation. It was probably used by monks when they armed for battle, whether spiritual or physical. As far as I know, it has never been written down or translated into English."

"Then how—you sang it in English!" By now Georgiana was standing across from the piano.

Mr. Markwood leaned forward. He looked toward the door, and seeing no figure there, he whispered, "Can you keep a secret, Miss Darcy?"

He was only joking, but for a moment she took him seriously. "I have never taken much interest in gossip, Mr. Markwood."

"My mother was Irish."

Georgiana smiled, and then she looked unconvinced.

"I do not know where she heard the chant," he said, "but she used to pray it with my brother and I as children every night before we went to bed. She prayed it in Gaelic. I didn't speak a word of her ancient language. But my heart knew what that prayer meant, and I memorized the sound of it. When we moved back to England, my father had a friend who was an Irish peer. He translated the words into English for me, and I rewrote them in order to make them rhyme. I set the verses to a tune my mother used to sing us."

"It's beautiful, Mr. Markwood. It ought to be sung in church."

"I doubt that will ever happen, Miss Darcy. At least not my

version. But I do intend to sing it to my own children one day, like my mother before me. . ." The vicar trailed off and grew melancholy.

"Mr. Markwood?" asked Georgiana tentatively.

He returned his eyes to her. "Forgive my distraction. I was thinking of my mother. She died when I was just seven years old. After that, it seemed everything in England reminded my father of her. And then one day, he came upon us at play on the moors, and he said, 'Boys, come inside, pick a few of your favorite things. We're leaving.' I didn't set foot on these shores again for almost fourteen years." He caressed the keys of the piano and seemed to grit his teeth. Georgiana wished she knew how to comfort him.

"But you and your father are on good terms now," she said, gently reminding him that he still had at least one parent.

"Yes. Yes we have reconciled, at least by letter. I suppose someday I will need to do the task in person. I have not had the opportunity, and he has not extended me an invitation to visit."

"Do you need to wait for one?" she asked. "Or do you think that, by now, the time has come to take the next step yourself without encouragement?"

She had not expected her words to have so great an effect upon him. She had not meant to make a judgment or to shame him. But she saw how hard he took the question. "I am sorry," she said in haste, "I had no right–"

"You have every right," he assured her, "to say what you believe is true." He slammed shut the piano's lid and rose from the bench. "You offer a very gentle chastisement, Miss Darcy. You mix wisdom with kindness, and make the truth palatable." He looked away from her and back toward the now hidden keys. He was nodding to himself. "You *are* right," he said finally. "It is time."

***

Dear Father,

Mr. Markwood stopped writing and began to chew on the edge of his quill. After a time, he continued:

> *As you probably know, Aaron visited me last month. Since then, I have been investing some very serious thought into a certain statement of his. He told me that I was stubborn to ask you to trust me without an explanation. He said you deserved better from me.*

The vicar paused again. He looked out his parsonage window toward Pemberley even though his view of the estate was obscured by both darkness and nearly a mile of woods. Why had it taken Miss Darcy's tender reproof to bring him to this moment? His brother had lectured him weeks ago, in no uncertain terms, and yet that had not inspired an adequate remorse. Both had said what he knew to be true, but only Georgiana's words carried a permanent weight. How and when, he now wondered, did her opinion come to have such power over him? He closed his eyes and bowed his head for a very long time, and then he drew himself up straight in his chair and dipped his quill in the inkwell once again.

> *Although I diligently sought a reconciliation with you, I never compassed my entreaties with terms of apology. Your inability to accept my word at face value injured me. I forgot, for a time, that the man who raised me up from my childhood, who worked incessantly to ensure my future, who never seemed to care what the world thought of him, but who only cared that he pursued the rough road of righteousness—I forgot, for a time, that that man was earthen clay. As am I.*

> *Forgive me, father, for expecting too much of you. Forgive me for thinking too much of myself. I must endeavor to remember that we live in a fallen world and not some simple paradise where to say a thing is always to mean it.*

I was not wrong to terminate my engagement with Miss Grant. She has secured Sir Andrew, and she is happier with him than she could have hoped to be with me. But whether or not ending our engagement was correct, I should have told you my reasons instantly. Had I done so, we would not have squandered seven months on a petty quarrel. Instead, I persisted in asking for reconciliation without repentance. And eventually, like the father of the prodigal son, you ran to the gate to prevent me, and you embraced me, and in your grace you kissed me before I could let a single rehearsed word fall from my unfaithful lips.

You understand my contrition; I will not dwell on it. This letter will precede me by but a week or two. I plan to journey to you myself. My visit can be only brief, as my duties in this parish are rather pressing. But I long to see you.

Your son,
Jacob

The vicar put down his pen. He sealed his letter in the candle's flame. And then he rose and carried that small light back through his empty parsonage to his silent bedchamber, where he would sleep that night, as he did every night, alone.

Chapter 25

Mr. Darcy asked Jacob Markwood if he would escort Kitty and her companion to London and then double back to Buckinghamshire to visit his father. A neighbour, the widow Mrs. Anderson, had agreed to accompany Kitty since she herself desired to visit a niece in the city. That, however, was not enough to satisfy Miss Bennet's brother-in-law. "It is unsafe for two ladies to travel that distance alone," he had told Mr. Markwood. "You may have the use of our carriage if you escort them." The vicar, ever glad to be of service, agreed instantly.

Kitty lamented that she could not share these hours of seclusion with the younger Mr. Markwood instead of his elder brother. But of course, such a happy circumstance could never arise; the Darcys would on no account permit her to travel with any young man who was not also a clergyman and trusted friend. Kitty did entertain the hope, however, that the vicar might call upon his brother before depositing her at the Gardiners.

The trio had barely been in the carriage four miles before they pulled up before a very modest cottage and stopped. Kitty asked the reason for the interruption, and the vicar replied that he must have a word with his curate. "It may take a few minutes," he said. "Would you two like to come inside with me?"

Kitty glanced disparagingly at the cottage. "We may take a short stroll," she replied.

Mr. Markwood helped the ladies down from the carriage. "Stay within sight of the house," he said. Miss Bennet consented and began to wander off a short distance, while Mrs. Anderson remained beside the carriage.

Kitty was not unaware of Mr. Bailee's affection for her. Since her return to Pemberley, the curate had attempted to address her after virtually every service. At first, she had made sport by encouraging his attentions until she feared he might take her too seriously. For the past two weeks, therefore, she had avoided him and had left the church immediately after services to immerse herself in the lingering crowds.

As Kitty strolled outside the curate's home, she came upon a very simple but beautiful garden. She noticed, too, that the exterior of the cottage had been exceedingly well maintained. Mr. Bailee appeared to have put a great deal of work into making his little home appealing to the eye. Gaining a new respect for the man who took such pride in his possession, Kitty watched as the clergyman opened the door.

Miss Bennet saw the vicar retreat into the cottage, and as the curate prepared to follow him, he glanced in her direction. The door's handle seemed to slip unintentionally from Mr. Bailee's hand, but in a moment he reclaimed it and pulled the door shut.

Later in the carriage, Kitty asked Mr. Markwood why he had needed to delay their journey with a visit to his curate.

"I had to go over some parish business with him. While I am gone, of course, he will be fulfilling all of my regular duties."

"Does he not fulfill them anyway?" She had the impression that curates were men who must constantly labor, with no leisure for pursuits like reading or walking or gardening. Those things, she thought, were for vicars alone.

"No," replied Mr. Markwood. "That is not the way with me. He does not need to be saddled regularly with another man's job."

Kitty was surprised to learn this information, and she thought it explained why Mr. Bailee had time to make his home so presentable. But she did not pursue the conversation. She had no interest in the industry of religion. Instead, she began to ask Mr. Markwood about his brother. The vicar was vexingly brief in his replies, and sometimes he just stared out the window as if he were not listening to her at all.

In reality, Mr. Markwood was attempting to gauge Miss Bennet's personality in order to determine whether she might really be a match for his brother. Aaron had shown an obvious interest in her, but she had not been the first woman to draw his attention, and Jacob doubted very much that she would be the last. The vicar therefore intentionally avoided talking about his brother in any detail to ensure that he did not encourage her affection.

As he gazed at the passing scenery, Mr. Markwood speculated about the extent of his brother's regard. Miss Bennet appeared carefree but basically moral—much like Aaron. She would be animated enough for him, but not so impulsive as to lead him astray. She seemed a shade immature, even for his brother, but she would grow out of that in time, especially with the society of her sisters to amend her. And, although she was not as beautiful as either of her elder siblings, there was something of the bright Bennet gleam about her.

"Miss Bennet," he asked, rather than answering another of her causal questions about Aaron Markwood, "what are your interests?"

"My interests, sir?"

"Your interests. What moves you? Music, painting, literature?"

"Ah. . . well, I like them all I suppose. I am best at playing."

"What instrument?"

"The pianoforte, of course."

"Of course. Nothing else?"

"Mr. Jameson is teaching me the harp at Mr. Darcy's instruction."

"And do you like it?" the vicar asked.

"Yes, though not so well as the pianoforte."

"What languages do you speak?"

"French and German," Kitty answered.

"Latin? Greek?"

"No, Mr. Markwood. Women do not learn such tongues!"

"No, indeed? I'm sorry. I had not realized. My mother read both."

"How odd, sir," she said with a slight laugh. "I suppose things may be different where you come from."

"I come from England. I only lived in the West Indies. But I suppose that under my father's roof, the status quo was rather altered. And I had somewhat of an insular upbringing."

"But your brother is educated," she insisted, glad to have an opening to mention the young Mr. Markwood. "He went to Cambridge!"

"Yes, and I to Oxford. The experience broadened our horizons, no doubt."

"Is your brother a successful barrister? Do you think he will plead in the inner bar one day?"

"I imagine he will," Mr. Markwood answered. "He has a talent for oratory. He belongs inside the dividing bar."

Though she pressed him, Kitty could not extract any further brotherly accolades from the vicar. Nor did Mr. Markwood succeed in discovering any more of her character, but perhaps the depths to be plumbed were truly that shallow. For his brother's sake, he hoped not.

When the three arrived in London, Mrs. Anderson was deposited at her niece's residence, and Mr. Markwood saw Kitty to her Aunt and Uncle's. Mrs. Gardiner suggested that Mr. Markwood call on his brother and that both rejoin them later. "Dine with us before you leave to see your father," she said.

It was more than Kitty had hoped. The vicar consented, but he seemed reluctant. Mrs. Gardiner feared his hesitation resulted from their position in society and their residence in Cheapside. Yes, he was a country vicar, but he was also the son of Sir Robert, and as a beneficiary of new money, he might be particularly sensitive about his reputation. They met amiably enough at Pemberley, but to be entertained in Cheapside. . . She began to make excuses for him. "Surely you are tired and wish to rest from your journey—"

"No, Aunt!" interrupted Kitty. "He can be no more tired than I, and I am perfectly energetic. I'm sure both of the Markwoods would be more than happy to join us. Isn't that right, sir?"

"I cannot speak for my brother. However, I would be honored to dine with you tonight, and I will return this evening at whatever hour, Mrs. Gardiner, you appoint."

Mrs. Gardiner named the time and the vicar agreed to it before returning to the carriage. Kitty watched him depart with a growing sense of happiness; surely, she thought, he could not return alone.

***

Mrs. Gardiner's misconception was quickly corrected when the two Markwoods arrived for dinner. Both gentlemen were perfectly agreeable, and neither seemed to be in the least bit affronted by either Mr. Gardiner's home or profession. Kitty's aunt, however, did observe how the girl behaved toward the young barrister, and she understood the elder Markwood's reluctance. She shot her niece a warning look, which silently advised her to distribute her attentions more evenly.

Aaron Markwood was more reserved than he had been at Pemberley, and Jacob thought some of the girl's novelty must have faded. As he watched their conversation, however, the vicar was forced to recant his former conclusion. His brother's reticence, he surmised, had nothing to do with a lack of affection. The barrister was clearly smitten. Why then was he not his usual flirtatious self?

Mr. Gardiner likewise observed Aaron Markwood's interest, and he began to entertain a hope that a third of his nieces might succeed in marrying well. But Kitty was not as resourceful as either Jane or Elizabeth, he thought. He would have to assist her.

"Mr. Markwood," Mr. Gardiner said to the younger brother, "are you too traveling to Buckinghamshire to see your father?"

"No, sir. I have visited him recently, and I have work here in London."

"Then I hope Mrs. Gardiner and I will be seeing more of you this summer, now that we have properly met."

"I as well," returned Aaron, but he wasn't looking at Mr. Gardiner.

***

Later that night, as the two brothers settled into the sitting room of Aaron's town home, Jacob glanced up at the painting of Pemberley mounted above the fireplace. Aaron had asked to purchase it from Mr. Darcy, and the gentleman had made a gift of the work. Jacob now looked upon it as a saint might look toward heaven, not the home he inhabits, but the home for which he longs. "So you don't miss Georgiana Darcy, do you?"

he asked. Was he asking his brother or himself?

Aaron, at least, took it as a flippant accusation. He was yanking off one of his boots, and he carelessly let it fly out of his hands so that it slammed against his brother's shin.

The vicar yowled. "You know that hurt."

"Only you can know that. I can only hope." Once he was in his stocking feet, Aaron swiveled around in his chair to face Jacob. He draped his legs over one arm and rested against the other. "So," he said, "you are going to visit father. The prodigal son returns. Only, you've already been assured of his forgiveness, and you're the elder brother."

"What of Miss Kitty Bennet?"

"Jacob, why do you often answer my questions with one of your own?"

"Did you ask a question?" The vicar smiled almost imperceptibly. "I thought you were merely making an observation."

"I suppose I was. But it cries out for a response."

"Everything you say cries out for a response. Now tell me, Aaron, what of Miss Kitty Bennet?"

The barrister sighed. "What do you wish to know of her? What shall I detail to you? Her glittering eyes? Her inconvenient and yet somehow endearing cough? Her delicate frame? Her effervescent personality? The aberrant direction of her sly little smile? What are you asking me?"

"First, your opinion of her."

"I think her quite pretty. She was, at first, merely above average, but she grows in beauty with observation. She's lively, which of course I like. Granted, she has space to mature. . . Shut that half opened mouth Jacob, I know what you are poised to say. So do I."

Jacob closed his mouth into a smile.

"Of course," continued Aaron, "that means she can only improve."

"Next, your intentions," said Jacob, resuming a serious air.

"Undecided."

"I don't care for that answer."

"Nor do I. Nevertheless, it is my answer. If Mr. Gardiner has any say, I suspect I will see more of her over this next month while she is in London, and I can sort out my intentions then."

"You will have two whole months," Jacob corrected him. "She does not return to Pemberley until August."

"I will be gone for the month of July."

"You can leave your cases for that long?"

"I'm leaving the bar, Jacob."

Mr. Markwood did not respond, but he grew tense. Was his brother now to pursue a new ambition? Would both sons reject their father's cause? It would devastate Sir Robert.

Aaron said, "If I needed the income, I would stay, but of course I don't. Father will support me."

"So you plan to be—what—a gentleman?"

"I will be what I am, Jacob. An abolitionist. I will seek a seat in the House of Commons when I am qualified. In the meantime, I will stir up support for Mr. Buxton's ideas, which I share. He thinks I can help his campaign and the cause by giving and writing speeches."

"It is certainly your gift," Jacob replied, relieved. His father's dreams would be fulfilled, and Aaron would leave behind the half-way house on the road to his own calling.

"It is your gift, too, Jacob. I heard you preach, remember, when you were a curate. And while I was in Derbyshire, I heard from others how your sermons stirred them up. And these were people I had suspected of complacency. Change the topic. That is all I ask. Join me in the cause. Leave your parish. You say you love God and believe that He has called you. Well, a man of God can travel the circuit just as well as—"

"Aaron, it's not that kind of calling. I tried to explain—"

"Think about it, Jacob! This passion you have for serving God; you can apply it to the cause. Other men have done so."

"There is more than one way to serve Him," the vicar insisted. "There is more than one injustice in this world. I believe in abolition. I will never stop believing. And I will do my part where God has placed me. I will assist you as I can, in my own sphere, according to its own pace. But I will not allow it to consume me as it has consumed our father. I will not—"

"Men *must* be consumed, Jacob. I've understood that about father even if you never have, even if he doesn't know you never have. While you choose to stagnate in a country parish, society grinds on in its callused way, propelled forward by the oppression of an entire race. The world isn't altered by your quiet wishing! There is a truth that must be proclaimed in every street of every town of every county in the land of England. And *you* are not proclaiming it!"

"Nor are *you!*" returned Mr. Markwood angrily. "You're all fire *now*, aren't you, Aaron?"

Aaron glared at him. He was angry because the words were true. He crossed his arms against his chest and continued to brood in silence.

"Aaron," his brother said softly. He was done with yelling, done with this foolish competition for a father's unequal affections. "I know you will do what you are called to do. I know you will find the courage. Do not hate yourself if you are not there this very moment. And do not hate me if I walk a different path. You are right. Perhaps some men must be consumed. Some, indeed, are called to be prophets—but others to be pastors. I have found my calling in this life. You have long known your own; you have long shared our father's passion. And you have long resented that he does not see that. But he will see, Aaron. He will see in time. The same way he saw, at last, what I was called to do. And I hope one day that you, too, will acknowledge my calling." This last the vicar spoke with pain, and Aaron heard the twinge within his voice.

The younger Markwood sat up in his chair and leaned forward. "Jacob, I have tried to understand the calling that you feel—"

"I don't want your understanding, Aaron. No one can *understand* another man's vocation. I want your respect."

Aaron was dumbfounded. His brother wanted *his* approval? It had never occurred to him that Jacob might crave his admiration. It was he, he thought, who had always looked up to the elder, who had always trailed behind him: the slower runner, the weaker fencer, the smaller thinker. When he could speak, he said with feeling, "Jacob, you have it. Have you ever doubted that?"

Mr. Markwood looked away. He would not let Aaron see his

face. Yes, he had doubted it.

"I am sorry," Aaron murmured, "if I made you feel. . . I have been too hard upon you. I have tried to put you, sometimes, into another man's mold. But I have always admired you. I have always known your strength. You are my elder brother, but that is not why I look up to you. And I do look up to you."

The vicar rose from his seat and came and placed a hand upon his brother's shoulder. "Where is my room?" he asked, and his voice hitched, and he controlled himself. He did not need to say what those words had meant to him. Aaron knew.

"Down the hall and to the left. Good night, Jacob."

"Good night," the vicar mumbled as he made his way down the darkened hallway.

Chapter 26

The streets of London were populated only by locals now. The wealthy landowners had long ago retreated to their country estates. The warm summer weather was not known to elicit the most pleasant of scents from the city. But by now, Kitty had become accustomed to the malodorous town, and she walked happily down its blocks, aware of little more than Aaron Markwood's presence.

Mr. and Mrs. Gardiner trailed a safe distance behind the couple, close enough to keep them in view, but far enough away to allow them a private conversation. The Gardiners had twice entertained Mr. Markwood in their town home, and he had this afternoon invited them for a stroll to a favorite inn, where he promised them an unparalleled lunch. Mr. Gardiner glanced knowingly at his wife and smiled. She returned his expression, but with greater hesitancy. "They will make a good match, do you not think?" he asked her.

"Possibly," she replied. "Certainly, she could not do much better, although he does appear slightly frivolous for my taste."

Mr. Gardiner laughed. "Oh my dearest, he is young. I was something like that in my youth, you know, and it did not offend you then."

"No," she confessed. "But I was fortunate you matured so quickly."

"I think Mr. Markwood will do the same. You have seen his brother, the vicar, who is but a year older, and think what a gentleman he is—at least, where being a gentleman matters. Neither of these men seem fully versed in social convention. But Mr. Jacob Markwood impressed me as being a true gentleman—that is, a man who has the concerns of others at heart."

"Indeed," she agreed. "But I think he is quite different from his brother, who seems to me somewhat more self-absorbed."

"And yet not selfish," said Mr. Gardiner. "I do not get the impression of any real conceit, and he certainly considers the feelings of others. You saw how he aimed to put you at ease last week when you expressed concern for our position in society."

"Yes, I will grant him that virtue. He was very kind. I think he may do her well. Though their tempers may be *too* alike. She needs a merry man, but perhaps not one as flirtatious as herself."

Mr. Gardiner only shook his head. He would not seek to convince her. He himself was only glad that a prospect had arisen; he would be relieved to have one more niece respectably married and one less potential future obligation. He watched as Kitty stumbled on a cobblestone and saw her steadied by the young barrister (for such Mr. Gardiner still regarded him, knowing nothing of Aaron Markwood's abolitionist fervor or of his future plans). He smiled to see that the man did not remove his arm immediately from her waist; it gave him hope that his matchmaking expectations might prevail. But gradually that smile faded, for the arm seemed to hang about her longer than was needed for a gentle reassurance of his affection. Mr. Gardiner glanced at his wife and saw her concerned expression. He began to walk faster toward the couple, and the instant he did so, the offending arm was removed from that intimate position, and Aaron Markwood had put a small distance between himself and Miss Bennet. Perhaps, thought Mr. Gardiner, the barrister had heard the impending footsteps, or perhaps he had merely realized his own impropriety and regretted it.

Mr. Gardiner slowed to allow his wife to reach him, but both were careful to keep a closer pace for the future. They were by now approaching one of the city centers, and they had begun to veer toward the left to avoid an embarrassing spectacle. A town crier stood, draped in hand painted signs, loudly and publicly protesting the sufferings of the common laborer. A small, curious crowd had gathered around him; most individuals, however, lingered just a moment before retreating from the scene.

As the crier's voice faded more comfortably into the background, Kitty said to Mr. Markwood, "I wish these people could comprehend how ridiculous they appear. They just make everyone uneasy. No one listens to them."

"These people?" asked Mr. Markwood, not quite sure whom

she meant. Laborers? Or public speakers who proclaimed with a passion what they believed?

She replied, "People like him, who stand shouting in the town squares. Political sentiments, certainly, have their place, but they are most discomforting when forced upon others, whether in the drawing room or in the public square. Do you not think such fanaticism is absurd?"

"Well," he said, "that depends on the message and the quality of the speaker, I imagine."

Alas, poor Kitty. She had no idea that Aaron Markwood, with his gentle frivolity and flirtatious nature, sported yet another, heavier face. She had fallen for but half the man, and she had never been tested by the whole. She was like a world traveler who sees a caged, smiling hippopotamus, and thinks it a humorous, endearing creature, never guessing at its fury in the wild. She sensed, of course, that she had said something wrong; she heard the hesitation and injury in his voice. But she could not guess why her words had offended him. Therefore, she simply agreed. "Oh, yes, of course," she hastened. "It certainly depends on the speaker and the circumstance."

This seemed to relieve him somewhat, and she shot him a disarming smile. He returned it happily. "You see," he confessed, "I myself have considered—"

Here Miss Bennet nearly took a stumble, and one would like to hope that she was too mature, by now, for it to have been intentional. Yet it did not appear that any impediment blocked her way. Mr. Markwood caught her, just as he had before, but he did not allow himself to hold her long. He did notice, however, the way her eyes danced when he touched her, and he liked that expression; he liked it very much.

One may wonder why a man of such zealous spirit should find himself so captivated by a half-formed creature such as Kitty Bennet. It seemed clear enough that she could never share his greatest passion and that she was unlikely to prove a buttress for his fervent soul. But Aaron was the kind of man who was willing to abandon himself to the moment. He understood, vaguely, the ultimate goals for which he strove, but it was the passion of the instant that propelled him. He had not succeeded, at this point, in reconciling his own diverse characteristics; he was hardly in a position to consider how he might combine his present infatuation with his life-long purpose. He was moving gradually toward a greater steadiness of character, but he had not yet arrived in the fullness of maturity.

He would depart London in a week and, when freed from Miss Bennet's inviting presence, he would have time enough to contemplate his future and her place within it. For the present, however, he forgot what he had been saying, and the walk continued. Their conversation resumed, but it took on a more trivial form, and it was neither her words nor his own that interested him. Instead he watched her, enjoyed her varied glances, and drenched himself in her obvious admiration, which warmed him more than the heat of June.

***

"You are looking quite well today, father," Jacob said as he sat down to breakfast. And indeed, Sir Robert's color had been nearly fully restored. When the vicar had first arrived in Buckinghamshire, he had been somewhat alarmed to find his father pale and frequently coughing.

"It comes in bouts, Jacob, you know that," Sir Robert had reassured his son. "If only I could predict it, I might have been in Parliament. As is, I must suffer unexpected relapses. But I always make my way through."

Jacob had begun his visit by doing penance for his past pride. Sir Robert had accepted the apology without hesitation and had prevented him from prolonging it, and then he had rushed Jacob into the library to show him his latest volumes; that is, as much as Sir Robert was capable of rushing at the time. He had to stop for breath along the way, and once he even leaned against the wall. But he arrived at their destination, and he delighted in making a gift of poetry to his son. He had little appreciation for verse himself, but he was thrilled to see Jacob's gratitude when he laid that first edition of Donne into his hands.

Now it was but a few days later, and Sir Robert looked

almost a young man. No doubt the presence of a beloved son had gone a long way toward making this recovery quicker than usual. Jacob's father motioned for him to come and sit beside him rather than taking a position across the table. "Look at this, Jake," he said, pointing at the day's papers. "Can you believe this editorial!"

Jacob diligently read the paper that had been extended to him. He knew the subject would be slavery. What else? "*Hmph*," the vicar mumbled. "Of course I disagree."

"Of course you do. Does it not enrage you?"

"Yes, although I could never express that so eloquently, you know, as Aaron."

"Aaron hasn't half your wit."

"Father, you underestimate him. He has as much wit as me and twice my passion, at least where the cause is concerned. Surely you see that?"

Sir Robert stood up and walked to the window with his back to his son. For the past few days, Sir Robert had tried to talk to Jacob about the cause, and the boy had constantly redirected the issue. Sir Robert did not wish to force his son to take up the mantle. However, he did wish to share with him his passion. He looked out at the sweeping landscape before him and tried to think how he could best communicate his desires. "Jacob," he said at last. "I well know that you will not become an active abolitionist. You are content with your pastoral calling. I can see that. Your former restlessness had been tempered. I will never again try to force you into my footsteps." He turned back to face his son. "But that does not mean I do not wish to speak with you about what presses on my heart and have you respond and share with me your thoughts. Do not think, if I try to speak to you of abolition, that I wish you to renounce your present calling. I only wish to speak with you. That is all. And do not offer up your brother as a suitable substitute. He is a different man."

Sir Robert's words relieved and disappointed the vicar simultaneously. He now better understood his father's intentions and was grateful to be reassured of his support for his calling. Yet Sir Robert still seemed unaware of his other son's vocation.

"Yes!" said Jacob, rising from the table and coming to stand beside his father. He looked Sir Robert fiercely in the eyes. "Yes, he is a different man. A man so like you, father! And I. . . I am not. I know you have always favored me. I cannot think why. Aaron is your mirror. And if you listened to him speak—"

"I have, Jacob! You think I have not noticed his fervor, his tone, his commanding voice? You think I haven't noticed how well versed he is in every rational argument against slavery?"

Jacob was astounded. He really thought his father blind to Aaron's gifts. "Then why—"

"All that means nothing, Jacob, if he can only speak in the presence of friends. Have you ever seen him speak among strangers? I never have. Never."

Jacob never had either, but he knew the day was coming. "He will," he said assuredly. "He will."

"When?" Sir Robert shook his head and returned to the table, slumping down in the chair and grabbing hold of the paper with one hand.

"Soon," answered Mr. Markwood. "Do you know he is leaving the bar? Did he tell you?"

Sir Robert jerked his head back round and stared hard at his son. "No. What do you mean by that?"

"I mean that he will start giving and writing speeches. He is to work with Mr. Buxton. He begins in July."

"Speeches on abolition?" asked Sir Robert.

"Yes."

"Public speeches?"

"Very public."

Jacob watched his father's face break forth into a joyful smile. The man had not looked this vibrant since before his illness. His father's happiness was contagious, and Jacob soon found himself grinning as well. The two looked at one another and began to laugh.

When their joy had subsided, Sir Robert urged his son to sit down again. "You've said little of your own life, Jacob, since you arrived here."

"I think it would seem rather dull, sir, by your standards. I could tell you about my parish duties. . .."

"Not that, my boy. Not that. You know the subject that interests me."

"Abolition? I am happy to speak of that now, father—"

"No, I mean the subject of your life that most interests me."

Jacob appeared honestly confused.

"You are now twenty-eight years of age."

"Indeed I am, sir, but that is no interesting subject."

"You ended your engagement with Miss Grant nearly two years ago. She is happily wed. Your heart, I hope, has healed?"

"Yes, sir, I believe it has."

"Then it is ready, I presume, to be lanced again by another."

Jacob laughed slightly and looked away from his inquisitor. "I don't think it could endure another lancing, father."

"Just a slight prick, my boy. Just enough to set it beating again. Have you found no one in all of Derbyshire to crack that stone?"

Jacob smiled half-heartedly to avoid answering. Sir Robert was really only teasing his son. Had Jacob had any love interest, his father thought, he would have mentioned it. He had assumed when he began his inquiry that Jacob's heart was unchained. But he saw now that his words were upsetting the vicar, and he wondered if he had hit too near the mark. Jacob appeared as though he might be in love, but he behaved as though he himself were ignorant of the fact. Lightly, Sir Robert said, "I see it is not a subject you desire to dwell upon. I have had the park redesigned. Do you wish to walk around it?"

"Are you well enough?"

"Never better, Jake. Never better."

The two rose to take their morning stroll. Mr. Markwood was relieved to have escaped an unpleasant conversation, but Sir Robert wondered warily about what his son was refusing to tell even himself.

Chapter 27

Summer had returned to Pemberley, and with it came all the beauty nature could afford. The sun threw a spotlight on the canvass of the world, which had been secretly and quietly painted with brilliant strokes from the Master Artist's brush. Jacob Markwood had returned as well after making amends with both his brother and his father. He had left his father's estate in Buckinghamshire certain, too, that Sir Robert would reconcile with Aaron, the son who had been with him always, but who had been just as lost and even more in need of his father's approval.

The vicar was now approaching Pemberley for one of his regular visits, and the calmness of the weather echoed the calmness of his soul. He saw Miss Darcy preparing to set out for a morning ride and waved to her casually. He had thought her beautiful since the day he had met her, but in the same way that a man thinks the grass is green. It is. So he observes it. Today, however, her beauty appeared starker than usual. Perhaps it was his general good mood. She returned his greeting and directed her horse away from him, out toward the expansive grounds of Pemberley. No more communication was necessary. He knew that she would shorten her planned excursion and come inside later to visit him and that he would have further opportunity of speaking with her. He did not think of this as his right, but nor did he regard it as a privilege. It was simply something experience had taught him both to expect and to enjoy.

But as he turned to approach the estate, his foot was staid, and his heart caught. He heard the frightened neighing of the horse followed by the startled scream of Miss Darcy. What had thrown her steed into such a terror he could not discern, but the animal had lost control and was bucking like an unbroken horse. Georgiana was desperately attempting to regain control, but despite her sound horsemanship, she could not stop the creature's mounting fury.

Mr. Markwood ran to her. He dodged the stomp of the hooves awkwardly but successfully and grabbed hold of the reins. The horse began to calm, but he did not know how long it might last; its eyes were still hollow with fright. He held out his arms to Miss Darcy. This might be her one opportunity to dismount safely, but she was not seizing it. She was still recovering from the force of several repeated jolts. Mr. Markwood sensed the horse was prepared to kick again, and he could not wait for Georgiana's consent. He grabbed her roughly from the horse and stepped from its path. The steed fulfilled the vicar's prediction: it kicked, and they narrowly escaped the blow. Georgiana tumbled backwards in his arms, and he broke her fall upon the rigid ground.

Running quickly into the distance, the horse soon slowed its gallop to a trot and finally a stop. It looked back at its mistress without repentance. There was no guessing what had caused the loyal horse to react so violently. The scattering of the field mice, perhaps. The vicar did not know, and he did not speculate. His concern was only for Miss Darcy, who had begun to tremble in his arms. He heard her gasp, sensed her breath catch, and was sure she would burst into tears as a sign of emotional exhaustion.

Yet no tears came. With a strength that astounded him, she steadied her nerves. By the sheer force of will, she mastered her fear in a moment. The trembling ceased; her breathing steadied. Instinctively he wrapped his arms more tightly about her. He did not know why he had done it. Not to protect her. She had calmed herself; she was not in need of his protection. She was not Talbot's sweet, innocent Georgiana. She was a mature woman, who kept a strong spirit hidden from the world, too humble to know her own worth.

Oh, yes, she was sweet, too, he thought, but not because she was ignorant of vice; innocent, but not because she had never sought to educate herself about the world. Her sweetness and her innocence were ultimately acts of will, which could not be negated by experience. They were born of choice, not naïveté.

In an instant, all the calmness with which he had met the morning was overturned. He knew what he had perhaps known before without admitting it to his conscious mind: he wanted this woman for his own. And at that moment, the scenes of all their past encounters traversed his mind in a torrid flash. And those days since Major Talbot's departure began to take on a new substance, which he could not now believe he had failed to perceive. He saw all their conversations in another light, and he came to a conclusion more frightening than his own feelings: she loved him too.

His arms began to burn against her with the heat of shame, and he drew them from her as if from scalding fire. He staggered to his feet and did not touch her except to help her from the ground. When she stood steadily before him, he released her hand. He stepped back, placing an immediate distance between them. In his previously tender eyes there fell an inflexible shield of forced indifference. The wall had been erected; the gate had been shut; the bolt had fallen. She watched him build it, watched him close it, watched him lock it, and she did not try to stop him. She knew it must be done.

***

Mr. Markwood accompanied Georgiana back to Pemberley and told the Darcys about the horse. They insisted that she rest in the sitting room and take some tea. Elizabeth brought her a letter that had arrived that morning, marked by the seal of Major Talbot. It had been a month since Georgiana had heard from him, and Mrs. Darcy knew she must not hesitate a moment before presenting the letter.

Georgiana took it and held it cautiously in her trembling hand. Mr. Darcy asked gently if she would share with them what she felt she could. He thought Mr. Markwood must desire to hear news of his friend, and he asked the vicar to sit.

Mr. Markwood took the offered chair and waited with severe uneasiness until Miss Darcy looked up from the letter. "He writes," she said excitedly, "that he has been in a place south of Brussels, called Waterloo. He has seen the victory of our forces. The war, he is certain, is as good as over. He writes he will have left for England by the time this letter reaches me and promises to follow it with his own person in a week." This news brought a glow to Georgiana's skin and a smile to her face. Elizabeth rejoiced in her sister-in-law's happiness, but she suspected also that it was not the happiness of a woman anxious to be reunited with her lover. It was the happiness of a girl relieved to learn a dear friend was safe.

Mrs. Darcy did not think to observe Mr. Markwood's expression. Elizabeth thought he could only be happy for his friend, and he was. But had she looked at him, she would have seen such a conglomeration of emotions play across his face that she would have been unable to read a single one.

Mr. Markwood remained as long as he could force himself to remain, and then he departed with the claim that he must meet his curate. It was true; he had an appointment with Mr. Bailee, although the man did not call at his parsonage until two hours later.

The two sat in Mr. Markwood's drawing room to discuss the duties of the parish. Mr. Bailee was always willing to take on more responsibility. His obligations, after all, had been more than halved when Mr. Markwood had first accepted the living. The curate thought the vicar took too much upon himself, and he did not understand the man's fervency. Peter Bailee performed his duties because he had to, and he resented not a one, but nor did he look forward to them as a calling. He was pleasant to all of his parishioners, and he was liked, yet they did not bare their souls to him, and he did not wish them to.

Although Mr. Bailee did not a have a clergyman's passion, he had an average man's perception and a good man's kindness. He knew something was troubling the heart of the vicar. He dared not ask what. Perhaps, the curate thought, Mr. Markwood needed to share his turmoil with someone, but Mr. Bailee was not the man. He asked, instead, if he could relieve Mr. Markwood of all his duties for the day and give him some space unto himself. He offered what he could, and the vicar took it.

The curate left quietly and left the vicar to himself. Mr. Markwood hardly moved to bid the man farewell, but Mr. Bailee could not take offense. The vicar sat there in that empty room, not knowing he had gripped the arms of the chair so tightly that his knuckles had paled and not knowing he was gritting his teeth until the pressure grew so hard that they slipped, and he bit his tongue.

How could this be happening again? How could God permit him to love another woman whom he could not rightly have? And after he had prayed, too, after he had wept, after he had petitioned God everyday for that one withheld blessing of domestic happiness. Send someone he had prayed, someone I can love as a man is commanded to love a wife, as his own body, as his one flesh. Someone who could greet him after he had been visiting his parishioners, after he had been amid the squalor and the hope, the sickness and the healing. Someone who could hear him with gentleness and patience, but who could also offer him a mind that would answer to his own. Someone like Georgiana Darcy. But someone who was free.

And what was Georgiana thinking at this moment? She was alone in her brother's library, alone among those countless volumes that had taught her about the world—not just the small, exclusive one into to which she had been born, but that mighty globe, which encompassed both the rich and poor, the powerful and the weak, both the society in which she was privileged to move and the society Mr. Markwood had chosen to serve.

She was holding in her hands *The Marriage of Heaven and Hell*, that first volume of Blake they had discussed so many months ago. Then, he had been to her only Major Talbot's friend, respected for his virtues and honored for his connection to the man who would be her husband. What was he now? Someone to be surrendered, to be put aside.

Major Talbot, she reasoned, was a good man. He would show her affection all her days, and he would be a pleasant husband to her. That had to be enough. It had to be.

***

One of the many duties Mr. Bailee took from Mr. Markwood, in order to allow the man some time to recover from whatever strange shock had affected him, was to call upon the widow Mrs. Warren. The curate found himself performing some odd jobs around the cottage, which had already been kept in good repair by a generous landlord and improved still further by the dedicated vicar. Mrs. Warren, however, was too old to do much about the house herself, and she could always point out a handful of tasks in need of neighborly attention.

Mr. Bailee, happy as he was with life in the abstract even if the particulars held for him no significant meaning, worked merrily. But even his easy spirit was, in time, mildly exhausted by the meddling of the widow, who loved to share the latest gossip and to probe the secrets of her guests. That the curate had today freed Mr. Markwood from this intrusion was a greater kindness than he could ever guess.

Mr. Bailee had been whistling to himself while he labored and had been largely ignoring the ramblings of Mrs. Warren, but he now found himself forced to answer a direct question. "Who was that pretty girl who came to the church this spring?" she asked him. "The one you were always talking to?"

The curate supposed it was conceivable he had spoken to more than one pretty girl in the spring, but there was, quite naturally, only one who occurred to him. "Miss Kitty Bennet," he replied with a smile and went back to work.

"Where did she go, then? I haven't seen her in many weeks."

"She is in London, I understand, with her aunt and uncle, but I think she will return soon." Actually, there was no speculation involved. He knew she would return soon, for he had made a point of the date.

"Isn't she Mr. Darcy's sister-in-law?"

"Yes, ma'am, she is."

"Well, you have some unction then, thinking you have a right to converse familiarly with her." Mrs. Warren was not by nature a judgmental or cruel woman, but age and isolation had somewhat eroded her finer sensitivities, and she allowed herself to be frequently cantankerous.

Mr. Bailee, for all his carefree feeling, found himself suddenly uneasy. "I. . . I don't know what you are talking about. I wish you would not be so presumptuous."

"Well, it was quite clear to me! Do you really think the sister-in-law of your landlord is likely to take an interest in you?"

"I have never had any such hope," he replied. The fact that he had said the words, however, did not make them true. He had entertained a faint hope, from time to time, but he had regularly beaten it back with the bludgeon of reason.

"I should think not. Why, she is likely to marry a gentleman, and I'd guess a rich one."

"I think you miss the mark there, Mrs. Warren. She is, indeed, Mr. Darcy's sister-in-law, but you are mistaken if you think she has a fortune of any kind or any more social standing than her relation to the Darcys can give her. I have more income to speak of than she can claim on her own, and I have almost as much education—albeit of the self-taught kind. If she should marry a rich gentleman, it will be her liveliness that captivates him and not any dowry, I assure you."

"Or her connections. Those can capture a man just as well as a pretty face."

"Perhaps," he said, "Perhaps. I think I shall work on your garden now." It was too warm, he knew, for her to follow him outside. He could escape her unwelcome prattling, do his duty by the vicar, and enjoy himself beneath the sun.

He went to work compliantly, neither unhappy with his labor nor fulfilled by it. He did not think of serving his fellow man in terms of service to God. He simply considered it to be as honorable a way as any to earn a living. So he fled the widow's presence without any real sense of having been offended, and he resumed his merry whistle as he labored in the sun.

***

Later that week, Georgiana Darcy stood outside the parsonage in Kympton, a small stack of books in her hand. Before Major Talbot arrived, she wanted to return all the volumes the vicar had leant her, and she wanted to return them today when she knew he would not be at home. It was his morning to assist with the instruction at the school, and she could leave the books with his manservant. She would never have to see him.

Except he opened the door.

"I. . . I thought you would be at the school," she stammered. "I was just going to leave these books with your servant. I had no idea you would be here."

"I instruct in the late afternoon now."

"Oh."

He was looking at her, not with the obvious love she had felt when she rested in his strong arms, but with a visage marred by hesitation and bitter struggle. Despite that painful expression, he appeared to her as handsome as ever. She held out the books to him, but he did not take them. Why did he not take them and let her leave?

He stepped back and opened the door wider. "Will you not come in? I was about to take tea." His actions appeared uncalculated. His expression had not changed. But he was inviting her inside nonetheless.

Why had he allowed that invitation to fall from his lips? She did not think she could resist it. He, too, regretted his unpremeditated words. It was fruitless to invite her inside, he thought. They could not sit and talk together without pain. What was more, he might fail to feign disinterest if she came too near. He hoped she would refuse. He thought she would not consent to be alone with him, not even if they sat formally in his drawing room, before many an open window. He was certain she would refuse.

And yet she did not. She took two steps inside the door, and he had closed it before she could retract them. He took the books from her hands and led her into the drawing room where he offered her a chair. While she was seated, he returned the volumes to a bookshelf he had built into the room. He had reduced his library through donation to the school, but there were still too many books to be contained in a single room. At least now, however, they were not randomly stacked against the walls.

He sat across from her and began to pour her some tea, but his hands were shaking, and it was a moment before he could steady the cup. Looking everywhere but at each other, they sat there sipping their warm beverages. The silence pressed in upon them. They felt like traitors. The best they could hope was to conduct themselves admirably, to mime fidelity even if they did not feel it.

Georgiana sensed she had to say something because the silence said too much. She put down her cup and picked up the book on the end table beside her. She read the title aloud, "*The Writings of St. Jerome.*" She opened the cover. They would have an innocent discussion about literature. That would shatter the oppressive silence.

She began to rehearse the subtitles the editor had given the individual letters. It was senseless, but at least it was noise. "Jerome's letter to Theodosius and the rest of the Anchorites." He listened to the rustling of the too crisp pages; it was not a well-loved book. He had been researching a reference, that was all.

He did not look her in the eye, but he watched her delicate fingers clutch nervously for the tip of the page so that she could turn it. "St. Jerome on the Song of Songs." Another page was grasped. The book seemed almost to creak with the turning. How could he hear such a tiny sound? He looked up at her. He wanted her to stop. It was maddening, this inane recitation, this unmistakable effort to avoid the truth that dangled like a two-edged sword between them. Still she read. "Jerome on Marriage and. . . "

He saw her cheeks grow crimson as she dropped the final word. He completed the title for her: "Sex."

The tension was corporeal.

She closed the book and placed it on the table. "Perhaps I should read it," she said hastily. "For as you know, I will likely be married within a month's time." Their eyes met. There was no indifference in his expression now; he could not disguise his sadness. It hurt her to hurt him, but it had to be said.

Although he appeared wounded, his words sounded light, and he even managed a frail smile. "Major Talbot would never forgive me if I encouraged you to read that."

"Why?" she asked, allowing her curiosity to supplant her discomfort.

"Because Jerome advises celibacy instead of marriage, and

he is of the peculiar opinion that even if a man should find himself wed, he would nevertheless do well to abstain."

"How awful of him!" she exclaimed, and then regretted her words. Not her words, but rather the vigor with which she had spoken them, an emotion that implied volumes about her own untapped sensuality.

She saw him drop his eyes from her face, and she thought he was lowering them in embarrassment. He had actually lowered them by instinct, and had settled them quite unconsciously in an inviting but improper place. He thought of how Major Talbot had once called her a vision, and how he had laughed. He was not laughing now.

Just as she began to feel the heat of his gaze, he recalled himself and dragged his eyes back to her face. He swallowed hard and before he could stop himself he had said, "Major Talbot will find himself a very fortunate man indeed if you can say so with such feeling."

This was too much to bear. She blushed with her whole body and rose clumsily, making her way hastily to the door. Alarmed and ashamed, he hurried after her. Just as she began to pull open the door, he extended one arm and pushed it shut behind her. He leaned with all his weight against it, trapping her between his body and the door. She could not very well go forward, and she could not very well go back. She stood facing the door, starring at the blank wood, and waiting for him to free her. She could hear only the sound of her own breathing, but she felt his breath warm her neck.

"Please forgive me, Miss Darcy," he said. "Please forgive me. I did not intend to be suggestive. Please say that we are friends."

"We are friends," she answered, but not in the way he wanted her to answer. He wanted her to assure him that she was not angry, that he had not lost her respect. Instead, she had willfully reminded him that they could be *no more* than friends.

"I am sorely sorry I have offended you."

"You have not offended me, Mr. Markwood," she said, and he sensed that she was speaking through tears. "You have never offended me. I do not think you ever could offend me. But you have embarrassed me. You are embarrassing me still. Please. . . please, let me go."

He heard the ache of love and confusion in her voice. He desperately desired to encircle her about the waist with his free arm, to pull her back against him, to whisper how much he loved her, how much he wanted her. But he resisted every improper urge; he resisted every overt act of betrayal.

He stepped quickly backward and left her sufficient space. She fled the parsonage without even shutting the door behind her. It fluttered there plaintively, and he slammed it closed. He let his head fall hard against the wood, and then he rebuked himself.

Chapter 28

Major Talbot returned to Derbyshire, and Georgiana greeted him with genuine joy and fondness. He did not notice that anything had changed in her, but of course he was not looking for a change. And perhaps what she had shown him in the past had run little deeper than affection. He did not seem much different either, but he was ever so slightly more reserved. His uniform was adorned with two new medals, which glistened proudly in the summer sun, but when she asked him how he earned them, he said only that he had done a soldier's duty by his men. He had seen, she imagined, countless horrors, and thought he should not share such things with her.

Each enjoyed the other's company, and when he tried to kiss her she consented, hoping to find she loved him after all. And though she found his lips agreeable, her being was not stirred. Infatuation could not weather a year of separation; a girlish fancy could not give birth to a woman's ardor. Talbot was dissatisfied by her response, but he knew not why. He buried every doubt and assured himself that their reunion was all he had desired and imagined.

Mr. Markwood saw the Major too and greeted him with honest pleasure, so glad he was that his friend had survived. But the clergyman did not dine with them at Pemberley; he had not, indeed, entered the estate since that awful day of self-discovery. Mr. Darcy accepted the vicar's word that he had been preoccupied with the concerns of the parish, but he insisted that Mr. Markwood dine with them the coming Saturday evening.

The vicar did not look forward to the meal. That past Sunday, Mr. Markwood had stood staring at the earthen floor of the chapel while his curate published the first of the banns, which heralded the impending union of Georgiana Darcy and Arthur Talbot. All who saw him studying the ground simply assumed he had allowed his mind to stray. It did not seem odd to them that he did not look toward the couple as Mr. Bailee read, "If any of you know cause, or just impediment, why these two persons should not be joined together in holy matrimony, ye are to declare it. This is the first time of asking."

That first reading passed; Mr. Markwood survived it, and he survived the week. Three more weeks remained until Miss Darcy would be wed. He performed his duties with less feeling than usual, but there was no neglect. What he did, he did for a people he would not disappoint; he no longer did it for the love of God. Saturday morning arrived, and he stood in his garden, glancing up the lane to Pemberley and wondering how he could seem unchanged at dinner that evening. He saw coming toward him Major Talbot, and he greeted his old friend warmly; if there were any coldness, it was only in his weary heart, not in his manner.

The two sat down in a pair of wicker chairs, shaded themselves from the sun, and began to talk. Mr. Markwood was amazed at how easily Major Talbot fell back into their former pattern of friendship. It seemed they could be apart for years and then resume their dialogue as if a day had never passed. But within himself, Mr. Markwood knew a day had passed, and it was a day of innocence. His friend was speaking to him with confident amiability, and all the while the vicar was housing within his breast a secret fire. If he covered it long enough, he wondered, would its flame die out?

Mr. Markwood heard about the Battle of Waterloo. He heard about Major Talbot's struggles and victories near Brussels. He heard about the exhaustion and the weariness, the toil and the glory. He heard, too, about how timid and beautiful a smile Miss Darcy had offered him when he arrived at Pemberley.

And then Major Talbot grew silent. The vicar feared his friend had sensed his secret. He therefore searched urgently for some words of pleasant conversation; he tried to imagine what he could say to sound as though nothing had been overthrown within him. But Major Talbot had not perceived a change within the vicar. He had only been considering a truth within himself. "Can I speak with you frankly, Markwood?"

The Major's sudden gentleness startled him. "Always," he

said.

"I'm not asking you to hear this as a clergyman," cautioned Major Talbot. "I'm not expecting an answer, and I'm not looking to change anything about the way things are. I am happy. I will be happy. But I need to speak these thoughts to someone."

Mr. Markwood let him know, without words, that he was prepared to hear anything.

"Georgiana. . . she's a wonderful girl. And she'll make me happy. But sometimes, I wonder if you were not right to imply that I was rushing into marriage. Sometimes, I wonder if I was not intended for the field and the field alone. If I remain in the profession, I will be made a Colonel. I have learned of uprisings in India, and I gather they have not been handled well; at least, that is to say, if I were there myself—" He looked tentatively at Mr. Markwood. He knew his friend would not judge him, but he was nervous nonetheless. "It is only a thought I have sometimes," he said.

Major Talbot adjusted his position to avoid the shifting sun. His chair groaned gently and he said, "I plan to retire altogether from soldering, of course. It would not be fair to her if I did not. But I cannot say I will not miss it." He smiled sheepishly and after a moment continued, "Yet it is done. I am committed, and I am determined to regret nothing. I long to be a soldier, Markwood, to serve my nation anywhere, to give my toil for its peace. But at the same time. . . that is a harsh life, one that must end with either death or age. And if it should end in age, what loneliness! Marriage may well be the better path for me. It will tame my wanderlust. And I do love her. As well as I am able to love any woman." The Major laced his fingers together and leaned back, waiting for his friend to speak.

"I hope this marriage brings you all the peace you seek," answered Mr. Markwood. "I do."

"Thank you." Talbot peered into his friend's face and saw a deepened struggle there. "Does something trouble you?" he asked. "You look as though you bear an awful weight."

Mr. Markwood longed to unburden himself. He felt that if his friend but knew the truth, if this quiet fire were let loose into the air, it might cease to singe him so intensely. He thought he could endure his friend's reaction—whatever it might be—better than he could shoulder secrecy.

Such candor, however, would have been too selfish, and under the present circumstances, it would seem manipulative. The Major had innocently revealed his doubts, and Mr. Markwood would not appear to take advantage of them. The vicar, therefore, said nothing at all.

Major Talbot, never one to coerce a man's responses, regretted his query and hoped a change of subject might bring his friend relief. He asked what he believed to be an unrelated question: "So, what do you think of her now?"

"Of whom?" Mr. Markwood asked, knowing well whom he meant.

"My fiancée, of course."

"She will make you an excellent wife."

The Major laughed. "You once would give her no more credit than that she seemed a sweet girl. But you've become her brother's friend. You've had a year to know her better. So tell me why she would make me an excellent wife. It will do me well to hear her praises sung."

Mr. Markwood told him why Georgiana Darcy would make an excellent wife, but he did not realize that he was not saying, precisely, why she would make *Major Talbot* an excellent wife. He spoke of her capacity for independent thought; he marveled in her unexpected wit; he praised her dedication to duty and extolled her devotion to her family; he remarked upon her gentle reverence, her quiet courage, and her strong humility. He said, at last, that she seemed to possess no worldly vanity, to seek no earthly glory, and to understand instead the pleasures of a quiet sphere.

"You love her," Major Talbot said.

Mr. Markwood's heart faltered; it heaved and calmed itself. His friend had perceived the truth. Yet, in the end, this fact brought no relief. There had been no rage, no confrontation. The words were not an accusation. Major Talbot had merely stated an observation and had stated it with pity.

The Major smiled and reached across the distance between them. He placed a hand on the young vicar's shoulder. "It must be a brutal blow," he said. "It is not the first time you have loved a woman who has loved another. I am sorry for you that things have turned out this way. I will work to make her happy. You must be content in that."

Anger would have been preferable to this gentle compassion. Major Talbot did not understand, could not understand, that the problem was so much worse than unrequited love. Mr. Markwood's soul was troubled. Should the vicar tell him the rest of the truth—that he believed Miss Darcy loved him too? What was his present obligation? To speak or to stay silent?

"Markwood?" Major Talbot asked, seeing that a strange quiet had befallen his friend. "You can be content with that, can't you?"

Mr. Markwood smiled wearily. "Yes," he said. "I can be content."

Miss Darcy had not revealed her feelings to the Major. Mr. Markwood felt he must not speak on her behalf. Moreover, what if he had been wrong? What if the love he thought he saw had been a figment of his imagination, a strange vision he had misconstrued? Whether or not her feelings were certain, he did not have the authority to reveal them. She had not chosen to; she might never choose to. Indeed, he did not doubt that she would choose instead to honor her promise. He did not doubt that she would strive to learn to love her husband truly. And perhaps she would succeed.

Major Talbot patted the vicar's back. "Go on now," he said. "Take an afternoon to yourself at last. You were telling me that garden needed weeding. Leave your parishioners to themselves for a day. I must leave to see Miss Darcy. But I will meet you again at dinner this evening."

When Major Talbot left, his step was even lighter than usual. He felt badly for his friend, but at the same time, their conversation had shored up his affection for Miss Darcy. His friend's regard had not offended him; instead, it had reminded him how worthy a woman she was. It was not long before he was actually running up the lane to Pemberley.

***

"You have mislead me, Markwood."

Jacob was in his garden where he was working the earth with his hands. He looked up and shut his eyes fast against the blinding sun. He turned his head away from the angry man who could not block its rays. Major Talbot had left the parsonage less than four hours ago, but now he was back, and it was clear that his entire outlook had been toppled.

"I never would have noticed it," the Major said, "never even would have thought to look for it, had you not revealed your feelings."

Mr. Markwood had been squatting on his bent legs; he did not rise. He opened his eyes but beheld only the earth beneath him. He listened as Major Talbot continued; he heard the ache of betrayal in that voice. "But I see it now. It is not merely you who loves her. That I would have accepted, because I knew you could endure rejection. Only that's not everything, is it?"

Mr. Markwood did not answer. He just rolled off his haunches and onto the ground, sat in the muddy earth, and drew his knees up beneath his arms.

"She loves you too." Major Talbot paced back and forth a few steps and then placed himself in front of the vicar, who still did not raise his eyes. "I talked about you when I was with her this afternoon. Not intentionally, you know. Just casual conversation. And I saw how she reacted. So I kept mentioning you. . . and I kept watching its affect on her. It became obvious even to me. So I asked her directly whether she loved you, and she did not lie."

The Major watched his friend's reaction, wondering if the vicar would triumph at the revelation, but Mr. Markwood would not let him see his face. "Had you not unintentionally revealed your part," said Major Talbot through clenched teeth, "I would have gone on in blithe ignorance at least until after the wedding." He laughed bitterly. "What did you think would happen, Markwood? Did you think she would forget she loved you once she had married me? Or did you think she would go on loving you but resist that feeling and do her duty by me like some sacrificial lamb? Do you think me so unfeeling that I would never sense the difference? And did you think yourself honorable this morning when you did not tell me how she felt? Did you think yourself honorable just because you threw back to me the very prize you stole from me?"

"She's not some *prize*."

"You know I did not mean my metaphor in that manner. But I suppose your self-righteousness comforts you." He waited for some reaction, and, receiving none, he ordered, "Stand up, Markwood."

Those three words entered the vicar's ears with an echo, like the sound of a loose pail falling down a well as it slips out of a thirsty man's hands and is lost in the depths of the darkness. Mr. Markwood rose slowly. He was terrified. It was not a fear borne of physical cowardice. He did not know what Major Talbot might do to him, and he did not care. It was his friend's judgment alone that he feared.

"I cannot help but think you have betrayed me," said the Major, acid in his voice. "I do not fault you for loving her. I suppose a man cannot control his feelings. But he *can* control his actions. You might have avoided her company. You might have made sure, by your absence, that she did not love you in return."

For the first time Mr. Markwood looked at Major Talbot, and there was a plea etched in his eyes. "By the time I knew there was any risk of that. . . it was too late."

"How could you *not* know? You would not *allow* yourself to know, because then you would have been faced with the difficult duty of giving up the company you had come to desire."

Was that accusation true? It might have been. It probably was. "I thought," Mr. Markwood protested, "I thought it was just time and distance that was making her. . . I didn't know it was me."

"Yes, well, it *was* you." Major Talbot looked away. He gazed up the lane toward Pemberley. He felt sad and angry, weary and hurt, but hurt by what? By the idea of losing Georgiana? He admitted that was not the root of his affliction. Her love for another man had hurt his pride, but it had not bred this sickness that crawled like a gnawing worm about his heart. He knew he would have been content with her, but he also knew he had never really staked his happiness upon her. If he were honest, he knew, too, that he would rather continue to lead a soldier's life than settle down with any woman. This feeling was not the pain of romantic heartbreak. It was the pain of disillusionment.

He had always regarded Jacob Markwood highly. His attitude toward him had appeared as it appeared to all men whom he liked—open and affectionate. But secretly, he had held for his friend a deeper respect, an unspoken admiration. Long ago he had witnessed Mr. Markwood's conviction in choosing the Church. When he learned that his friend had broken his engagement with Miss Grant to free her for another, he had been overawed by the chivalry. If, then, he could no longer trust Jacob Markwood, whom could he trust in all the world?

"I will end the engagement," he said quietly. "My heart will not shatter if she is not my wife. But hers, I think, will. . . if she is not yours."

Mr. Markwood had been bracing himself for a blow. And he had received one, but not through a fist. That would have been easier to absorb. This news, however, floated lightly as a leaf on the surface of a troubled current. He received it with the ashamed gratitude of a man accepting a gift he knows he does not deserve.

"Have you nothing to say?" Talbot asked, not knowing what he wished to hear.

"I'm just a man, Arthur."

"I thought you were the best of men."

"What is best with men?" The vicar's voice was sadly quiet as he spoke. "The best thing a man can imagine or attain is like a dim reflection."

"No," Major Talbot shook his head and stepped back. "No, I do not accept this excuse. I did not expect too much of you. You failed. Not my expectations. *You.*" He turned on his heels and walked hurriedly away. The vicar watched him in silence.

***

A few hours later, Mr. Markwood wound his way up the lane toward Pemberley. He did not know how he would face Major Talbot casually over dinner. But Major Talbot was not there. He could see from the look on Georgiana's face that he had been there. He had broken off the engagement just as he had promised. He had said he was heading to India to resume his calling as a soldier.

Mr. Markwood watched her as she ate in silence; he saw her relief swallowed by sorrow and her hope eclipsed by guilt. He drew her eyes to his by force of his intensity, and what she communicated in that single moment added the final weight to his already sinking spirit. She said, without a word, *I love you. But I cannot be yours. Not like this. Not like this.* She had seen the Major aching; she did not know—she could not believe— that she was not the cause.

The hour passed awkwardly. The Darcys perceived something momentous had occurred; each guessed the Major had broken the engagement, but neither said a word.

Major Talbot did not come to dinner that evening, and he did not come to church the following morning. He was not there when Jacob Markwood took the bread and prepared to break it, when he said those words he must have said some hundred times before: "In the night He was betrayed. . ." He was not there when the vicar kneeled before his curate and became the last of all to receive the bitter-sweet wine, which burned his throat and fell like sparks decaying into ash.

Chapter 29

The light was like a shadow now. Or at least, that is how it seemed to Mr. Markwood, who had obscured himself in darkness of the empty church. But the intruding moon had shone through a pane of glass, and that faint beam, which so imperfectly reflected the far greater power of the sun, now moved from off the floor, played across his cheek, and rested there like a mark.

He had been there for hours. He had remained behind after evensong, which had passed like another ritual mechanically performed. He had been sitting in that rigid pew with one hand extended across the back. He was staring at the outline of the cross and wondering when this dullness in his soul would turn to sorrow or remorse or to any great emotion that would enable him to pray. There were no groanings of the spirit now, and if his lips let fall any words at all, they were the essence of every prayer—"Lord, have mercy"—but he did not feel them.

This, he thought, is what St. John of the Cross had referred to as "the dark night of the soul." But he now believed the term was wrong; "dark" was too poetic. It implied a kind of angry passion, but there was no passion—no emotion—nothing now.

He heard a footstep in the church. He did not turn. He had been hearing ancient footsteps all his life, and he had turned before and never seen what he had longed to see. Always symbols and shadows and fractured mirrors casting dim reflections.

Someone sat behind him. He did not turn. He had felt a presence all his life, and he had turned before, but he had always found the spot empty with signs of sudden vacancy.

Once, all these shapeless whispers had been enough. They were enough no more. He did not turn.

But this time, there was a voice. "I leave for India tomorrow," it said, "and I cannot leave like this."

Mr. Markwood let loose a quivering sigh; he closed his eyes. Major Talbot leaned forward and said, "Tell me why it hurts like this."

The vicar, who could sense feeling returning slowly to his soul, said, "Better it should hurt. Better it should hurt."

"I do not understand you," said Major Talbot, who now rose and came and sat beside him. "You thought I should not be so sorely disappointed. You thought I wanted too much of you. You thought I set my standard far too high. And you were right. Had I not, there would not be this pain."

"No, *you* were right," said the vicar, looking at his friend. "The pain is better than surrendering the dream."

"Not if it destroys a friendship."

"It doesn't have to. You have come to me. Have you come because you've tempered your expectations?"

"No."

"We can accept the shadows only as long as we know there is a substance. We can trust in the echo if we believe that some-where behind it lies a voice. This pain, this dissatisfaction, it is a symptom of your longing for the ideal. If the longing were to stop, that would be the true tragedy."

Major Talbot leaned back in the pew. He stretched his arm out too, behind the vicar. He looked at the cross. "You know I am not a religious man," he said, "but I think I understand you."

"I think we have always understood each other."

"You will marry her?"

"If she will have me," the vicar answered.

"She will have you."

They were quiet for a time. Major Talbot's pain was easing, Mr. Markwood's spirit was reviving.

"What does it feel like?" asked Major Talbot.

"I feel a kind of sensation now, a reviving of—"

"No. I mean, what does it feel like to be in love with a wo-man? I thought I was. I think now it was just affection. Not that affection is a light feeling. A marriage can be built on that alone and endure."

"Yes," the vicar agreed. "Better, too, than it can endure on passion alone."

"But you do not feel passion alone. You feel that, and affection, and esteem, and. . . something else."

"Yes."

"What is that something else?"

"I have no word. We English call it love."

"We call so many things love."

"So many things *are* love, Talbot."

"I love my country," said the soldier. "Somewhat like you love your God. But you can diffuse that love and love a woman too. I cannot seem to do that."

"You do not have to," Mr. Markwood insisted.

"I know that now. And that knowledge comes as a mighty liberation." The Major removed his arm and sat forward. "Tell Georgiana," he said carefully, considering his words, "tell her when you see her tomorrow that I did care for her, that it was not a frivolous thing with me, that—had I been able to love any woman in the way she desires to be loved—I would have loved her. Tell her I saw mostly her innocence and her sweetness, and the soldier in me longed to protect her. Tell her I do not resent her loving you, because you saw everything in her—the innocence and the sweetness but also the strength and the courage, the wisdom and the depth. And you longed to protect her, but also to love her, even to learn from her. Tell her you and I are friends again, and always will be, though an ocean may divide us. Tell her I am at peace, more than a soldier can ever hope to be."

"It would be better if you told her yourself," Mr. Markwood said as he turned his eyes to his friend. "She is feeling a great deal of guilt. She saw how pained you were; she is sure she has been unfaithful, in thought if not in deed. She thinks she was the cause of that wound. Tell her yourself. I cannot heal her of that. She cannot accept those words from me."

Major Talbot shook his head. "I cannot see her again. I must leave too early in the morning. I ride to Brighton and sail from there. There will not be many more opportunities. I must leave early. And it is too late to call now."

"Please—"

Major Talbot looked at Mr. Markwood, saw the desperation in his eyes, and understood. If Georgiana was not brought to comprehend these things, their marriage could not be. She would not build it on the ruins of another man's heart; she would not build it in the wake of her own perceived infidelity.

"Let us go back to your parsonage," the Major reassured him. "Give me a quill. I will write this all out in my own hand for her, in my own words. You may bring her the letter in the morning. She will recognize my writing. She will accept it just as if I had spoken to her."

Although the letter was written in under an hour, both men remained awake late into the night. They sat up talking, while Major Talbot stretched out on the rug and Mr. Markwood slumped easily in a chair. There was light in the window and laughter under the roof, and the hours passed without observation, washed in the glow of an unshakable friendship.

∗∗∗

The following morning, Mr. Markwood was guided into Mr. Darcy's study. The master of Pemberley put aside his work and greeted his friend. "I was going to ride out this morning. Do you wish to join me?" Mr. Darcy desired to be away from Pemberley and alone with the vicar so that he might ask him openly about his friend Major Talbot and learn what his sister would not tell him.

"No, thank you. . . I have come to call upon your sister, if I may."

"Oh," said Mr. Darcy softly, and worry marred his brow. He had deduced from his sister's expression that the Major had ended the engagement, but he had not guessed why. Mr. Darcy did not think his sister loved Major Talbot in the manner that he loved his own wife, but he had thought she cared for him and that she would be content to pass a life beside him. He assumed she must be wounded by his rejection, and perhaps the vicar only wished to comfort her. But he thought he heard in Mr. Markwood's voice something telling him that the story was not so simple, and he resented that he did not know the plot.

"May I see her?" Mr. Markwood asked again.

Mr. Darcy was standing with the tips of his fingers resting on his desk. He tapped them in distraction. "Major Talbot, I presume, is not with you."

"No. He departed for India this morning. He will be working there to quell mutinies. He will settle there."

Mr. Darcy's hand froze in place. After a moment, he lifted it, and stood back from his desk. "I do not know what is transpiring here," he said. "And you do not seem particularly inclined to tell me. Apparently you feel the need to speak with my sister first. I will trust you know what you are doing. But once you have spoken with her, I want you back in this study. I'll stay here until you return. You will find her in the east sitting room."

"Thank you," Mr. Markwood said, and he turned to leave.

"My sister is very dear to me," said Mr. Darcy from behind him. He was not sure why he had said it. It might have been a warning, or it might have been a plea. He could not know how he himself had meant it because he did not know what was happening.

"I know," said Mr. Markwood as he left. It was a reassurance that revealed nothing.

***

He found her in a corner with a book, but of course she was not reading. She had heard him come in, had recognized his footfalls. She did not look up until he was seated beside her. She saw his hand first, not his face, and then she saw the letter. She reached out for it, reflexively. He let go of his end and rose to look out the window while she read. She still not had not seen his eyes.

Mr. Markwood had thought she would say something when she was ready. But he had stood there so long, gazing at the distant pond, and there had been no sound. He could wait no longer, and he turned. She sat there, gripping either side of the pages, crying silently. They were not tears of sorrow or of guilt. But they were tears nonetheless, and he could not bear them.

He came to her. He took the letter from her, folded it, and placed it on the table by her side. He kneeled before her and reached up to her cheek, brushing the tears from her face with a gentle touch. He waited until her eyes were dry before he spoke, and it was a long time. His own were damp, but the tears captured in them did not stifle the fire she saw smoldering there. "Will you," he said, and he looked abruptly down. He felt as though he could not breathe. Why was this so difficult? He looked up at her again, and again he could ask no more than, "Will you?" And she could do no more than nod.

He drew her too him with a zealous gratitude. She felt his arms possessively enfold her, this time by conscious will and not reflex. His flesh was hot against her own, but now it was not shame that made him burn.

He did not ask, "May I?" as Major Talbot once had done. He did not think to ask. He did not think at all. But she received his kiss without surprise, without rebuke. And she responded with a passion she did not think she owned.

***

"I don't like this at all," said Mr. Darcy from across the desk. Mr. Markwood was sitting in the very same chair Major Talbot had inhabited just over a year before.

The smile that had graced the vicar's face twitched, caught, and then completely faded. By the time he had left Georgiana, he had been so exuberant that his happiness could not be contained; it had not occurred to him that anyone else could do anything but share in it.

"Do you mean to tell me," Mr. Darcy continued, "that you have been wooing my own sister, in my own house, under my own roof, while she has been engaged to your own friend?"

"I. . ." Why hadn't he realized this would be Mr. Darcy's reaction? Georgiana's brother knew only a very small fraction of the story; he knew only that Major Talbot had come and gone and that the engagement was at an end. He had not been there the night before when the two friends had reconciled; he did not understand the depth of Major Talbot's calling; he had not witnessed either the vicar's struggles or Miss Darcy's past efforts to suppress her feelings; he had not known how determined both had been to find and do the thing they thought was right. "I. . . have not wooed her—"

"Well, then, you are quite the Casanova to win a woman without wooing her."

"I mean, not openly—"

"Obviously not openly; all this was done in secret, it would seem. You think that makes it less wrong rather than more?"

"I meant not intentionally. I did not seek to woo her. I did not know she was being won. At least, I did not know I knew. I did not—I would not—I never could betray Major Talbot in that way. Or you. Or her. I did some wrong, I know; I failed to be precisely the friend I should have been, but I strove. So did she. It did not happen as you think."

"How then did it happen?"

Mr. Markwood struggled to explain himself—to explain it all. It was not easy. How can a man put into words the trials of the heart and soul, the troubles and the triumphs of a friendship? In the end, Mr. Darcy believed him simply because he wanted to believe. He was satisfied. He sent a servant to call in Miss Darcy, and she came and stood beside the one she loved, with her hands held anxiously together, and she looked at the brother she admired, and she waited for his judgment.

The questions he was about to pose might have been better asked in private, but he wanted Mr. Markwood to hear the answers. "Do you love this man?" he asked.

"Yes," she said, and though he knew it, it was the first time the vicar had actually heard her acknowledge it with words. Mr. Darcy saw his eyelids lower, as if those dark lashes were actually genuflecting.

"And you have consented to marry him?"

"I have," she said.

"Do you realize that even though he is wealthy and likely to become even more so, Mr. Markwood has chosen a life of simplicity and relative anonymity?"

"I do," she answered.

"Are you fully aware, Georgiana, that his choice to live this way will also lower your standing in society and that some will consider your marriage an unwise act of condescension? Do you realize that in being married to a mere country vicar, you will be regarded with less esteem than you have been accustomed to receiving? Are you prepared to face the same society from a humbler position, to move among the same people and within the same houses, knowing, now, that they are perhaps quietly condemning you?"

Mr. Markwood was studying the patterns in the wood on the desk. He might have thought Mr. Darcy was being too hard upon him if he were not already rebuking himself. Georgiana's brother wanted to make it clear to the vicar just what, precisely, he was asking of his sister. And until that moment, it had been far from clear to him. He had never considered it a sacrifice to leave his father's estate and to walk into a country living. He had taken it for granted that Georgiana would step into that life just as seamlessly.

"I cannot pretend it will not affect me," she said.

Mr. Markwood laced his fingers tightly together and stared harder at nothing. Would she ask him to renounce his calling for her, to become a member of the landed gentry, to pass his days in playing whist and holding balls? That, after all, was what Major Talbot had been loath to do. And when it came to that—did he love her any more than had his friend? He could no longer envision his life without her. But nor could he envision her without his life. To him, it had been a single dream.

"I cannot pretend there will not be moments when that fact stings," she continued. "But I have never really wanted this— this kind of life. I have loved Pemberley because it is beautiful, because it was my childhood home, because you are here, and now Lizzy, too. I have not loved it because it is larger than a parsonage, or because presumably superior people have called within its walls. I do not love it because I have a host of servants to satisfy my every want or because I desire to spend my waking hours in a stately drawing room as I entertain important guests, always on my guard, always afraid I will violate some social custom. Oh, I do not say that wealth and reputation are worthless, or that I have not been grateful for my station in this life. But I never chose it. And here's a life that I can choose. A quiet life that will suit a quiet soul."

"Very well," said her brother, and there was a hitching in his voice, as though joy had been mingled with the dregs of guilt and pain. Mr. Darcy feared that he had, at times, pressured his sister to be the very person she had not wished to be. And now there was this man, this friend, who would take her from him, but he would not take her far; and he would love her deeply, and he would give to her the very life her own brother had never guessed she sought. "You both have my blessing," he said, and there might have been tears in his eyes, or it might have been a mere defense against the growing sun.

He gestured to her and she came and let her brother hold her tight, let him whisper, "You cannot know how happy it will make me to know that you are happy in this life. To know you can experience the kind of love that I—Georgi, not many people get such chances in this world."

Mr. Markwood witnessed this overflow of emotion, so uncharacteristic of the reserved man, and retreated from the room. He shut the door with gentle ease behind him. He would have a lifetime to spend with Georgiana. Her brother could have this moment.

Chapter 30

The happiness of Jacob Markwood was thus ensured, but what of his brother Aaron, and what of Kitty Bennet and that somewhat lesser prospect Peter Bailee? It is true that the young Mr. Markwood had seen much of Miss Bennet that summer in London, although their courtship had been uncertain. It was evident he fancied her, but he had also been careful not to commit himself. Kitty was frustrated by the young man's failure to proclaim his love, and she could not conceive of an acceptable reason for this egregious omission.

The fifth time Aaron had called at the Gardiners, he had encountered her alone. That, Miss Bennet thought, should have been an ideal opportunity for a confession. She had anticipated a proposal. She received, instead, a shock. He told her he would be absent from London for the entire month of July and gave her no reason for his departure other than a nebulous reference to having business to conduct in Sussex. Yet he had seemed to regret leaving her, and he had looked back at her fondly as he descended the stairs of the Gardiner's home.

Kitty had passed a moody month in London before she returned to Derbyshire at the end of July. Aaron followed in September for his brother's wedding. His father could not accompany him; Sir Robert had experienced a relapse, and, although he was not in any danger of death, he could not make the journey from Buckinghamshire. He sent his warm congratulations and his hearty blessing along with an invitation to his soon-to-be daughter to visit his estate the following spring. He must see the woman who could captivate Jacob.

Aaron, however, came hastily and happily. He was quite excited for his brother, but his joy at the vicar's bliss would not prevent him from taunting Jacob whenever the opportunity arose. He recalled how the vicar had scolded him for his own attentions to Miss Darcy, and his aim, now, was to suggest to his brother another motive for his past moral sensitivity.

It was her fortune, Miss Bennett thought, that young Mr. Aaron Markwood could not remain with his brother after the wedding and that he must, instead, reside as a guest of Pemberley. Kitty now hoped for the opportunity to secure him more completely, and she outlined all the ways that she could wrest from him some word or action from which was no retreat.

$$***$$

The wedding was not a large affair, but it was elegant, and Mr. Darcy had offered up his sister with the full confidence that Mr. Markwood would love her well. Even so, when Mrs. Darcy found her husband late that evening in the portrait gallery, he appeared to be brooding.

"What are you doing alone here, love?" she asked, placing a hand gently on his shoulder.

He pointed to one of the portraits, which showed an innocent looking young girl who was making an unsuccessful effort to stand with composure beside her very dignified older brother. "It seems like only yesterday she was a child."

"Perhaps, to you, my dear. But Georgiana is a woman."

"I know. And she has found a worthy husband." After awhile he looked down at her. "Did you have any idea, Lizzy, before it happened?"

"I knew she did not love the Major deeply, but I thought she might be happy with him. I noticed that she was attentive to Mr. Markwood, but I had no idea how deeply she loved him, and I certainly had no inkling of his feelings for her. It came as a shock to me as much as it did to you."

"How could we have been so blind while all of this was happening before our eyes?" Mr. Darcy asked.

"They were somewhat blinded themselves, my dear. And I am in no position to think well of my own perception. I didn't have the slightest idea how you felt about me until the day you proposed."

He shook his head. "You made that clear enough."

She put her hand tenderly in his. "I'm sorry," she said. "I did not mean to remind you of that."

"Don't apologize," he replied, glancing at her tenderly. "Sometimes it is good for me to remember how far we have journeyed together. That knowledge deepens my gratitude." He now looked back at the portrait. "And see how far she's journeyed," he said quietly.

Elizabeth began to tug his hand gently. "Come along," she said. "You cannot stand here all night. It's growing late."

"I'm not tired."

"Nor am I," she replied.

Mr. Darcy continued to gaze absently at the painting until the implication of her words dawned upon him. He looked down at Elizabeth, and the understated twinkle in her eyes lit his own. He was still amazed at how quickly, and with what little effort, she could ignite his ardor. He wanted to take her immediately into his arms, but he could not conceive how to do so with a burning candle in his hand and nowhere to set it down. Instead, still holding her hand, he began to walk quickly down the hall.

Elizabeth laughed at his impatience. "The chamber will still be there when we arrive. It's not going anywhere."

"No, but we are," he said, and now that they had arrived at a windowsill, he put the candle down and blew it out. The room was clothed in darkness, except for the bright glow of the moon, which lighted the hallway just enough to guide them through the house. Mr. Darcy swept his wife from off the ground and began to carry her down the hall.

"Mr. Darcy!" she exclaimed, in sincere surprise.

"Why," he asked, as he clutched her tighter to his chest, "do you so often address me by my last name?"

"Because, my dear," she replied, "Fitzwilliam sounds so very awful."

He struggled to appear affronted, but instead, a great laugh erupted from the depths of his being, and Elizabeth returned his merriment. The sound of their laughter mingled with his heavy footfalls and echoed through the mansion.

✱✱✱

Mr. Markwood granted himself time to enjoy the company of

his new wife, and he had, for at least a week, failed to open a single book, to write a sole exemplum, or to entertain a lone parishioner. He had not thought anything could draw him from his duties, but he allowed himself this short respite and felt no guilt in doing so. He knew he would return to his calling soon. For the moment, however, his hours were wholly preoccupied with original pleasures, the likes of which he had not even begun to imagine.

Consequently, the Sunday following the wedding, Peter Bailee was forced to preach a sermon. He did not mesmerize the congregation as the vicar often did; he spoke with amiability but with no deep feeling; he made some useful observations but released no rousing revelations. He was articulate if not poetic, soft spoken, and more than glad to step down from the pulpit in the end. His sermon was well received. Kitty was glad to see him succeed and even told him so after the service. She did not fear that her accolade would excite any false expectations, for Aaron had been her constant shadow, and she trusted that the curate understood her intentions.

Mr. Bailee did, in fact, consider himself a highly unlikely candidate for her affections, but he could not suppress his delight when he received her compliment. He was thrilled that she had bothered to offer him reassurance. "Thank you," he said, with a sparkle in his eye that was brighter than usual. "Though I am afraid it was a very short sermon."

"They are the very best kind," Kitty replied, and then wished she had not. Her sisters were teaching her to be proper, and it was probably not proper to make flippant remarks to the local curate. She was relieved therefore when he laughed heartily. He looked as though he wished to converse with her further, but Aaron Markwood caught hold of her arm and told her it was time to return to Pemberley. She heeded him without remorse and enjoyed his conversation as they walked toward the estate, but she could garner from him no proclamations.

After lunch, the ladies withdrew, and Kitty tried not to be distracted. Jane Bingley was once again a guest of Pemberley, and she watched her younger sister's anxiousness with gentle amusement. When Kitty had asked a second time if the gentlemen would soon be joining them, Jane replied, "Do you not enjoy the company of your sisters?"

"Of course I do," said Kitty. "But you are all married now, even Georgiana. You see your husbands all the time. I do not often have the privilege—" She caught herself. She was going to say she did not often have the privilege of seeing Aaron Markwood. She did not deceive herself into believing that her interest was concealed, but she knew better than to be so obvious as to proclaim it.

"They will join us before long," Jane reassured her.

"Long!" cried little Jonathan Bingley, who was learning to parrot his mother.

Jane's prediction was proven almost immediately as the three gentlemen entered the room. Mr. Bingley lifted his son from the floor and kissed him happily. When Jonathan grew weary of his father's embrace, he began to squirm. Mr. Bingley put his son down, and the boy toddled off into a corner to play with a wooden toy.

Kitty Bennet was hurt that Aaron did not take a chair beside her. Instead, he sat next to Charles Bingley and began to converse amiably with the gentlemen.

"Do you enjoy your profession?" Charles asked him.

"I have taken a hiatus from the law," said Aaron. He then spoke loudly and with far more self-confidence than he actually felt. "I am at present fully occupied with the abolitionist cause. I have discovered I have more talent as an orator than as a barrister. As my father's wealth supports me, I am at liberty to follow my conscience." When he finished making this pronouncement, he glanced at Miss Bennet but not long enough to read her reaction.

"I did not know you were an abolitionist," replied Mr. Bingley.

"I am," said Aaron firmly, now watching Miss Bennet with more concentration. She seemed neither appalled nor pleased by the revelation.

"Mr. Markwood," Kitty said. "I will be in London again in the spring."

"I'm afraid I will not be there. I will be in the north country for most of the season."

Kitty's countenance fell. Was he implying that he had no desire to see her? Mr. Darcy looked from Aaron Markwood to Miss
Bennet, and he was surprised to find that the young man seemed to be placing a distance between them. The pair had not
spoken much during dinner, but then Mr. Markwood had been
seated at a distance from Miss Bennet, and he had certainly
looked at her a great deal. Perhaps, thought Mr. Darcy, the
young man had lost interest. The master of Pemberley did not
think that Kitty's heart would break; she would, however, feel
the insult.

***

Aaron and Kitty did not exchange any further words that eve-
ning, but Miss Bennet encountered him alone in the portrait
gallery the following morning. "You are awake early," she said.
"Yes," he replied. "I found it difficult to sleep." He motioned
to the portrait of the late Mr. Darcy. "Your family is very distin-
guished."
"My brother-in-law's family," she corrected him.
"Your own is not?"
She certainly did not want to impair her chances with Mr.
Markwood, but, before she could control herself, she had said,
"My father is a gentleman, but he has not provided for my for-
tune. I am not likely to marry well."
"I think you are wrong," he replied. "The Darcys and the
Bingleys both see to your education. You have. . . you have natural beauty and talents that will attract a suitable husband."
Kitty was astonished by the compliment. He had seemed so
indifferent to her the previous evening; she thought surely he
had ceased to care for her. "Thank you."
"A suitable husband," continued Mr. Markwood, "is one who
can both support his wife and shower her with appropriate attentions." He turned from her and gripped his hands together
behind his back. He stared straight ahead at the wall. "I can do
the first. But I cannot do the second."
"What do you mean, sir? Do you not intend to be a suitable
husband yourself one day?" Kitty had learned much, but she

had not learned to be subtle.

"Miss Bennet," he said, turning to her again. "You now know that I am an abolitionist. That was my business in Sussex in July, that is my business in Derbyshire today, and that will be my business in Yorkshire in the Spring."

"Your abolitionist beliefs are of no consequence to me."

He knew what she meant. She was saying his opinion on slavery was no obstacle to her regard. Yet he took from her statement a second meaning. "Yes, so I gather," he said. "But they are of very considerable consequence to me. They require me to be often away from home. They require most of my energy, most of my passion, and most of my time."

"So you do not wish ever to marry?"

"What I wish and what I can justly accomplish are two very different things."

"I am quite capable of entertaining myself in a husband's absence, Mr. Markwood."

"You think so now," he replied. "But you will not think so in time. You will learn that you desire more."

"If you are telling me you do not want me," said Kitty. "I wish you would be more direct and not waste my time."

Mr. Markwood laughed uncomfortably at her frankness. Then he replied with some candor of his own. "I am telling you, Miss Bennet, that *you* do not want *me.*"

"How can you know what I want?"

"Your wants and your desires, Miss Bennet, may change with time. I should not have spoken of wants. I should have spoken of needs. I can guess what you need, and I can assure you with confidence that I am not it."

Kitty's face colored with anger, almost as if she were a child prepared to throw a temper tantrum. But her voice was calm. "Won't you let me make that determination for myself?"

"Yes, but not this time. I'll let you choose the next one."

She did not smile at the joke.

"However," he continued, "I will give you a nudge in the right direction. Did you notice how attentive the curate was to you after church yesterday?"

"A curate! I can do better than that!"

"My brother tells me Mr. Bailee is a good man, that his income is rather more than what one might expect, and that although he knows how to enjoy himself, he is a good steward. His duties are fixed, his profession is stable, and he would always be so grateful that he had won you that he would never cease to treat you with the devotion that is due you. Were I you, Miss Bennet, I would at least speak to him after morning-song today."

"And will you strive to push us together this morning?"

"I will not attend the service. I leave in an hour. I must make a speech in Lambton and then another elsewhere in Derbyshire later this evening."

"Then I suppose this is farewell."

"Yes, I suppose it is."

She coldly offered him her hand, and he kissed it. Her skin was soft like a child's, but her eyes were fierce like a betrayed woman's. *How beautiful she is!* he thought as he stepped away and bowed before her. He hated to leave her like this, hating him. But he knew she would forgive him in time, and she would find a better life even if she had to share it with another man.

Chapter 31

"I won't detain you long," said Aaron as he watched his brother's new wife retreat into the parsonage. The two brothers sat down in the comfortably worn wicker chairs that rested outside the Markwood home. The autumn weather was a little dreary that morning, but Jacob preferred to bid his brother farewell out of doors.

"I am glad, Aaron," the vicar said, "that you have finally surrendered to your calling. I suppose, however, that we will not see much of each other now that you will be so often traveling."

"No. We never saw one another as often as I would like anyway. Our paths lead in different directions."

Jacob only nodded in response, and the men were silent in one another's company. Aaron seemed to his brother to possess a heavy heart, but Jacob did not quite know how to probe his thoughts.

"How was your romantic holiday?" Aaron asked at last.

"Delightful but all too brief. Duty compelled me home again, and Mrs. Markwood understands that."

"It must be a beautiful thing indeed to have a wife who understands your calling, who will support you in it, and who will truly share that life." Aaron looked out at the trees, watched a single leaf drift wearily to the ground, and saw it fade into the earth.

Jacob gathered his resolve and chose directness. "You have rebuffed Miss Bennet?"

"I. . . I finally found the strength to make it clear to her that I have no intention of marrying her."

"And what happened to your former resolution?" Jacob's question was half-teasing, half-serious. "When you were fencing that day, remember, you said that if any of those women had anticipated a proposal, you would have given her one. You said you could make yourself love anyone."

"Ah, but that is not the problem. I *do* love her. It is only that I love the cause more. It is only that everything that means everything to me. . . it means nothing to her."

"How then do you say that you love her?"

Aaron shook his head. "Perhaps I am lying to myself there, too. But what I have felt certainly extends beyond a fancy. I have fancied before, Jacob, but I have never. . . I have never found it hard to walk away from a woman. Telling Miss Bennet what I told her. . . I think it was the hardest thing I have ever done. And yet I love her enough not to offer her the kind of life that will, in the end, fail to content her. Do you think I did wrong?"

Jacob was silent.

"Answer me. I can bear it."

"I do not think you could make her happy without renouncing your calling."

Aaron laughed lightly; it was impossible to discern the feeling in that laugh. It was not amusement, nor bitterness; it was not quite pain. "She vowed she would find ways to entertain herself in my absence."

"She may have said so," the vicar replied. "But I do not think she is mature enough, at the present moment, to understand the price she would have had to pay: not just the cost of your constant absence but also the price of being subject to the hatred of those who publicly oppose you. When she does understand that, she will be glad—I do not mean to be cruel, but she will be glad—to be free of you. I do not wish to insult Miss Bennet. She is a good woman. I believe that one day she will possess maturity and a greater depth of character than she does at present, but I doubt she will ever possess the kind of strength required of an abolitionist's wife. "

"So you *do* think I did right," insisted Aaron.

"I think you did right, but I think you did it too late."

Aaron bowed his head and roughly raked his fingers through his hair. It was a far gentler rebuke than he deserved. He had allowed Miss Bennet to believe his intentions were. . . well, he had not known what his intentions were. But had he been more mature, and a stronger man, he would have understood his destiny sooner, and he would have had the courage to pronounce it. Then he would have known, before he had deeply excited Miss Bennet's affections, that he was not meant for her. And perhaps he had known it ever since that day in the London public square. But he had been fond of her, and he had hidden that knowledge from himself. He had allowed her smiles and sighs and little touches to overwhelm his reason, and he had permitted temporal pleasure to push the permanent truth back into a mental dungeon. In so doing, he had hurt himself, and, what was worse, he had hurt her. "She did not receive my refusal well," he said. "I do not blame her. I did much wrong. But I would have done a greater wrong to marry her. For either I would cling to the cause and alienate her, or I would abandon the cause and alienate my own conscience."

His brother did not gainsay him. But still Aaron persisted, "If Georgiana had asked you to give up being a clergyman to marry her, would you have done it?"

"If she had asked it then she would not have been who I thought she was."

"Did she not ask something similar of your friend the Major? Is. . . I am sorry, Jacob, but is that not why he broke the engagement?"

"He offered to leave soldiering when first he proposed to her, before he was truly aware that it was his calling. But that is not why he broke the engagement. They did not love one another, and that is ultimately why." He did not divulge his own role in the situation, and Aaron did not prod him.

Jacob continued, "I think I could not love a woman who did not appreciate my zeal. I do not say this to judge you or to suggest that you are deceiving yourself when you say you love Miss Bennet. I think you do love her, but I think your heart is unlucky because it did not alight on a woman who could support your purpose and who could be happy doing so. Georgiana and I meld together in that way. She makes me better at my calling, but my calling also permits me to establish a steady, quiet home, which is precisely what she desires. One day, perhaps, you will find the kind of woman who craves the things your heart craves. But I believe you are right to think that Miss

Bennet will grow to resent you if you marry her and do not abandon the cause. A woman cannot go on making that kind of sacrifice, Aaron, unless she too is committed with a passion to abolition."

Nothing more was said on the subject of Miss Bennet. Jacob could see the guilt his brother choked down and the regret he felt because he had not acted more quickly. But Aaron, the vicar thought, would soon enough immerse himself in the cause, and, though he may not directly forgive himself for his transgression, the memory of that error would fade. As for Kitty Bennet, she would eventually cease to resent the young rake who had once courted her. When she came to understand her own desires, she would likely seek an uncomplicated life.

The chair creaked as the vicar rose. Aaron soon followed and the two brothers shook hands. "God bless you, Aaron. You have a rough road ahead."

Aaron nodded. He gripped his brother by the shoulder. "Goodbye, Jacob. Thank you for hearing me."

The vicar watched his brother turn and walk toward his horse. The usual, amused cockiness of his footsteps had morphed into a determined stride. The abolitionist mounted his horse swiftly and looked back to wave one final farewell. There was a hint of sadness in the change that had overcome Aaron, as must always be when the frivolity of youth gives way to maturity. But there shone now in his eyes an open and unflinching purpose, and with it danced a powerful hope for the future.

***

The weeks passed, and Miss Bennet gradually healed herself. The offense perpetrated against her had inflicted a sharp abrasion, but it had scarred her ego far more than her heart. She had reluctantly accepted Aaron's advice and had spoken to the curate after morning song; she had spoken to him, indeed, after every service for two months. Aaron's rejection had jarred her out of her naiveté, and now something unprecedented seemed to be happening to her. She was growing up.

Jacob Markwood observed the progress of his curate and

wished Mr. Bailee due success. He himself could highly recommend the state of matrimony, and he meditated upon his blessings daily. He was, in fact, ruminating upon that very subject now after a productive day of visiting his parishioners. With a quickening step he approached the door of the dwelling he could at long last call a home.

Georgiana rushed to greet her husband when she heard him entering the parsonage. He dampened her ardor, however, by holding up his hands before her, which were caked with dirt down to his wrists. He had been once again weeding the widow Warren's terminal garden. Mrs. Markwood, therefore, settled for a quick kiss, which she executed with precision, careful not to come in contact with those darkened hands.

She followed him as he made his way to their bedroom, where he proceeded to transform the basin of clear water into a murky pool. As he dried his hands, he turned to face her. She had grabbed hold of one of the bedposts and was leaning against it with a book clasped in her free hand. A single tendril of her luxurious hair had fallen loose and curled about the side of her face. For an instant he was enthralled, until he gradually blinked himself back into sentience. The initial intoxication of marriage had by now subsided, but there were still moments when he found her presence mesmerizing. It had come as a startling revelation to him to learn that her beauty was no longer a fact to be accepted but rather a joy to be experienced.

He put down the towel and came and stood across from her. He wrapped his hand around the bedpost just above hers.

"When did you first begin to love me?" she asked.

He smiled slightly. He did not answer because he did not know the answer. He reached down and took the book from her hand. She seemed to be in a romantic mood. He wondered what she might be reading.

"*A Journal of the Plague Year!*" he grumbled.

"We need not always have the same taste in literature, my dear."

He let go of the bedpost, transferred the book to his other hand, and tossed it away from himself onto the bed. He scowled. "Little wonder your mind is preoccupied with romance. It is such an uplifting volume." The vicar leaned forward and closed the last distance between them. He claimed her by placing an arm around her waist and drawing her tightly against his chest. He kissed her cheek and whispered, "I never can predict you, my love. You never give me just what I expect."

His nearness inspired in her the same thrill she had felt so many months ago when they had selected books for the school and he had descended that ladder to land close beside her. Now, however, neither duty nor fear compelled her to step a-way. Instead, she rested her head upon his chest and snuggled just beneath his chin. With the ghost of a smile outlining her lips, she asked, "You would not like it half as much, would you, Mr. Markwood, if I were a model wife? For then you could not entertain yourself by mocking me."

"Oh," he replied, pushing her away just enough to look into her eyes, "but you are a model wife, Mrs. Markwood."

This profession she rewarded with a prolonged kiss. She then drew coyly away from him, walked to the side of the bed, and reached over to reclaim the book he had tossed aside.

"What *did* you expect me to be reading, Jacob?"

"Well," he murmured, watching her intensely but not follow-ing her, "when you came in after me with that book in your hand, I thought perhaps you intended to soothe me after a weary day by reading aloud some romantic poetry."

She replied, "I only had the book in my hand because I hap-pened to be reading it when you came in. But once you had entered, I fear I was too engrossed with other thoughts to return it to its proper shelf, and here I am, just me and Mr. De-foe."

"And your husband." He leaned back against the bedpost, grabbing hold of it for support. He gestured for her to come to him with the tilt of his head, but she pretended not to notice. He tried again and she looked innocently baffled. Finally he sur-rendered and commanded aloud, "Come over here beside me, Georgiana." She could not pretend to ignore the hunger in his voice.

When she stood again next to him, she asked, "What would you like me to read you?"

"John Donne."

"Any poem in particular?"

He placed his mouth against her ear, kissed it, and whispered, "Elegy To His Mistress Going to Bed."

She allowed her lips to arch into a smile and said, "I fear I cannot read it to you. You have a first edition. As you know, at that time, the poem was thought too indecent to print. But if you happen to have it memorized, I suppose you could recite it to me."

"I do not have it memorized," he said, slipping his arms around her and lazily permitting one hand to caress her back, "but I can recall the substance." He watched the sparks climb into her eyes as he spoke. "If we cannot have a reading of the poem, dearest Georgiana, then perhaps, as a compromise, we might settle for an enactment."

***

The following Sunday, Jacob Markwood asked his curate to accompany him up the lane to Pemberley. He and Georgiana had settled comfortably into the parsonage, and he had resumed his pastoral duties with all his former passion—indeed, with more. Marriage had made him a better minister. Georgiana had awakened his heart to a new kind of love, and, far from finding himself selfishly consumed or permanently distracted by these unique delights, he had learned on the deepest level possible what it meant to live for another. This lesson, in turn, made him still more sensitive to the needs of his parishioners. Having already bidden his wife ahead to Pemberley, where they dined every other Sunday, the vicar now lingered after services.

"I cannot be welcomed there," said Mr. Bailee, shocked by the invitation.

"I only meant to ask if you would accompany me to visit one of the servants. Mr. Darcy's cook has fallen ill. She and her husband are both in need of comfort."

Mr. Bailee sighed with relief. He had feared the vicar had completely forgotten his place. He knew that Jacob Markwood possessed no snobbery and that he was equally comfortable with both the lowly and the great. But he hoped the vicar knew the limitations of society and respected them. "Good," said the curate. "That I can do. I was afraid. . . no, you are more sensible than that."

"Than what?"

"Nothing. Let us go."

Mr. Markwood wondered at his curate, but he felt no need to insist on an explanation. They walked quietly together to the estate, and, coincidently, Miss Kitty Bennet happened to be strolling in the very garden they were forced to pass on the way to their own destination. Or, at lest, Mr. Markwood had said it was on the way.

The vicar saw his curate notice her and hesitate. He watched Mr. Bailee's footsteps taper to a halt, but he himself did not pause. He called back to Mr. Bailee, "Meet me later, if you will, by the back door to the kitchen." The curate nodded; both knew he would not meet the vicar later.

Peter Bailee turned and trailed after Miss Bennet, who, upon observing him, greeted him with a welcome smile. "Will you walk with me?" he asked, extending her his arm. She took it, and they strolled slowly in the garden. Both looked with admiration at the wonders nature had wrought and observed the wild beauty of the gardens, which had been tamed but not suppressed through the application of human order.

At length, they approached a small stone bench. "Shall we rest for a moment, Miss Bennet?" Mr. Bailee asked. She consented, and the two sat down next to one another.

"I love these grounds," said Kitty. "And I love the inhabitants of this great estate. Some day I will have to have a home of my own. I cannot rely on my sisters for their charity forever. And yet I would hate to leave all this."

"You are Mrs. Darcy's sister. She will have you visit here no matter where you settle."

"Yes," she said, and smiled at him somewhat apologetically. "She will have me visit, I suppose. . . perhaps even if I should marry a man of lowly station."

He looked away. These past few weeks she had given him a hope, and now would she crush it with this petty blow? She saw his pain; she had not meant to cause it. "You are much respected," she said.

He smiled weakly. "By whom?" he asked.

"By all the parish, I imagine. And by me."

Now his smile brightened; his jollity returned. He shook his head and laughed and said, "We are speaking in some kind of cipher. Let us be direct and say all that must be said, make a decision, and continue with our lives—whatever they me be. I cannot play this silly game; it isn't in me."

Kitty laughed a little too. His directness pleased her.

"You are a sensible woman, are you not?"

"Not many think so, Mr. Bailee. If you did, you would be the first."

"I mean only that you are not unrealistic, are you? Carefree, yes, and a bit flirtatious, but well aware of what is practical?"

"I have always known that a day would come when I would have to settle upon a husband for support, if that is what you mean."

She expected her frankness to unsettle him, but he seemed wholly at ease. "And have you found one to settle upon?" he asked.

"Not at present."

"And is you heart chained to any other?"

"Not any who will have it. And, if I am honest, perhaps not any heart at all."

"You say you respect me. I gather, though, you do not love me."

Kitty looked away. That was a little too blunt. But best to speak the truth, she thought. "I like you very much," she said.

"Well enough. That is a beginning with solid promise. You know, Miss Bennet, I *can* support you. Not like this," he laughed, raising a hand toward the majestic estate before them. "But better than many men you have a chance of marrying. I have a deep affection for you, Miss Bennet. You are quite pretty; I cannot quite rid your picture from my mind. Your liveliness delights me, and I see you are growing in intelligence. I would be quite content to have you in my home, you know, to have you for a wife. I'll call that love; I don't know what else to call it."

She did not answer. His remark about her chances of marrying had stung a little even though she knew it to be true. But perhaps he needed to humble her a bit. She had always tried to humble him.

He continued, "I know you care for me, Miss Bennet, though you do not yet love me. And I know you wish to be settled. In this world of ours, not every union can commence with passion, and not every woman can afford to wait for that dreamed-of knight who may or may not actually exist."

He lazily plucked a blade of grass from the ground below. "Romantic love. . . I know that's what you young girls want. But that is rare and mostly found in picture books." He wrapped the slender thread around his fingers as he spoke and watched it, not her. "And when you think you've found it, half the time you haven't; you've only had a fancy and puffed it into something less than real."

The curate had turned his body half-away from her. He was resting his elbows on his knees, leaning forward, and toying with the blade of grass. His posture was bashful but his words were bold. "Those who find what the writers call 'true love,' they are the truly fortunate. But the rest of us must seize what happiness we can, and nurture it, and hope it grows into something more. Passion fades, Miss Bennet. It is born; it dies; it revives and dies again. But respect and simple affection endure. They do not waiver. They do not change with the seasons." He broke the blade apart and let the divided pieces slip casually to the earth's green floor. At last he turned his eyes to her. "A woman can teach herself to love, Miss Bennet, if she has the conviction."

Kitty gave him no encouragement. His speech was strangely full of candor, and she was astonished by it.

"You will not reply?" he asked.

"What would you have me say?"

"I would have you say. . ." he looked down at his hands, bit at his lip, and fell silent. Eventually he stood, turned, and stared straight at her with those quiet eyes.

"I would have you say," he repeated, assembling his words, "that because I love you, you will allow me to teach you to love me too. I would have you say that yes, you will be my wife."

Kitty was stunned. He had been leading to this, no doubt; the fact was as clear as the cloudless English sky. But now she had to answer.

"You. . . I have mistaken you, Miss Bennet?" He was surprised by her reaction. She seemed frozen in her place. Finally her senses returned to her. It seemed a long time. "You have not mistaken me," she said and looked up at him with a smile in her eyes. "I am no romantic, and I want a husband. You will do."

He let out a roar. She loved that laugh, at least—that much she knew. "I will do," he said. "I will do." He sat back beside her, placed an arm around her, and shot her an amorous glance. He leaned forward and whispered, "Well, you shall see how I will do."

Chapter 32

"I now pronounce you man and wife," announced the vicar as he watched the joy further diffuse across his curate's already ruddy face.

Peter Bailee turned to his young bride Kitty and took her hand affectionately in his. She responded with a smile of her own, which was tinted more with satisfaction than with love. She had accomplished the first major goal society had assigned to women of her kind. She was a wife.

Later, when Kitty Bennet entered the curate's little cottage for the first time, her eyes surveyed the surroundings. It would be a lie to say she was not disappointed. A slowly developed good sense had inspired her to accept the bird in hand rather than beating a thorny bush that might, at last, prove uninhabited. She knew her husband would be a good and kind man and a steady, if not abundant, provider. She knew—and this was more than most women could claim—that he would love her. And yet she was the sister of the mistress of Pemberley. She possessed both a longing for society and some lingering sense of a right to it. She had a thirst for the glamour of London, with its theaters and its circles and its sophistication. And when she saw the inside of that tiny cottage—as ordered and as warmly welcome as it was—she could not help but feel the future loss of all her girlish fancies.

Peter Bailee saw the look that marred her pretty face. He had a quick ability to read the thoughts of others, and he had a large enough heart to care for their pains. These two qualities in combination would have made him the best of clergymen if only he possessed the inclination, as well, to reach out and heal. But he felt no firm calling to his trade; the curacy was his bread and butter, and indeed a duty to be performed justly, but it was not a passion that enveloped him. He wanted his own happiness and the happiness of those who at any given moment were beside him. But he did not want to wade through the ugly refuse of the Crucifixion to get there. So he settled for something that was a little less than real joy but a great deal more than discontent.

He smiled softly at his bride. "When I have saved a little more," he said, "perhaps in a few months, we may go to London for a brief holiday."

She nodded to him in return as though to indicate that it would be enough and that she had meant no insult by her fallen look. She felt now the warmth of her husband's hand encircle hers as he tugged gently to persuade her to follow him. They stood soon at the doorway to the largest room in the house, a not unfashionable bedroom, which the curate had, quite obviously, taken pains to ornament to her satisfaction. "This is yours," he said. "I hope it pleases you."

"It is quite beautiful," she replied, not insincerely. "But where will you sleep?" For she had looked about the cottage upon entering and, beyond a drawing room and a kitchen, had seen no other room but one small alcove, which, through the open door, she perceived housed a wardrobe and something like a cot.

"There," he said, pointing across the way to the closet-like habitation she could not imagine he would claim. "I previously used it as a kind of library—not that I have much of one—and for general storage. But I have moved my books strategically about the cottage, and I have managed to organize very effectively, and. . . well, it will do."

Kitty felt a sudden warmth for this generous curate, who with what little resources he had was aiming to please her. "Peter, really, I did not intend to monopolize the greater part of your cottage."

"Our cottage," he corrected her. "Our home." Then, after a considerable pause, he ventured, "We might have shared a single room, and used the other for a den of sorts, but I. . . I did not want to presume. I thought you would likely prefer your privacy."

He said this with such a tender mixture of hope and hesitancy that she could not help but be struck by his tone. Most men assumed their wives won by virtue of an accepted proposal, but Mr. Bailee seemed determined only to begin his courtship now.

He had won her hand, certainly, but it was rather the heart for which he aimed, and it was the heart he was determined to secure.

A shock of his earthy hair had fallen loose across his eyes, and with an instinct of affection, Kitty reached out and brushed it back from his brow. She let her fingers rake through his hair and back down across his ear.

He felt the warmth of her fingers against his flesh and knew, at least, that she was not shy. He reached an arm around her and drew her toward him and prepared to plant his lips upon her own. She smiled in amused expectation. It would be their first kiss. She thought of herself as the more experienced party because she had accepted his proposal in a condescending mood and because she had already first been courted by another. She was prepared to receive his light, hesitant kiss with a warm but non-intimidating generosity and to grant in return a mild recompense.

And so it was that she was taken utterly by surprise, and stripped of her own sense of worldly superiority, when his mouth bore down on hers with hungry passion. She had never anticipated—let alone experienced—anything like that kiss. This tame man, with whom she expected to make a somewhat droll but decidedly livable home, obviously had more than frivolity stored in his jovial frame. And since passion can sometimes thrive even where true love has not yet forged a road, Kitty found herself responding in a way she had not planned.

***

In the year of the vicar's marriage to Georgiana, the Atwoods held another New Year's Eve ball. Mr. Markwood returned to the gilded halls of Hartethorn without a memory of pain, and he danced across its open floors, holding fast the unexpected answer to his prayers. Jacob Markwood's first foray into Hartethorn had been a painful one, but now he could return with a healed heart and with gratitude for the fact that God did not always answer his prayers as he expected. He had once loved Sarah Grant (now Lady Atwood), and that love had been sincere; but he realized now that he and Lady Atwood would never have been an adequate match.

Both women were beautiful, and both were intelligent. Yet there was a boldness in Lady Atwood that was replaced by a humility in Mrs. Markwood, and Jacob's former love boasted a lively, perhaps even adventurous, nature that in his present wife took the form, instead, of a quiet but courageous dedication to the good. For the vicar of a country parish who had chosen the provincial yet fulfilling life of a painstaking divine, Georgiana was the perfect complement.

When he was not dancing with his wife, whom he must occasionally allow another partner, Mr. Markwood took his station alongside his brother-in-law. Mr. Darcy was more his old, aloof self at this ball than usual; Elizabeth was not there to extract his liveliness. She rested at home, for it would be less than four months before a child was born to her. The two men stood side by side in quietude as they sipped their drinks and watched the activities, one with a dreamy vacancy upon his countenance, the other with a look of concentrated observation.

Mr. Darcy at last fractured the silence. "Your brother dances very well."

Aaron Markwood had returned from the north with his coffers full of money for publishing abolitionist pamphlets. Something of a gypsy now, he seemed to have no permanent home, and he was presently lodging with his brother at the parsonage. He planned, however, to return soon to London where he still let a town home. There his talents as an easy charmer would be put to use as he moved about society and sounded out its many inhabitants to determine where they stood on the issue of slavery and to guess what aid or obstacle they might provide.

"He has had much practice," replied Mr. Markwood with a smile as he considered all the time Aaron had spent as a socialite before dedicating most of his energy to the cause. Now, however, the young abolitionist was taking but a brief respite from his travels and speeches. Aaron's elder brother smiled to see him behaving as his old easy self. The vicar could enjoy this glimpse into a more frivolous past because he knew his brother would soon resume the hard work of his calling.

While Aaron Markwood danced across the floors of the ballroom, Kitty Bennet remained at home with her husband. The embers of the fire were dying, and it was long past their usual time to retire. But Kitty still sat on the sitting room couch gazing forlornly out the window down the path that led, some miles away, to Hartethorn.

Her husband sat in a chair across from her and pretended to read. He was a quick witted man, but he was not a great reader; were he not waiting for his wife to speak of her discontent, he would rather be doing some active, small thing than living vicariously the adventurous life of a fictional hero. Nor did he spend much time among the theologians; his religion was practical and admitted little room for speculation or controversy. He read when he must pass the time and when he must, on those rare occasions, write a sermon.

But Kitty would only mope. She would not say to him that she wished she had been invited to the ball or that she knew the reason she had, this time, been excluded. She had offended him once or twice in the past weeks by dropping hints that she felt her social situation had deteriorated; she had vowed not to raise the subject again.

Kitty had made progress: she had learned, in some measure, to be grateful for her husband, who gave her sustenance and patient love. Yet she still sometimes played the whimpering child who coveted what the other children possessed. This defect Peter Baillee's tenderness had not dissolved, and he was reluctant to apply the honest austerity that might be required to overthrow it.

At last he spoke. "You cannot look out that window all night, Kitty. Dearest, I am tired. Let us go to bed."

"You go on without me," she replied as her face formed a visible pout. She did not intend to wound him, of course, but she naïvely thought that, perhaps, she could win her way with such expressions.

"I desire your company."

This was a more direct statement than Kitty was accustomed to receiving. Normally he would have tried to persuade her with a show of gentle concern for her possible exhaustion, or with another mild reference to the late hour. But now there was no hesitation in his voice, and his decisive tone left her only with the choice of either pleasing him or displeasing him. Since she had never intentionally sought to dissatisfy him, she rose to follow him.

He lay in bed and watched her as she brushed out her long and curly hair. Captivated by the attractive image, he barely heard her when she said, "Peter, in Lambton the other day—remember I saw that beautiful dress?"

"M'hmm. . ." he murmured, thinking more of her lithe figure than any dress she wished to clothe it in. "You desired it, I know, but of course you know we cannot afford it."

She turned around on the bench and looked sheepishly down at her hands, which clutched the brush. There was no fear in her expression but only coyness when she said, "Do not be angry, Peter, but I bought it yesterday."

Mr. Bailee blinked. This he could not believe. He knew she had often wanted such things, and at times he had too easily acquiesced because he was so delighted by the joy his gifts brought to her eyes. His once careful frugality had kept them stable and free from the snare of debt until last week when, for the first time, he had asked Mr. Markwood for a loan to pay some existing bills. He had been determined to forgo anything but necessities until he paid it back. "Owe no man anything," said the Bible, and that was the kind of straightforward advice Peter Bailee could understand and appreciate. So when Kitty had asked for the dress, he had simply said no and had not been swayed by any amount of petting or pleading.

"Did you say you bought it?" he now asked.

"Yes, dear. With the money from Mr. Markwood, which you had left in the study. I know you did not think we could afford it last week, but I assumed since you had borrowed some money from the vicar that you would be more than willing for me to have just this one little thing." She smiled at him lightly and said, "Do not be angry with me, Peter," but it was clear from her flirtatious expression that she had no expectation he would be. After all, he had never expressed anger to her in the past.

This time, however, her expectations were defeated. "That

money," said Mr. Bailee deliberately, "was to pay our outstand-ing bill with the butcher and for the repairs to the cottage."

"Oh, but darling," she said, with a foreign nervousness in her voice, "you know Mr. Markwood will give you more if you ask. You are such a useful curate to him, and he is so generous."

"I will not ask him, Kitty." He threw the covers violently from off the bed, rose, and walked rapidly to her side. He was not a tall man by any means, but she felt as though he towered a-bove her because his eyes were so strangely stern, so unlike the mild, twinkling lights she had taken for granted.

The tears came: not a fake fountain meant to win her a girl-ish request by girlish means, but real tears born partly of shame and partly of fear. What was happening to her control over him? Was she losing it, and, worse yet, was it right that she should lose it?

At first he regarded the tears to be but another trick. "This will not work, Kitty. This will not work. You will return the dress tomorrow."

But when she turned her head away from him so that he could not see the streams that wetted her face, he knew she was truly ashamed. Had it been a ploy, she would have gazed at him with welling eyes until his poor heart could not bear the sight and he submitted.

"Kitty," he murmured, more gently now. "Kitty, you would not wish to be wed to a man who did not insist on maintaining his dignity, would you? Such a man would be looked down upon by the very society you so covet because he could not pay his debts or manage his own house. I may not be invited to the great estates, Kitty, but I *am* respected by their inhabitants. I will not surrender that respect, not for a pretty dress for the woman I love, not for all the dresses in the world. You must ac-cept that. You must trust me to provide for you, and you must be content with what I can afford to give. If you do not do these things, you will be miserable and our marriage will be miserable."

She wiped her wet cheeks with the front and back of both of her hands and gasped for a breath. She was ashamed, scared, and disappointed, but with all of those emotions there was mixed a strong sense of relief. She had felt affection for her husband previously, had considered him a respectable man, and had even enjoyed physical intimacy with him, but she had not admired him until this moment. She had liked the easy man, but now she thought she just might be able to love the strong man.

"You are right," she said quietly, "and I hope you will forgive me. I will return the dress tomorrow."

He sat down beside her and stroked her cheek. His gentleness seemed all the more beautiful because she no longer took it for granted. She understood that he could have responded more harshly and that other men would have responded more harshly. His lips covered hers, and she responded with more than a physical passion; the kiss she returned him contained the first bloom of love.

Epilogue

It would seem a sin against literary convention to press on at this point. After all, we have had our climax, and we have seen something of a denouement. We have been assured of the reconciliation of our two friends, and we have had more than a hint of the future happiness of our most important characters. And yet, an author cannot help but care about every character. Though she may press her audience's patience to persevere far beyond the headiest moment of the story, she must do so; for there are fates yet to be written, and lives yet to be altered.

Have you, dear reader, forgotten Niles Davidson? No doubt you have tried. It is, I believe, the desire of most decent souls that the scoundrels of this world should experience both repentance and redemption, but, barring that possibility, the second most pleasing act to witness is their punishment.

Yet in this life the wicked sometimes prosper, and they are not cut down in the midst of their arrogance, at least. . . not as we expect. Niles Davidson did not meet with failure in his profession; he was not lost to the world in some unseemly accident; he did not experience humiliation at the hands of some superior. Rather, he received an unanticipated inheritance from a distant uncle, which enabled him to retire a very wealthy man. There was a single snare, however, which he could not escape, and that was marriage at a time when he least required it. But Caroline Bingley could be a forceful woman, and, in the end, she would not be denied.

Mr. Wickham, too, must not be forgotten. He never experienced the conversion of character for which Mr. Markwood had hoped. Forgiveness inspired in him not so much a feeling of gratitude as a sense of relief. He continued to incur occasional debts though he did, at least, manage to avoid the most unsavory of creditors, and he never again dared to cross Mr. Darcy's path. His wife retained a modicum of respectability, and his daughter remained safe from any odious threats.

Aaron Markwood continued to travel throughout the country, and his reputation as an orator grew. He would never be elected to the House of Commons, but he soon learned that his influence as both a speaker and a writer far outstripped any power he would have had as a politician. He lectured at the universities; he wrote editorials for the city papers; he cried out in the town squares of countless shires, and he turned the hearts of innumerable men. In his forty-fifth year, he saw his dreams realized when Parliament abolished slavery in all the British colonies. He then emigrated to America so that he might pursue the cause upon those foreign shores, and there he met with Colonel Fitzwilliam, who was persuaded to assist him. Had Aaron lived but six years longer, he would have seen in America the bloody end of what Dr. Livingston had once termed the open sore of the world.

Aaron's brother Jacob soon came to realize that he did not have to run his parish single-handedly. The vicar still insisted on—and took great pleasure in—performing many of the most mundane tasks of the parish, but he acknowledged that even Moses had learned to delegate authority. The vicar began to place more trust in his curate, which freed his own time so that, without abandoning his pastoral calling, he could still recruit others to assist his brother's cause. He even convinced the Darcys to become involved, which took far less effort than he had anticipated.

The sanguine Mr. Bailee performed his duties assiduously, if not passionately, and in his spare time he taught his wife to love. Colonel Talbot meanwhile had settled in India, as much as he could 'settle' anywhere. He had found a purpose in his life, and he did not lose touch with his distant friend. Though his letters were infrequent, they were always warm and full of adventurous tales.

A few months after the New Year's Ball, Mr. Markwood stood before Elizabeth Darcy, who was kneeling at the altar. The vicar smiled warmly and began to say to her, "Forasmuch as it hath pleased Almighty God of his goodness to give you safe deliverance, and hath preserved you in the great danger of Childbirth:

you shall therefore give hearty thanks unto God, and say. . ."
here he began to read the 127th Psalm, interrupted occasionally by the endearing cooing of a tiny baby girl, whom Mr. Darcy
held proudly in his arms. "Lo," said the vicar, continuing with
the Psalm, "children and the fruit of the womb are an heritage
and gift that cometh of the Lord. Like as the arrows in the hand
of the giant: even so are the young children." Mr. Markwood
glanced at Mr. Darcy, whose attention was absorbed by his
daughter. "Happy is the man," he read, "that hath his quiver
full of them. Glory be to the Father, and to the Son: and to the
Holy Ghost; As it was in the beginning, is now, and ever shall
be: world without end. Amen."

Mr. Markwood addressed the small congregation that had
come to join in this religious event. "Let us pray. Lord have
mercy on us."

"Christ, have mercy upon us," they returned.

Mr. Markwood intoned again, "Lord, have mercy on us."

"Christ, have mercy upon us."

"Lord, have mercy on us," said the clergyman one last time,
before all prayed the Lord's Prayer. Then he looked at Mrs. Darcy. "O Lord," he said, "save this woman thy servant,"

"Who putteth her trust in thee," the congregation answered.

"Be Thou to her a strong tower;" he continued.

"From the face of her enemy."

"Lord, hear our prayer."

"And let our cry come unto thee."

"Let us pray," said the minister, looking now toward heaven.
"Almighty God, we give thee humble thanks for that thou hast
vouchsafed to deliver this woman thy servant from the great
pain and peril of Child-birth: Grant, we beseech thee, most
merciful Father, that she, through thy help, may both faithfully
live, and walk according to thy will, in this life present; and also
may be partaker of everlasting glory in the life to come;
through Jesus Christ our Lord."

The vicar's amen was solidified by a gurgling cry from Han-
nah Elizabeth Darcy, and the small circle of family and friends
could not help but laugh, however solemn the occasion.

Timeline of Historical Events:

1804—Napoleon crowned emperor

1807—Bill passed to abolish the slave trade

1811—Prince of Wales begins acting as regent for George III

1812—U.S. Congress declares war on England

March 1814—Napoleon abdicates and is exiled on Elba

December 24, 1814—Treaty at Ghent (ends War of 1812)

January 1815—Lord Byron marries Annabella Milbanke

January 7, 1815—Battle of New Orleans

February 16, 1815—U.S. Congress ratifies the Treaty of Ghent

February 26, 1815—Napoleon escapes from Elba

March 17, 1815—Great Britain agrees to contribute troops to an invasion force to be assembled in Belgium near the French border

March 20, 1815—Napoleon again ascends to the throne

June 18, 1815—Napoleon is defeated at Waterloo

April 1816—Lord Byron divorced from Miss Milbanke, exiled from England

1818—Thomas Buxton elected MP from Weymouth

1823—Buxton forms the Society for the Mitigation and Gradual Abolition of Slavery and persuades William Wilberforce to join his campaign

1833—Slavery abolished in all of the English colonies

Literary References:

- "Be Thou My Vision." As sung today, it first appeared in the *Irish Church Hymnal* in 1919. The original words come from Irish monastic tradition and date from around 700 AD. The modern prose translation was published by Mary E. Byrne in 1905, in Volume II of the journal *Erin*. It was versified by Eleanor H. Hull and published in *Book of the Gael* in 1912. Mr. Markwood, of course, would not have created the same verses as did Eleanor Hull almost a century later; therefore, the lyrics you see here are the result of the author's own versification based upon the 1905 English prose translation, and they could therefore realistically represent the fictional vicar's translation from the original Gaelic. The modern version of "Be Thou My Vision" is set to the tune of "Slane," an old Irish folk song included in Patrick W. Joyce's collection, which was published in 1909. Mr. Markwood, obviously, would have set his version to a different tune.

- William Shakespeare, *Hamlet*, *King Lear*, *Richard II*, and *Much Ado About Nothing*. Early 17th century.

- *The King James Bible*, 1611, would have been the version read during the time of *Conviction*.

- *The Book of Common Prayer*, 1662, would have been used in the Anglican church during this time.

- Daniel Defoe, *A Journal of the Plague Year*, 1722; *Moll Flanders*, 1722.

- John Donne, *Poems*, 1683.

- William Blake, *The Marriage of Heaven and Hell*, 1790-1793; *Songs of Innocence and Experience*, 1798.

- Sir Walter Scott, "Lay of the Last Minstrel," 1805.

- Mary and Charles Lamb, *Tales From Shakespeare*, 1807.

- Lord Byron, "Written after swimming form Sestos to Abydsos," May 9, 1812.

For more exciting historical novels
visit doubleedgepress.com.

The following pages feature some of our recent releases.

DOUBLE EDGE PRESS

Extraordinary Stories. Extraordinary Writing.

Shall Die by the Sword

by T.S. Beckett

This medieval action-adventure story takes place in 14th century France. Knights, damsels in distress, swordfights and smallpox all catapult you into a time where honor and integrity were the most valued possessions of the day, and a knight really would find, and fight for, his fair maiden.

Available through all major book retailers or on-line at Amazon.com

ISBN: 0-9774452-0-8 Soft cover - 242 pages

In the Brief Eternal Silence

by Rebecca Melvin

Romance, suspense, murder and intrique against a backdrop of Victorian England, 1863. Non-stop action as Dante Larrimer, Duke of St. James, searches for the murderer of his parents and finds betrayal within the Queen's closest circle—and love in a most unexpected manner.

Available through all major book retailers or on-line at Amazon.com

ISBN: 0-9774452-1-6 Soft cover – 440 pages

Sworn fo Mackinaw

By James Spurr

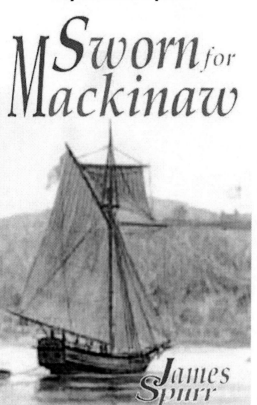

The tall ship *Friend's Good Will* sails you into the peril and excitement of the War of 1812 on the Great Lakes in this well-researched historical novel. Master William Lee and owner Oliver Williams have their convictions put to the test as their ship becomes a pawn in the struggle between men and nations.

Available through all major book retailers or on-line at Amazon.com

ISBN: 0-9774452-2-4 Soft cover – 280 pages

Printed in the United Kingdom
by Lightning Source UK Ltd.
126103UK00001B/206/A